KT-178-649

BOMB HUNTERS

BOMB HUNTERS

IN AFGHANISTAN WITH BRITAIN'S
ELITE BOMB DISPOSAL UNIT
SEAN RAYMENT

Collins

First published in 2011 by Collins
HarperCollins Publishers
77–85 Fulham Palace Road
London W6 8JB

www.harpercollins.co.uk

1 3 5 7 9 10 8 6 4 2

A catalogue record for this book is
available from the British Library

HB ISBN: 978-0-00-737478-6
PB ISBN: 978-0-00-739527-9

Printed and bound in Great Britain by
Clays Ltd, St Ives plc

Mixed Sources
Product group from well-managed
forests and other controlled sources
www.fsc.org Cert no. SW-COC-001806
© 1996 Forest Stewardship Council
FSC

FSC is a no[n] profit international organization established to pr[o]mote the
responsible [management] of [the world's] forests. Products carrying the FSC
label are [independently certified] to assure consumers that they come
from f[orests that are managed] to meet the social, economi[c] and
[ecological needs of present and future generations.]

Find [out more about HarperCollins and the environment] at
[www.harpercollins.co.uk/green]

In memory of all of those who have taken
the long walk and never returned.

Dedicated to Josephine Rayment

Contents

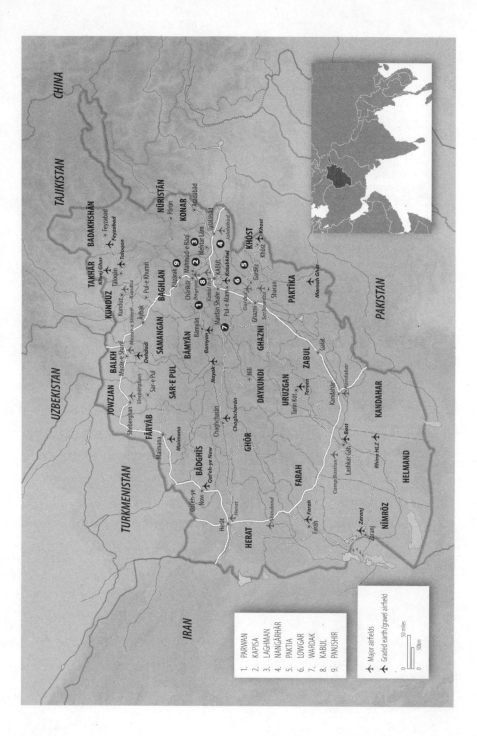

CHINA

TAJIKISTAN

UZBEKISTAN

TURKMENISTAN

IRAN

PAKISTAN

BADAKHSHĀN
Feyzabad
✈ Feyzabad

TAKHĀR
Khvej Ghar
Taloqān ✈ Taloqan

KUNDUZ
Kunduz ✈

BALKH
Mazār-e Sharīf ✈
Dehdadi ✈

JOWZJAN
Sheberghan
Sheberghan ✈

SAR-E PUL
Sar-e Pul

FĀRYĀB
Maimana
Maimana ✈

BĀDGHIS
Qarʻeh-ye Now
✈ Qarʻeh-ye Now

SAMANGĀN
Aybak

BĀMYĀN
Bāmyān
Bāmyan ✈
Nayak ✈

GHŌR
Chaghcharān
✈ Chaghcharan

BAGHLĀN
Pul-e Khumri

Bāzārak ⑨
Chārīkār
Mahmūd-e Rāqī
Bagrām ✈
② ③ Mehtar Lām
⑧ Paghmān
KABUL ✈
Kābul ⑥⑤
① Pul-e ʻAlam
Maidān Shahr ⑦

NŪRISTĀN
Pārūn

KONAR
Asadabad
✈ Jalālābād
④ Jalalabad

KHŌST
Khōst ✈ Khost
Gardēz

PAKTIA
Gardēz ✈
Sharan
Sar-e Kowsar

PAKTIKA
Sharan
✈ Mamun Ghar

GHAZNI
Ghaznī
Ghazni ✈

ZĀBUL
Qalāt
Qalāt ✈
Shinobar

DAYKUNDI
Nīlī

URUZGĀN
Tarīn Kōt
Terēen ✈

KANDAHĀR
Kandahār ✈

HELMAND
Lashkar Gāh ✈
Bost ✈
Camp Bastion ✈
Rhino HLZ ✈

FARAH
Farāh
Farah ✈
Shindand ✈

HERĀT
Herāt
✈ Herat

NĪMRŌZ
Zaranj
✈ Zaranj

1. PARWAN
2. KAPISA
3. LAGHMAN
4. NANGARHĀR
5. PAKTIA
6. LOWGAR
7. WARDAK
8. KABUL
9. PANJSHIR

✈ Major airfields
✈ Graded earth/gravel airfield

0   50 miles
0   50km

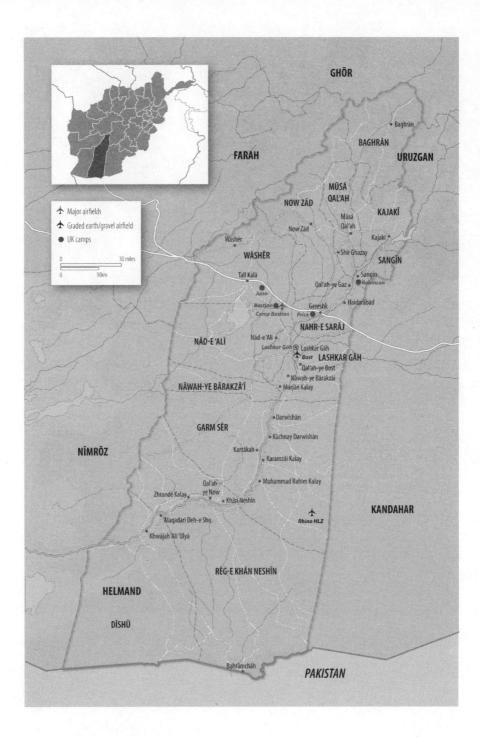

GHŌR

Baghrān

BAGHRĀN

FARAH   URUZGAN

MŪSĀ
QAL'AH

NOW ZĀD   KAJAKĪ

Mūsá
Qal'ah

Kajaki

Now Zād

Washēr   Shir Ghazay   SANGĪN

WĀSHĒR

Tall Kalā   Qal'ah-ye Gaz   Sangīn
                                              Robinson

Juno

Bastion   Gereshk   Haidarābād
Camp Bastion   Price

NĀD-E 'ALĪ   Nād-e 'Alī   NAHR-E SARĀJ

Lashkar Gāh   Lashkar Gāh   LASHKAR GĀH
            Bost

Qal'ah-ye Bost

Nāwah-ye Bārakzāi

NĀWAH-YE BĀRAKZĀ'Ī   Marjān Kalay

Darwīshān

GARM SĒR   Kūchnay Darwīshān

Kartākah

Karamzāi Kalay

NĪMRŌZ

Muhammad Rahīm Kalay

Qal'ah-
ye Now

Zhrandē Kalay   KANDAHAR

Khān Neshīn

'Alaqadari Deh-e Shu   Rhino HLZ

Khwājah 'Alī 'Ulyā

RĒG-E KHĀN NESHĪN

HELMAND

DĪSHŪ

Bahrāmchāh

PAKISTAN

Major airfields
Graded earth/gravel airfield
UK camps

0   30 miles
0   30km

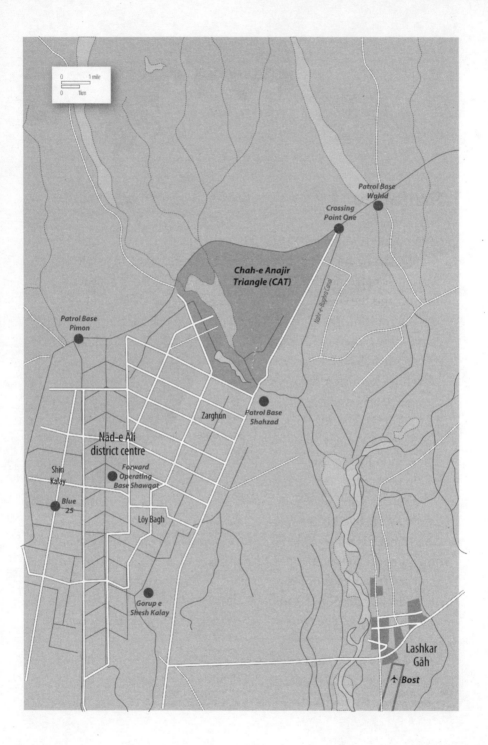

- 0   1 mile
- 0   1km

Patrol Base
Wahid

Crossing
Point One

Chah-e Anajir
Triangle (CAT)

Nahr-e-Bughra Canal

Patrol Base
Pimon

Zarghūn

Patrol Base
Shahzad

Nād-e Ālī
district centre

Shin
Kalay

Forward
Operating
Base Shawqat

Blue
25

Lōy Bagh

Gorup e
Shesh Kalay

Lashkar
Gāh

↑ Bost

Prologue

0500 hours, 16 August 2009, Sangin.

Fully swung his mine detector and listened for the high-pitched alarm before taking a step. The sun had yet to rise from beneath the horizon and the Green Zone, fed by the waters of the Helmand River, was still cool and damp and a friend to the soldiers. Silence. That was good – it was the sound he wanted to hear as he continued his slow, probing search along the dried river bed.

Swing, step, listen. Swing, step, listen.

Lance Corporal James 'Fully' Fullarton was point man – the loneliest job in Helmand. Stretched out behind him in a silent, human chain were 130 men of A Company, 2 Rifles, each literally trying to follow in Fully's footsteps as he steered his way through the Taliban killing fields surrounding the British base.

Fully was good at his job, probably the best point man in the company. He had lost count of the number of patrols he had undertaken since arriving in Helmand five months ago. He had seen and done it all in Helmand. Now he had just one more month to push and then it was back home to his fiancée. Two months earlier, while on R&R, he had popped the question and Leanne, the love of his life, had said yes. The couple were planning to marry the following year.

Strong as an ox and with a ready smile, 25-year-old Fully was undaunted by the knowledge that he alone was charged with picking a safe route through one of the most dangerous and mine-ridden areas of Helmand. He had grown used to the surge of fear that rose up from his stomach every time he left his base in Sangin for another operation into the Taliban badlands. He had learned to live with the terror of knowing that one step in the wrong place could mean instant death or mutilation.

In Afghan, as the soldiers call it, it was good to be scared. Being scared meant you cared, about yourself and mates. Fear heightened the senses and challenged complacency. Fear kept you alive.

Step, swing, listen. Step, swing, listen.

Fully always insisted that the next man in the patrol keep at least 15 ft behind him – close enough to hear the whispered words of command, but hopefully far enough away to avoid being fragged if Fully stepped on a pressure-plate IED, the Taliban's weapon of choice in the Sangin Valley.

The pre-dawn mission on that late-summer morning was intended to clear a route south-west of Sangin town. Several of the soldiers had been physically sick while waiting for the order to move out from the secure surroundings of Forward Operating Base (FOB) Robinson, a fortified compound rumoured to have once belonged to an Afghan drug lord. Others traded banter but the majority were silent, hoping that today it would not be their wife, mother or father who got the knock on the door with the news that their husband or son had fallen victim to a Taliban bomb.

It was a dangerous mission and everyone knew it. Fully's section of eight men from 2nd Battalion Royal Regiment of Fusiliers, attached to the Rifles as vital reinforcements, were at the vanguard of the operation. The soldiers solemnly filed out of the base into the early-morning darkness. No one spoke; only the soft crump of boot steps walking through the talcum-like dust could be heard. After just a few hundred metres many of the soldiers, weighed down by ammunition, water, and radios, were breathing heavily, their desert-camouflage uniform clinging to sweat-soaked bodies.

Fully knew the route well and had little trouble navigating his team across the cold waters of the waist-deep Helmand River and into the wadi that lay beyond. As the point man in the section Fully also had to scout ahead, searching the shadows and the reed banks for any sign of the enemy.

Step, swing, listen. Step, swing, listen.

No one knows whether Fully heard the tiny click as the two plates forming the conducting elements of the low-metal pressure plate touched. But even if he did, there was no time to react. The circuit was made in an instant, electricity flowed, and the detonator buried inside 20 kg of home-made bomb exploded. The blast tossed Fully 40 ft through the air. He flew like a rag doll, and when he landed his legs had gone.

Staff Sergeant Kim Hughes, a bomb-disposal expert, took cover as the sound of the explosion rumbled along the valley. A thick brown plume of smoke and dust mushroomed into the lightening Helmand sky.

'Fuck. IED,' he involuntarily muttered under his breath. After four months in Helmand during which time he had neutralized eighty bombs, Staff Sergeant Hughes could tell the difference between the sound of home-made and conventional explosives detonating. A shiver ran down his spine.

Brimstone 20 – the callsign, or radio codename, of the bomb-hunting team led by Staff Sergeant Hughes – had been attached to the company to provide support in case IEDs were discovered during the operation. The team was composed of the IED disposal team and a Royal Engineer Search Team, or REST. Without prompting, the searchers began preparing for action. Two minutes later they were called forward to begin clearing an emergency HLS, or helicopter landing site, and only then did they know that a casualty had been taken.

Up ahead, at the scene of the explosion, a form of controlled panic had descended. Fully was lying motionless, bloodshot eyes staring at the sky. Blood trickled from his ears. Fusiliers Louis Carter, 18, and Simon Annis, 22, two of Fully's best mates, soldiers who had become closer than brothers, inched their way towards their stricken commander. Their faces filled with horror as they saw the extent of his injuries. Fully was alive, just.

An urgent message was sent back to battalion headquarters. 'Contact! IED strike. We have one double amputee, wait out.'

'Don't worry, Fully, we're gonna get you out, mate. Everything will be OK,' said Fusilier Annis as the soldiers lifted Fully's shattered body onto a stretcher. Tourniquets were applied to what remained of his legs. Morphine helped to dull the pain. The two soldiers lifted the stretcher and were moving as quickly as possibly towards the HLS when a medic saw that Fully had stopped breathing. 'Come on Fully, mate, breathe,' cried Fusilier Annis.

They were the last words he spoke.

With Fully revived, the stretcher bearers moved off again and almost immediately detonated another massive IED. Fusiliers Carter and Annis were killed instantly. Then the screaming started.

'What the fuck's going on?' said Sergeant Pete Ward, as the distant sounds of panic grew louder.

'God knows,' replied Staff Sergeant Hughes, 'but it's bad.'

Sergeant Ward was a Royal Engineer Search Advisor, or RESA, and a key member of Brimstone 20. The two men looked at each other but no one spoke. It was a silent confirmation that the worst had just happened.

The men readied themselves for action. Staff Sergeant Hughes checked his equipment. He made sure his snips – wire-cutters – were tucked securely into the front of his body armour, next to his paint-brush and hand-held mine detector. The rest of his essential equip-ment was contained in his man bag. Their preparations were interrupted by a red-faced fusilier who emerged out of the gloom with the unmistakable look of fear etched across his youthful face. 'We need the search team up ahead,' he stuttered. 'We've got multiple casualties.'

Staff Sergeant Hughes swallowed hard, turned to his colleague, and said, 'Pete, be careful. We don't know what we've got up there.'

Forty-eight hours earlier Hughes had been enjoying the last few hours of his R&R back in his home town of Telford. He and his team of bomb hunters were due to form the High Readiness Force (HRF) back at Camp Bastion for at least a week as they reacclimatized to the Helmand summer. But then his close friend Staff Sergeant Olaf Schmid and his team had been stricken by a bout of diarrhoea and vomiting and were pulled out just before the operation, which meant the remainder of Brimstone 20 were called forward.

Hughes gathered his team together for a final briefing. 'Fuck knows what's going on but it doesn't look good. Everyone stay sharp.' Turning to one of the searchers who had remained with his team, he said, 'We don't know if anything has been missed, so I want you to clear a route up to the incident. Stop about 30 metres short of where the injured are and we'll make an assessment. Everybody move in single file and stay switched on.'

The reeds on either side of the bank grew taller and thicker farther along the river bed and channelled the screams of the injured back towards the bomb hunters. As they moved closer to the scene of carnage, they began to pass soldiers sitting on their haunches or crouching in fire positions. Some had been crying. Others stared blankly into the distance. The look of abject terror on their faces told its own story.

The lead searcher stopped and Hughes moved up to his side. Neither man spoke. Searchers were slowly clearing safe lanes to the dead and injured. Beads of sweat ran down the staff sergeant's face and he breathed heavily as he took in the enormity of the devasta- tion. The dead and injured – some six soldiers – were spread over an area of 200 square metres. Uninjured soldiers were also trapped inside what was effectively a minefield. They too would also need to be freed. In the distance the sound of uncontrolled sobbing could be heard. Only the searchers were moving, their silent concentration broken by words of encouragement for the wounded.

The body closest to where Hughes was standing had no legs and only one arm. It looked more like a bloody bundle of camouflage rags than a British soldier. On the other side of the bomb crater lay another soldier, clearly dead, his body grotesquely twisted, his legs gone. The two soldiers had been blown about 20 metres in opposite directions and so Hughes knew from experience that it was a device composed of 20–30 kg of HME, home-made explosive. For the first time in his career as a bomb hunter Staff Sergeant Hughes was confronted with a mass-casualty IED incident.

He willed himself not to be distracted by the screams of the female medic whose leg was snapped in two by the force of the second blast. Loitering menacingly at the back of his mind was the death of Captain Dan Shepherd, a bomb-disposal expert killed while on operations three weeks earlier.

Now was the time to concentrate, to formulate a plan, to try to work out what the hell was going on. The size and positions of the two explosions told him that the bombs must have been wired up to a central power source. But where was it? The injured were the priority, the dead would be collected later: it was always the same routine. But the key now was to ensure there were no more casualties. One of the searchers had cleared a safe route, searching the ground almost inch by inch, to the injured female soldier when he discovered another device. 'Got one, Kim.' The device was about an arm's reach away from where the injured medic was lying.

Time was now crucial. Everyone knew the Taliban would be moving towards the sound of the explosion and hoping to ambush the casualty evacuation. There was no time to put in a protective cordon, use remote vehicles, or for Hughes to don his protective bomb suit. It was a Category A action, a practice only conducted in one of two circumstances: either a hostage scenario where explosives have been strapped to an innocent individual, or a mass-casualty event where not taking action is certain to result in further casualties.

In both situations the emphasis is on saving other people's lives even at the expense of the operator. Staff Sergeant Hughes knew what had to be done. Take the power source out of the equation, he thought to himself. He began a fingertip search up to where he believed the first bomb had been buried, locating first the pressure plate and then the 20 kg bomb itself. As he searched he told the young woman that she was going to be fine, urging her to remain calm. He found a wire and cut it, all the time hoping that the Taliban hadn't upped the ante and created a collapsing circuit. If they had he knew he would be dead in seconds. But there was no bang.

Even before completing the neutralization, a searcher located another device between Fully, who was still alive, and the Royal Military Police soldier, who was lying on the ground writhing in agony. As Hughes cleared a route to the device, a wire leading into the areas where the bombs had been placed had been discovered. There was every possibility that the recovery operation was now being targeted by a hidden insurgent.

The searchers had to accept that any further devices could contain little if any metal and as such they could no longer rely on their mine detectors. By now the sun was starting to rise in the sky and the bomb hunters were warned by intelligence officers from the battle-group headquarters that the Taliban were moving into the area. Staff Sergeant Hughes pushed on to the next device. Once again it was a pressure-plate, or PP, IED, linked to what was a central power source. It immediately struck Hughes that he was dealing with a complex device not seen in Helmand before. He was now in a whole new dangerous world with only his wits and skill to rely on. All the bombs were laid out in exactly the same way and were composed of a pressure-plate IED which sat directly on top of a 20 kg main charge of explosive. There was every possibility that if one bomb detonated they would all explode at the same time.

Again Hughes conducted a Cat A neutralization, and again any error would have proven fatal. Less than two minutes after the second device had been neutralized a third was discovered near one of the dead soldiers. The device was located on the extraction route over which the casualties would have to pass. For the third time in less than twenty minutes Hughes carried out a Cat A task.

As the sun began to illuminate the wadi, dark patches of disturbed soil could be seen all around. Hidden beneath each site was a bomb. In an area of 40 metres by 50 metres the bomb hunters found seven bombs. In addition they identified the locations of another six devices from 'ground sign', disturbed earth left after a bomber has planted a device, and left these in situ.

Hughes was moving back along one of the cleared routes close to where a fallen soldier lay when a platoon sergeant asked him to remove the soldier's dog tags. The soldier had sustained a triple amputation and his face was covered in severe lacerations. Hughes rolled the dead soldier onto his front and pulled out the two dog tags from beneath his body armour. He took one off, threw it to the platoon sergeant, and put the other back securely on the dead soldier so that he could be formally identified later. He rolled the body back into its original position and gave him a comforting pat on the back.

Before the wounded could be evacuated, two more devices which had been discovered on the extraction route needed to be neutralized.

Despite the carnage, Hughes managed to maintain his composure until a stretcher party arrived to collect the bodies. It was clear that one of the young soldiers on the team had been good friends with at least one of the dead. The fusilier began to sob uncontrollably when he saw his friend lying dead in the dust of the dried river. Suddenly the full enormity of what had happened began to dawn on everyone involved in the operation. Up until that point Staff Sergeant Hughes and his team had been wholly concentrating on locating and neutralizing Taliban bombs. His focus broken, he turned away, his eyes welling up with tears. No one spoke. The bomb hunters hung their heads as the young soldier was carried away. Everyone knew there were many more tears to come.

Just forty-five minutes after Hughes arrived at the scene, thirteen devices had been located and five had been cleared, three by a Cat A action. After the bombs were neutralized, the injured and dead were removed. Fully didn't make it – he died shortly after he was evacuated from the battlefield. The three other wounded soldiers all recovered. The team didn't know it at the time but they had just completed what was later described as the single most outstanding act of explosive ordnance disposal ever recorded in Afghanistan, for which Staff Sergeant Hughes was later awarded the George Cross. By the end of his six-month tour he had cleared 118 bombs.

Chapter 1: **Living the Dream**

'Bomb disposal – it's the best job in the world.'
**WO2 Gary O'Donnell GM and Bar. Killed in action
September 2008.**

0345 hours, 10 March 2010, Helmand, Afghanistan.

The Hercules drops like a stone through the black Helmand sky, its four overworked engines groaning. Most of my fellow travellers are boyish-looking soldiers in crisp new uniforms – fresh meat for the Afghan war machine. Many of the soldiers are battle casualty replacements (BCRs), sent to Helmand at short notice to replace those killed or injured fighting the Taliban.

It's a sombre journey. We all cling to our seats as the aircraft descends at an impossible angle. Beneath the dim, green glow of the safety lighting, a silhouetted soldier begins to vomit. The acrid smell of a partially digested meal drifts through the cabin and I feel my gag reflex kicking in. My comfortable, peaceful civilian world is inexorably slipping away. I begin to sweat profusely beneath my helmet and combat body armour, or CBA, scant but necessary protection against a missile strike or ground fire from an anti-aircraft gun. The lumbering aircraft begins to pitch and roll in a desperate attempt to avoid missile lock-on.

One of the crew is monitoring the ground outside with night-vision goggles, searching for the tell-tale flashes of anti-aircraft fire.

A missile strike at this altitude would not be survivable. I wonder if the rest of the passengers, like me, are urging the pilot to fly faster. No senior military official will admit it publicly but the current thinking in the Ministry of Defence is that is just a matter of time before the Taliban acquires surface-to-air missiles and manages to shoot down a troop-laden Herc flying into Helmand. Such a cata-strophic event, the loss of dozens of British troops in a single inci-dent, could finally kill off the dwindling public support for the war in Afghanistan and signal the beginning of the end for the entire NATO mission.

A young Army officer sitting on my right conjures up a nervous smile but his eyes tell another story. It's his first tour in Helmand and he has never flown in a Herc before. I attempt to allay his fears by giving him the thumbs up. But, in truth, I'm probably just as worried as he is. I'm not a good flyer at the best of times and all sorts of 'what if' thoughts are running through my head. Six hours earlier, when we arrived in Kandahar Air Force Base, known within the military as KAF, the young officer reminded me of a timid boy attending his first day at school. Fresh-faced and awkward, among no friendly faces, he sat by himself for several hours with his head buried in a Dick Francis thriller, before boarding the flight to Helmand.

I'm on board what they call the 'KAF taxi' – effectively a military shuttle flight into Helmand from the sprawling Kandahar Air Base. I'm one of more than 100 passengers flown into Afghanistan on an ageing RAF TriStar – it first came into service in the early 1980s and was already second-hand. Hopefully the aircraft's engines are in better shape than the passenger cabin because that is well and truly knackered. If the TriStar was a civilian plane, I'm pretty sure it would be grounded. Parts of the interior are held together by 3-inch-wide silver masking tape and the toilet doors have a tendency to fly open while in use – 'The in-flight entertainment,' some wag commented – but, frankly, it's good enough for 'our boys' flying off to war to fight and die for Queen and Country. The TriStar is straight out of the military manual of 'making do'. It's what happens when the armed forces have been underfunded for decades. It is, as one senior officer told me, a third party, fire and theft, rather than fully comprehensive, insurance package.

Afghanistan has its own unique smell – it's the dust in the atmosphere – and it's on the plane thousands of feet above the desert; for me it's the smell of fear, death and courage, and there is no other smell like it. The fear, and also the excitement, of being in a war zone are already beginning to build inside me and giving rise to a mix of emotions. I have yet to arrive and already part of me is wishing that I was back home, in a warm, safe house with my family. Instead I'm just minutes away from landing in one of the most dangerous places on earth.

Fourteen hours ago I was sitting in the bleak departure lounge at RAF Brize Norton along with several hundred soldiers. All tired, all sad. For them the long goodbye had come and gone – they were just at the start of their six-month tour. Six months of fear, broken up by bursts of excitement and long stretches of unimaginable boredom. There is nothing romantic about front-line life in Helmand: it is hard, dangerous and dirty. Generals and politicians fighting the war from their desks in Whitehall might talk about the importance of nation building and national security, but for the soldiers at the bullet end of the war it's all about survival. From the private soldier, who joined the Army because it was the only job available after eighteen years on a sink estate, to the Eton-educated Guards officer, winning is coming home alive and not in a Union Jack-draped coffin. Soldiers in Helmand fight for themselves and each other – grander notions are for others to hold.

It was the same for me when I served as a young officer in 3rd Battalion Parachute Regiment in Northern Ireland in the late 1980s. Every member of 3 Para knew why the British Army was on the streets of Ulster. We understood the politics, the tribal tensions and the history, but it mattered little to any of us. Soldiers do not fight for Queen and Country: they fight for each other. They do not fix bayonets with the government's foreign policy objectives ringing in their ears: they do so because they are professionals trained to obey orders. It's the same in Helmand today. Every soldier still wants to win a medal but he also wants to make it home in one piece.

But with glory comes a terrible price. In Helmand, a front-line soldier stands a one-in-ten chance of being killed or injured; those are not good odds. Looking around the departure lounge at RAF Brize Norton, I wondered which of my fellow passengers would not survive the six-month tour, and I doubt I was the only one with that thought in their mind. The atmosphere was subdued, depressing even. Some soldiers entered the room with eyes reddened by tears, doubtless wondering whether they would ever see their loved ones again. Part of me, sitting here now descending into the Helmand desert, wonders the same.

There was once a time when I thought that as a journalist I was safe in a war zone. It's a foolish notion. Why should I be less at risk than anyone else? But I believed it nonetheless. I have worked in several war zones – the Balkans, Iraq, Northern Ireland – and I always thought death and injury were something that happened to others. Mainly soldiers or journalists who forgot to obey the rules or who simply pushed their luck too far.

That was until one of my best friends, Rupert Hamer, was killed while on assignment in January 2010 after the US armoured vehicle in which he was travelling was destroyed by an IED. He was working as a reporter alongside photographer Phil Coburn, and the pair were both attached to the US Marines Expeditionary Force when he was killed. They were part way through a two-week assignment and were returning from a shura, or meeting of elders, when the tragedy struck. Phil and Rupert were sitting beside each other inside a 30-ton heavily armoured Mine Resistant Ambush Protected (MRAP) vehicle when they hit a huge improvised explosive device.

The main charge was composed of ammonium nitrate powder and aluminium filings, and when these are mixed together in the right quantities the result is lethal. The explosive was packed into several yellow palm-oil containers buried about 15 cm beneath the ground. The detonator was probably made from a Christmas tree light, or something similar, with the bulb removed. The bomb was one of the largest ever seen in Helmand.

The MRAP more or less remained intact – the front and rear wheels and axles were blown off – but the shock wave which tore through the vehicle was devastating. Despite wearing helmets and body armour and being strapped into their seats, Rupert, Phil and four US Marines all suffered multiple injuries. Phil and Rupert were sitting side by side, but while Rupert died Phil survived, though the bones in his feet were smashed beyond repair and both feet were amputated. Four US Marines travelling in the vehicle were seriously injured and a fifth was killed.

Death in Helmand is random – it has killed the best in the British Army, possibly even the best of the best. Every soldier from private to lieutenant colonel – all the ranks in a battlegroup – have been killed in action in the province since 2006. Not since Korea has the British Army been in such a bloody fight, and every indicator suggests it's going to get worse.

I last spoke to Rupert less than two weeks before he was killed. It was an unusually warm day in early January. He had called me from Kabul while waiting for a flight to Helmand. I was sitting on a chair in my garden, guffawing with laughter as he relayed in detail all the hilarious events that had befallen both him and Phil in the short time that they had been in Afghanistan.

Rupert was in good form, joking about the Marines' lack of organization and saying that by comparison they made him look organized. My last words were, 'E-mail me when you can, and look after yourself.' As he set off for Helmand, I went to Austria for a week's skiing holiday with my family. Rupert was killed on the following Saturday, 10 January.

The first thing my wife, Clodagh, said to me after I told her Rupert had been killed was, 'It could have been you.' At that moment I vowed never to return. Fuck it, I thought to myself. It's not worth it.

Not for a few stories for a newspaper. But even as the words formed I secretly I knew I would return. The problem for me is that I find war zones exciting places. There is a thrill to being under fire, even risking your life, always in the knowledge, of course, that, as an observer, rather than a protagonist, I was somehow invulnerable. Rupert's death shattered that illusion, but as the shock of his loss gradually lessened I was soon beginning to convince myself of the need to return.

Rupert always said to me, 'If you are going to report the war, then you have to see the war,' and he was right. Just before I left, my 6-year-old son asked me why I was going to Afghanistan. 'To carry out research for my book and to report on what is happening in the country,' I told him, hoping that he wouldn't ask me if I was going to do anything dangerous. 'Why can't you just get the information off the internet?' he responded, looking confused. 'Because that's what somebody else has seen and witnessed,' I replied. 'I need to see what is going on for myself so that I can write about it.' 'Oh,' he said, 'I think I understand.'

So here I am on a C-130, ten minutes away from landing in Helmand, the centre of a war zone where every day British troops are being killed and injured. So much for never returning. And the news from the front line is not good. In Sangin, a town in the north of Helmand, six soldiers have been killed in the first week of March. Four of the dead were shot by snipers. Taliban shooters are good, and the Army is understandably nervous. Enemy snipers are feared and hated by all armies and run the risk of summary execution if captured. Snipers will go for the easy kill or one designed to shatter morale: the young soldier, the commander, the medic. Morale in Sangin had understandably suffered. Soldiers were being picked off at the rate of one a day. Although the sniper is guaranteed to generate fear, in Helmand the IED, the unseen killer, remains the soldiers' worst nightmare. A step in the wrong direction, a momentary lapse of concentration, can mean mutilation, the loss of one or more limbs, or death.

Lose a leg in what is known as a traumatic amputation and you have just four and a half minutes for a medic to staunch the wound before you fatally 'bleed out'. The time decreases with each additional limb lost, and that is why no quadruple amputee has yet survived.

IEDs are now being manufactured on an industrial scale – it is no longer a cottage industry. Bomb factories in some parts of Helmand can produce an IED every fifteen minutes. Made from pieces of wood, old batteries and home-made explosive, they are basic and deadly. The Taliban have already produced IEDs with 'low metal' or 'no metal' content, which are difficult to detect. So, as well as using equipment to detect bombs, troops also need to rely on what they call the 'Mk 1 eyeball', hoping to spot ground sign.

In Helmand the IED is now the Taliban's weapon of choice and the main killer of British troops. The field hospital in Camp Bastion now expects to treat at least one IED trauma victim every day. Between September 2009 and April 2010 there were almost 2,000 IED incidents.

The human cost of this war has never been higher. Since 2006 more than 350 soldiers have been killed and more than 4,000 injured. Of these, more than 150 have lost one or more limbs. And those are the statistics for just the British forces. Every country with troops in Helmand – the United States, Estonia and Denmark – has suffered similar losses.

In one week alone in February 2010 there were 200 IED incidents – that is, bombs being detonated or discovered. Do the maths – that's over 9,000 a year. Or more than one IED for every British soldier serving in Helmand.

The job of battling against this threat falls to the Joint Force Explosive Ordnance Disposal Group, part of the Counter IED, or CIED, Task Force. At the tip of the spear are the Ammunition Technical Officers, or ATOs, the soldiers who defuse the Taliban IEDs – the bomb hunters. Also called IED operators, the ATOs work hand in glove with the RESTs. It is a fantastically dangerous task, not because the devices are sophisticated but because of the volume of bombs. The number of IED attacks started to go through the roof in 2008, a development which was entirely unpredicted. Back then there were just two bomb-disposal teams in Helmand because someone, somewhere in the Ministry of Defence did not regard Helmand as a 'high-threat' environment. That was the official version of events but in reality Iraq was still the priority and there were simply not enough bomb hunters to serve in both theatres. The following year IEDs were killing more soldiers than Taliban bullets. By the middle of 2010 the CIED Task Force began suffering casualties on a scale which had not been seen for thirty years.

I've come back to Helmand to try to understand why anyone would want to become a bomb hunter. I want to get inside their heads, learn about their fears and concerns, the unimaginable stresses they face every day and what drives them on knowing that one mistake, one single slip, can mean death. For three weeks I will be an embedded journalist working alongside both the bomb-hunting teams of the CIED Task Force and the Grenadier Guards battlegroup.

It is virtually impossible to report from Helmand without being embedded. The risks are so great that independent travel is a nonstarter. Travelling independently through Helmand could only really be achieved by striking some sort of deal with the Taliban in order to pass safely through areas under their control. Even if that were achievable there would still be every chance of hitting an IED or finding yourself in the crossfire of a battle between the insurgents and British troops.

Being an embedded reporter has its advantages, the most important being safety. To a certain extent journalists are exposed to the same risks as soldiers, but because you are not playing an active part in a battle you are not fighting through Taliban positions, so you have to be fairly unlucky to be killed or injured. But there are disadvantages. All of my copy will be scrutinized by censors who will check it for anything which could be construed as a breach of operational security. Before any journalist can embed with the British

Army, he or she must sign the 'Green Book', a contractual obligation stating that the Ministry of Defence will scrutinize all copy, pictures and video before publication.

Most journalists don't have a problem with this, even if it does run counter to the idea of a free press, and I for one would not want to write anything which might put a soldier's life at risk.

The C-130 slams into Camp Bastion's darkened runway, and the relief on board is tangible. The engines once again begin to scream as we slow to a halt. Beneath the green gloom of the safety lights, the troops begin to ready themselves for disembarkation. The Herc's rear ramp opens, like a giant mouth, revealing a kaleidoscope of orange, yellow and white lights blinking through the desert dust. This is not a military camp, it's a small city, dominated by the monotonous drone of departing aircraft, some carrying troops, others bearing the coffins of the fallen.

One by one we silently disembark, keeping our personal thoughts private, each wondering what the future will bring. Beneath a star-lit sky we are led in single file from the airstrip to waiting buses, before being driven to one of the 'processing centres' where fresh troops undergo their final preparations for war. The week-long Reception, Staging and Onward Movement Integration (RSOI) programme is effectively designed to fine-tune the soldier so that he can hit the ground running. In effect it's the last chance to get things right before coming face to face with the enemy.

A two-tier war is being fought by the British Army in Helmand. The 'teeth arm' troops, those involved in the day-to-day fighting and killing, live in small patrol bases, where the conditions range from sparse to austere. Toilets are often holes in the ground, soldiers keep clean with a solar shower – a bag of water which has been left to bake in the sun – and meals are a mixture of fresh food and Army rations. Six months on the front line is a dangerous existence with few comforts.

But those troops who remain in bases like Camp Bastion or Kandahar Air Base live, by comparison, in air-conditioned luxury, with hot showers and fresh food, and where off-duty hours can be spent in one of the many gyms or watching premiership football on satellite television. 'Life in the rear,' as the American troops in Vietnam observed, 'has no fear.' The majority of those soldiers based at Camp Bastion will never set foot beyond its gates, but while they might not take the same risks as the front-line soldiers their job is just as vital. They keep the war machine moving by ensuring that the right food, water and ammunition arrive at the right place at the right time. It's a job which lacks the 'glamour' of battle but is just as important.

The coach snakes its way through the camp, passing row upon row of huge tents which were once white but have now taken on the hue of the desert. I've been coming to Camp Bastion since 2006, and every time I return the place has grown. Someone once said that the best decision the British Army ever made in Helmand was to build the base in the middle of nowhere. Had it been near a town or an area of habitation, the chances are that it would have been mortared or rocketed every night.

Our belongings are dumped in the desert dust by an Army lorry and chaos ensues as 100 individuals search for the bags in the pitch blackness. The soldiers are told to collect their kit and move into one of the briefing rooms – I say goodbye to the young Army officer, shake his hand and wish him luck, silently hoping that he makes it home safely in six months' time. The weary soldiers file into a tent to begin a series of briefings through which many will sleep. I'm left with the lasting impression that Camp Bastion is one giant processing centre. Every night hundreds of tired, nervous and confused troops arrive to feed the war machine, and every day, or almost every day, the dead, the wounded and the lucky fly out.

Twenty hours ago I left my home in Kent and kissed my wife and sleeping children goodbye and said a silent prayer as the first cuckoo of spring sang the dawn chorus. Now I am in another world, where the threat of death and violence is always present. Not for the first time I ask myself, what am I doing in Afghanistan? It's 5 a.m. Helmand time, and finally I get some sleep.

Rupert Hamer was not the first person I have known to be killed in Helmand. While embedded with the Grenadier Guards in November 2009 I met Sapper David Watson, who was a member of a REST. He struck me as a quiet but professional soldier who was completely committed to his job. He was killed in an explosion in the Sangin area on 31 December. I met Sergeant Michael Lockett in 2008 when he was awarded a Military Cross after serving in Helmand in 2007. He returned in 2009 but was killed in action on 21 September, just a few weeks before he was due to return to the UK.

In July 2008 I was embedded with the Parachute Regiment for a short period at FOB Inkerman, just north of Sangin town. There had been a spike in Taliban attacks over the past two months and just two weeks before my visit a suicide bomb had killed three members of the regiment. On one early-morning patrol in which I took part, I met Lance Corporal Ken Rowe, a member of the Royal Army Veterinary Corps, and his dog Sasha. Everyone immediately warmed to both man and dog. I think there was something about Sasha that reminded everyone of home, but less than a week later both were killed in an ambush.

Then there was Warrant Officer Class 2 (WO2) Gary 'Gaz' O'Donnell. War is one of the few human endeavours that create real heroes, and one of those was Gaz. He was a high-threat IED operator – one of just a handful of soldiers gifted with the skill of being able to defuse home-made bombs in the most deadly place on earth.

I first met Gaz in Helmand in July 2008. I was told that Gaz was worth chatting to because he had a 'nice collection of war stories'. I wasn't disappointed. My lasting memory is of him sitting astride a quad bike dressed in just his body armour, helmet, shorts and a set of cool civilian shades. It was on one of the training grounds in

Camp Bastion, where troops coming fresh into theatre are taught the basics of 'Operation Bama' – the process of locating and confirming the presence of IEDs in Afghanistan.

Gaz's dress code broke all the rules, and the smile on his face said he was loving it. I liked him as soon as he shook my hand. He was a combination of unruffled calmness and mischief. His thick red hair was long and unkempt, as was his moustache. His obvious disregard for dress regulations was the flip side of his professional life, where his unwavering allegiance to a set of rules and self-discipline kept him alive. Gaz was already a veteran of Iraq, Northern Ireland, Sierra Leone and two tours in Helmand. He was a legend in the counter-IED, or CIED, world even before he arrived in Afghanistan.

Blazoned across his broad shoulders was a tattoo: 'Living the Dream'. It was his motto. He had already won the George Medal in Iraq and was destined for another top gallantry award for his work in Helmand. Gaz lived to defuse bombs – it was his calling.

At 24 years old Gaz joined the Army relatively late in life. The delay was due in part to a failed experiment as a rock guitarist – another tattoo of a cannabis leaf, also on his back, was a memento of a more hedonistic life.

From the day he joined up Gaz wanted to become an IED opera-tor. But it was to be a long haul. After passing basic training he was posted to Germany to serve in 3 Base Ammunition Depot, learning the trade of the Ammunition Technician. But when the opportunity came to take the Improvised Explosive Device Disposal Course, he passed with flying colours. A feat he also managed to achieve on the IED High Threat course, to become one of just a handful of bomb-disposal experts to pass the course first time.

Like every bomb-disposal operator, Gaz was keen to get involved in the thick of the action in Iraq, but he was forced to wait until 2006, by which time he was a staff sergeant, before he finally got his wish. The war had gone belly-up, primarily because of the complete absence of post-operation planning. After defeating the Iraqi Army and deposing Saddam, the US and British forces managed to snatch defeat from the jaws of victory. A Shia insurgency in the south quickly followed a Sunni revolt in the north. Reconstruction of the shattered state ground to a halt and al-Qaeda, the Islamist force behind the 9/11 attacks, managed to gain a foothold in the country.

By 2006, attacks against the multi-national forces in the south were a daily occurrence. With the help of the Iranian Revolutionary Guard the Shia insurgents managed to develop a range of highly sophisticated improvized explosive devices called Explosively Formed Projectiles, or shaped charges, which could penetrate armour and were detonated by infrared triggers.

These IEDs took a terrible toll on the British troops, killing and maiming hundreds, especially those travelling in the now notorious Snatch vehicles. These were lightly armoured Land Rovers once used to patrol the streets in Northern Ireland during the Troubles. Snatches were originally designed to protect troops from small-arms fire, rocket-propelled grenades (RPGs) and shrapnel. When the insurgency exploded in 2004, the British Army found itself without a vehicle in which troops could conduct patrols in urban areas, and the Snatch was sent to fill the gap. But such was their vulnerability to attack that within months the troops had dubbed the vehicles 'mobile coffins'.

By 2006 reconstruction plans for Iraq had become a faded dream. Troops rarely ventured out of their bases without being attacked. The first sign that the Iraqi people in the south were not as welcoming as the government and the top brass might have hoped had come on 2 July 2003, when six members of the Royal Military Police were attacked and killed by a 300-strong mob in the town of Majar al Kabir.

By the end of his tour Gaz was estimated to have saved the lives of hundreds of British soldiers and was subsequently awarded the George Medal. By 2008 he was in Helmand, one of only two bomb-disposal experts who could be spared to work alongside soldiers fighting in the most mined country on earth. In April of that year Gaz was deployed to the province as a member of the Joint Force

Explosive Ordnance Disposal (EOD) Group team. A month later he had obtained almost celebrity status after defusing eight IEDs in six hours.

The operation began on 9 May, when a Danish vehicle patrol approached a track junction in the Upper Gereshk Valley in central Helmand. It was a classic vulnerable point, or VP, an ideal location for the Taliban to plant one or more IEDs. At the top of the junction, on a ridge line overlooking the valley, was a position which had been used many times before by the Danish troops to monitor movement in the notorious Green Zone. A fertile plain bordering the Helmand River, the Green Zone was where the Taliban held sway. It was 'Terry's Turf,' Gaz said, 'Terry Taliban' being a nickname for the insurgents.

The patrol stopped short of the crossroads and two British soldiers from 51 Squadron Royal Engineers, who were accompanying the Danes, began to scan the area. The two British engineers knew that in all likelihood the Taliban had probably buried at least one IED and, using their standard-issue Vallon mine detectors, the pair began searching the area. Moving forward in slow, measured steps, the two young sappers began swinging the detectors from left to right.

Within minutes one of the alarms screamed, signalling the presence of a suspect device. The Royal Engineer knelt down, pulled out a household paintbrush – a vital piece of equipment for every soldier in Helmand – from the front of his body armour, and gently began to brush away dust from the area where the detector had gone off. Within a few minutes the tell-tale shape of an IED pressure plate emerged. The device was marked and the two soldiers moved, one to each side of the track. Minutes later the alarm sounded again. Over the next two hours a total of eight booby-traps were found in a 75-metre radius. It was the largest multiple-IED site ever seen in Helmand.

Back in Camp Bastion, while Gaz was tucking into a pot noodle, his favourite snack, and watching the TV, a 'ten-liner' requesting an IED operator suddenly popped up on a computer screen in the operations room of the Joint Force EOD Group. The ten-liner is so named because it reveals ten lines of information about an IED: date, grid reference (location), description, activity prior to find, rendez-vous location and approach, incident commander, tactical situation, threat assessment, initial request, requested priority (immediate, pre-explosion, post explosion, urgent, minor, routine, no threat).

Gaz and his search team were on HRF standby and at a drop of a hat they could deploy to anywhere in Helmand to defuse IEDs armed with only the information contained within the ten-liner. And on the morning of 9 May 2008 Gaz was called to the ops room, where Major Wayne Davidson, the officer commanding the EOD squadron, told him he had a task. 'Sounds relatively straightforward,' were the major's parting words as Gaz went to brief his team. The ten-liner stated that there were one or more pressure-plate IEDs in a vulner-able point in the Gereshk Valley.

Within ten minutes Gaz's team, which consisted of his No. 2, or second in command, the electronic counter-measures (ECM) opera-tor and the infantry escort, the last basically his bodyguard, were ready to move. A few moments later the REST and the RESA had assembled in the briefing tent.

'This should be interesting,' Gaz said, then explained the situa-tion. 'We've got multiple IEDs in an area which looks like an over-watch site into the Green Zone. Chances are it's been used by ISAF before and a pattern has been set. We'll learn more when we arrive. Questions?' There were none – everyone knew the score. 'Good – let's go.'

Within forty minutes Gaz, his team and the search team were airborne, heading for the IED site in a Chinook helicopter.

Even before leaving the safety of Camp Bastion, Gaz knew the 'bomb suit' – an all-encompassing piece of body armour designed to protect ATOs from the effects of an explosion – was not an option. The bomb suit weighs almost 50 kg and the temperature was already 45°C. He knew that he was unlikely to last more than twenty minutes inside it. Besides, a bomb suit is really designed to protect the operator when either walking to or away from the bomb. Gaz took his chances; it was a calculated risk but one which he believed favoured him.

'By the time I got to work,' he explained later, 'the wider area had been cleared by the search team and the area was secured. An incident control point had been cleared and I was happy. I moved forward, took a moment to gather myself, and then began to work methodically through the area. I have been an ATO for a long time and worked in some pretty nasty environments, but I had never encountered nothing like that before. It was pretty tense.'

Gaz spent hours on his hands and knees, his face just inches away from the IEDS. Had any one of them exploded, he would have been killed instantly.

It was the same routine for each bomb. Walk down the cleared lane, locate the device with the hand-held metal detector, and try to isolate the device from the power supply. Operators must always be aware of the potential for other threats in the area. There have been occasions where another device has been placed to target the operator, such as a so-called command IED, which could be something as simple as a hand grenade with a piece of wire or string tied to the ring pull at the end of which is an insurgent waiting for the right time to strike.

This is the most risky period for any IED operator. Once they 'go down the road' or 'take the long walk' to the bomb, they are on their own and effectively isolated – and make a very inviting target. Everyone else in the team, including supporting troops, must be outside the blast radius.

'It was 11 a.m. and it was getting pretty hot,' Gaz explained. 'I wanted to save as many of the devices as possible so that we could extract the maximum amount of forensic information.' Just when he thought he was finished, he discovered another IED. But this time it was attached to a command wire, which can either be pulled to initiate the explosion or linked to a power source such as a battery and detonated electronically.

Gaz was stunned. 'At that stage I didn't know whether I was being watched by the Taliban who were waiting for me to get close to the device. It was a very sobering feeling. You're there staring at something, knowing that it could go bang at any moment and that would be it: "game over". But Gaz pushed on and successfully disabled the command IED. 'I don't know if I was being watched and the Taliban just decided not to detonate it. But I think it was there to catch out an IED operator. Maybe I was just lucky that day, and that suits me just fine.'

By early evening Gaz had finally completed the mission. He was physically and mentally shattered, dehydrated, his face red and sore after hours in the intense desert sun. It was only when he returned to the incident control point (ICP) for the final time that the fatigue hit him like a left hook. 'I eventually finished at 6 p.m. I was out there for seven hours but to be honest I didn't really notice the heat because I was so focused on the task. It was only when I got back into the ICP and it was time to return to Bastion that I realized I was knackered. My arms and legs felt as though they were made from lead and I had a thumping headache.'

But it was a successful mission. Every IED operator wants to recover a device intact so that it can be forensically tested. At this stage, obtaining forensic information left on the device during its manufacture was still in its infancy, but within two years this skill would become key to defeating the bombers.

A smile spread across Gaz's face as he continued, 'I managed to disrupt all eight IEDs and all of the forensic information was recovered. That is absolutely vital. We need to know who is making these bombs and we can get a lot of that from the equipment. It was exactly the same as with the IRA. So if I can recover a device and we can get some forensic, then gleaming [soldier slang for brilliant or great], and I sleep well.'

Two months earlier Gaz had been called to deal with a roadside bomb which was blocking a convoy route, leaving large numbers of troops stationary and vulnerable in hostile territory. Wherever

possible the Taliban will try to place their fighters in positions close
to where they have planted IEDs so that they can follow up a successful detonation with an ambush.

Gaz, knowing the risks and the need for speed, worked solidly for
twenty-four hours and discovered eleven devices. One of the bombs
was attached to a command wire, which the Taliban attempted to
initiate as he walked towards it. Gaz survived only because the device
failed to detonate properly. Despite knowing that the Taliban were
clearly watching him, he continued working until the entire area was
made safe.

'It was a tough job but in situations like that you just have to be
methodical, keep a clear head, and trust your own judgement. I
might be the person who goes in to disrupt the IEDs but it's a real
team effort. You have to have total confidence in your search team –
and everyone shares the same risk.'

Sitting in the ops room in Camp Bastion, Gaz explained to me
how the Taliban were beginning to change their tactics and how he
believed the war in Afghanistan would change because the insurgents couldn't win using conventional tactics.

As I sat sipping a cup of tea in the cool of the air-conditioned
room, Gaz disappeared for a few minutes before re-emerging with
a large plastic bag. 'This is an IED,' he said, holding it up for me to
see like an angler with a prized catch. 'I defused this one and
brought it back a few weeks ago,' he told me with a beaming smile.
Before me was a man in his element, but it was clear that Gaz really
had no concept at how extraordinary he was. Even those around
him, IED operators more senior and experienced, seemed to be in
awe.

'This is the pressure plate,' he said as he pulled what looked like a
shallow rectangular wooden box wrapped in plastic torn from a
dirty bag. 'This is basically a large switch. You have a power source
connected to these two pieces of metal and to a detonator. Step on
this and the whole thing goes bang – it's that simple, but it works and
it's deadly.'

The pressure-plate IED's design is frighteningly simple. Inside the wooden case, which is about 40 cm long, 8 cm wide and 5 cm high, are two rusty saw blades about 15 cm long. The idea is that when pressure is applied to the box, the blades touch, the electric circuit is completed, and the device explodes.

I'm stunned. 'Is that it?'

Gaz nods, smiling.

'What's the explosive composed of?' I ask.

'Anything Terry can get his hands on. Mortar rounds, artillery shells, land mines. This place has been at war for thirty-odd years, so there's a lot of stuff lying around – and if they can't find any explosive they'll make their own.'

What's it like being an IED operator? I ask Gaz. 'Bomb disposal – it's the best job in the world,' he replies. 'I wanted to do it from the moment I joined up. I love the challenge: when you go down the road it's all down to you – your wits against theirs – and providing you stick to your training and don't become complacent you should be OK. The Taliban are always developing their tactics, so we need to make sure we are really on the ball. I'm never nervous when I'm on a job, but I'm never complacent either.'

As we chat away in the ops room, leaning on a table which also doubles as a huge map board, Gaz tells me about an incident which even he admits was a little close for comfort.

Members of 2 Para based in the area of the Kajaki Dam, in the north of Helmand, had discovered an IED on a track leading to their base. As normal, a ten-liner was sent out by the troops and Gaz's team were dispatched to the scene.

'It was a routine job – sort of thing I'd done many times before,' he said, lifting his feet onto the end of the bench. 'I went through all the normal drills, making sure everything was secure, and so I set about trying to render the device safe. I always work in the prone position – lying down. I find it more comfortable and you don't present too much of an easy target to the Taliban. I was working away trying to isolate the power source. The device was different to others I had seen. In this case the trigger was an everyday clothes peg with two metal contacts fixed to the closing parts of the peg. The peg was being held open by a piece of rubber wrapped around the opposite end. I thought, I haven't seen that before – that's quite clever. While the contacts were held apart the device was safe but it was also connected to a power source, so it had to be isolated as well.'

As Gaz set about working on the device, he noticed out of the corner of his eye that the rubber started to move backwards along the peg. He had less than a second to react. Just before the rubber clip holding the arms of the peg apart snapped, he pushed his finger between the contacts, stopping them from snapping shut and detonating the bomb. With his other hand he pulled out a pair of pliers from the front of his body armour and cut the wiring to make the bomb safe.

'I saw the ends of the peg moving,' Gaz said. 'I didn't have time to think. I had to act straight away, so I jammed my fingers between the two contacts. I had to make an assessment that there wasn't a secondary circuit. Then there was no other option but to cut the wires manually. Even for me that was a bit of a close shave.'

The device was wired to an 82 mm mortar and a 107 mm Chinese-made rocket: enough explosive to wipe out a dozen men. Had the peg closed Gaz would have been blown to pieces.

Facing death was part of every IED operator's daily routine, yet the stress associated with working in Helmand in 2008 left Gaz unfazed. Just before I left him in the ops room, I asked Gaz if he ever worried about being killed. 'It never enters my mind,' he replied. 'You can't do this job and worry about getting killed.'

On 10 September 2008, less than a week before he was due to fly home to his family, Gaz was killed while trying to defuse an IED on a routine mission in Musa Qala. He was awarded a posthumous Bar to his George Medal on 4 March 2009.

Gaz was the first ATO to be killed in Afghanistan, and everyone who worked in bomb disposal knew from that moment on that his death wouldn't be the last.

* * *

I awake, drunk with fatigue, to an announcement over the PA system: 'Op Minimise is now in force.' Operation Minimise is launched every time a soldier is killed or seriously wounded. When it's in force all connections to the outside world – e-mails and phone calls – are suspended until twenty-four hours after the next of kin have been informed. There was a time, when the mission in Helmand was still new, when the launching of Minimise would temporarily silence laughter in the canteens and prompt soldiers to speak in hushed tones. Not any more. Today in Helmand violent and sudden death is a reality of life, and such announcements appear to barely register with the troops.

Stepping out of the large tent, I am greeted by a cloudless sky and the distant but distinctive 'wokka-wokka' engine tune played by an RAF Chinook landing on the flight line. Camp Bastion is now a fully-fledged multi-national base. It probably boasts a high ranking on the list of the world's fastest-growing towns. In 2006, when the soldiers from the Royal Engineers began turning raw desert into a military base, it probably housed just 2,000 troops. Since then it has grown tenfold, although I doubt anyone really knows how many troops are actually based inside at any particular time. It now comprises Camp Bastion 1 and Camp Bastion 2, and the US Marines have grafted their own base, Camp Leatherneck, onto one side.

Bastion is richly endowed with creature comforts. There is Pizza Hut, a Chinese and an Indian takeaway, NAAFI and foreign equivalents, and the American PX store, which sells everything the modern fighting soldier needs. Soldiers with time on their hands can go to the gym, play computer games, jog in complete safety around the camp perimeter, or watch a premiership football match courtesy of the British Forces Broadcasting Service. The Danish battlegroup, which also has a headquarters in Bastion, put on a rock concert. There is even talk that the US Marines are planning to build a swimming pool to increase the comfort of those serving during the summer in Helmand, where temperatures can reach up to 50°.

Soldiers being soldiers, this has led to relations between male and female troops, and in 2009 at least ten British servicewomen fell pregnant and had to be sent home. Numerous canteens each disgorge hundreds of meals every day. British troops even have a choice for breakfast: the continental version for the health-conscious or the 'full English' for those who enjoy a heartier start to the day.

The troops live cheek by jowl in air-conditioned tents, sleeping cocooned within individual mosquito nets on camp beds rather oddly described as 'cots'. The base even has its own police force to ensure that soldiers are properly dressed for meals – open-toed sandals, for example, are forbidden in the dining halls – and those who break the camp speed limit of 15 mph face being issued a speeding ticket by the camp police. The base has also earned the distinction of becoming the UK's sixth busiest airport – after Heathrow, Gatwick, Edinburgh, Birmingham and Luton – with more than 400 helicopter and aircraft flights every day. It is a far cry from April 2006, when a two-man control team from the RAF's Tactical Air Traffic Control Unit activated the dirt-track landing strip. Some ninety minutes later the first of hundreds of thousands of flights arrived. Today combat operations, medical evacuations and logistic sustainment flights all operate from what has become a vital military hub.

Discreetly positioned in one area of the base is the headquarters of the CIED Task Force. The operations room is in the same place as the last time I visited, two years ago, when I met Gaz O'Donnell. But there are now more than a dozen IED Disposal, or IEDD, Teams in Helmand, whereas when I interviewed Gaz there were just two. Despite the increase, the IED operators and the RESTs are kept busy all the time, working out beyond the perimeter of Camp Bastion. Most of the teams are deployed to various battlegroup locations in Helmand, while the High Readiness Force – which is composed of a four-man counter-IEDD team, seven-man high-risk REST, and a RESA – is on duty in Camp Bastion, ready at a moment's notice to fly to anywhere in the province.

The living quarters of the CIED Task Force consist of rows of tents. Above each tent is a board which identifies the team living there. One board reads: 'IEDD Team 4 – warfare not welfare' and identifies the ATO as 'Badger'. Another reads: 'Team Inferno – First to go, last to know.' There is little for the soldiers to do in this part of the camp and it is clear that most of the tents are rarely inhabited. Any downtime is usually spent sleeping, preparing for the next operation, or relaxing in the 'bar', which, although there is no alcohol on sale, just fizzy drinks and chocolate, has become a gathering point for residents and a place to relax for those passing through.

Another board reveals the location of one of the RESTs and reads: 'Team Illume – Loves the jobs you hate!' The sign also reveals that three members of the team are battle casualty replacements – soldiers flown in to replace those who have been killed or injured. It is clear that black humour is one of the life-support systems for anyone involved in IED work, but even though soldiers are flippant about the risks it is an unwritten rule that they never joke about their dead or injured colleagues.

Within a few minutes of arriving at the Task Force Headquarters I meet up with Staff Sergeant Karl Ley – a man who, at 29, has become something of a legend in the IEDD world. Badger, as he prefers to be called – and I'll explain why shortly – has come to the end of his six-month tour of duty and in that time he has defused 139 Taliban bombs. It's a record.

Chapter 2: **Badger's War**

'I thought, this is where I cop it; I'm going to be hit in the back and the lights are going to go out and that's going to be it. No more life, no more wife, no more kids.'
Staff Sergeant Karl Ley, ATO, 11 Explosive Ordnance Disposal Regiment, Joint Force EOD Group

The dust cloud mushroomed into the air, momentarily enveloping the armoured column snaking east across the flat desert plain.

The logistics convoy, one of many that day traversing the arid expanses of Helmand, had paused at the head of a dried-out river bed which for centuries had served as a transit route into the town of Musa Qala, home to an isolated British base in the north of the province.

Like the many bases which pepper Helmand, the one at Musa Qala was wholly dependent for its survival on Combat Logistics Patrols (CLP) – vast, 100-vehicle armoured convoys which delivered food, water, fuel, ammunition and mail to every isolated compound in the province. As there were too few helicopters, resupply by CLP was vital. The men and women of the Royal Logistic Corps who still today keep the convoys moving, often risking daily ambushes and IED strikes, really are the unsung heroes of the Afghan War.

As the dust cloud began to settle, troops from the front two vehicles jumped from the back of their Mastiff armoured troop carriers and scanned the surrounding desert. Gunners provided cover with .50-calibre heavy machine guns and automatic grenade launchers were trained on potential enemy ambush sites.

There were only a few routes into and out of the wadi and the Taliban knew them all. Each was a natural ambush site and had to be cleared of IEDs before convoys could proceed. Briefed on the task ahead, the first group of soldiers began preparing to clear routes while others moved into position to provide covering fire should the Taliban attack. The mid-morning sun had already begun to blast its intense heat onto the desert. Searching vulnerable points was a routine event for the soldiers but there was always a need to guard against complacency. For those tasked with route clearance there were no short cuts. At least once a week a soldier in Helmand was either killed or injured by an IED and many of the casualties were searchers – specifically selected and trained for the task of finding hidden bombs.

In the shade of an armoured vehicle the soldiers checked their Vallons by swinging them over a metal object, the high-pitched whine of the alarm indicating they were in prefect working order. Searching for IEDs is now a well-established discipline. Working in pairs, the soldiers moved along the dried river bed, swinging the mine detectors in sequential arcs, always left to right. The carefully choreographed movements of the searchers – each focusing on the imaginary lane stretching out before him – should ensure that any device would be detected, but it was going to be a slow process. Depending on the amount of metal debris in the ground, which, along with other factors, could cause false readings, searching could prove a very long job but one that could never be rushed.

After about forty-five minutes, when the soldiers had pushed about 100 metres into the wadi, an alarm sounded. The whine was loud and the meter reading indicated a significant metal device in the ground. The soldier knew instinctively that just half a metre in front of him was an IED. Speaking nervously into his personal role radio, he said, 'I've got a strong signal – I'm going to confirm.' Back at the head of the convoy, his section commander responded, 'Go easy, no need to over-confirm. Just do what you need to.'

The soldier was now an isolated figure, made all the more distant by the watery effect of the heat haze. His colleagues had already withdrawn to a safe distance in order to minimize casualties if the bomb detonated.

Bending down on one knee, he put the Vallon to his right and from the front of his CBA removed a paintbrush. Gently, and with a technique learned through hours of practice, the soldier began brushing and flicking away the fine desert sand. Almost every thought emptied from his head as he focused on clearing the dust away from the area where he suspected the device was buried. A fist-sized stone was sitting right on top of the spot where he believed the bomb was hidden. He stopped and stared. What to do? Licking the sweat from his top lip, he realized that whatever was causing the Vallon to shriek was buried in the parched desert directly beneath the stone. The initial inspection revealed little. If he was to investigate further, the stone would have to be removed. Gently wrapping his gloved hand around the object, the soldier began to lift.

The unmistakable sound of metal grinding on metal emerged from the ground beneath his feet. He froze. Just 5 cm beneath the soil an IED was about to explode. The two metal contacts, which would complete the electrical circuit when connected and detonate the 20 kg of home-made explosive, had moved to a distance of less than 0.5 cm apart. When the contacts touched, the device would explode.

Beads of sweat rolled down the soldier's face. His eyes widened and his pupils began to dilate, a natural reaction to the adrenalin beginning to surge through his veins. *Motherfucker! What the fuck do I do now? Don't panic – absolutely do not panic.*

It wasn't a PP IED that had been discovered, but a pressure-release, or PR, device, one of a new generation of IEDs recently devised by Taliban bomb makers, and the stones were the trigger. Pressure-release bombs operate in the opposite way to pressure-activated devices. Detonation occurs when pressure, such as a weight, is removed.

The soldier released his grip on the stone and hoped for the best – in theory if the pressure was reapplied the electrical contacts should remain apart. He held his breath and carefully, his eyes tightly shut, began to withdraw his hand. The grinding stopped. He almost collapsed with relief. Grabbing his Vallon, he stood up, took two steps back, and let out a long breath before turning around and retracing his steps through the safe lane he had cleared earlier, back to the head of the convoy.

'I think it's a PR,' he told his section commander, his eyes still filled with fear and relief. 'I nearly set the bastard thing off. For fuck's sake give us an ash.'

Back in the cool, air-conditioned ops room at the HQ of Joint Force Explosive Ordnance Disposal (JFEOD) Group, the first details of the ten-liner – in this case a request for an ATO – started to emerge on the computer screen via the secure J Chat e-mail system. Dispatching a team of bomb hunters to clear a route for a logistics convoy was standard procedure for the EOD headquarters. It was a routine job and no one in the ops room batted an eyelid. In September 2009 bombs were being discovered every day, sometimes every hour of every day, in Helmand. No one was going to get excited about a bomb in a wadi. Had a similar scenario played out in Ulster some fifteen years earlier, the clearance operation would have been a major event, the Defence Secretary would have been informed and the story would have led the news.

Staff Sergeant Karl 'Badger' Ley and his IEDD team, callsign Brimstone 32, were fresh into theatre. That was obvious to every one of the several thousand soldiers garrisoned behind Camp Bastion's concrete and barbed-wire walls. For a start their complexions were too pasty, their uniforms were crisp and starched, but most of all they didn't look knackered. Badger's team had just completed their RSOI training and were now officially classed as ready to deploy, as the HRF, to anywhere in Helmand. In theory teams new into theatre should have a few days, maybe a week, to acclimatize and sort their kit out before starting on their first operation. But the reality was different. Badger, like every ATO who had gone to Afghanistan before him, was beginning to realize that what he had learned on his High Threat course bore little resemblance to the reality of daily life on operations.

Within twenty-four hours of completing RSOI, Badger's team received their first shout. Earlier that morning he and the other soldiers in Team 4 – No. 2 operator Corporal Stewart Jones, Lance Corporal Clayton Burnett, who was the ECM operator, and Lance Corporal Joe Brown, by trade a driver but acting as the infantry escort – had spent most of the morning packing and repacking their operational equipment, trying to get the weight down and fit everything they needed into two Bergens. All the operational kit went in one of the rucksacks while personal items, such as clothing, rations, water, sleeping bag and mat, and what soldiers call 'comfort items' went in the other. Around 10 a.m., just as Badger was thinking of heading over to the welfare tent for a coffee, the operations room's runner poked his head through Team 4's tent and said, 'Badger, you've got a shout on. You need to get to the ops room for a briefing.'

Within the hour Team 4 and their equipment, along with a seven-man team of specialist Royal Engineer searchers, were on a Chinook heading for a desert HLS close to where the convoy was being held up. The chopper landed amid a dust storm of its own making and within seconds the soldiers were off. Badger's tour had just begun.

Although Badger and his team had been in Helmand for only a few days, the rest of the search team were coming to the end of their tour. The partnering of teams fresh into theatre with those that have a few months' experience under their belt ensures a continuity of expertise. Both the bomb-disposal teams and the Royal Engineer searchers form part of the CIED Task Force, which also includes weapons intelligence specialists, members of the Royal Military Police and Royal Engineer bomb-disposal officers. The Task Force's main, although not only, task is to dispose of or defuse regular munitions, such as artillery shells, rockets, mines and hand grenades. As well as finding and dismantling the IEDs, it creates a database of suspects based on forensic evidence obtained from devices 'captured' intact. Every time an ATO manages to 'capture' a device complete information is obtained which can be fed into the database, and this may one day identify the bomb makers and bomb emplacers, as well as reveal from where the components of the device have been sourced.

Badger was just beginning his first operational tour to Afghanistan, but he had deployed to Iraq as a No. 2, worked in Belize and Northern Ireland, and defused many IEDs back in the UK as a member of Nottingham Troop and Catterick Troop, both of which are part of 11 Explosive Ordnance Disposal Regiment, the unit responsible for dealing with IEDs in the UK.

As soon as he was out of the helicopter Badger automatically began to assess the situation around him. Rather than just focusing on the bomb, he was also assessing the tactical situation, the terrain, and the disposition of friendly and potential enemy forces.

The convoy commander explained the situation to Badger, who immediately suspected the device was a pressure-release IED; that, he thought, would explain the sound of grinding metal. Badger was aware that the Taliban knew that British soldiers and members of the Afghan National Army (ANA) or Afghan National Police (ANP) would sometimes move rocks or stones when trying to confirm a device. Someone, somewhere had set a pattern and the Taliban were trying to exploit it. Badger knew he would have to be on his guard. Like all ATOs operating in Helmand, he was acutely aware that for the Taliban there was no greater prize than killing a member of a bomb-disposal team.

The ANP had already developed a reputation for having a robust approach when dealing with IEDs. Rather than call for assistance from the British or US, many commander, would attempt to deal with the devices themselves and several of their number had been killed or seriously wounded by the devices. It seemed that many police commanders viewed calling in an operator to deal with an IED as a slight on their honour, and that seeking help was tantamount to an admission of cowardice. So instead the ANP would try to deal with the device – sometimes they were successful, and, tragically, sometimes they weren't.

The convoy had pulled back to a position around 150 metres from the device, but Badger and the RESA wanted to set up their ICP as close to the area as possible while still remaining in the safe zone. They commandeered one of the Mastiffs and moved to within 80 metres of the bomb so that they could get good 'eyes on' the area.

The first stage of the operation was to select and clear the ICP, which the engineers did quickly and without incident, and when it was declared secure they moved off to conduct an 'isolation' of the bomb to make sure there were no others in the area. Scanning the area with a special wire-detecting device, the engineers moved cautiously in a wide arc around where the device was believed to have been buried. The engineers were hoping to detect command wires attached to IEDs positioned close to the main charge. Trust is key in this particular operation. The ATO must be absolutely sure that the area is clear of all devices. His life is in the engineers' hands and he must be free of any external concerns if he is to be able to focus on defusing the device. Around half an hour later the engineers returned. 'Everything's clear. Over to you, Badger,' said the team commander.

Adrenalin trickled into Badger's veins and his heart beat a little faster as he made his final preparations before moving towards the device. He checked his personal equipment one last time, touching each piece of equipment as he went through a mental checklist. He tightened the strap on his helmet and adjusted his knee pads. It was the same routine every time – check, check, and check again. That was the mantra of the IED operator. There were no short cuts – not in Helmand.

By now it was stiflingly hot and neither Badger nor any of his team was properly acclimatized to the heat. Even in September the temperature in the Helmand desert could soar above 40°, and while the raw, unforgiving heat of the summer might have passed, the midday sun was still avoided by anyone with any sense.

'I thought it was meant to get fucking cooler in the autumn, Stu,' Badger said to his No. 2. 'This heat is crippling, so I'm going to take it really slowly. The last thing I want is to pile in halfway through the job. Make sure everyone back here is properly hydrated. The last thing we'll need on our first job is a heat casualty.'

Badger picked up his Vallon, switched it on, and gave it the mandatory test by swinging it over a rifle lying on the ground by his feet. The alarm sounded and he smiled. Everything was set.

'Right, see you in a bit,' Badger told the rest of the team, who were now settled in the ICP. They watched silently as he moved off into the distance, swinging the Vallon in front of him and waiting for the alarm to sound. The approach was slow and measured, everything being done in accordance with the rulebook. After reaching the device Badger cleared an area around it so that he could work comfortably, also ensuring that he had enough room for his feet.

His plan of attack was simple. The device was probably a pressure-plate device, so Badger went to work using his fingertips and a trowel, working carefully but as quickly as possible. Within fifteen minutes he had located a wire and then the power source – eight 1.5-volt batteries taped together and wrapped in plastic. A small smile of satisfaction moved across his face as he prepared to isolate the bomb from the power source.

Badger checked and rechecked that the firing mechanism was properly armed and that the electric cable connected to the rear end of the device was intact. Happy, he moved back to the ICP, where he handed the other end of the cable to Stu. 'It's all set up,' he said to Stu and the RESA as he wiped the sweat from his face. 'I've found a wire – the device seems fairly straightforward but I'll know more once the power source has been isolated. I tell you what, this heat is some-thing else – I'm absolutely fucking baking.' As Badger sat down and drank lukewarm water from a plastic bottle, Stu connected the wire into the green box known as a firing circuit.

'There's going to be a bang in about fifteen seconds. Stand by, stand by,' Stu shouted before pressing a black button on the green box, which he held in his hands. Less than a second later a bang, not unlike the sound of a shotgun, echoed around the valley.

So far so good, Badger thought. He had stuck to the book and so far everything had gone like clockwork. 'We'll give it a few minutes and then I'll go back down,' he told the team. This is known as the 'soak' period. In Northern Ireland, operators would wait several minutes before attempting to defuse a bomb. That luxury was not available in Helmand, where the Taliban were always watching. As Badger waited in the sweltering heat, it now became crystal clear to him why ATOs did not wear bomb suits in Helmand. Like the rest of the team, he was struggling to keep cool wearing just body armour. In the summer even this acted like a thermal jacket, making it feel like the temperature was about 10° hotter. With a bomb suit weighing around 40 kg and the thermometer in the mid-40s for nine months of the year, it was simply a non-starter for almost all ATOs. The fact that it was blue was also not lost on the team, all of whom knew there was nothing a Taliban sharpshooter would like to bag more than an ATO.

Badger returned down the cleared lane and checked to see if the wires had been cut. Yes, the IED weapon had done its job perfectly. He taped the ends of the wires to ensure that a circuit could not accidentally be created, removed the battery pack, and then began to extract the device itself. Extracting a pressure plate is achieved with a hook and a line. Basically a hook is attached to the plate, the ATO retreats to the ICP with the other end of the line, then he and usually his No. 2 pull on the line until the plate is pulled free. If the device detonates for any reason, no one is hurt. It's a simple but safe and effective method.

When Badger returned for a third time to the device, he was astonished by what he found. The pressure plate contained a central metal contact which could be detonated by pressure being either applied or released. This was the first time such a bomb had been seen in Helmand, and the device had been specifically designed to target ATOs and soldiers attempting to confirm its nature.

Beneath the pressure plate were several rocket warheads which would have killed anyone in a 20-metre radius of the device, and the chances are that there would have been very little, if anything, left of Badger. He took photographs of the site, the plate and the explosive, which was later detonated by the side of the track.

It had been a long, very hot day. The device had taken around two hours to disarm but it had been worth it. To obtain a brand-new device intact was a real coup. The weapons intelligence specialists who pored over bomb-making material hoping to obtain forensic data would be delighted. But, most importantly for Badger, the day had gone without a hitch, the team had coped well in the heat and under pressure, and there had been no accidents.

I met Badger as he was coming to the end of the tour. It had been a gruelling six months for the CIED Task Force. Six members had been killed and more than twenty injured, and several of these had sustained life-changing injuries. Not since the bloody days of the Troubles in Northern Ireland in the early 1970s had the world of Army bomb disposal lost so many men in such a short period of time. The losses had taken their toll on everyone serving within the Task Force, for bomb disposal is a close-knit world where the loss of even a single colleague is a bitter blow. Although ATOs are some of the most highly trained and professional soldiers in the British Army, no one in the field of bomb disposal had foreseen the huge surge in the use of IEDs by the Taliban. In 2008–9 these changed the face of the war in Helmand. Huge tracts of the country had been turned into minefields and the workload of bomb hunters went through the roof. It wasn't unusual for ATOs to defuse ten or twenty IEDs in a day, while under fire and working in temperatures in the 40s. The situation was unsustainable, and casualties inevitable.

A six-month tour in Afghanistan is both physically and emotionally exhausting for every front-line soldier. For Badger it was no different. In the six months from September 2009 to March 2010 two of his closest friends were killed and several more were injured. He came under fire on numerous occasions and had several close calls with IEDs, but he went home without as much as a scratch even though he had defused 139 IEDs.

Badger, with his compact, wiry frame, short brown hair, keen eyes which sparkle with mischief, and a mellow Sheffield accent, had acquired his nickname as a young soldier eleven years earlier following a drunken incident in a nightclub involving a bottle of Tippex, his pubic hair and a group of divorced women. It has remained with him ever since.

The South Yorkshireman joined the Army on 14 November 1999 as a private in the Royal Logistic Corps. His academic prowess at school – he obtained A-levels in geography, history, sociology and general studies, having earlier gained nine GCSEs – could have taken him to university and then on to the Royal Military Academy Sandhurst to train as an Army officer. He had been offered places at university, including King's College London, to pursue war and peace studies, but the idea of spending three years 'locked in lecture halls' and then facing a large debt at the end of his degree didn't appeal.

'I just had this vague notion of wanting to join the Army,' Badger told me. 'Some of my friends had already joined, so I went to an Army careers office and they must have been short of ammunition technicians that week because they sold it quite well to me.'

Ten years later Badger was posted to Helmand as part of Operation Herrick 11. His bomb-disposal team was one of dozens of units attached to 11 Light Brigade. Somewhat surprisingly, given the scores of soldiers killed by IEDs, Badger describes the task of defusing home-made bombs as his 'comfort zone'. 'The infantry think my job is scary, they are terrified of IEDs because they are this unseen threat in the ground which just keeps killing and wounding them, but they are my comfort zone. It is all about what you are used to.

'The infantry expect to get into firefights with the Taliban and many of them actually want to. That's what they joined the Army to do – go to Afghanistan and kill the Taliban. And when the shooting kicks off you can actually see that some of these guys are really in their element, it's what they were made for. But not me. Firefights terrify me. Give me an IED to defuse any day. It's all about your comfort zone. I hate coming under fire, it terrifies me. I will try and dig a hole with my spoon to get into some sort of cover.'

In September 2009 Badger was dispatched to Patrol Base Woqab, near Musa Qala, to attend to a device which had recently been discovered by the local infantry battalion. The bomb was a PP IED and in itself didn't present much of a challenge to the bomb hunters. Outside of Sangin, the Musa Qala Taliban were regarded as the 'hardcore' element in Helmand – always ready to take on ISAF, the International Security Assistance Force, and experiment with new devices in the hope of catching out an ATO. It wasn't lost on Badger that this was the same area where Gaz O'Donnell had been killed on 10 September the previous year.

It was an ordinary shout. The search team deployed, cleared the area, checked for command wires, but none were found. Badger cleared a safe lane down to the device and began defusing the pressure plate, which went without a hitch. The plate had been cleared and the time had come for Badger to destroy the home-made explosive *in situ*. 'We don't recover the main charge. It's just too risky, so what we do is destroy it using conventional military high explosive. I set up the explosive, the last thing I did was to connect the detonator, then moved back to the ICP, where Stu fire-connected it to the firing circuit and detonated the main charge.'

As soon as the explosion rumbled across the valley, the local Taliban sprang into action, assuming that one of their devices had been triggered and that ISAF or the Afghan National Security Force (ANSF) – which draws on the ANA, the ANP and other police units – would have casualties, in which case they would be vulnerable and therefore ripe for ambush. What they found when they arrived at the scene was a lone, unarmed British soldier walking slowly in open ground – the perfect target.

Around fifteen minutes after the explosion Badger had made his way back to the site. 'I went back down the road to check that everything had worked and then the Taliban opened up good and proper. It was a case of "fuck me". The Taliban opened up with everything. The bullets were cracking above my head. There was single shots, automatic fire, RPGs coming in. I could hear the bullets zipping past me. It was absolutely terrifying. I was thinking, "How they can they be so close without hitting you?" And you're saying, "Those cunts, those cunts." I thought, this is where I cop it; I'm going to be hit in the back and the lights are going to go out and that's going to be it. No more life, no more wife, no more kids. And so I've gone from being in my comfort zone – defusing an IED – to being absolutely shitting myself in less than a second, and all the time I'm sprinting like a crazy man trying to get back.'

Badger was on his own in open countryside, 80 metres from his team and safety. There was no cover to hide in, and if he moved out of the metre-wide safe lane he risked triggering an IED. The only option was to turn and run.

'I ran like the wind itself – Usain Bolt had nothing on me. When you're neutralizing an IED and the Taliban start shooting, the best thing you can do is to drop to your belt buckle and let the infantry win the firefight. In the past that's what I'd done. As long as the rounds are landing too close, you're pretty safe. I always ask the infantry commander what he wants me to do if we get involved in a contact and nine times out of ten he'll say, "Sit tight, hide and we'll win the firefight." They don't exactly expect us to do a great deal of fighting.'

Badger came bounding back into the ICP and, although he was terrified, the rest of the team were in fits of laughter. 'I was shaking like a shitting dog,' he told me, a broad grin on his face. 'I'd come about as close as you would want to come to being shot, and all your mates are laughing at you. It was because of the look on my face as I came running in. I was knackered and out of breath and you think, that was too fucking close.'

Although his team frequently came under fire, Badger maintains that he never got used to being attacked. A month later, in October, he was teamed up with Warrant Officer Class 2 Dave Markland, a 36-year-old who had served in the Army for almost twenty years. Dave entered the world of ordnance disposal at a relatively late age. Much of his early career had been spent as a Plant Operator Mechanic – they're known as 'Planties' – and passed his RESA course in the spring of 2009. Badger and Dave became firm friends – their different characters seemed to complement each other – and developed a working relationship that was the envy of many within the task force. Dave was physically large – 6 ft 4 in. tall and weighing in at around 16 stone – 'but his personality made him even seem bigger', according to Badger. He was one of those individuals whose greatest enemy was boredom – and the long, dull days of inactivity in Camp Bastion.

In late November 2009 Badger and Dave were dispatched to FOB Keenan, near the town of Gereshk in central Helmand, to take part in Operation Gumbesa. Gereshk sits astride Highway One, otherwise known as the 'Afghan ring road'. It forms part of the old Silk Route and still has key strategic significance for both the Taliban and ISAF forces. It has been at the heart of many battles, with the military initiative constantly switching between the British troops and the Taliban. The presence of ISAF troops has brought some stability to the area. The town has a hospital with both male and female doctors and has around twenty schools, which are attended by around 20 per cent of the population.

Taliban bomb teams were targeting FOB Keenan, and dozens of devices had been laid in the area with the aim of restricting the movement of the Danish battlegroup based locally. The FOB is sited directly behind a hamlet and the inhabitants of this were in just as much danger from the IEDs as the ISAF forces. Part of the CIED mission is to clear IEDs out of civilian areas. The local population is only too well aware of the damage the devices can cause, since hundreds of civilians are killed and maimed every year. An IED is totally indiscriminate, and although the Taliban will arm some devices only at certain times of the day to avoid civilian casualties, most are not monitored and will kill and injure anyone – man, woman or child – who detonates it.

The first day of Operation Gumbesa began at around 0700 hours when Badger, the IED Team 4, WO2 Markland and the Royal Engineer searchers, together with their infantry force protection, patrolled out of the base. The cruel heat of the summer had subsided but the temperature could still reach the mid-30s in November, although by that stage Badger was fully acclimatized.

The operation went as planned on the first day. Badger, Dave and the search team managed to find, defuse and recover seven devices in about ten hours. They were delighted with their efforts. That night interpreters in FOB Keenan could hear the Taliban angrily discussing the team's success over their Icom radios. The Taliban's two main methods of communication are mobile phones and Icom radios. The second broadcast on known frequencies and can easily be intercepted with an Icom receiver. The intelligence obtained, known as Icom chatter, sometimes proves useful and can forewarn troops of attack, but it needs to be used carefully. Because the Taliban know that their radio communications are monitored by the British, much of their chatter is designed to confuse.

'The Taliban were furious,' Badger recalled with a broad grin. 'They had spent ages planting loads of IEDs and we came along and started to remove them all. It had been a long, arduous day, really gruelling, and everyone was exhausted by the time we returned to base. You come back in, drop your kit, have something to eat, attend the evening briefing, prepare for the following day, and then try and hit the sack. You're always knackered – either through the sheer length of the task or through fear of being attacked. No one ever has any trouble sleeping. One of the skills you quickly learn is to get sleep when and where you can.

'Large-scale clearances are always the same. You really have to guard against switching off. Sometimes you can wait for hours and nothing happens. It can be so boring, and then you have to switch into work mode in an instant. But the effort was worth it when we were told how pissed off the Taliban were.'

The following morning the whole process began again and the IEDD team deployed to the same area. Dave made his assessment of the locality and began directing the search team, while Badger relaxed nearby in a spot that he assumed was safe. While the two were shooting the breeze, unbeknown to them the Taliban were on the move.

'All of a sudden the Taliban opened up on us – it was close, really close,' said Badger. 'Because we had been chatting we had not been paying much attention and we were suddenly caught on our own. We both hid behind some banking and I was trying to get as low as possible – the rounds were fizzing just above our heads. It was like, "Shit, where did that come from?" But Dave was a big bear of a man, huge – and I looked over at Dave and, although I was terrified, I suddenly started laughing – I mean really pissing myself, and I started taking the piss out of him. He was always going on about how much bigger he was than me. The bullets were whistling and cracking above our heads and it was not a good time to be big when you are trying to hide behind something so small.'

Badger and Dave had no other option but to sit tight until the enemy position could be suppressed by soldiers from the Royal Anglian Regiment who were providing security for the bomb hunters. Once the enemy fire had stopped the two of them sprinted back to where the infantry were based and the search began again. By the end of the second day Badger had defused a further fourteen devices, followed by another seven on the third day – twenty-eight devices in three days.

Badger is due to return home in the next few days and he has the look and behaviour of a man who has just won the lottery. He's relaxed and carefree and looking forward to meeting his family. I ask him whether, given the buzz of the job, he wishes he was staying. Will he miss the unique bond of brotherhood, which is forged in war zones among soldiers who have faced death on a daily basis and seen their closest friends fall and die in battle? 'Will I miss Afghan? Not for a fucking second. I'll miss my mates, but that's about it. No one wants to stay here for a moment longer than necessary. I just want to get home and hug the wife and kids – and to be honest I wouldn't be bothered if I never came back here again. I've lost mates, really good mates, and that's been hard, but compared to some people I've had it easy.'

I'm chatting to Badger in a vast green Army tent crammed full of cots ready for fresh troops coming into theatre. The whole of Camp Bastion is in a state of flux because the several thousand men of 11 Light Brigade are leaving and the men of 4 Mechanized Brigade are beginning to arrive. It is a routine handover, known as a roulement or relief in place (RIP), which takes place every six months. It's easy to spot the difference between the two sets of troops. Those who are coming to the end of their tour appear more rugged and suntanned, their uniforms are worn, and their eyes tell a different story from those of the new guys. The RIP is a fantastically busy period, and Camp Bastion swells to almost twice the number of British troops, many of whom are going through RSOI training. After a journey through the night they are pitched into a series of lectures in tents where the temperature hits 32°. Some of the men have not slept for twenty-four hours, and they struggle to stay awake. The troops are warned of the various dos and don'ts in Helmand – such as do drink plenty of water and do wash your hands every time you go to the toilet and don't approach Afghan women, ever, or pick up anything which may be remotely interesting from the ground while on patrol because it might be attached to a bomb. Those troops going to the front line are pitched into a series of day and night live-firing exercises on ranges beyond the camp wire.

Overall it is an exhausting and sometimes frightening experience, but especially so when they get onto CIED training. Much of this will have been covered in numerous exercises before their deployment, but here in Helmand the training is somehow more frightening. Everyone knows that the next time they carry out the same drills will be for real. The instructors – members of the CIED Task Force – have a captive audience. No one wants to miss out on a piece of information, a tip with the benefit of someone's experience. Mistakes on exercises back in the UK are acceptable but in Helmand they may cost an arm, a leg or a life.

The soldiers are taught how to search, confirm and recognize buried IEDs using Vallons. Over the next six months the soldier will learn how to recognize the detector's various alarm tones. Again and again the instructors remind them to look for the 'absence of the normal and the presence of the abnormal'.

As we sit talking inside the 30-ft-long tent, which even in the dry heat of Helmand still smells damp, Badger tells me of the worst period of the tour. In the space of three weeks one of his best friends had been killed, another had been wounded and sent back to the UK, and a third had suffered a double amputation after stepping on a pressure-plate IED. The three men were all ATOs and were all doing exactly the same job as Badger when they were killed. The first of Badger's friends to fall was Staff Sergeant Olaf Sean George Schmid. Oz, as he was known, was one of the true characters of the bomb-disposal world – he was known to everyone and loved by most. He was a huge personality, cocky and scruffy, but he was also an excellent bomb hunter. He had spent several years serving with 3 Commando Brigade and proudly wore his Para wings and famous Green Beret and revelled in his status as an Army Commando.

Oz was irrepressible. His favourite saying when morale would take a bit of a dip was 'Let's man-up and get on with it.' Every morning without fail those who walked past his bed in his tent in whatever part of Helmand he was working would be greeted with one of two phrases: 'Suck us off' or 'Two sugars with mine.' He once attended a memorial service in Sangin for a fellow soldier killed in the area a few days earlier but fainted through exhaustion. When he came round, a padre was standing over him, asking if he was OK. Oz opened his eyes and responded with, 'Get off my fucking hair.'

It was as a chef that Oz originally joined the Army in 1996, but while serving with an infantry unit in Northern Ireland he saw a bomb-disposal team at work and felt he had suddenly found his calling. Oz arrived in Helmand in July 2009 on Operation Herrick 10 and immediately took part in Operation Panchai Palang, or Panther's Claw, a multi-national operation designed to push the Taliban out of central Helmand before Afghanistan's ill-fated presidential elections. Oz, known as 'Bossman' by his team, was one of Badger's closest friends. The two had known each other for around eight years and were on the same High Threat course before being deployed to Helmand.

'Oz filled the room, absolutely filled the room,' Badger said, a broad smile lighting up his face. 'He was a fantastic bloke, a great laugh. He was the loudest man I knew, he was brilliant. Before you go on any course in the Army, you get a set of joining instructions and at the back of that is a course list. I would always flip to the back and look at the list and if Oz's name was on it you knew it was going to be a good one. It would be two weeks of hard work but two weeks of hard drinking. Oz worked hard and played hard, that was his way.'

In August 2009 Oz was attached to the 2nd Battalion Rifles battlegroup, based in Sangin, which was quickly developing a reputation as a graveyard for British troops. Since June 2006, when members of 3 Para moved into the valley, barely a week has passed without the Taliban launching some sort of attack. Sangin held special significance for the Taliban. It was one of the main opium centres in Helmand and thus had the potential to provide the Taliban with the hard cash they needed to sustain the insurgency. The Taliban knew they couldn't defeat ISAF troops in a stand-up fight but what they could do was make commanders question whether holding on to Sangin was worth the growing casualty rates.

Every battlegroup which deployed to the Sangin Valley knew they would not return to the UK without sustaining losses. By the end of their tour in April 2010, 3 Rifles battlegroup, based in the Sangin district centre, had suffered more fatalities than any other unit that had served in Helmand since 2006.

The Taliban operating in the valley had developed a fearsome reputation for being ruthless and inventive, especially in their use of IED ambushes. Some soldiers have likened them to the IRA in South Armagh in Ulster during the Troubles in the 1980s and 1990s. The South Armagh Brigade was the only IRA unit which was never infiltrated by British intelligence. It was close-knit, tough and fearless, with commanders who were always seeking new ways to attack British bases and kill soldiers with specially designed bombs and mortars.

For the ATOs Sangin was probably the least popular and most challenging of all the battlegroup locations in Helmand. Such were the dangers of serving there that IED teams were changed every six weeks and no new ATOs or search teams were ever sent to the area for their first tour.

The narrow alleyways, the rat-runs and the lush fields of the Green Zone, criss-crossed with irrigation ditches, streams and canals, were exploited to the full by the insurgents. Patrolling British troops were channelled into classic ambush sites almost from the moment they left the front gate of the base. Once inside the Green Zone practically all movement was restricted to foot, and the field of view, especially in the summer with the crops tall, could be as little as a few metres. Fighting was at close quarters and often brutal – bayonets were always fixed and often used.

IEDs are produced in Sangin in prodigious numbers and are used to channel and restrict the movement of British troops. The Taliban bomb makers in the area were regarded as the best and most innovative in all Helmand. New devices were often tested in Sangin before being exported to other parts of the province. The Taliban would watch every move the soldiers made, noting their favoured routes, crossing points and rendezvous points. They understood British tactics, knew how troops would respond in a firefight, knew how long it would take to call in an air strike and the Army's casualty evacuation procedures. There were only so many places where a helicopter could land and evacuate an injured soldier, and the Taliban knew them all. Routine patrolling through some of the built-up areas close to the base was impossible. Rather than walk along a track or road, troops moved from compound to compound by scaling 15-ft-high walls in a bid to beat the bombers. The soldiers knew this activity as 'Grand Nationaling'.

Pharmacy Road in Sangin town was the most deadly street in the whole of Afghanistan. Since the British first moved into the area, hundreds, possibly thousands, of devices have been planted on it, killing dozens of soldiers. Any operation which required troop movement on this road had to be carefully planned and searched. By April 2010 160 soldiers of the 281 soldiers killed in Afghanistan since 2006 have died in Sangin town and the surrounding area. I have been on patrol in the area on several occasions, taken part in operations, and have come under fire on several occasions and I can still recall the sense of relief I felt every time a patrol ended.

The main British base in the Sangin area of operatons, FOB Jackson, sat on the periphery of the district centre and was bisected by the Helmand canal, which offered the troops based there temporary respite from the summer heat and boosted morale. Dotted throughout Sangin are smaller patrol bases, such as PB Tangiers, an ANA base close to the district centre, and PB Wishtan, at the eastern end of the notorious Pharmacy Road. The casualty rate in PB Wishtan was so high in the summer of 2009 that troops, with their customary black humour, renamed it PB Wheelchair.

The soldiers who have to patrol in Sangin day after day, sometimes twice or three times a day, often after having witnessed a fellow soldier having one or more limbs blown off, need truly remarkable courage. And it's worth remembering that many of them are just 18 or 19 and on their first operational tour.

Despite the risks, Oz Schmid was in his element and relished the challenge. This easy-going, fast-talking Cornishman had an infectious smile and a fantastic sense of humour. He had named his squad 'Team Rainbow' after the gay pride emblem, because he claimed they were the only 'all-gay IEDD team in Helmand'. The team members were nicknamed Zippy, Bungle and George, and their mascot, a duck, was known as Corporal Quackers. It was all part of the coping mechanism adopted by Oz and his team.

Like every ATO in Helmand, Oz knew that death lurked around every corner. Every bomb had to be treated as a unique event. Taking short cuts or making assumptions could end in a trip home in a body bag. As if to emphasize the dangers Helmand held for ATOs, Captain Daniel Shepherd, 28, was killed defusing a roadside bomb in Nad-e'Ali a month after Oz arrived in Helmand. He was the second ATO to die in Afghanistan. Like Gaz O'Donnell, who had died eleven months earlier, Captain Shepherd hadn't made a mistake; he was just unlucky. As one soldier later told me, 'That kind of shit can just happen in Afghan.'

In an interview he gave before he was killed that appeared in the *Sunday Times* on 8 November 2009 Oz referred to Dan Shepherd's death and how it had shaped his view of the role of ATOs in Helmand: 'There are times when I'm actually thinking about Dan and I'll go down the lonely walk, as they say, get to the target and think, what am I doing here? But it's a flash through my head, if you like.' Oz was typical of most ATOs I have met: they never think about their own safety and are far more concerned with the lives of their fellow soldiers.

'Nine times out of ten, in fact 99.99 per cent of the time, I'm down there and I'm doing it as quick as I can, because obviously the longer the guys are down on the ground the more they present themselves as a target.

'And then obviously once we're out on the ground, other things, atmospherics around us, you know I'm getting dicked as well – they're trying to look and see what I'm doing, so it's a lot of focus into what I'm doing and why I'm doing it. My brain's always thinking about the device: how I'm going to render it safe. It's not necessarily wandering off to: am I going to get home? Every device is different in its own little way ... you have got to find exactly what it is and come up with the best way of dealing with that, so your mind is constantly focused on that. I don't really think about the enemy. There have been a couple of piss-take jobs, though, where they are trying to have a bit of a joke. I found a dollar on top of a pressure plate in Nad-e'Ali the other week.'

On 9 August 2009 Oz took part in an operation to clear Pharmacy Road, which runs east from Sangin town centre out to PB Wishtan. By this time the area directly around the PB had become one of the most dangerous parts of Afghanistan, with one in three of the soldiers based at Wishtan being killed or wounded that summer. Several of those had been killed or injured close to the base and the dozens of IEDs which had been laid in the area meant that patrolling was almost impossible. PB Wishtan was cut off from resupply by land. Bomb-damaged vehicles had been turned into a basic but effective roadblock and Pharmacy Road was riddled with IEDs. Three previous attempts to clear the road, which is lined by 15-ft-high mud walls, had all failed.

The operation began at 5.30 a.m., just before the sun appeared over the horizon. Specialist Royal Engineer searchers, flanked by soldiers from the Rifles, pushed out from FOB Jackson and began the search. The troops made steady progress until they came to a military digger which had been blown up by the Taliban during a previous operation. All around the vehicle the ground was littered with IEDs. At around 0800 hrs and with the temperature already in the mid-40s, Oz set to work. Within 100 metres he found and cleared the first IED of the day.

Oz had planned to use a remote-controlled vehicle to clear another device but as it moved into the danger area the robot struck an IED and was destroyed. Knowing that the Taliban were probably in the area and monitoring the progress of the operation, Oz moved forward again and cleared a route to within 5 metres of the vehicles.

'We started searching forwards along the road again,' he explained. 'We found another bomb half a metre away from the lane that I'd used to search up to the vehicle. We sent two little robots out and they got blown up, so I went on my feet.'

His team then moved into a compound adjacent to the stricken vehicles and began preparing to take them off the road. Another device was quickly discovered, which Oz also cleared. The engineers in the compound blew a hole through the outside wall and winches were used to drag the vehicles off the road. Clearing bombs from the route to the vehicles had taken an hour, during all of which time Oz had been completely reliant on his own eyesight and his understanding of enemy tactics. As the light began to fade he once again led a high-risk clearance of the stretch of road from which the vehicles had been taken away and removed a further two devices.

The whole operation had lasted eleven hours. It had been fraught with danger, and luck had also played a large part in ensuring that there were no British casualties. Oz and his team were drained, physically, emotionally and mentally; they had discovered a total of thirty devices and defused eleven, but the road was open and C Company, 2 Rifles, were resupplied. Although it was clearly a team effort, the mission would have failed if it had not been for Oz's heroic and selfless acts.

Despite the danger, Oz, like every other ATO working in Helmand, never wore his protective body suit. 'It's too hot to wear a suit out here and it's tactically not feasible,' he said. He saw the suit as an easy way for the Taliban to identify him. 'Every time we're out on the ground we're obviously denying them their kill against us, so in effect we've become a high-value target for them, as they are for us. Certainly a few times, certainly in Sangin, we've been targeted and over the old Icom they say, "The bomb team is here, let's hit them." They call us the bomb team, according to the interpreter – probably "wankers" in the local language.'

Over the next few months Oz's team were called out to dozens more IED incidents, some where soldiers had been killed and wounded and others where by luck the device had failed to explode.

'I have been to a couple of devices that have been very unstable. The bomb makers' construction of the devices isn't brilliant. A loose wire in the wind could create a short, so when I have my fingers in there I have to pay attention.'

On 8 October 2010 Oz was dispatched to the district centre to deal with a device which the ANA had discovered while on patrol. The IED consisted of an artillery shell placed close to seven large cans of diesel. If the bomb had detonated it would have devastated the area. On arrival the ANA soldiers led Oz directly into the IED's killing area. The Afghan soldiers had not warned the public for fear that the device might be detonated by the Taliban once they knew it had been found. Oz realized that he was not only at personal risk but so were around forty civilians who were in the immediate danger area, and time was not on his side.

Oz moved up close to the device and quickly assessed that the shell was part of a live radio-controlled IED. It was also clear that the bomb was almost certainly being overwatched by the Taliban. Oz felt that he had no choice but to conduct a manual neutralization. To do this he employed a render-safe procedure which is only ever used in the gravest of circumstances and is conducted at the highest personal risk to the operator. Oz insisted that his team move back out of the safety area before neutralizing the bomb. Once again the heroism he displayed went beyond the call of duty.

After the incident Oz said, 'My heart's not racing at all when I go in.' But then he corrected himself: 'No, that's not true, there are some points when it does. There's a lot of apprehension, a lot of adrenalin going through you at the time, especially when the device is something a little bit different, when you know that it is targeting you, but it's important to appear calm. The guys look at you, they draw strength from you. For an infantry commander on the ground, it's a hell of a weight off his shoulders when you come in.'

Defusing was not Oz's only task, however. He also had to gather the vital forensic evidence which enables military teams to trace the militants who smuggle, make and plant IEDs. Forensic evidence was

what Oz called 'the big picture in the IED loop', and it's their expertise in gathering this that sets British high-threat IED operators apart
from any others.

'As British teams, we'll get everything out of the device because
our skills and drills are the best in the world, believe it or not.
Because of our background and what we've learned over the years in
places like Northern Ireland, it allows us to adopt some techniques
in order to gain vital information from devices. It's all about getting
the forensics, matching it, and going that way round it as opposed to
just making it safe. We want to capture them, to get criminal
convictions.'

After Oz's work in the Pharmacy Road operation – as well as
defusing a large IED in the centre of a bazaar which, had it exploded,
would have killed many civilians – rumours began to circulate in the
Task Force that he was in line for a gallantry medal. 'I am just looking at getting home with my legs,' was his response.

Working in Sangin was beginning to take its toll on Oz and his
team. Barely a day seemed to pass which didn't require Oz to put his
life on the line. Back in Camp Bastion his boss, Major Tim Gould
QGM, the officer commanding the JFEOD Group, was concerned
about Oz's mental and physical health. ATOs need to be managed
very carefully. In 2009 they were a scarce resource and they remain
so today. Oz insisted that he was tired but fine and wanted to stay in
Sangin.

On the evening of 30 October Oz called home and spoke to his
wife, Christina. She later recalled that he sounded uncharacteristi-
cally strained after being left exhausted by yet another four-day
operation in the Sangin area. With tears leaving tracks down his
dust-covered cheeks, he said, 'I'm hanging out, hun. Can you come
and get me, babe?' Of course she couldn't, but she reassured him that
he had just two days to push before he was due to return home for
his two weeks' R&R.

On 31 October, Halloween, the day before he was due to fly
home, Oz and his team were called out on another task, one which

required him to defuse three devices. As the day drew to a close the team were about to return to the base when one of the searchers discovered a command wire running down the alleyway they had been working in. Oz's team had unwittingly walked into a trap. They had no idea at which end of the alley the device was located and so had no safe route forward or back. Oz immediately seized the initiative and traced the command wire to a complex IED. The device was linked to three buried charges designed to take out an entire patrol. His team withdrew and cleared an ICP while Oz moved forward. That was the last time he was seen alive. Oz was killed instantly while dealing with the first device. In five months in Afghanistan he had defused sixty-four IEDs; the sixty-fifth killed him.

His wife was told later that evening that Oz was dead. Later Christina recalled, 'I wasn't surprised. I got this gut feeling after he called me for the last time. He never speaks like that. He was exhausted. He said he had been out there too long and could I come get him. I told him I couldn't.'

At about 9.30 p.m. on 31 October 2009 Christina watched as two men wearing green berets approached her house. 'I thought, oh my God, what are they doing here?' Laird, her 5-year-old son, thought it was Oz, his stepfather, returning home. 'I can remember saying he's definitely not here. It's not Daddy, I told my son. I asked them why they were there. I said, "Just tell me he can talk. I don't care about his legs and arms. Can he talk?" They looked at me and said, "Let us in." I didn't cry. No one else was hurt. I remember thinking what a relief that was.'

In the moments after Oz's death the news began to filter back to the CIED Task Force headquarters in Camp Bastion. The J Chat said that a Brimstone callsign – indicating an IED team – had suffered a fatal casualty. Then the screen displayed 'SC' – the first two letters of Oz's surname – followed by the last four digits of his Army number, which together made up his Zap number, a personal coded number given to operational troops. Oz was the third ATO to be killed in action in Helmand in thirteen months. It was an attrition rate that had not been experienced by the world of bomb disposal for almost 40 years.

Later that evening, at FOB Price, near Gereshk, Badger made his routine evening call to the ops room just to let them know everything was OK. 'I called in and Major Gould, my boss, answered and said, "Badger, I've got some bad news. Oz is dead." It was like being hit in the stomach with a cricket bat. I was devastated.' Badger found himself a quiet corner and began to cry. 'I knew I had to tell the boys. They all knew Oz, so it was important they were told as soon as possible. So you have to man-up, wipe your eyes, wash your face, and break the news. There were a lot of tears – it was a very difficult evening for everyone in our community.'

Four days after Oz was killed I arrived in Helmand for a three-week embed with the Grenadier Guards. I had never met Oz, but I knew that as an ATO he was an extraordinarily brave soldier. While I was waiting to transit forward from Camp Bastion, a special service was held for Oz before his body was repatriated to the UK. Hundreds of soldiers attended and many of those who served with him were in tears. I have attended several of these services, and they are all moving, sometimes traumatic events. But Oz's was different: it was transparently clear that the Army had lost someone very special.

Lieutenant Colonel Rob Thomson, the commanding officer of the 2 Rifles battlegroup, described Oz, in the hours after his death, as 'simply the bravest and most courageous man I have ever met. Superlatives do not do the man justice. Better than the best. Better than the best of the best.'

Two weeks after Oz's death, Captain Dan Read, a fellow ATO, was wounded by shrapnel when a soldier standing close by detonated a victim-operated IED. Captain Read was a very popular officer who had joined the Army as a private but later passed the officer selection course and attended the Royal Military College at Sandhurst. Although his injuries were not serious, as most of the shrapnel hit his arms, he was sent back to the UK to recover.

Soon the casualties were coming in so thick and fast that the battle casualty replacements couldn't keep pace with the rate at which soldiers were being wounded. A senior officer later told me, 'We were unprepared for such large numbers of casualties. We didn't have the resources in place and we couldn't cope with the volume of casualties. We were in trouble.'

Morale within the CIED Task Force had taken a bashing. 'It was a very bad period, a dreadful few weeks,' said Badger. But for him it was not just the loss of mates that was worrying. 'Oz was at the top of his game,' he said ruefully. 'They were doing the same job as me and part of you does think, if it can happen to them, then it can happen to me.

'After Oz was killed I had to phone my wife and tell her that there had been an incident and one of the lads had died. I said to her, "Don't worry, I'm OK." I've told her plenty of times that if they hear bad news on the TV or radio, then it means I'm OK because she would be told first. But all the wives are worried, worried all the time. I think it's harder for them. Every time there's a knock on the door their heart stops.'

The period between August 2009 and March 2010 was one of the bloodiest in the British Army's history of bomb disposal. It wasn't just the British ATOs who had taken casualties either. Both US and Canadian ATOs have also been killed in southern Afghanistan. An SAS sergeant told me that he was in awe of the bomb-disposal units. He went on to describe an incident in which a US bomb-disposal officer was killed while taking part in a mission. 'We were going into a compound and we had a US ATO with us. He got to the compound and he said, "I'll go in first and clear it. You guys wait here." He went in with his mine detector on his own, and about a minute later there was this huge bang. We followed up and he had been blown in half by the bomb. His bottom half had been completely separated. You're like, "What the fuck?" Thankfully he had been killed instantly. We all owe our lives to him – if we had gone in the bomb would have taken out an entire SAS team.

'These guys are incredible – people think our job is risky but it's nothing compared to what these guys do. We always have plenty of intelligence, more often than not we know exactly what will be waiting for us. But these guys have to go in on their own. It's incredible. The incident happened just before Christmas in December 2009. And his wife and two children buried him the day before Christmas Eve. Whatever way you cut it, that's just shit.'

A few days after Oz Schmid was killed, Dave Markland and Badger, lying on their beds in the FOB, made a pact. They promised each other that if either of them was killed – blown to pieces by an IED – nothing would be left behind. For the one event which terrifies ATOs and everyone in the world of bomb disposal is the prospect of their body parts being left on the battlefield after an attack. The size of the bombs being used by the Taliban in Helmand can literally blow a human to pieces. Everyone involved in bomb hunting accepts such a fate as a fact of life, and many take comfort from the fact that, if their number is up, they will know very little of it.

While chatting about nothing in particular, Badger turned to Dave and said, 'Oz, Dan Shepherd and Gaz O'Donnell were all at the top of their game, Dave, you know that. They were as good or better than me. So let's make a pact. If I get blown up, I get blown out of the safe lane and we are under fire and taking casualties, promise me that you won't leave me behind. You've got to promise me that.' Badger was now sitting up and staring at Dave, who nodded and replied, 'The same goes for me, Badger, mate. Now, enough morose talk. Let's go and get a brew and check on the lads.'

Badger and Dave had hoped to work together for the rest of their six-month tour. The two soldiers had developed a very special working relationship during the ten weeks they had spent together. But that plan was interrupted by their R&R after Christmas. Badger took his leave first and when he returned Dave departed. The planning for Operation Moshtarak, a military drive intended to clear the Taliban from central Helmand, was already underway and bomb hunters were urgently required for the so-called 'shaping operations' which took place a few weeks before the main event – the large-scale thrust into the heart of Taliban territory. Both men were due to take part in a shaping operation together but Dave's return from R&R was delayed and Badger deployed with another search team.

Dave arrived a few days later, but with little to do he quickly became bored and frustrated and was soon asking to be sent out on an operation. Badger recalled how Dave was 'bouncing off the walls'. 'He kept going up to Major Gould saying, "Boss, you've got to put me out on the ground – I'm doing my nut here." Eventually a task came up and he was told he was going out – he was delighted. I remember him going up to Gould and shaking his hand before he went out. Major Gould looked him in the eye and wished him good luck – these things are important in our world.'

The two bomb hunters were deployed to Battlegroup Centre South, in the Nad-e'Ali area of central Helmand, Badger to the north and Dave to the south. Both search teams were involved in a series of straightforward routine search and clearance operations. On 8 February Dave's search team was dispatched to clear a route where a suspected device had been uncovered. It was a routine operation, the ICP was cleared by the searchers and the mission was going according to plan. But a mistake had been made. A pressure-plate IED which had been missed was detonated by Dave as he moved across to one side of the ICP. The blast was huge and devastating, killing Dave instantly. Badger was a few kilometres away, conducting a similar route-clearance operation, when he learned the dreadful news.

Badger recalled, 'I kind of found out by accident that Dave had been killed; no one officially told us. We heard a "nine-liner" saying that someone had been injured from a Brimstone team. We enquired and the Royal Anglian's operations room told us that there had been an incident with a Brimstone callsign. At that point your heart starts racing and you are just praying that whoever has been injured is going to make it. We looked on the J Chat and I knew straight away that it was Dave.' Seeing Dave's Zap number, they realized straight away whose it was.

'Dave was working with six Gurkhas,' Badger continued, 'so I immediately knew that he was the casualty. The J Chat said he was KIA. My heart sunk and I felt sick. I immediately got in touch with the ops room to try and find out what had happened and I was hoping against hope that a mistake had been made. It shouldn't happen but it's not unheard of for people to get Zap numbers wrong. But they confirmed that Dave was dead.

'I never got the full details, just that he had been taken out by an IED and that it was quick – that's all you can hope for really. It's a small comfort and you just have to crack on. I was on my own when it was actually confirmed for definite that he was dead. I gave myself five minutes, had a little cry, and then you just have to man-up and go and tell the boys. I called the team together – we had all worked with Dave too and we were all very close. Everyone was gutted but we all had to remember that there was a job to do and we would be back out on the ground in the morning. As hard as it sounds, we couldn't let ourselves be distracted by Dave's death because we all knew that we could be the next to be killed.

'Obviously you think about it when you are on your own or lying in bed at night but you have to trust your drills and assure yourself that providing you do your drills correctly you should be OK. But Dave did nothing wrong.'

With tragic irony Dave's name was added to the memorial which he designed and built and which still stands in the quiet corner of the compound where the JFEOD Group is based. When the mission is over and the troops come home, the memorial will come with them.

After a few weeks' leave Badger will return to his unit where he will be given a pager and will command one of the many teams which provide IED coverage over the whole of the UK. Even back in the UK Badger will be called out two or three times a week to deal with devices ranging from a Second World War grenade found in a granny's cabbage patch to a suspicious package left on a train.

'It has been a gruelling six months,' he says. 'I've spent a lot of time sleeping on floors and I'm not getting any younger. You are working most days and it's the sheer number of tasks you are asked to do which slowly grinds you down, and at the back of your mind you know you can't make a mistake. It's going to take time to settle into home life again – for the last six months I've been making life-and-death decisions, now it's a case of shopping in Tesco's and deciding which cereal I want – funny how life changes.'

I say goodnight to Badger and we arrange to meet tomorrow. His tour is over but mine is just beginning. In a few days' time I will once again be on the front line. I've only been in Camp Bastion for less than a week but already I feel it's too long. I want to get out into bandit country again but this time will be different. This time I will be with the bomb hunters searching for IEDs. The promises I made to my wife and myself after Rupert's death are already beginning to evaporate. Rather than finding reasons not to go into the danger zones, I'm doing the opposite.

Chapter 3: **Bomb Makers**

'I, and probably most soldiers, could tell the difference
between home-made and military-grade explosive.
I knew that a 5 kg bomb would take a leg off, a 10 kg
bomb would take off both legs and anything bigger and
you were dead.'
Sergeant Major Pat Hyde, A Company, 4 Rifles

I'm sitting on a makeshift wooden bench within the quiet enclave of
Camp Bastion which is home to the Joint Force EOD Group. The
sun is shining brightly in a cloudless sky and the temperature is a
comfortable, almost perfect 26°. I'm drinking tea with Staff Sergeant
Karl 'Badger' Ley, one of the ATOs who for the past six months has
been defusing home-made bombs in what the soldiers call the 'heart
of darkness'.

In the crisp morning light I can see that Badger is tired, both
physically and mentally. He doesn't tell me this but I can see it in his
eyes and the way he talks, in the lengthy pauses during our conversation and the way he stares into the distance. It's not just the hours
spent defusing bombs for the last six months which have left him
exhausted but the deaths of six of his colleagues and the horrific,
often life-changing injuries suffered by many of those within the
CIED Task Force. He is tired of Helmand and, like many ATOs, tired
of watching his commanders writing letters home to the families of

the dead, and explaining why the sacrifice of a son, husband or brother was not in vain.

I've met soldiers like Badger before – men who carry the burden of having lost friends in the cause of duty. It is a burden they will carry for ever, always wondering whether they could have done more to save the life of a comrade or prevent another from being injured. It is another tragic, hidden cost of war.

The wounds left by the deaths of his fellow bomb hunters are still raw. Badger served during one of the bloodiest periods in EOD history. Before the war in Afghanistan, twenty-four British ATOs had been killed in action, twenty-three in Northern Ireland and one in Iraq. Since 2008 five ATOs have been killed in Helmand, and many more have been injured. The attrition rates in Helmand now mirror those of the early years of the Troubles.

'IEDs are basic but deadly,' Badger states matter-of-factly. 'Take for example the pressure-plate IED. What is this thing which has killed hundreds of British troops? Let's break it down.' He speaks quickly and fluently. I can tell it's a conversation he has had many time before, probably with senior officers wondering why the Taliban are able to make IEDs in such vast numbers and with apparent ease.

'A bomb is a switch with a power source connected to a detonator which is placed inside a main charge of explosive,' Badger continues. 'An IED consists of anything which will keep two metal contacts apart – we have seen strips of wood and clothes pegs – which are used to form a switch. The contacts can then be moved together by applying pressure or releasing pressure. So the most simple devices we have found consist of two pieces of wood, maybe 1 in. wide and about 1 ft long, with an axle blade nailed to each piece. The pieces of wood are kept apart by a piece of sponge or another piece of wood, anything which will allow the two axle blades to come together when pressure is applied – the same theory works if the device is pressure-release. Wires are then connected to the two blades and to the deto-nator, which can often be the most complicated part to make. It's not commercial, something improvised. The detonator is then placed inside some home-made explosive, often a mixture of ammonium nitrate – which is a common fertilizer widely available in Helmand – aluminium filings and sugar, and this is known as ANAL and this is the main charge. The explosive needs to be put in a container, something which will keep it dry, and commonly in Helmand the Taliban are using palm-oil containers. At this stage the explosive is very stable. You could throw it against a wall and nothing would happen. You could burn it and it would burn furiously but it wouldn't explode – for that you need a detonator. The detonator is then inserted into the container, usually by cutting a hole in the side, and then resealed. The device now needs to have a power source – so what's available? Batteries. Eight 1.5-volt batteries are often enough.'

Badger speaks with a hint of anger or at least irritation in his voice as he continues, 'So you now have a simple circuit, which an 11-year-old boy could easily knock together, consisting of a power source connected to a switch – the pressure plate – which is connected to a detonator. And that is your bomb. Flick the switch by bringing the two metal contacts together, which allows an electric current from the batteries to flow to the detonator, causing a small explosion inside the main charge, which explodes with enormous force. The power can be increased by adding more ANAL, conventional explosives or conventional munitions such as artillery shells, mortar bombs, hand grenades or rocket warheads.'

Badger has described the construction of an IED with a 'high metal' content. These were the first generation of devices and are relatively easy to find with a Vallon. But the Taliban are an adaptable and inventive foe. War and fighting are part of their culture and heritage. Their fathers and grandfathers fought the Soviets and then each other in a civil war, and now they are fighting NATO. Just like the IRA, who, let's face it, were also insurgents, the Taliban will always try to build on success rather than failure. So it was only a matter of time before they began to build IEDs with 'low metal' content. Instead of using saw blades or other strips of metal as the switch, the Taliban have begun to use the carbon rods from inside batteries. And they work really well.

In addition to victim-detonated devices, such as pressure-plate and pressure-release IEDs, there are also those which can be triggered by remote control. Some devices can also be turned on and off remotely. In some parts of Helmand, for example in Musa Qala, pressure-plate bombs are armed remotely just before a British patrol arrives in the locality. If the patrol takes another route, the device can be switched off and the track is then free for local people to use. By adopting this tactic the Taliban can reduce their collateral damage, for they need to keep the local population on their side in the areas they control. The threat from these devices, which is potentially considerable, is lessened by the use of electronic counter-measures, or ECM. These were developed during the 1980s and 1990s, during the bloody days of the Troubles, and their use still remains an extremely sensitive subject.

The next group of devices are the command IEDs, which function 'on command' rather than being victim-operated like a pressure-plate device. Again the main charge is often, though not exclusively, home-made explosive. Command IEDs break down into two categories. The first is the 'command pull', where the device is triggered by an insurgent pulling on, for example, a piece of string or wire. This can be as simple as dislodging any non-conductive material that is keeping two electric terminals apart. When the terminals touch, the bomb functions. The other category is the 'command wire' device, which is detonated by an insurgent connecting the bomb to a power supply, such as a car battery, when a potential target is in range. In Helmand, command wires up to 200 metres long have been found. With the power source, which often contains a high proportion of metal, so far away from the explosive, these are very difficult to discover with a metal detector.

IEDs can also be detonated by a trip wire. One example of this kind of device is the Russian-made POMZ, which is effectively an anti-personnel fragmentation grenade mounted on a wooden stick.

When a soldier approaches the device, an insurgent gives the wire a gentle tug to pull the pin out of the grenade, causing it to detonate in less than a second. These devices can also be detonated by the victim walking into a trip wire.

'IED production has gone beyond being a cottage industry,' Badger continued. 'They are now being knocked out on an industrial scale at the rate of one every fifteen to twenty minutes. This is something which is very difficult to target because, when you see the nature of the devices, they are so simple but very effective. I wouldn't say the bombs are bodged – but they're not far from it. But that doesn't matter. They are still very effective and they do the job. They don't have to be state-of-the-art – quality control is minimal – but the beauty of these things is that they work. You can leave a pressure-plate IED buried in the ground for a month, maybe more, and it can still kill.

'During the Northern Ireland period the IRA were incredibly sophisticated – the IRA wouldn't put a device on the street unless they were 100 per cent sure that it would function. In Helmand there is absolutely no quality control. The bombs are knocked together with any old rubbish, which can make the device very unstable. You could sneeze and it would function, you could be working on it and the ground around you could collapse and it could function, or it could function just because you are moving the earth close to it. The IRA built devices with "ready-to-arm" switches but we haven't seen anything like that here. The bombs might not be much to look at but they are very effective and they are killing and injuring lots of troops and civilians.'

Intelligence has emerged suggesting that Iran has been training Taliban snipers and bomb makers, a worrying development with similarities to the situation facing the allies in Iraq. Iranian intervention in Iraq was responsible for killing and injuring hundreds of British troops.

During 2006 and 2007, IEDD teams deployed to Afghanistan for four months. Back then there were only two British bomb-disposal teams in Helmand. Iraq was still the main focus for IED disposal. But that changed in 2008, when Helmand was redefined as a high-threat environment and the tour of duty was extended to six months. In the space of two years the number of Taliban attacks had surged by more than 300 per cent. Soldiers were being killed and injured almost daily and the IEDs were also being used to target ATOs. When news that the tour was to be longer was announced, none of the ATOs being sent to Helmand complained; they simply did as they were told.

By January 2010 serious concerns were beginning to be voiced over the pressure facing ATOs and other members of the bomb-hunting teams. Everyone working in EOD was aware that all three of the ATOs who had so far died in Helmand had been almost two-thirds of the way through their tours. It was the same story for an ATO who was seriously injured. The exception was Captain Dan Read, who deployed to Helmand on Operation Herrick 11 and was injured in October 2009 and was sent back to the UK as part of his recovery. He returned to Helmand in early January 2010 and was subsequently killed in action in Musa Qala on 11 January. The counter-IED world had not seen so many deaths in such a short space of time since the early years of the Troubles, in the 1970s. The question being asked was, 'Were they exhausted or had they become ambivalent to risk?'

'In the days when Northern Ireland was a big problem, an ATO would be lucky if the number of devices he defused on a tour reached double figures,' Badger explained. 'Now guys are doing fifty to 100 devices. I've disposed of 139 in six months. A year ago, the idea that an ATO might dispose of 100 bombs on a tour in Helmand was unthinkable, but soon it will be the average. The pressures on ATOs are huge, the room for error zero.

'We had not lost an operator since 1989, but now we are back to the attrition rate of the early 1970s. It is a demanding and gruelling job and I think we will see, in the years to come, cases of post-traumatic stress disorder beginning to emerge. The stress is unquantifiable. It is one of the major worries. We don't know what sort of toll this war is having on bomb-disposal teams. We won't know that for a long while.

'The Counter IED Task Force was established to deal with the IED threat in Helmand. In 2006 there were just two ATOs and two search teams; that number has increased but we still need more. At the moment we are very pressed and we can't deliver enough effect.'

By 'effect' Badger meant the ability to defuse bombs at the right time in all the areas necessary, both to allow British troops to move about safely and to give the local people some freedom of movement.

'We desperately need more ATOs and search teams,' he went on. 'These are the people who allow soldiers to interface with the locals, which is all part of counter-insurgency. CIED is about a lot more than just getting rid of bombs – it is about opening up the country to allow ISAF and the Afghan security forces to secure the local population.

'Bomb hunting teams could clear thousands of IEDs every month and it wouldn't have any effect at all – the key is to make sure you clear the right ones. We still do not have enough IED operators here, and that's a source of frustration. In theory each company should have a team, but we simply don't have the numbers. It takes up to seven years to recruit and train an Ammunition Technician – that's as long as it takes to train a doctor.'

The woeful shortage of ATOs was caused in large part by a catastrophic decision to halt recruitment into the Royal Logistic Corps at both officer and soldier levels. The net effect was that bomb-hunting units were left with a 40 per cent reduction in manpower at a time when British troops were on operations and facing a significant IED threat in both Iraq and Afghanistan.

Bomb-disposal experts are a scarce resource; there are only a finite number in the Army. As well as taking part in operations in Helmand, bomb-disposal teams are also based on the British mainland and in Northern Ireland, ready to deal with an IED 24/7. A select group of bomb hunters, known as Team Alpha, also work with the SAS. One of their roles is to defuse IEDs attached to hostages and suicide bombers. They specialize in 'Category A', or manual, neutralizations, which are undertaken only when no other option is available, for example when a bomb is strapped to a hostage or to prevent a mass-casualty event. ATOs who choose to work with Team Alpha must be prepared and ready to tackle any device and do whatever is necessary to save life – even if it requires self-sacrifice.

Before deploying to Helmand, ATOs must successfully complete a gruelling eight-week High Threat course, which just 20 per cent pass at the first time of taking. While on the course ATOs learn how to dispose of all types of IEDs they can expect to meet in theatre and also undergo rigorous psychological testing to assess their suitability to operate in an environment where they will often be the target. There have been several qualified ATOs who have failed to make the grade on the course because they lacked the mental fortitude to deal with the unrelenting demands of a high-threat environment.

As well as the bomb hunters and RESTs, the CIED Task Force works alongside a number of units, including the Joint Force Engineer Group, to clear IEDs. The Python is a rocket-propelled mine-clearance system which is mounted on a Royal Engineer Trojan armoured vehicle and has been used in Helmand to blast a route through IED belts along which troops or convoys of armoured vehicles can safely pass. An alternative route-clearance system is the Talisman programme, which consists of a fleet of vehicles designed to clear routes for combat logistic patrols. Each Talisman suite is composed of a Mastiff 2 protected vehicle in which the IEDD team travel; a Buffalo mine-protected vehicle with a rummaging arm, which can be used to locate IEDs; a JCB high-mobility engineer excavator, used to fill in ditches or potholes; a T-Hawk micro air vehicle, which is a man-portable drone that flies ahead of the convoys and observes suspicious vehicles; and a Talon, a tracked remote-controlled vehicle which is used to disrupt or disarm IEDs. The Python and Talisman are perfect for clearing routes through banks of IEDs for combat logistic patrols or for major advances into enemy territory. But they have little use for the majority of bomb-disposal work in Helmand, which takes place on public roads and in small villages and hamlets, where most British casualties occur.

The use of robots has also met with limited success in Helmand, because almost every piece of equipment used by bomb-hunting teams needs to be man-portable and the only robot light enough to be carried without a vehicle is the Dragon Slayer. Officially the MoD claims that the Dragon Slayer is a fantastic piece of equipment which will prove to be a huge aid to bomb-disposal teams and is the 'best remote-controlled bomb disposal robot on the market'. But I have yet to come across an ATO who was impressed by the Dragon Slayer. Most complained that the device, which weighs 10 kg, often broke down or was too weak to pick up large quantities of explosives. On paper the idea of disposing of IEDs with robots is obviously the ideal solution, but the reality is different. A similar argument is used for the bomb suit, which is meant to protect bomb hunters from the effect of a blast. While it might be suitable in the relatively controlled environment of Northern Ireland, and to a certain extent Iraq, it is completely impractical in Afghanistan. ATOs need to be highly mobile. They need to be able to climb walls, crawl into culverts, and run for their lives when the Taliban attack – all of which are almost impossible while wearing a 50 kg bomb suit.

The terrain and the distances IEDD teams need to travel also make the use of robots difficult. Most operators I met used robots at every appropriate opportunity, but those opportunities were few and far between and many teams never actually used robots on operations. In fact Badger never used a robot for any of the 139 bombs he defused during his six-month tour.

'In an ideal world,' Badger told me, 'it would be better to deal with IEDs from 100 metres, by using robots and remote weapon systems, but the nature of the operation here means that cannot always be achieved. We have robots but they are of limited use if you have to climb over a 6ft wall to get into a compound where a bomb has been placed.' Badger checks his watch. 'I've got to be going – got a flight out of here and I'm not missing that.' We shake hands and Badger wishes me a safe trip.

IEDs kill in various ways, depending on the type of charge, and in Afghanistan those are composed of artillery shells or mortar bombs filled with either military-grade explosive or home-made explosive. These devices have a high metal content and are relatively easy to discover by soldiers trained to use Vallons. When one is detonated the effect is similar to that of an artillery shell exploding and it often causes lethal fragmentation injuries. The effectiveness of the explosion and the range of the shrapnel are severely limited because the device is buried beneath the ground. To compensate for the limitations imposed by the need to conceal the bomb, the Taliban often use multiple mortar bombs or artillery shells.

The other type of device which is now increasingly seen in Helmand is one where the main charge is usually home-made explosive concealed in a plastic container. The only metal content in these devices will be that used within the pressure plate, if one exists. For this reason they are much more difficult to detect, although not impossible. The containers typically contain 5, 10 or 20 kg of HME, but can be stacked in multiples to produce a bigger explosion. Any device with a charge of between 5 and 10 kg will take off a leg; 10 kg will take off both legs and most of a soldier's behind. Anything larger will cause instant death. Soldiers who trigger these devices are killed or injured purely by the effect of the blast or by the pressure wave caused by the explosion, which is powerful enough to tear off one or more limbs. In some cases, especially if the bomb weighs more than 20 kg, the blast can blow a soldier to pieces. In Helmand there have been occasions whem only small body parts of soldiers have been found because they have been so close to the point of detonation. Many soldiers have also suffered severe blast wounds because they were close to a device when it exploded. In one example a soldier lost an arm and suffered severe blast injuries to the rest of his body after a colleague stepped on a pressure-plate IED. The soldier who triggered the device survived but lost both legs in the blast.

Soldiers now accept that there is a high probability that they will be wounded by an IED, especially if they are based in areas such as Musa Qala and Sangin. They know that they might lose an arm or leg but also accept that, while such an injury may be life-changing, it need not diminish their quality of life. But the greatest fear which eats away at soldiers is the horrible prospect of losing their genitals in a blast. Human genitals are made from soft tissue and are easily damaged or blown off in an IED blast, especially when the explosion has already resulted in a traumatic amputation. Many soldiers privately told me that they would rather be dead than return to the UK without their testicles.

'The first thing everybody checks after they have been blown up is their wedding tackle, that's providing they are conscious,' a soldier confided while we were chatting about the numerous threats they faced in Helmand. 'Virtually the first thing a soldiers asks is, "Have I still got my bollocks?" It happens on the battlefield or in hospital. Nobody want to go home without their nuts – it's a big topic of conversation among the soldiers. You will get guys asking, "What would you rather lose, your legs or your nuts?" There are some guys who'd prefer to lose both legs, both arms and be blind but still have their nuts. Others say if you don't have any nuts you no longer have the urge for sex because you don't have the right hormones in your blood, so if you do lose your nuts you won't miss sex anyway. It's all part of the reality of life in this fucked-up place.'

Many other weapons will have a disproportionately greater effect when used in multiples. Here the Taliban subscribe to Aristotle's dictum that 'the whole is greater than the sum of its parts', and this is precisely the case with IEDs. IEDs are used by the Taliban as a single bomb but it is when they are used in multiples that they have the greatest effect. The Taliban have learned to be meticulous in the planning of ambushes. After fours years of fighting the British, they are now able to predict, often with unerring accuracy, how troops will respond when ambushed. Insurgents are good students, always watching and learning. When a NATO soldier is seriously injured, the Taliban know that the standard operating procedure is to call for a helicopter evacuation. For the aircraft to land safely, space and flat ground are needed. So what better place to plant several more IEDs than an obvious helicopter landing site?

The Taliban know that soldiers will rush to the aid of a colleague who may be, say, a triple amputee and bleeding to death. Soldiers being soldiers, they may well disregard the threat to them and not clear a safe route to a casualty in order to provide life-saving first aid. Such blind loyalty among the British troops has often been exploited by the Taliban, with the consequence that those who have rushed to help a stricken comrade have ended up as casualties themselves.

As one soldier put it, 'It's easy to lose your head and forget your drills when your best mate has had both legs blown off and is screaming in agony. We have had to drum it into soldiers to make sure they always clear a safe lane when going to an injured colleague. Where there is one device there are often more.'

Over lunch in one of the many tented canteens dotted about Camp Bastion, I ponder over what Badger has told me. Only now am I really starting to understand the sheer enormity of the task facing the bomb hunters. On paper the odds look stacked against any of them surviving a six-month tour, but bomb hunters are a breed apart – not that they will tell you that. The most effective weapons they have in their armoury are training, skill and courage, but also luck, and of that they will need bucketloads.

British troops are monitored by the enemy's 'scrutiny screen' of various degrees of sophistication practically every time they leave a base. In some areas, such as Sangin, the monitoring, or 'dicking' as the soldiers call it, is very sophisticated. Dicking is often conducted by young men, sometimes boys just 10 years old, armed only with a mobile phone, who report directly back to the local Taliban commander, and all for a few dollars a day. Soldiers are dicked when they cross obstacles, search VPs, chat to locals, when they enter compounds and when they leave compounds. With such a vast network of willing assistants the Taliban could monitor the movement of British troops all day every day.

'Everything we do is watched by the Taliban in Sangin,' Captain Rob Swan, the commander of Brimstone 31, one of the ATOs working with the Task Force, explained to me while we were relaxing in the Joint Force EOD Group's 'bar' – a large tent with a television and armchairs but no alcohol.

'The Taliban are well aware that if one of their devices is found, then it is highly likely that an ATO is going to be almost certainly called in to defuse it, especially if the device is in an area used by ISAF. So we get called in and basically the Taliban will sit and watch from a distance. He will watch every move, every procedure, every action I make.' Captain Swan smiles and shrugs. 'And there's nothing we can do about it. We can't stop them, we all know they are doing it. It's infuriating watching them sitting with their backs against a compound wall 40–50 metres away, just watching what the operator is doing. They will watch what actions I carry out on that device and they will try to think of ways to catch me out. They will look at areas I may or may not have searched. And you know they are thinking: he didn't search there – maybe I should place an IED in that area. So I have to be very careful all the time, constantly changing my drills and making sure I don't set patterns – it's basically a game of chess with serious consequences for the loser. I always have to stay one step ahead. It's cat and mouse.'

Rob Swan and his team had been sent to Afghanistan as BCRs. The team consisted of Corporal Kelly O'Connor, at that time the only female No. 2 in Helmand, Lance Corporal Sebastian Aprea, 24, the specialist electronics operator, and Ranger Charlie Clark, 27, a reservist serving with the London Regiment (TA) who in civilian life was a tree surgeon but in Helmand was the infantry escort and therefore responsible for covering Captain Swan's back while he was defusing bombs.

In the weeks before Christmas one ATO had been killed and two
had been injured, one severely. Three separate attacks had reduced
the CIED Task Force's bomb-disposal capability to 30 per cent,
exposing the fragility of the JFEOD Group. Replacements were
urgently needed.

Rob, Kelly and Seb had all trained together on the High Threat
course a few months earlier and had expected to deploy to Helmand
in March 2010. But, following a run of casualties, the order came
through that the team should expect to move at short notice and the
three eventually flew out on 16 December 2009. Shortly after they
arrived, Charlie, the fourth member of the team, turned up.

'Being deployed as a BCR wasn't something that really played on
my mind,' added Rob as we chatted in a rare moment of inactivity
while his team relaxed while on standby for the High Readiness Force.
'In fact coming out early was a bit of a bonus – the sooner you come
out the sooner you get home, and my wife is seventeen weeks pregnant so I really want to be home in time for the birth of the baby.'

'Yeah,' interjects Kelly, 'we were just keen to get out here. Better
than sitting on our arses back in the UK.' The other three members
of the team all nod in agreement.

Rob joined the Army in 2003 and after leaving Sandhurst a year
later was commissioned into the Royal Logistic Corps. He says he
had a vague understanding of the nature of bomb disposal but it
wasn't until he was deployed to Iraq in 2005, when he was attached
to the Light Dragoons battlegroup, that he became interested in joining the profession. 'I volunteered to be an escort for an ATO who'd
been tasked with defusing a device which had been taken into a
police station by an Iraqi police officer who had found it on a bridge.
I watched the ATO at work and I found it really intriguing, so when
I returned to the UK I did a bit more research and found out about
the course. As far as the RLC is concerned, it was a bit more of the
pointy end of the sword, so I volunteered for the course.'

Seb, the Royal Signals specialist electronics operator, is 24 and is
chatty, personable and intelligent. He studied science subjects at

A-level, gaining an A and two Bs. 'I thought about going to university but the Army seemed to be a better deal,' he tells me with a broad, youthful smile across his face. 'You get paid to learn and the stuff I'm learning at the moment is pretty much degree level. By the time I have finished my training I will get a Master's – it's all degree-level physics. So it's the same thing as being at university except I'm being paid for it and I'm doing something beneficial for others.'

Seb, who possesses a maturity beyond his years, says he was happy to face the risks that come with being a member of a bomb-disposal team because he believes such a dangerous and demanding job will ultimately assist him in his progress within the Army. He explains, 'This is regarded as quite a prestigious posting for my trade and usually only the top 1 or 2 per cent of each course get selected. I did pretty well in training, I joined up in March 2007, so I've only been in three years. This is my first posting. I went to speak to my troop warrant officer and told him I was interested in going into EOD. I knew it would be good for my career. He made the phone calls and I asked to go to Catterick because it is quite close to where I live and I would be able to see my mum. My mum is threaders at the moment, though. Every time I phone she is in tears. She worries a lot. I try and tell her I'm OK but she still worries.'

One of the most testing days of Brimstone 31's tour took place in early March 2010 in Sangin. Taliban activity in the area was at an all-time high. Almost every patrol from one of the numerous British-occupied bases in the area was subject to some form of attack and the casualty rate was going through the roof. For most of 2009 and half of 2010 the mission in Sangin was to simply contain the Taliban, and the plan to bring security and prosperity was a slow, difficult and often bloody process. Schools were opening and there was more activity in the bazaar which ran through the centre of the town. But security for Afghan civilians had been paid for with the blood of young British soldiers, and the sacrifices being demanded of them were becoming increasingly questionable. Between October 2009 and April 2010, the 3 Rifles battlegroup, which was composed of 1,500 troops from a number of different units, suffered the worst casualties of any British unit involved in the Afghan War to date. More than thirty soldiers were killed and over 200 were injured. Battles would occur almost every day, occasionally several times a day, and the population, whose hearts and minds the British were trying to win, were often caught in the middle. Sangin remains a complex environment where the Alikozai tribesman fears murder if he shops with an Ishakzai trader. It is a society riven with tribal infighting, drugs and corruption, as well as the insurgency, and caught in the middle were the British.

The troops of A Company, 4 Rifles were warned in early 2009 that they would be needed to support the 3 Rifles battlegroup for the winter tour of October 2009 to March 2010. News that the company would be based at FOB Inkerman was met with some relief. Every soldier in the British Army was aware of Sangin's reputation as a graveyard.

FOB Inkerman is the outermost of the many patrol bases which satellite the town of Sangin, and it sits in the edge of Route 611, around 8 km north of the town. Since it was first occupied by the Grenadier Guards in June 2007, barely a day has passed in which troops based there have not been involved in fighting. Inkerman was established with the primary function of interdicting the movement of insurgents into the town, a tactic which had met with some success. The Taliban had responded by seeding the route between Sangin and Inkerman with IEDs, making travel almost impossible for locals, the British, and anyone else.

Because resupplying the FOB via Route 611 was becoming increasingly difficult, in October 2009 A Company attempted to establish a new resupply route through the desert over a distance of about 8 km. The bomb-hunting team charged with clearing the route was led by Staff Sergeant Olaf Schmid, but it proved to be a tortuous and difficult undertaking. Within hours of leaving Inkerman they discovered a run of six IEDs. Progress almost ground to a halt as banks after banks of IEDs were encountered. The mission took eight days to complete and it was immediately clear that resupplying Inkerman via the desert was unsustainable.

Within weeks of arriving, A Company suffered one of its darkest periods when two 20-year-olds, Rifleman Philip Allen and Rifleman Samuel Bassett, were killed on 7 and 8 November respectively. Both soldiers were killed by IEDs during routine patrols in the Inkerman area. Rifleman Bassett was killed while clearing a route to resupply one of the small patrol bases in the area. He was at the front of the patrol, clearing the way with a Vallon, when he stepped on a device. The blast resulted in a double amputation, but although Bassett survived the initial blast and remained conscious throughout the casualty evacuation he later died in hospital, such was the severity of his wounds.

An American Task Force Thor route-clearance team also attempted to clear Route 611 by detonating scores of IEDs as their heavily armoured vehicles drove along the road between Sangin and Inkerman. While Task Force Thor's vehicles managed to eradicate pressure-plate IEDs, they had no effect at all on command-wire IEDs, a fact which was discovered when a massive 150 lb bomb detonated beneath a Mastiff carrying six British troops. Everyone in the vehicle survived, but the commander, a young lieutenant, lost a foot in the blast.

Even after the route had been cleared, the Taliban soon returned and began burying even more IEDs, by locating blind spots which could not be monitored by the British and by using children to bury devices.

Brigadier James Cowan, the commander of 11 Light Brigade, and Lieutenant Colonel Nick Kitson, the commander of the 3 Rifles battlegroup, in conjunction with Major Richard Streatfield, the officer commanding A Company, decided that the only alternative was to try to secure Route 611 by occupying a series of compounds adjacent to the road. The operation was launched shortly before Christmas 2009, and by early January a total of nine compounds and patrol bases had been created.

Initially the Taliban did little. They simply watched and waited, as they had done in the past. Intelligence later emerged that they thought the British were going to create a series of bases securing the route all the way to Kajaki, some 25 km farther north. But when occupation of the compounds stopped, the insurgents attacked.

Like the IRA, the Taliban would always repeat those tactics which met with success, while immediately abandoning any practice which met with failure. Insurgent commanders would learn, adapt and improvise. The Taliban began to attack the British with improvised claymore mines, which the troops dubbed 'party poppers', and when these failed to make an impact 107mm Chinese rockets were fired at vehicles from a range of about 100 metres. Dummy IEDs were also used to lure bomb-hunting teams into ambush sites. In addition the Taliban began to devise ways of dropping pressure-plate IEDs into old bomb craters and quickly covering them with a thin coating of earth, and this was often done in broad daylight just metres from the PBs.

'The Taliban were very inventive,' said Pat Hyde, at that time the company sergeant major of A Company. 'They were the equivalent of the South Armagh Brigade of the IRA. They would give anything a try and even resorted to using some of the old IRA tactics. They began to plant massive bombs in culverts. We had to occupy a compound to guard the culverts to prevent the Taliban from planting IEDs inside. That base, "Hotel-18", was being attacked twenty-five times a day. Two soldiers were killed guarding that culvert and a further twelve were injured, including a triple and a double amputee.'

Taliban attacks were also becoming more adventurous and increasingly complex, with multiple phases. The insurgents' confidence seemed to be growing daily, which perhaps indicated that they were receiving outside help. One such Taliban ambush took place in early March 2010, during a routine resupply mission, when a combat logistic patrol slowly weaved its way along a cleared path along Route 611 from Sangin, north towards FOB Inkerman.

As the convoy passed close to PB Ezeray, the Taliban were waiting. Dickers farther down the route had given them plenty of warning that an easy target was approaching. As the convoy approached, the insurgents manoeuvred a 107 mm rocket along an alley and waited for the target to show itself. When the target, a vehicle known as a Drops (Demountable Rack Offload and Pickup System), emerged, the Taliban couldn't miss.

These vehicles lift and carry ISO containers (steel shipping containers) to bases around Helmand and form the backbone of the supply chain, but they are slow and cumbersome and make easy targets. Almost immediately the Drops burst into flames, forcing the two Gurkha soldiers to flee for their lives. The convoy pushed on to Inkerman, leaving the stricken vehicle to burn for the next thirty-six hours.

WO2 Hyde, 34, had joined the Army as a 'junior leader' and had been a soldier for seventeen years. He had served in Iraq, Kosovo, Northern Ireland, and previously in Kabul. He originally joined the Gloucester Regiment, which was later amalgamated into the Royal Gloucestershire, Berkshire and Wiltshire Regiment, before being merged again, this time with the Devonshire and Dorset Regiment, the Royal Green Jackets and the Light Infantry, to form the Rifles. Hyde was a seasoned operator, who thought he had seen it all until his company arrived in Helmand. He and his six-man team, callsign Hades 49, which also included two women, Corporal Hayley Wright, a Mastiff commander, and Lance Corporal Jody Hill, the team medic, were dispatched to recover the damaged Drops and bring it back to Inkerman. Despite being the most senior rank in the team, Hyde always positioned himself as top cover, manning the .50-cal. The position provided him with the best view of the area but also made him the one most vulnerable to attack. The shortage of troops within the company also meant that he only ever deployed on route missions with three troops per vehicle.

'We had just come in off a ten-day op when we were told to go and recover the Drops,' he recalled. 'We were stinking. There was no time to wash, shave or change our clothes. We knew no one had been near the vehicle because it had been blinking hot and we had various sentries and sangar positions observing that area, so we felt pretty happy about it.'

As the vehicle was dragged clear, lots of strips of metal began to fall from the burnt-out hulk. Within minutes around 150 people, mostly children, descended on the area, grabbing at anything which could be carried away.

'We recovered the Drops back to Inkerman – no dramas, everything went to plan. Once we got it back we then had to go out again on a routine resupply run. But this time we started to pick up some Icom chatter: "The tanks [as the the Taliban call Mastiffs] are coming. Get ready." As we were driving along we were expecting a 107 mm rocket to come winging out of the alleyway at us. They had done that before and we thought that was what the Icom chatter was about. But instead of a rocket we got a double-stacked anti-tank mine.'

The mines were planted by the Taliban when the area was flooded with locals picking up pieces of scrap metal during the recovery of the Drops. In just twenty minutes, in broad daylight in an area which was under constant observation, the Taliban had managed to lay a complex multi-IED ambush. The insurgents had seen that the ground was being dug up as the vehicle was dragged away and immediately decided to exploit the situation. Instead of having to dig the bombs into the ground, they could place them in some of the welts carved out of the ground and loosely cover them with soil.

'There was this huge bang,' recalled WO2 Hyde. 'I was on top cover and the blast really took it out of me. The shock wave went right through the vehicle and I was left feeling like I wanted to vomit. The difference between high explosive and home-made explosive is unbelievable. The noise was deafening and inside the vehicle all the lights had gone. The blast had also taken off the front of the vehicle, the wheels had gone, and we were going nowhere. Fortunately we were in a Mastiff. If we had been in a Snatch or anything else we would have been dead.

'I knew I was all right and I quickly checked to make sure everyone else was OK. And then it's time to take a chill pill, calm down, everyone stays inside the vehicle, no one moves, everyone makes sure they are OK. On this job there were three vehicles in the convoy – another two behind us. At this stage I'm thinking that we can't afford to let this vehicle fall into Taliban hands and get wrecked even further because we were running out of Mastiffs – they were our lifeline. By now we had around nine patrol bases along the road and we had to supply water to them all because there were no wells. So all the water, ammunition, rations, everything had to come from Inkerman.'

Hyde contacted the ops room and informed them that he had been in an IED contact. He knew that the chances of a follow-up attack were high and asked if there was ISTAR (Intelligence, Surveillance, Target Acquisition and Reconnaissance) in the shape of a unmanned air vehicle such as a Predator, fast jet or attack helicopter.

'I wanted any ISTAR to have a look on the ground around us to see if the Taliban were forming up for an attack, or whether there was someone waiting on the end of a command wire. I decided to get out and begin clearing the area and at the same time I was trying to formulate a plan as to how we were going to get back. At this stage I was also concerned about a secondary device. The Taliban in Sangin aren't just going to plant one device, they are always thinking three or four moves ahead. I was clearing the area and I discovered a command wire running about 4 metres in front of me to a shape in the ground. It was another anti-tank mine ready to hit the team who were going to be sent in to recover us.'

Hyde had no idea how many other devices were in the immediate area, but it was clear that he and his team could not extract themselves from their position without help from a bomb-hunting team. The time now was around 5 p.m. and the sun was beginning to set. Rob Swan and Brimstone 31 were a few kilometres away in FOB Jackson, waiting for a flight back to Camp Bastion, when they were told they would be needed for another mission. With darkness falling, Captain Swan and Lieutenant Colonel Nick Kitson, the commanding officer of 3 Rifles battlegroup, decided to wait until morning to extract the sergeant major and his team.

'The only real option was to stay in the vehicle. There was sensitive equipment inside, we couldn't really extract ourselves safely, so we settled down and waited. There were six of us inside the vehicle and we had support from sangars overlooking the position. It was cosy but smelly – we had been out for ten days and we all stank.'

That evening Captain Swan attended the orders group, where the plan for the recovery of the vehicle and the clearance of other IEDs was spelt out. The plan was as simple as any could be in Sangin. The troops would be moved out of their base just before first light and make for the ambush location. One of the main obstacles was a wide irrigation ditch, which is where the Rifles, the IED team and the Royal Engineer searchers all expected to be ambushed. The ditch was an obvious choke point. That was where the British soldiers would be most vulnerable, and everyone knew it.

The Taliban didn't disappoint. The recovery operation had made good progress up until the irrigation ditch. Both sides had been secured and half the patrol had crossed the ditch when the Taliban opened up. An RPG whizzed overhead. 'It wasn't a very good shot but we all jumped into the river and we were up to our waists in water,' Rob Swan recalled.

'I was more worried about my fags than anything else,' said Kelly. 'They were in my pocket and they were the only packet I had left.'

The soldiers took up fire positions on the bank to suppress the enemy, and a ferocious battle ensued. Troops in the two sangars overlooking the road began to engage the Taliban, WO2 Hyde was pumping .50-cal rounds into the enemy positions, and the ground troops were engaging the insurgents with every weapon at their disposal. The battle raged for about an hour before the Taliban withdrew, allowing Swan to move forward and begin clearing the devices.

He added, 'It's rare, particularly in Sangin, to go out on a job and not be hit at some stage during the task. When it happens you don't think, oh shit, I'm under fire, you just get on with it. It doesn't feel real, just like another training scenario. Once the enemy were suppressed we moved forward into another ditch and set up an ICP and pushed the cordon up to the Taliban's fire positions.'

Once the ICP had been cleared and established, the search team moved forward in the hope of clearing a safe lane to the vehicle, but within 30 metres of the ICP another pressure-plate IED was discovered.

'It was the same device which had been used to blow up the Mastiff – a double-stacked anti-tank mine attached to a pressure plate,' said Rob. 'So I cleared that – it was quite a big device and would have easily taken out another vehicle. The Taliban had been quite clever. About 60 metres back they had exactly the same set-up – a pressure-plate IED with an anti-tank mine – that was designed to target the recovery or just an opportunity target. But in between the two there was a command-wire IED as well. That device had been designed to take out the recovery team – to kill soldiers. It was a pretty complex set-up.'

In the weeks that followed, the Taliban changed tactics again and began to plant IEDs in culverts running beneath roads. Pat Hyde had predicted that they would begin to exploit this opportunity, and he was proved right. Members of the Rifles were daily forced to risk life and limb clearing the tunnels, and on almost every occasion the Taliban were lying in wait.

One of the other great frustrations among the troops in FOB Inkerman was the lack of a permanent IEDD team. A team was based in FOB Jackson, where every day they would clear devices that were a threat to locals or the soldiers. But in Inkerman they had their own problems to contend with. WO2 Hyde explained, 'There were days when I would have to drive down to FOB Jackson to pick up an ATO – but to do it I almost certainly had to drive close to or even over IEDs. We would have IEDs to clear and no one to clear them. I think, of all the problems we faced in Helmand, IEDs were the worst – a problem made worse by the shortage of ATOs.

'By the end of the tour I, and probably most soldiers, could tell the difference between home-made explosive and military-grade explosive. I knew that a 5 kg bomb would take a leg off, 10 kg would take off both legs, and anything bigger and you were dead.'

By the time Operation Herrick 11 came to an end in April 2010, Pat Hyde had earned the dubious distinction of being the most blown-up soldier in the British Army. He survived eleven IED strikes on a vehicle, two 107 mm rocket attacks and two bomb attacks while on foot patrol. The only injury he sustained was when some red-hot rocket shrapnel dropped down the back of his body armour and burnt his back. A Company, 4 Rifles held the stretch of road between Sangin and Inkerman until April 2010, when they handed it over to 40 Commando, Royal Marines. During their six-month tour the company of 131 soldiers and the various attachments from the engineers, the artillery and 3 Rifles sustained fifty-three battle casualties and ten soldiers killed in action. The company had been involved in more than 500 small-arms attacks and 200 IED incidents. Sangin was later handed over to US Marine Corps control in September. All of the bases built by A Company, 4 Rifles were subsequently closed.

Rob Swan's stay in Sangin was short-lived and eventful, but in terms of sheer fear did not compare with the action he'd seen a few weeks earlier during Operation Moshtarak – NATO's big push into central Helmand.

The build-up to the operation had been getting plenty of attention in the media, with commanders hoping that the net effect would be that the Taliban, realizing they would be killed if they attempted to stand and fight, would depart. Before the operation, practically everyone taking part was hoping that the Taliban would have fled.

Brimstone 31 were attached to Right Flank, one of the Scots Guards companies involved in the operation, whose mission was to conduct a heliborne assault in the area of Sayedabad, around 5 km south of FOB Shawqat, a British base located close to Nad-e'Ali district centre. Troops from other battalions would be conducting similar operations near by. In the days leading up to the mission Rob Swan went to seemingly endless meetings and planning conferences. Nothing was being left to chance. Everything which could be rehearsed before the op was being rehearsed.

In the early hours of D-Day, 13 February 2010, Brimstone 31 and the other elements of Right Flank flew into three pre-reconnoitred compounds under the cover of darkness. The plan was for the three platoons to each secure and hold one compound, establish a foothold on the ground, and begin clearing the area of IEDs.

Rob and the RESA were attached to Right Flank's tactical headquarters, while the rest of the IEDD team were dispersed among the other platoons. The first phase of the operation went without a hitch and all three platoons managed to secure their objectives within minutes of landing. In those few hours before dawn the sense of relief was tangible – but it was short-lived. As the sun rose over the Green Zone, the Taliban attacked en masse.

'Within about twenty minutes of sunrise every compound came under accurate fire,' Rob recalled. 'We cut murder holes in the walls to try and observe the enemy's movements but the fire was so accurate that it was actually coming through the murder holes. It was unbelievable. That level of accuracy is something you just don't expect – we were pinned down and unable to move. It was top-class sniping fire. A gun team was sent out to put down some suppressing fire but they were hit straight away and one of the guys was hit in the leg. He had to be casevaced [casualty-evacuated] out and we basically had to sit it out for that day.

'It was absolutely horrendous. We were all pinned up against one wall. We had a guy in the compound get shot through one of the murder holes, and how he didn't get hit is beyond me. It went straight through his trouser leg and came out his backside. He was convinced he had been shot in the nuts and we had to convince him that everything was exactly where it should be. We've been under fire before where you know you are pretty safe and the bullets are thudding into the walls and you're not worried, sometimes almost laughing – I actually have laughed while I've been under fire – but there was nothing remotely funny about this situation at all. I was very stressed. I thought I actually might cop it in there. It was about as bad as you could imagine it to be. If I had moved just a few inches to my left or right I would have risked being killed.'

At this point Seb added, 'You don't feel very safe sat in a compound when the enemy knows exactly where you are. It was 360 degrees, the bullets were whizzing past, coming in and hitting the walls above us and to the side. There was only a very small area which was safe, and we were in it.'

Even Kelly, who was renowned for her laid-back, unflappable nature, recalled, 'I was just hoping we weren't going to get hit, it was that bad. You couldn't move. It was a shit fucking day. The Taliban had us exactly where they wanted us and there was bugger all we could do.'

Then Rob spoke again. 'I don't like small-arms fire. When I'm dealing with a device I feel like I'm in control, I know what I am doing. I was sat rigid in a compound – there were about forty of us against one wall for about thirteen hours. We didn't need to be told not to move because you could see that if you did you would get hit. If you needed a piss, you did it where you were sitting.'

It is often noted in the British Army that 'a plan rarely survives first contact', and therefore one of the principles of warfare is 'flexibility'. Right Flank were stuck fast and surrounded, with all three locations under fire. Urgent action was needed, and the company commander decided that the safest bet was to move the whole company into one location and robustly defend it. The soldiers knew that the Taliban attacks would fizzle out after dusk, because with little or no night-vision equipment they were in no position to take on British troops in the dark. As night fell, the insurgents melted away and the troops reorganized themselves.

'We had loads of stores with us,' said Rob. 'We bought a generator in, a quad bike for casevac and loads of fuel but we couldn't take it with us. So we had to help the engineers "dem" the generator and the quad and we blew it all up. We took what kit we could carry and began the move into another compound. It took about seven hours to move across and get into the same compound. When we met up I made sure everyone was all right really.'

Seb added, 'You look back and you think that was pretty close, but the infantry are pretty good and they always look after you well.'

The fighting rolled on for a further five days. Some of the battles were lengthy, while on other occasions the fighting was small-scale and sporadic. But the obvious threat from small-arms attack effectively grounded Brimstone 31. Such was the scarcity of bomb hunters in Helmand that no commander would risk putting them out on the ground to clear IEDs when the Taliban were obviously in the area.

The owner of the compound which the troops had occupied, paying him a daily rate for its use, remained within one of the buildings and the troops hoped that he might provide some useful information on the local Taliban, such as their strengths and the type of weapons they possessed. But the man was insistent that he knew nothing about the Taliban, meeting any questions put to him via an interpreter with either a shake of his head or a shrug.

On the fifth day of the operation the officer commanding Right Flank, Major Iain Lindsay-German, told Captain Swan they had received intelligence suggesting that there was a Taliban bomb factory in the local bazaar, just 30 metres from the compound. The area was searched with ISTAR, in the form of both fast jets and attack helicopters which scoured the countryside for signs of the Taliban.

Once the all-clear was given, the troops moved out of the compound and began to secure the bazaar, which earlier in the week had been a hive of activity but miraculously had emptied overnight. The Scots Guards also pushed smaller units out to a distance of some 200 metres from the compound to secure fire positions in case the Taliban attacked.

Rob explained, 'We went out and searched the bazaar: there were about forty shops in total. Some still had bread in them, and groceries. It was a long, arduous process. You can imagine what it was like, moving from one shop to the next, always having to be careful that the place hadn't been booby-trapped. We had received intelligence suggesting that there might be a bomb factory in the bazaar. You hear that a lot, but there was no real sign of anything suspicious. Then just as we were thinking, the intelligence is shite, we found a shop which had thirty-eight pressure-plate IEDs – and you're like, "Fucking hell, good job." The shop also had lots of other bomb-making components. There were batteries and wires. Lots of metal saws for the pressure plates, rolls of wire, pieces of wood had been cut up. There were lots of power packs. All the paraphernalia you would expect to be associated with a bomb factory.

'I went in there and cleared all of them, looking out for booby-traps at the same time. I made them safe and put them to one side, one after the other. Just as I finished that, the guys were searching a shop on the other side of the bazaar and found about another 20 kg of HME, so there were two separate areas in the bazaar, one with a switching system and pressure plates and the other where they made the high explosives. We were 3 km behind an IED belt at Kalshal Kalay, where they have had lots of finds of IEDs. The feeling was that the bomb-making factory we discovered was where they were making the devices, putting them together and then carrying them forward to where the Grenadier Guards were operating and were putting them in the ground and trying to kill the soldiers, so it was quite good that, although we were there for a week and were under a lot of fire, we took thirty-eight devices out of that area, and destroyed 250 kg of HME and 100 kg of conventional explosive in the form of artillery shells and mines.

'The Taliban are knocking out IEDs on an industrial scale. We can't keep up. There must be dozens of factories out there churning hundreds of devices out every day. Most people back home think these things must be sophisticated because they're killing and injuring lots of soldiers. But they're not. They're really basic – there is no quality control, no standard. They are just thrown together, but they are effective and deadly.

'I've seen bomb factories where there are shelves of pressure plates, shelves of detonators, shelves of main charges. It was a case of come and grab what you need and take it away and bury it and go away and do the same again. The Taliban look at areas they want to deny to us – they could be areas of tactical significance or a small community which they want to keep under their control. And so they lay IEDs in belts knowing that we will avoid them or work hard to clear them.

'The compound we occupied was 20–30 metres from the bazaar and the guy who owned the place where we were based lived 30 metres from a bomb factory. We asked him if there were Taliban in the area and he said no. The OC held a shura for all the elders and they were like, "Yeah, there's nothing in there. Go in and search it, you won't find anything." I think most of them were just frightened. They knew that they could ultimately be killed if the Taliban discovered they had helped us. And that's the same everywhere you go. I think the majority of the local nationals want to help but they are all too scared to be honest. They're playing the long game – they know we will leave one day but the Taliban aren't going anywhere.'

Talking with other officers on previous trips, I have seen the same frustration as Rob is expressing over the actions of the locals. One of the greatest challenges commanders in Helmand face is trying to convince the Afghans that they are better off with ISAF than the Taliban. The insurgents counter this by claiming that ISAF will leave in a few years but the Taliban will remain in Afghanistan for ever. Faced with that situation, who would you back? The Taliban often say that their greatest weapon is time. 'You have the watches, but we have the time,' they claim.

As we chat the subject drifts onto the countries from whom the Taliban are receiving support and assistance. Rob smiles as he says, 'The Taliban's bomb-making knowledge hasn't been developed in Afghanistan. It's far too good for that. The current thinking is that it has come from Pakistan, and possibly Iran. The belief is that the majority of the advances in IED technology are coming from

Pakistan. There are lots of intelligent people in Pakistan, who are thinking outside the box, and the Pakistani secret service have helped the Taliban, we know that. There are a lot of bomb-makers in Quetta [in Pakistan] and other Taliban strongholds developing new devices all the time. But they have to come up with a simple blueprint for a bomb which can be made out of easily obtainable material and which is not over-complex. If the material wasn't a problem, then we would have real problems here. The Pakistani Taliban could easily produce devices similar to those we faced in Iraq, and that would cause us enormous difficulties.'

News reaches me via my media escort that our helicopter flights into FOB Shawqat in Nad-e'Ali in central Helmand are confirmed for tomorrow around midday. The excitement of leaving Camp Bastion and moving closer to the action grips me once again. I am acclimatizing to the war zone. Promises I made to myself and my family about not going on patrol or doing anything dangerous are beginning to evaporate. England, my family and my office in Victoria almost feel like a lifetime away. That's good in a way, I tell myself with little conviction. Better not to think about my family than to miss them. I suppose that's how the soldiers cope too.

I am told that our group, which includes the *Sunday Telegraph* photographer Heathcliff O'Malley and Captain John Donaldson, known as JD, the Grenadier Guards' media officer, will be flying into the FOB in a Sea King. I'm not filled with confidence. These aircraft are ancient, having been in service with the Royal Navy for more than thirty years. They were sent out to Helmand in a belated attempt to boost the number of helicopters available to British troops for operations following numerous claims and allegations that troops were dying unnecessarily because they were being forced to travel by road instead. There is a certain truth in this. Even before the surge in use of IEDs by the Taliban, Afghanistan was one of the most land-mined countries on earth and anyone going overland was risking death or injury. It became clear to me as early as October 2006, when I first visited Helmand, that there were too few helicopters there. A senior officer from 16 Air Assault Brigade in 2006, when British troops first entered Helmand en masse, was privately furious that his force was so poorly equipped with helicopters.

He was a tough former member of the special forces, and one of the few British Army officers who had fought against the Taliban in Helmand prior to 2006 and thus had a thorough understanding of the terrain. Shortly after he returned to the UK from southern Afghanistan he told me how his personal planning for the entire mission had been undermined by equipment shortages.

'I knew the mission was going to be difficult given the resources I had,' he explained, as we chatted over a pint in a pub in Mayfair. 'I knew it would be a close run thing. I fired off numerous memos up the chain prior to our deployment requesting more support helicopters but I don't think the people at PJHQ (Permanent Joint Head Quarters) really understood the problem. There was no real understanding there (at PJHQ) of the terrain in Helmand, the distances involved and the fact that there were no roads. The main effort was always going to be Iraq and I think a lot of people in PJHQ simply thought Afghanistan was a side-show. So the mission was always going to be problematic even before the Taliban got involved.'

I have interviewed numerous senior commanders in Helmand since 2006 and everyone of them has privately told me that the lack of British helicopters had cost lives and hampered operations. When I asked whether I could report their concerns 'on the record', every single officer naturally refused. The general consensus was that publicising their complaints would not result in any increase in the number of support helicopters, and would only generate unwanted 'heat' from Whitehall. The more honest among them also admitted that such a claim might also have a severe impact on their military careers.

I return to the tent and begin to pack and repack my kit, trying to work out what I will need for the next phase of my embed, when I move beyond Camp Bastion and into the action. It's much warmer both at night and during the day than I had predicted, so the winter fleece can be dumped. During my last visit in November I travelled too lightly and my warm clothing consisted of a down-filled waist-coat and a lightweight fleece. Needless to say, I was absolutely freez-ing at night – primarily because I was sleeping in a steel ISO container which was effectively a large fridge.

Chapter Four: **The Front Line**

'Everyone wants to get involved in a firefight when you first come out but when it's happening every day you start to wonder how long your luck will last.'
Guardsman, 1st Battalion Grenadier Guards

The RAF Merlin is flying 'nap of the earth', at low level, over the Helmand desert at an altitude of around 100 ft. The chopper is bobbing and weaving like a prizefighter trying to dodge a punch, twisting one way, then the other. In Helmand the safest journeys are the shortest, including those by helicopter.

I've flown out of Camp Bastion in a helicopter on dozens of occasions over the past four years but it remains a nerve-racking experience. RAF helicopters are pretty well protected. Most have at least two machine guns, one fore and one aft, a host of defensive aids, which should be able to handle any surface-to-air (SAM) missiles, and armour plating on the floor and sides of the fuselage. But there is always the risk of the Taliban getting a lucky hit. As I write this in June 2010, they have managed to down a US Black Hawk that was trying to extract a wounded British soldier. As the helicopter came down to land, when it is at its most vulnerable, a hidden Taliban RPG team managed to fire a rocket that hit the tail rotor. Four of the crew were killed in the crash. It will not be the last time that a helicopter is shot down on a routine mission.

The British military have already drawn up contingency plans for a mass-casualty event if and when a British Chinook laden with upwards of forty troops is brought down by enemy fire. It is feared that such a catastrophic event would kill off the diminishing support for the mission among the British public and lead to a full-scale withdrawal of British troops. So far the British have been lucky, whereas both the US and Canadian militaries have lost helicopters, either to enemy fire or to mechanical failure, at the cost of many good men. In war good luck always runs out.

I begin to think once again of Rupert and his last journey and wonder whether I will have the same fate. 'Once you go beyond the wire there are no longer any guarantees,' someone once advised me before I embedded with an infantry unit. 'You share exactly the same risk as everyone else.' The fear and concerns that gripped me are no longer so intense. I'm becoming acclimatized to the dangers Helmand holds, though I'm not sure whether that is a good or a bad thing. I know the fear will return, but I also know that I will be ready for it.

The landscape below is Old Testament. Rectangular, mud-made compounds baked as hard as concrete after decades, possibly hundreds of years, beneath the sun. The dwellings are purely functional; there is no exterior decoration, no outward sign of wealth or individuality. There are no roads, just tracks worn by years of use. Rectangular emerald fields magically appear on the flat, bleak moon-like surface of the desert. Afghan children wave excitedly, while the adults, mostly men, carry on tilling their fields and planting their crops in exactly the same way as their ancestors would have done centuries earlier. Farmers have been working the land here for decades, turning the barren desert into a fertile oasis. The lush, green fields are the first indicator that we are approaching the Green Zone. What should be a thing of beauty is anything but, for this is Taliban country.

In Helmand I've always found the concept of a so-called front line – the Army term is the Forward Line of Enemy Troops, or FLET

– something of a misnomer. The reality here is much more fluid, for there are no real fixed lines and, at least as individuals, the Taliban have complete freedom of movement. The insurgents can come and go as they please into the villages, or kalays, which make up most of Helmand. Some have even ventured close to Camp Bastion. In 2008 a suicide car bomber attempted to destroy a two-vehicle Snatch Land Rover convoy on a routine run between Bastion and Camp Shorabak, where the Afghan National Army are trained. A captain in the Royal Irish Regiment who survived the attack told me of the horror he felt at the extraordinary sight of the bomber's face lying in the middle of the road. He said that he wouldn't have believed this was possible unless he had seen it for himself. The force of the blast had sliced the bomber's face from his skull.

The Taliban's cunning was laid bare in their killing of a British soldier on the ranges close to Bastion a few months before I arrived. As part of the RSOI package, units will often march the 5 km to the ranges, a fact which was noticed by the insurgents. So, in the dead of night, when the ranges are unguarded, they sneaked in and laid an IED in a position where they knew British soldiers would be training. The following day, as members of the Coldstream Guards arrived for a day's live firing, Lance Corporal James Hill, who had flown into Helmand four days earlier, detonated a pressure-plate IED containing an estimated 5 kg of explosive and was killed instantly, proving once again that nowhere in Helmand is safe.

The Merlin continues to jink and twist through the air in an attempt to foil any group of hidden insurgents tempted to shoot down a NATO chopper. On each flank Army Air Corps Apache attack helicopters – called 'mosquitos' by the Taliban – are riding shotgun. The Apache is a fearsome £12-million killing machine. Each bristles with a vast array of weaponry which has been adapted for the war in Helmand. The Apache has a crew of two – the pilot who flies the helicopter and a co-pilot or gunner who controls the weapons systems in battle. The aircraft was originally conceived during the Cold War and came into service with the US armed forces, who have 800 compared with the British Army's sixty-seven, in the early 1990s. Its primary role was to destroy columns of Soviet tanks should they swarm over the north German plain on their way into western Europe. That threat no longer exists, so here they are in Helmand using their Hellfire anti-tank missiles to obliterate Taliban strongholds.

The Apache also carries a 30 mm automatic cannon with a cyclic fire rate of 620 rounds per minute. It takes just one second to take out a target at a distance of 500 metres. A helmet-mounted display enables the cannon to be 'slaved' to the pilot's eye line for manual firing. The flight helmet's clip-on arm drops a small screen in front of his right eye – the helmet-mounted display, or HMD. At the centre of the HMD is a cross-hair sight, like a sniper's. As the pilot's eye moves, so the cannon swivels to follow his line of sight. All he has to do is to look at the target, select the weapon and range, and pull the trigger on the pistol-grip control column.

In addition the Apache is equipped with weapon pods, each of which can carry nineteen CRV7 rockets. These can be fitted with an armour-piercing warhead or packed with eighty 5-in.-long tungsten darts known as flechettes. So a salvo of just eight of these rockets releases 640 flechettes, saturating an area the size of a football pitch. The existence of these weapons is not overtly advertised by the Ministry of Defence because of the effect they have on a human body. The darts strip human flesh to the bone. Those Taliban fighters who aren't killed instantly die a long and lingering death, and woe betide any innocent civilians who find themselves caught in the killing zone in the midst of a battle. The pain and suffering human beings are prepared to inflict upon one another in war is truly appalling, yet I'm secretly reassured to know that we have these weapons.

Like many of the trips by helicopter I have made in Helmand, my flight was delayed by twenty-four hours owing to the helicopters being retasked for a more urgent mission. I've known people who have been stuck in Camp Bastion for up to a week until a flight became available, so a twenty-four-hour delay is viewed as minor-league stuff. Helicopters are a 'mission critical' capability in Helmand, and the British operation has been under-resourced since operations in southern Afghanistan began. The government always maintained that commanders had enough helicopters for the job, and, when asked 'on the record', commanders would concur. But 'off the record' they would then declare that the numbers of helicopters were pitifully low and that troops were being forced to take unacceptable risks travelling in vehicles which were not sufficiently protected against Taliban attack. But, much to the dismay of the military's rank and file, not a single serving senior officer was prepared to put his head on the block by stating what everyone knew to be a fact. General Sir Richard Dannatt, when he was Chief of the General Staff, came closest to directly criticizing the government's failure to equip the military with adequate numbers of helicopters for the mission in Afghanistan. During a visit to Helmand in 2009 he stated publicly that he had visited UK troops located in various outposts by travelling in a US helicopter because no British helicopters were available.

Only now do commanders believe they have the requisite number of helicopters to achieve mission success. The bulk of the troop-carrying capacity is conducted by the half dozen or so RAF Chinooks – the twin-engine workhorse which keeps the Helmand mission alive. They are supported by a clutch of Army Air Corps Lynxes, which at first couldn't fly in the summer owing to the intense heat but have since been adapted, ageing Royal Navy Sea Kings, and RAF Merlins, the latest addition to the British military rotary fleet. The size of the helicopter force has at least doubled since 2006, when NATO forces first ventured into Helmand. But troop numbers have tripled since then, so there is little if any overall gain.

Just fifteen minutes after leaving Camp Bastion we arrive at FOB Shawqat, the British headquarters in Nad-e'Ali. The Army likes to show off Nad-e'Ali because it is one of the few places in Helmand where the British and NATO strategy is flourishing. The Taliban have been forced from the district centre and the whole area is ringed by police and Army checkpoints. When any British VIPs arrive in Helmand, they are routinely shipped off to Nad-e'Ali. Few ever make it into Sangin or other areas where the Taliban presence is more apparent.

The helicopters touch down in a haze of green smoke on two adjacent landing sites within the base. It is rumoured that Shawqat was built in the ruins of a fort occupied by British troops during the First Afghan War, in 1840. Strange to think that 170 years later the British Army is still fighting over the same ground. The fort's 40-ft-high walls are made of red-brown clay bricks, probably fashioned by hand for a seventeenth-century Afghan warlord. Some of the huge round turrets are still intact and have been turned into fortified observation posts by the Afghan National Army, who provide security at the base.

FOB Shawqat has hardly changed since I was here in November 2009, but it does have two important additions: working showers and toilets, crucial for morale. At that time only solar showers were available, but because the water is heated by the sun, a warm shower was impossible in the morning as the temperature then hovered around zero. Soldiers in FOBs were under orders to shave every day but the only means of heating the water was with an ancient 'puffing billy' water heater. This device, which was probably in service with the British Expeditionary Force when it retreated from France in 1940, heated enough water for about twenty soldiers on a base which contained several hundred. It was first come first served, and everyone else had to wash and shave in water chilled to almost freezing by the bitter Helmand night. I can still conjure up the agonizing cramps which momentarily crippled my hands when washing and shaving in the icy water.

The toilets represented an interesting departure in the task of disposing of human waste. Beyond Camp Bastion, apart from at the base at Lashkar Gah, which is home to the brigade headquarters and an infantry company group, plumbing was absent in all the FOBs. Until November 2009 soldiers defecated in foil bags. One of these was placed over a normal toilet, and when the job was done the bag was sealed and thrown into a fire pit. Simple but effective. Before the arrival of poo bags, soldiers were forced to use cubicles which had an open pit beneath them. The stench in the summer was unbearable, but, even worse, the open nature of the pit meant that disease was rife and many troops were struck down with the dreaded D and V, diarrhoea and vomiting.

Within seconds of our touching down, Lieutenant Colonel Roly Walker, the commanding officer of the Grenadier Guards, appears at the HLS, dressed in full battle rig and clutching his rifle. His eyes are obscured by military-issue wraparound sunglasses, but I still recognize his smiling face. 'Thought you weren't going to make it,' he says, his hand outstretched, before adding, 'Good to have you back, Sean. Right, there's no time to waste. You're coming with me – we're off on a bit of a convoy up to Chah-e-Anjir. We'll be staying out overnight, so grab what you need. You've got five minutes.'

Chah-e-Anjir, in the north of the Nad-e'Ali district, is home to Inkerman Company. The base is located at the apex of an upturned triangle which is known by the Army as the CAT – the Chah-e-Anjir Triangle. When I last visited Inkerman Company gun battles with the Taliban were almost a daily occurrence and the FLET was less than 100 metres from the base's forward position. This position was in an area known as Five Tanks, named after five large storage tanks which were part of the mass of machinery left behind by the Americans when they left some fifty years ago.

Roly, a white Kenyan educated at Harrow and Sandhurst, is, at 39, one of the youngest battlegroup commanders in Afghanistan. He is passionately committed to the Afghan mission and is fully signed up to the vision of General Stanley McChrystal, who at that time was the US commander charged by President Barack Obama with breaking the stalemate in Afghanistan, until he was sacked and replaced by General Petraeus in June 2010.

Within minutes of stepping off the Merlin I'm strapped into the back of a Ridgeback armoured vehicle. There are four of us in the rear of the vehicle, each wearing body armour and helmets, so it's a tight squeeze, but I feel secure. The Mastiff and Ridgeback come from the same class of vehicles and are almost identical, but the Mastiff is larger, with six wheels to the Ridgeback's four. The Ridgeback is one of the latest British Army vehicles to arrive in Helmand and is packed with state-of-the-art technology. It has an armoured V-shaped hull which should help deflect blasts from mines and IEDs, while bar armour on the sides should protect those inside from RPG attack. It is also equipped with a remotely controlled 7.62-mm chain gun which is mounted on the roof and controlled by the vehicle commander through a pistol-grip control. A camera mounted on the gun gives the commander a crystal-clear 360-degree view on a drop-down computer screen. To engage the enemy he positions the cross-hairs on the target, flicks off the safety catch and presses the red trigger with his forefinger. The commander does not experience any recoil and the gun, which can fire sixty rounds per minute, can kill anything within a range of 1,200 metres. Thermal imagery allows the weapon to be used at night.

Every now and then WO1 Ian 'Faz' Farrell, the regimental sergeant major of 1st Battalion, the Grenadier Guards, and who, for this trip, is the vehicle commander, manoeuvres the cross-hairs onto some unsuspecting target. It's a pretty awesome weapon – straight out of some hi-tech computer game. I feel detached from the outside world – it is almost a surreal experience, and the various TV screens just add to that sense of dislocation. It's almost like watching an 'in-vehicle movie'. Other cameras positioned on the exterior of the Ridgeback allow the troops inside a similar 360-degree view through two Situational Display Units.

Our vehicle is third in a convoy of six and I should feel secure, but I don't. At the back of my mind there is a nagging, almost irritating uneasiness. It's been there since I first arrived in Helmand, and I was hoping by now that it would have disappeared. On previous trips I have happily boarded an aircraft or climbed into the back of an armoured vehicle, but I'm now wondering whether this trip will be my last. All I can do is hope or return home. Rupert Hamer was travelling in a similar vehicle – a US MRAP – when he was killed and Phil Coburn was injured. The MRAP comes from the same family as the Ridgeback but is probably even more protected. So if Rupert was killed on a routine trip, just like the one I am about to undertake, why should I be any safer?

On previous excursions into Taliban country I have often paid lip service to the array of safety harnesses and seatbelts in the back of an armoured vehicle, many of which don't even work or fit properly. But this time I ensure that I'm properly strapped in, and this time it's the sort of seatbelt you might find in a Formula One racing car. I also do a quick check to make sure that everything else inside the vehicle is secured so that if we do hit an IED, nothing, including the passengers, moves around.

The convoy pushes out of FOB Shawqat and heads north. Turrets swivel as commanders scan the roads ahead for likely enemy fire positions. Ditches, compounds, vehicles, walls – almost anything which offers the insurgents cover – is a potential firing point.

I'm told the journey is expected to take forty minutes, which comes as something of a revelation. The last time I was in Nad-e'Ali, just some four months earlier, a trip of a similar distance had taken six hours. Every unsecured piece of road needed to be searched for IEDs by soldiers using mine detectors.

'I bet you didn't think we would have this sort of freedom of movement,' Roly says with a wide smile on his face. 'If we had come along here before Operation Moshtarak we would have had Apaches flying top cover and we would have been greeted by the mother of all ambushes. It would have been a very tough fight and there is no way we could have continued, but look at it now' – he points at one of the display units – 'it's pretty benign.' I ask Roly whether he thinks the Taliban have fled or simply gone to ground. 'I think it's a mixture of both,' he says, hedging his bets. 'We really won't know how successful Operation Moshtarak has been until after the summer or even well into next year. I think the local Taliban have probably returned to their farms, packed the Kalashnikov away and will get on with the poppy harvest and wait for us to make the next move. But I think we have sent a very clear message. They know they can't win here and we've got to get them to understand, and the local population, that this is not a short-term exercise. Up until recently the Taliban have seen themselves as the shadow government around here, but now they've been evicted. We must make sure that they don't creep back in. The real test is not now but in the months to come.'

Moshtarak, which means 'together' in Dari, the language of Afghanistan, was devised to remove the Taliban from central Helmand in areas not previously cleared by ISAF forces. Success would mean that the writ of the government was extended, ISAF would have greater freedom of movement, and a major Taliban stronghold would be destroyed. Unlike previous ISAF operations, prior to Moshtarak the Taliban were given plenty of warning. General McChrystal, the US commander of ISAF forces, wanted them to leave rather than stand and fight. By telling Taliban commanders that the largest NATO operation in Helmand was about to be launched, it was hoped that they would see sense and flee. Less fighting would mean fewer civilian casualties, which was central to McChrystal's strategy. The operation had two key objectives: the US Marines would seize the district of Marjah, while a combined multinational force led by the British would seize a series of objectives around Nad-e'Ali and in the Babaji area of central Helmand. Preparations started as early as September 2009, when members of the Canadian Army began training some 400 members of the ANA.

Shaping operations began in mid-January, and by D-Day, in the hours before dawn on 13 February 2010, the first of ninety helicopters left Camp Bastion to seize a series of objectives in an operation which would eventually involve up to 15,000 ISAF troops. Most of the British objectives were seized almost immediately, and opposition was light. But Marjah, farther south, was proving to be a tougher fight. Marjah was one of the most important areas to the Taliban. It was their key stronghold in the region and a centre of IED production and development. But it was also crucial to the production of opium, the sale of which was helping to fund the insurgency. The US Marines had by far the tougher challenge and the fighting, albeit on a small scale, continued for many months, and, by late July 2010, British soldiers were again being killed in areas from which the Taliban had supposedly been cleared.

While Operation Moshtarak was successful in the short term, the jury is out on whether it has achieved its long-term aims. At the time of writing, the end of July 2010, Operation Tor Shezada has just been launched to clear the Taliban from the southern area of Nad-e'Ali close to and around the town of Sayedabad, which was one of the last large Taliban strongholds in the area. As with Moshtarak, the Taliban had already fled, not surprisingly, by the time the British troops moved in.

As our convoy trundles through a small kalay en route to Patrol Base Shahzad there is a loud clang against the vehicle just behind where I'm sitting. WO1 Farrell turns to the driver and, with a wrinkled brow, says, 'Was that an RPG?' He is more curious than concerned. The driver shrugs and responds, 'Dunno, sir.' The sergeant major swivels the turret over to the left and using his display unit searches the terrain for Taliban fighters. 'Probably just a kid throwing a rock,' he mutters. I'm now waiting for all hell to be let loose, thinking that we have just driven into Roly's 'mother of all ambushes'. I turn to Roly. '*Was* that an RPG?' I ask, trying not to appear nervous. He seems not the least bit bothered. 'If it was, it didn't detonate. Pretty good shot, though,' he says admiringly. 'It must have been at least 100 metres away. Could have just been a stone being flicked up.'

The convoy pushes on without stopping to investigate further and within a few minutes we are crossing a shallow river several hundred metres from the outskirts of the PB. On the right are rows and rows of traders selling everything from motorbikes to fizzy drinks. It is a scene of typical Afghan chaos, but business is clearly booming. 'Last time you were here this market was dead. Now look at it, it's flour-ishing,' Roly tells me. 'The locals had to change the markets' days because some were being run on the same days and they were "steal-ing" trade from each other. That's a real measure of success – that's how you counter the insurgency, it doesn't have to be all done by fighting.' He's really giving me the hard sell about what has been achieved since my last visit. And why not? His battalion has worked relentlessly for almost six months, they have taken casualties, and several of his men have received life-changing injuries. So they should feel proud of what they have achieved. But it would be a mistake to think that success in Nad-e'Ali is the beginning of the end for the Taliban.

Minutes after arriving, we are ushered into a large tent for a pre-lunch shura with the district governor, Habiullah Khan. Mutton haunches and rice is the menu of the day, along with what the soldiers call 'toenail' bread, joking that it is made with the feet of the locals. There are no knives or forks and, sitting cross-legged on a carpet the size of a squash court, we all tuck in, cupping the fingers of the right hand to scoop up the greasy but delicious rice. I'm amazed at the vast size of the portions, with the standard for consumption being set by the governor, who is famed for his large appetite. After lunch a steady stream of locals arrive and begin to fill the tent. They have come to listen to the governor and Roly. The message is one I have heard many times before, except this time the circumstances are different. For the first time in years the locals in this part of Helmand can live their lives in the knowledge that the Taliban no longer rule. Yet rather than jubilation there is suspicion, for the insurgents' parting message was 'We'll be back' and the locals believe it.

First to speak to the 200-strong audience is the governor. Habiul-lah Khan has a kind, friendly face, but he is also cunning and has acquired a good grasp of modern politics. He knows that in the audi-ence he has both supporters and detractors, as well as members of the Taliban who are on an intelligence-gathering mission. The people of Chah-e-Anjir have always seen themselves as a class apart from the rest of Nad-e'Ali. In the 1950s US aid groups pumped millions of dollars into southern Afghanistan under the Helmand River Project, which was, somewhat ironically, responsible for the growth of the Green Zone – now regarded by the Taliban as its territory. Various ethnic groups moved into the area and today, with its thirteen different ethnic groups, it is one of the most ethnically mixed parts of southern Afghanistan. Even after the US pulled out, the good times continued, until Afghanistan descended into thirty years of self-inflicted chaos. There are still elders living in the area who can remember when Chah-e-Anjir was a thriving, almost autonomous community, and they have no interest in being 'ruled' by what in their eyes amounts to an 'outsider'. So the governor was also doing the hard sell.

'What have the Taliban done for you?' he asks the all-male audience, but his question is met with silence. 'You could not trade without being taxed, you had no freedom, your children couldn't go to school, life was not good. But now, now you can trade and you keep your money and your children can get an education, and that is good for our society. You must tell your children that the Taliban offer us nothing, only misery.' The governor's speech rambles on for almost an hour and I begin to feel that I am losing the will to live. The lack of sleep, the heavy lunch and the rising afternoon temperature are beginning to take their toll. I look over at Roly, who stifles a yawn. I'm glad I'm not the only one suffering.

Then it's Roly's turn to address the shura. Speaking through an interpreter, he begins by thanking the audience for allowing him to speak and for attending the meeting. He is slick and smooth, but, most importantly for the locals, sincere. He explains why Operation Moshtarak was needed and apologizes for any inconvenience it caused, speaking in the knowledge that collateral damage in this area during the kinetic phase of the operation was nil.

Roly then turns to the insurgency. 'I have no argument with the Taliban. If I could speak to the Taliban commanders, I would do it today. We would then sit down like grown men and discuss our differences and in the way of the world we would solve our problems by talking, not fighting. But I have offered and no one has come to my door. We are not here to fight the Taliban. We are here, at the invitation of your government, to protect the Afghan people. But if the Taliban attack us, we have a right to defend ourselves.'

The speech goes down well and afterwards there is a long queue of elders ready to thank Roly and shake his hand. 'That seemed to go well,' I told him afterwards. 'Hope so,' he said. 'Only time will tell. We've got to make the most of this transition period, we've really got to show the elders that there is an alternative to the Taliban, but, more importantly, we've got to convince them that we are not going to pull out any time soon.'

After the meeting I join Roly's headquarters party, together with Major Ed Boanas, the officer commanding Inkerman Company, on a patrol beginning at Five Tanks and going across the FLET into a beautiful village called Abdul Washid Kalay. Up until Operation Moshtarak, crossing the FLET would have immediately provoked a full-blown firefight and British casualties would have occurred. Dense vegetation makes this 'close' country where the field of view is limited to about 100 metres at most. It's classic insurgent country, made for ambushes.

When I last visited Five Tanks, in November 2009, I was spotted by a Taliban commander, primarily because of my blue body armour. An Afghan interpreter monitoring Icom communications heard a commander call for a sniper to be brought forward to engage two people dressed in blue. The blue body armour, which was supposed to identify me as a journalist, had merely made the Taliban assume that the photographer, Heathcliff O'Malley, and I were VIPs. This time I'm wearing khaki body armour in the hope that I won't be so obvious.

It takes just a few minutes to walk up the road to the kalay. The road, a rock-hard muddy track, was once heavily laced with IEDs, the whereabouts of which were known only by the Taliban and local people. The track has since been cleared and secured, but walking along it still leaves me with an uneasy feeling. Abdul Washid Kalay was one of the first villages to fall on D-Day of Operation Moshtarak. The Taliban knew what was coming, and left. Those members of the community who were either sympathizers or actual members of the Taliban have put away their weapons and returned to their fields.

'When I first entered the village I wanted to give them an unequivocal choice – they could carry on fighting and face the consequences of all that involves, or they could put down their arms,' Major Boanas explains to me as we peer through the camouflage netting of a heavily fortified sangar position which provides a fantastic view over the surrounding area. 'So far they have decided to do the latter. When we arrived they acknowledged that there had been no civilian casualties in their area, and they were grateful. They are looking at us to see what we do next – that's why I call them floating voters. If we leave now we will lose their trust, and the Taliban will come in and say, "We told you ISAF wouldn't stay."'

This lush and fertile area is important to the illegal but flourishing narcotics trade which has been steadily increasing in Helmand since the arrival of the NATO force in 2006. 'That's poppy, that's poppy,' Major Boanas says, pointing at the sea of green fields surrounding the patrol base. 'All of those fields over there are poppy. Pretty much poppy all around,' he says, smiling. 'But that's not our problem, that's for the counter-narcotics people to resolve. The last thing we want to do is to bound in here and steal their livelihood.'

Back in November I took part in a routine patrol to the north of the PB. It was fairly straightforward, the sort of minor operation undertaken by thousands of British troops every day in Helmand. But it is while on exactly this type of patrol that our soldiers sustain the most fatalities and injuries. Every day, sometimes twice a day, troops leave the safety of their base armed to the teeth and ready to do battle with the Taliban. After six months very nearly every man will have been involved in a firefight and seen his brothers-in-arms killed and injured in battle. It is during these routine, everyday events that soldiers demonstrate real courage.

On 30 November 2009 Lieutenant Douglas Dalzell of 1st Battalion Coldstream Guards was leading a patrol into the Padaka, an insurgent stronghold in Babaji. As the patrol moved along a track, the soldier directly in front of Lieutenant Dalzell triggered an IED. The blast punched him to the ground, leaving him stunned and disorientated. Staggering to his feet, he saw that the young soldier who had stepped on the bomb had lost a leg. Lieutenant Dalzell, who was just 26 and on his first operational tour, rallied his guardsmen while coordinating the evacuation of the wounded soldier. The plan was to move back down the same alleyway with the injured man being carried by a stretcher party composed of Sergeant Paul Baines, who was attached to the patrol, Sergeant John Amer, the platoon sergeant, and four other soldiers

As the troops moved off, Sergeant Amer stepped on a second bomb, which blew off both his legs and left him with mortal wounds. The soldier on the stretcher lost his remaining leg in this blast and every member of the stretcher party suffered serious shrapnel injuries, including Sergeant Baines, who was bleeding heavily from wounds to the head, neck, and legs. It was a scene of utter carnage and as Dalzell and Baines composed themselves, Taliban machine guns rattled into life. Dalzell immediately took control of the situation, directing his men to return fire and clear a safe route to a helicopter. While medics began treating Amer, Baines picked up the other double amputee and carried him in his arms across a ploughed field to a waiting helicopter. In total five casualties were evacuated, four of whom carried rank. Baines immediately recognized the weakened nature of the patrol and refused to be extracted. Instead he picked up his rifle and helped Dalzell in the move back to the PB. Only then did Baines reveal the extent of his wounds and submit to evacuation. A week later he discharged himself from the field hospital in Camp Bastion and was back on the ground fighting. Back in the PB, Lieutenant Dalzell had the difficult task of informing his men that his close friend and their platoon sergeant had died. Four hours later the platoon was back on patrol.

The above account illustrates graphically the grave risks soldiers have to take in order to conduct the most ordinary of tasks. Every unit which has served in Helmand can probably tell similar tales. Lieutenant Dalzell carried on leading 2 Platoon until his twenty-seventh birthday on 18 February 2010, when he stepped on an IED while on patrol in Babaji and was killed instantly. He was posthumously awarded a Military Cross.

During the first three weeks of June 2010 fourteen soldiers were killed in action during routine patrols across Helmand. In Sangin alone, while much of Britain fretted over the future of the English football team at the World Cup in South Africa, four Marines were killed on four consecutive days. The Ministry of Defence refuses to provide timely details of the number of troops wounded in Afghanistan, but instead publishes monthly figures stating the number of soldiers wounded in action, describing them as either 'very seriously ill' or 'seriously ill'. The details of the appalling injuries being suffered daily in Helmand, such as double and triple amputation, blindness, paralysis, brain damage and battle shock, are excluded.

I have been on many patrols, both as an embedded journalist and, back in the late 1980s, as a serving soldier. To walk out of the relative safety of any military base into hostile enemy territory takes courage. While serving in Northern Ireland I learned to live with the knowledge that I, like every one of the other 13,000 or so soldiers based in the province at that time, was an IRA target. Hard targeting – rapid acceleration of a vehicle through the gates of a British Army base in order to provide a 'hard target' for an IRA sniper – at Woodburn RUC Police Station in West Belfast in 1989 as the second in command of B Company, 3 Para, or commanding a Close Observation Platoon in a covert reconnaissance patrol on the home of a known IRA player, was an unnerving experience. To control my fears I would focus on the detail of the planning of the patrol, the target, and my own personal administration tasks, thereby filling my head with positive information rather than allowing fear to take control. But back in those days it was fairly rare for British troops to be killed by the IRA: between 1989 and 1991, 3 Para, which was the resident battalion in the Belfast area, had four soldiers killed by terrorist attacks and a fifth killed by a joyrider. In Helmand a battlegroup can lose the same number of soldiers in a day.

In November 2009 I went on patrol with the Grenadier Guards' Inkerman Company in the Chah-e-Anjir area. It was a routine local security patrol, the bread-and-butter work of the majority of soldiers in Helmand. But routine does not mean safe. A week earlier Kingsman Andrew Campbell, 18, from Wigan, serving with the Duke of Lancaster's Regiment, had been shot through the face while taking part in his very first patrol. The bullet struck him in the cheek and exited through the back of his head. Miraculously, he survived and walked away from the battlefield, and after being evacuated back to Selly Oak Hospital in Birmingham made a full recovery. A week before that attack, Sergeant Nathan Cumberland, of the Grenadier Guards' Reconnaissance Platoon, lost both legs after detonating an IED while on patrol. His section was moving across a field on a track used by locals and Sergeant Cumberland was number three in the line. The first two soldiers walked over the device and he stepped on the pressure plate. One of his legs was blown off immediately, while the other was attached by muscle.

In the weeks after he was injured I spoke to Nathan and he told me that he could actually see one of his legs in a field a few metres away. 'I knew immediately what had happened and at that stage you wonder two things: will I live, and how much damage has been done? One of the first things I checked when I got back to the hospital at Camp Bastion was whether I still had the family jewels, and thankfully I did. But then the Taliban opened up on us – some of my lads were pretty shocked – I could tell by the look on their faces, but when the Taliban hit us I had to grip them and started telling the guys to return fire. We were at a real risk of taking more casualties.' The follow-up attack after an IED strike is a classic Taliban ambush, and while it seems a brutal and cowardly tactic it makes perfect sense from the Taliban's point of view. The British troops were extremely vulnerable – they had a seriously injured soldier and were probably more focused on casualty evacuation than on a Taliban attack.

Another time, in a somewhat bizarre shooting incident, Lieutenant Paddy Rice was shot and wounded while trying to move a radio on the roof of a checkpoint called Compound 23 in Chah-e-Anjir. Paddy, aged 25 at the time, was shot by a Taliban sharpshooter through a murder hole of a compound a few hundred metres away. The bullet struck him in the back, just beneath the armhole in his CBA, travelled up through his back, along the outside of his spine and through his neck, which was sliced open, exiting his body just beneath his right ear. The bullet then passed through his helmet. Paddy realized immediately that he had been shot but was unaware how lucky he had been until he was taken back to Camp Bastion. The wound required twenty-nine stitches, but three weeks later he was back on duty.

The patrol I accompanied was composed of around a dozen members of the Grenadier Guards company, together with a section of troops from the Afghan Task Force (ATF) – a semi-covert unit of Afghan soldiers specially selected and trained by members of the British Army base. The plan was for the patrol to move from the company headquarters, located at PB Shahzad, into the surrounding countryside, visit some of the British checkpoints and examine a small bridge which had been blown up a few days earlier by the Taliban.

Patrolling through the Green Zone is an unnerving experience for everyone. Attack can come from absolutely anywhere and almost always without warning. I can recall my nervousness walking through the gates of the camp and expecting to be hit at any moment. My stomach was turning, shivers were running down my spine, and sweat was dribbling down my back. In some parts of Helmand the threat from IEDs is so great that soldiers throw up before going out on patrol, and I was certainly feeling weak-kneed and nauseous myself. But for one of those who was on patrol with me, fear is no longer the enemy it once was. Guardsman David Walton, a fresh-faced 18-year-old, had learned through experience that there was no point in worrying about what might happen. David was already a veteran of several battles and appeared to enjoy life as a soldier in Helmand. He once aspired to play professional football and was a member of Coventry City's youth team, but those dreams were shat-tered when he broke his leg badly during a match.

'I enjoy it most of the time – the Army is like a big family, so it's quite a lot of fun,' David told me, wiping sweat from his brow as we took shelter from the intense sun during a break in the five-hour patrol. 'It's not often in life that you really get a chance to help people and defend the country, and that's what I think we are doing here. But it can be a bit scary. A few weeks ago one of my mates stepped on an IED but it wasn't connected. If it had been we could have all been killed. That was a bit of a wake-up call.'

As the patrol moved along the dusty tracks, the sound of gunfire and explosions could be heard in the distance but neither the soldiers nor the farmers toiling in the fields took any notice. It seemed that everyone had grown used to the sounds of war.

'My parents do worry about me,' David added. 'Especially my mum. When I call home and she asks me how things are, I always play it down and just say, "I'm OK, everything's fine." There's no point telling her about the deaths and the injuries, she would only worry.'

Our route should have taken us along a track with a 5 ft mud wall running along either side. The patrol was about 1.5 km from the main base and close to the FLET. The two Vallon operators moved forward and began to scan the walls and the track. Within a few metres they began to get high tones, so a halt was immediately called. Captain Florinin Kuku, who was leading the patrol, decided that to proceed on the planned route was too risky. The Nigerian-born captain is one of the few soldiers in the British Army who has actu-ally detonated a pressure-plate IED and managed not to lose a limb.

He was blown up in 2007 near Gereshk, during the Grenadier Guards' first tour in Helmand. Fortunately for him, IEDs were still in their infancy.

'We are getting some pretty high readings along the walls and the track, so we are going to change our route and cut across that field,' Captain Kuku told me after we arrived at one of the bases we were visiting on the patrol. 'I doubt whether there are any IEDs along that route because it's obviously being used by the locals and you would think they would know. But sometimes they just avoid the bombs and continue to walk along the same route because they know exactly where the bombs are. Frankly, for us it's not worth the risk.'

As we cut across the ploughed field I begin to feel horribly exposed and vulnerable. I'm staring at the ground, trying to walk in the footsteps of the person in front of me. The nausea returns and my stomach begins to turn over. Images of myself reeling in agony on the ground, holding two bloody, mutilated stumps, begin to fill my head and it takes all my inner strength to carry on walking. I'm expecting an explosion with each wincing step. It is a feeling I've had many times before and my only solace is that I know it will pass. Later I take comfort from the soldiers who tell me that they have exactly the same feelings every time they leave the base. 'Only a fool wouldn't be scared,' Captain Kuku tells me.

As we move towards the first checkpoint on the patrol, Captain Kuku spots a tourniquet lying on the ground. He tells one of the soldiers to take a note of the grid coordinates of the tourniquet from his satnav, and then explains that there's a possibility the tourniquet could be linked to an IED. 'That,' he says, pointing at the tourniquet, 'is unusual. It could have fallen from a soldier, or could have been used and discarded after someone was injured. But it's definitely Army-issue. We know that the Taliban are attaching IED to pieces of NATO military equipment so that if it's picked up by a soldier it will be detonated. The IRA used to do the same sort of thing. The basic rule is: "Never pick up anything on patrol." We mark and avoid and then call in the details when we get back to the PB. Next time we have an ATO up here, if there is time, we'll take him on patrol and get him to clear all the suspected IEDs. Until then we'll just leave it.'

After we move into the checkpoint, a small compound occupied by a section of Grenadier Guards, I strike up a conversation with a corporal from another unit, working alongside the ATF. He tells me that he was here a few months ago, before the arrival of the Grenadier Guards, when the area was swarming with Taliban. 'We were just moving across a field, which we just crossed and we were ambushed. It was pretty cheeky. I was almost cut off from the rest of my section – one of the Tiger Teams. But the lads did really well. They put into practice everything they had learned in training and we managed to extract under fire.' Tiger Teams are the specially trained units of the ATF and they are in great demand across the whole of Helmand. The Tiger Teams' members are all volunteers, mostly from areas outside Helmand, and they are trained and selected by special units within the British Army. Those who make the grade join the ATF, while those who fail are used as members of force protection teams guarding the camp.

'This is the best job I've had in the Army,' the corporal tells me. 'I'm on my own working with these guys. We share the same tent, and eat the same rations. I try to teach them a bit of English and they try to teach me a bit of Pashto, which is spoken by Pashtuns in the south of Afghanistan and northern Pakistan, but I always have an interpreter with me. They are really up for it. Every commander wants a Tiger Team in his AO [area of operations] because they have a unique skill set. They can spot things that we wouldn't see or would take us months to learn. I've been out with them when they have seen someone on a motorbike and just said, stop him. When we've checked the guy out we've found bomb-making equipment on him. They saw that he didn't quite fit in and they noticed the reaction of the locals to him and that's what they picked up on. The villages are very insular, everyone knows everyone. Sometimes you just have one long extended family and the locals will immediately notice someone new. It's the sort of thing we might be able to do if we spent two years here, but we don't. They [Tiger Teams] are one of the real success stories of what we are doing out here.'

As we chat, the soldiers return from viewing the bridge which had been destroyed by the Taliban a few days earlier. One of the officers explains that the Taliban were trying to extort money from one of the local farmers, who refused to pay. 'They blew up the bridge which we built a couple of months ago. The bridge helped him get across his land and the improvements we made to the banks helped with irrigation. What the farmers really want here is better irrigation so they can grow crops and make money. But the Taliban want their cut. This farmer refused to pay up, so they blew up the bridge. We can fix it but it's likely to happen again unless we get rid of the Taliban or at least police the area properly.'

By the time we return to the PB I feel exhausted. We probably walked no more than 3–4 km but the heat and the constant threat of attack were an extra burden.

Within the hour the convoy is on the road again for an overnight stop at PB Tapa Parang, in the district of Basharan, in the north-west of the district. By the time we arrive it's dark but I can still make out some of the features and hear the sound of the river at the bottom of the hill on which the base is located. Once again I'm struck by the stunning natural beauty of the landscape and I remain convinced that if Afghanistan sorted out its act it could make a fortune from tourism.

A group of soldiers, part of the commanding officer's tactical headquarters, who are providing the security for the trip, are cooking Army rations over a small fire in the corner of the compound. I walk over with a foil sachet of pasta in tomato sauce and ask if I can share their hot water.

One of the group is an SAS sergeant – the special forces liaison officer attached to the battlegroup whom I met earlier on the patrol. 'Of course, mate, fill your boots. Want one of these?' he says and offers me an Army biscuit. The soldiers are chuntering about leave and R&R. They seem to be split over whether a two-week break in a six-month tour is worth it. I dunk my silver sachet in the boiling water and the conversation reignites.

'By the time you get home and get your head sorted, it's time to come back. And what have you done? Spent two weeks on the piss with your mates trying to forget about this fucking place and answering questions from tossers who want to know what it's like to fucking kill someone. I'd rather do six months straight and get a bigger bonus at the end.' The soldier who says this looks as if he is barely in his twenties but this is his second time in Afghanistan. The bonus he mentions is the tax-free operational bonus all troops serving in Afghanistan receive, irrespective of rank, at the end of their tour.

The soldier continues, 'R&R just fucks you up even more. Can any of you honestly say that you felt better afterwards? By the time it's over you're in a shit state because all you've done is cane it for the last two weeks.'

The SAS sergeant laughs as he says, 'You're obviously not married, mate. Wait till you're married and have kids. That's when you'll find that R&R is important.' Then he turns to me. 'You'll get two differing opinions. Married blokes want R&R, especially if they have kids. In the US Army they get two weeks a year and the divorce rate is going through the roof. In SF [special forces] the divorce rate is already pretty high. Young blokes, guys who are single, are willing to stag on for the full six months, but they want a bigger bonus at the end. Some blokes would do nine months if the tours came around less often – once every three years – but nine months is a big lick out.'

I ask the group whether a six-month tour is too long. 'Two weeks is too fucking long in this shithole, mate,' says one of the soldiers, and the group grumbles in agreement. 'Afghan is a fucked-up dump and nothing we do is going to change anything.' I ask, 'Don't you think things have improved since you were last here?' 'Yeah, I suppose it's quietened down a bit – it couldn't have been much worse.'

Another of the group disagrees. 'Come on, it's a lot quieter now than it was before Moshtarak. Then we were being hit about ten times a day.'

'Most of your commanders say this is what young soldiers join up for,' I say. 'Yeah, but you can have too much of a good thing,' someone says. 'Everyone wants to get involved in a firefight when you first come out but when it's happening every day you start to wonder how long your luck will last. And then there are the fucking IEDs – they're everywhere, man. It's like you can't fucking move without hitting one.'

As we chat, one of the men begins to complain about the so-called REMFS – rear-echelon motherfuckers – back in Camp Bastion. These are guys who never leave the camp apart from going on R&R and returning home. Their role is to support the troops in the field but some front-line soldiers find it difficult to stomach the knowledge that those who remain on the base are entitled to the same medal and the same tax-free bonus as the soldiers who have to go out and fight the Taliban every day.

Then we start to talk about kit, which by and large the soldiers think is pretty good. 'When I first went to Iraq,' says a sergeant, 'the body armour was pants. All you had was this small plate protecting your heart and the blokes used to say, "The Iraqis will have to be a good shot to hit that." But this stuff is shit hot. We're getting new kit all the time – but that won't stop the blokes buying their own. A soldier will always want his personal kit, especially when you're on an op like this.' The sergeant's opinion is more or less shared by everyone else. The SAS sergeant then adds, 'If you really want good kit, lad, you should join the SF – we get what we want.' 'Yeah, the fucking SAS – more pay, best kit and you're allowed to grow your hair long. Bunch of cowboys,' says someone. That brings the response, 'Right, next one who says the SAS are a bunch of cowboys gets it right between the eyes,' and everyone falls about laughing.

The soldier who served with the Grenadier Guards in Helmand in 2007 says, 'The vehicles we had in 2007 were shite, especially the

Snatch – great for Northern Ireland, not so good for Helmand.' A Snatch usually carries four soldiers – the driver and commander plus two more who can provide top cover through a hatch in the roof. The vehicle made its way into the public's consciousness during the Iraq War, when the insurgency began to derail any attempt to undertake reconstruction in southern Iraq. The Army needed a versatile, manoeuvrable patrol vehicle, and the Snatch fitted the bill. It was regarded as a success until it began to be targeted by insurgents armed with Iranian-built improvised roadside bombs. Knowing its deficiencies, senior officers shamefully allowed the Snatch to resurface in Helmand, where it was again being used on operations until it was effectively withdrawn from service in 2008 after four soldiers – Corporal Sarah Bryant, Corporal Sean Reeve, and SAS reservists Lance Corporal Richard Larkin and Trooper Paul Stout – were killed when their Snatch was destroyed by an IED.

'I'd refuse to go in a Snatch now,' said one of the younger soldiers. 'We all know the risks in Afghan and we're all prepared to take them, but I wouldn't want to travel in a vehicle which won't offer any protection if you get blown up. You know that if you get hit when you're in a Snatch you're dead.'

'There's no such thing as a bomb-proof vehicle,' adds another soldier, 'and if there was you would still have to get out of it at some stage. Even the Mastiff has been taken out and blokes have been injured. Terry [Taliban] will take one out one day, it's just a matter of time, it's just about building a bomb big enough. In Iraq the Sunni managed to blow up US Abrams tanks. If you can blow up an Abrams, you can blow up anything.'

The conversation eventually peters out and one by one the soldiers go off to sleep, like me, beneath a pitch-black desert sky twinkling with millions of stars. A full night's sleep is impossible. The ANA soldiers are jumpy and believe they have seen gunmen moving through the fields which ring the camp. Every hour or so a parachute flare is fired into the air, an event which is usually a precursor to a gun battle, but not tonight.

By 8.30 the following morning we are back in Shawqat and I meet up with Staff Sergeant Gareth 'Woody' Wood, who is an ATO. Woody has just returned from a four-day clearance operation in Chah-e-Anjir, the area from where I have just returned. He is exhausted and in need of a shower and a good night's sleep but he greets me with a smile.

'We're going to do some bomb-hunting tomorrow,' he says to me. 'Coming along?'

'Can't wait,' I reply, and I'm genuinely excited.

Chapter 5: **The Asymmetric War**

'In Afghan, you always want to be lucky – being lucky is better than being good. Plenty of guys good at their job have been killed out here but the lucky ones survive.'
Sapper Richie Pienaar, 33 Engineer Regiment (EOD)

It's 8 a.m. in the vehicle park of FOB Shawqat and a team of bomb hunters are preparing for their latest mission. The sun is shining brightly in a cloudless sky and the temperature is already on the rise. It may well reach 30° today and it's still only early March.

One by one the soldiers begin arriving and form a small, tight group next to one of the vehicles. They all look tired and drawn and their uniforms have seen better days. As each man arrives, he drops his kit in a central pile and lights up a cigarette.

The bomb-hunting unit is composed of an IED disposal team – Brimstone 32 – commanded by Staff Sergeant Wood. Woody's squad has also acquired the nickname 'Team Massive' because none of its members is taller than 5 ft 8 in. The team's No. 2 operator is Corporal Kevin 'Boonie' Boon, who is 22 but looks much younger, and the third member is Lance Corporal Joe Rossiter, the infantry escort, the soldier who watches Woody's back while he defuses the bomb. Joe is effectively a bodyguard who must remain 100 per cent focused all the time Woody is working. He is also doubling up as the ECM operator.

The remainder of the bomb-hunting unit is formed by Brimstone 45 – a high-risk search team coming to the end of their six-month tour in Helmand. The team consists of Corporal Adam Butler, who is the acting team commander, Lance Corporal Michael Brunt, and Sappers Richard Pienaar, Gary Anders, Dan Taylor-Allen and Gareth Homewood.

The callsign for all bomb-hunting teams has the prefix 'Brimstone', followed by a number. For Brimstone 45 there is one more operation to complete, one more bomb to find and defuse, and then it's home. It's been a long six months and the soldiers have had a belly-full of Afghan. The trauma of war is etched on their tired, dusty faces. Every member of the seven-man search team – working with the six members of Brimstone 45 is Kev O'Dwyer, the RESA – has had a friend either killed or wounded on operation and no one wants to become a casualty at the end of the tour.

The soldiers, all in their twenties, come from small, anonymous towns and villages across the UK. To a man they nearly all joined up because the Army was the only decent job on offer. It was either the barrack room or the dole queue – the same deal for many soldiers now serving in Helmand. Those with GCSEs or A-levels, and higher IQs, are offered the opportunity to learn a trade in a corps, such as the Royal Engineers, Royal Logistic Corps or the Royal Signals, where promotion can be rapid and the pay better. The rest, either through choice or necessity, end up serving in the infantry, where, if he's sent to Helmand, life for the private soldier is six months of boredom interspersed with spikes of extreme terror. These guys have been drawn from 33 Engineer Regiment (EOD), based in Wimbish in Essex. The unit is the specialist explosive ordnance disposal and advanced search regiment for the Royal Corps of Engineers. The soldiers are regarded as something of an elite within the Royal Corps of Engineers and they carry themselves with a certain swagger.

Every search team works in conjunction with a Royal Engineer Search Advisor, who helps plan the search and the clearance of the device. The relationship between the ATO and the RESA is crucial – their lives depend upon it. The RESA working with Woody is Staff Sergeant Kev O'Dwyer, who is barking out a series of orders in his heavy Cornish accent. He is bald and thickset and has heavily tattooed forearms. His helmet is battered and tatty and his chin-strap hangs loosely beneath his jaw. Kev has the look of a man who was made for war. His eyes are red and angry and I learn later that he is 'not the sort of bloke you want to fuck with'. Kev moves among the soldiers as they prepare for action, cajoling and encouraging them, ensuring that all the correct checks have been conducted. He keeps a mental checklist of dos and don'ts. He's done it a hundred times before but he can't afford to stop now – not on the last mission, not when the team are so close to making it back home in one piece.

The bomb hunters work silently, sometimes in pairs, and every-one knows exactly what to do and what is expected – in this outfit there are no passengers. Weapons, radios, ECM, and especially their Vallon mine detectors are checked and rechecked. Every soldier also makes sure that his Combat Application Tourniquet (CAT), which will save his life if he loses a limb in a blast, is close at hand, together with his personal morphine injection. The same routine is under-taken before every mission. Check, check and check again is the soldiers' mantra.

The latest mission is to clear an old Taliban firing point believed to have been booby-trapped with a pressure-plate IED. The soldiers' lives will depend on their skill as searchers and their equipment, so problems need to be discovered within the safety of a base and not in the middle of an operation.

I notice that one of the soldiers, Sapper Gareth 'Gaz' Homewood, a Geordie, has scarring on his face. It looks fresh and I later discover that he was injured when his team commander was killed in a bomb blast. He appears naturally quiet but not timid and I wonder how badly the death of his commander affected him, indeed affected them all.

Banter breaks out and Lance Corporal Rossiter, a former lorry driver and territorial volunteer serving with the London Regiment, is getting a fair amount of stick for planning to join the Royal Military Police when he returns to the UK at the end of his tour in July. The RMPs are known widely in the Army as 'Monkeys' and some of the searchers are making monkey noises and asking Joe whether he has any bananas. Corporal Richard Lacey, the investigator from the Royal Military Police Weapons Intelligence Section – WIS, pronounced 'Whiz' in Army-speak – who is also coming out on the patrol, tells Joe not to worry. 'Pay no attention. They're just jealous.' Joe just smiles to himself as he tests his ECM. The others in the team say he's always smiling.

Mostly, however, the troops are subdued and pensive. No group of soldiers serving in Helmand is more aware of the risks that IEDs pose than the Royal Engineer Search Teams. For high-risk searchers, no mission is routine. They can never lower their guard, never have a bad day, never afford to make a mistake. Everyone has a story of a soldier whose luck ran out.

Against the growling engines of the six Mastiffs which will ferry us to the front line, Kev barks out a series of orders and makes sure that everyone knows what they are to do if we get ambushed on the way or strike an IED. They are the last words of advice, the last reminder before we head out into what the troops call bandit country. I'm filled with a sense of fear and excitement. Finally, after months of planning and waiting, I'm going on a bomb-hunting mission with some of the most highly trained soldiers in the world.

The convoy heads north along an arrow-straight dirt track which serves as one of the main roads in the area. The track cuts a brown swath through the otherwise lush, green countryside, where fields of poppies, wheat and melons – the cash crops of Helmand – are fed by the clear waters of the Nahr-e-Burgha canal. Children are playing on the paths outside their compounds and farmers are tilling their fields. This is a good sign, and the Army would describe this scene as 'positive atmospherics'. Basically it's the presence of the normal and the absence of the abnormal – in short, normal everyday life – and this means an attack is unlikely. It is when the soldiers sense the presence of the abnormal and the absence of the normal that they begin to worry. Communities are very closed in Helmand and in some cases consist of just one extended family. Strangers are immediately identified and anyone acting suspiciously will attract attention immediately. Warnings are passed rapidly by word of mouth and children are quickly ushered into compounds until the threat has passed. A soldier's ability to develop a sixth sense that allows him to pick up on 'atmospherics' will help to keep him alive during the six-month tour.

Within fifteen minutes of leaving FOB Shawqat the convoy arrives at Blue 17. This patrol base is on extended loan from an Afghan farmer, who will be paid handsomely for allowing the British to use his home, possibly up to $400 a month, a sum which is likely to triple or quadruple his annual income. The base is roughly triangular, consisting of three 15-ft-high mud walls, reinforced with military Hesco blocks. Inside are three buildings in which the fifteen Guardsmen and twenty members of the ANA sleep and eat. It is a basic but comfortable existence and the soldiers have done their best to turn it into a home. National flags – the English Cross of St George, the Welsh Dragon and the Scottish Saltire – adorn the walls in the sleeping quarters, fighting for space with topless models and footballing icons, but mainly topless models. In another room the axiom 'Necessity is the mother of invention' is in practice and the soldiers have somehow rigged up a widescreen TV to a power source so that they can view the latest DVDs sent from home.

On the roof of one of the buildings a reinforced sangar provides a 360-degree view of the fields and smallholdings which surround the isolated PB. The terrain is pancake-flat and the sangar dominates the surrounding countryside. But it is also an obvious target and when I last visited Blue 17, in November 2009, the Taliban had tried but failed to destroy the sangar in a brave but ill-conceived rocket and machine-gun attack. The rocket-propelled grenade missed and detonated in a nearby field and the Taliban gunmen were outflanked by a section of British troops, who were dispatched from the PB within two minutes of the attack being launched. Today, however, Blue 17 is a relatively safer place. Rather than being within shooting distance, as it was in November, the forward line of enemy troops is around 2 km to the west.

Woody heads straight for the operations room to receive a briefing on the location of the bomb. The initial briefing is one of the most vital stages of any bomb-disposal mission. Woody, like all ATOs, is coming to the situation with just the information contained within the ten-liner, and often it is inaccurate.

He is met by Lance Sergeant Paul Hunt, a section commander in the Grenadier Guards, who greets him warmly and offers him a brew. In the ops room Lance Sergeant Hunt points to a large-scale aerial photograph of the area surrounding the base. 'The device is in Compound 23,' he says, indicating the compound position in the photograph. 'It's just behind the door. We need to clear it because the compound owner wants to move back in. The guy came to us the other day and said that he wants to return home. So I passed the message up the chain [of command] and said that the device needs to be sorted.'

Woody is concentrating on the map, seemingly oblivious to the briefing from the lance sergeant, yet he is absorbing every word. His gaze still fixed on the photograph, he asks, 'Is there any history to this?' in an attempt to find out why an IED should be placed inside an empty compound. One of the most important parts of the ATO's job is to elicit facts from troops on the ground. Every single piece of intelligence the bomb hunters can extract from soldiers who have seen the IED will help Woody and the RESA formulate their plan and potentially save a life. Only when Woody begins to understand why a bomb has been placed in a given position can he begin to plan his clearance operation.

Woody continues the questioning, 'Are there any other entrances? Is there any other way I can get in? How high are the walls?' He is trying to build a mental picture of the task ahead based on all the intelligence he can glean. Every snippet of information is vital.

'We've got "eyes on" from here actually,' reveals Lance Sergeant Hunt. 'Come up into the sangar and make your own assessment. You'll be able to see the ground much better than I can explain it.' Access to the sangar is via a rickety makeshift ladder which would break every health and safety regulation in the book back in the UK. We all climb up into the sangar. The lance sergeant points out the lie of the land and the road leading down to the compound.

Kev and Woody discuss their plan of attack. The two are locked in a barely audible conversation, eyes fixed on each other. Kev speaks first, pointing and moving his arms in a sweeping movement. The role of the RESA is to help the ATO plan and organize the search. It is vital that each has a complete understanding of how the other operates. This particular mission is relatively straightforward – it is something that Kev and Woody have done countless times before – but both know there is no room for complacency. Within a few minutes Kev has formulated his plan. 'I think we can get in from across that field,' he says to me, pointing at a gap between two trees around 50 metres from the PB. 'We'll move out of the patrol base across that field. Put an ICP in there,' he adds, pointing at a position in a green wheat field around 80 metres in front of the compound where the bomb has been hidden, 'and Woody can get in by climbing over the wall.'

Woody turns to Lance Sergeant Hunt. 'Have you got any ladders?' The lance sergeant shakes his head and says, 'They've all gone back to the FOB, but that wall is climbable. Just so that you know, when we found the IED we came up north into the open area and we pushed along over the northern side of that compound and the ANA went, "Whoa, whoa, stop, stop, IED, IED," and they pointed it out to us. I haven't seen it. The bloke who has seen it has gone back home. But what you have got is the charge and one prominent wire sticking out.'

Woody asks, 'What does the charge look like? What size is it?' Hunt makes a shape with his hands and says, 'It looks about this big – the size of a shoe box.'

'We can get the ANA to stop the traffic while you're working on the bomb. You should also be aware that we've been hit on a few occasions from that tree line over there,' says Lance Sergeant Hunt, pointing to a clump of trees around 400 metres to the north. 'What we can do is push some of our guys into that wood line because that's the only area not covered from the sangar, that's the only vulnerable spot around here.'

'OK,' says Kev, staring at the wood line in the distance, 'I think we're going to need that covered. If they [the Taliban] move into the wood line we are going to be sitting with our arses exposed.'

After the briefing I ask Woody how he feels, sensing that something is niggling him. He tells me, 'I've given up trying to get the information I need off a ten-liner because everybody ends up missing some stuff off. That's fairly normal. I always feel much happier when I can get out and have a look. It's relatively straightforward but there may be a bit of an issue when I get in the compound. That is always a threat. If you have an IED on a road, that's straightforward. But with this I'm going in on a route that they [the soldiers] haven't been in yet, so I'm the first one going in, so I'll have to clear my own way through that compound, which, depending on the ground, could be tricky. There may be more than one in there, something the Taliban might use which I wouldn't necessarily expect, so I have to outthink them. It's just like chess – you always play two or three moves ahead and never let yourself get boxed in.'

Back on the ground, Kev gives one of the searchers a minor bollocking. 'Where the fuck have you been? I've been calling you on the radio. Didn't you hear me tell you to come up here and see what's going on? Right, get a fucking grip, stop pissing around, and get the lads together.'

I can feel the tension rising in my stomach at the prospect of leaving the safety of Blue 17 and heading into the field where the Taliban have booby-trapped the isolated compound.

The final briefings are conducted and the soldiers prepare to leave. They lift their CBA from the floor and get ready for action. Radios and Vallons are checked once again. Before we move out, the soldiers wait for the traffic to be stopped by the Afghan troops. I can feel the tension rising. Everyone just wants to get out and get stuck in and I can empathize with that feeling. Get in, clear the device, and get out – no dramas.

Woody thinks it will take around twenty minutes to isolate the compound and to check for the presence of command wires. The ground is pretty flat and the terrain is uncomplicated. 'But it depends on what we find in the compound,' he adds. 'You never really know what you're going to find until you are face to face with the device, so you need a clear plan, but you also have to remain flexible.'

In the two months that he has been in Helmand, Woody has already defused around thirty bombs, but he is experienced enough to know that no device, no day, is ever the same in Helmand. 'Start thinking like that,' he tells me, 'and you'll be going home in a body bag.'

Woody is 28, with close-cropped hair which is beginning to recede at the temples. He is about 5 ft 8 in. tall and does not have an ounce of fat on his small, wiry frame. He is blessed with a naturally happy face and a slight gap between his front teeth which adds a hint of mischievousness to his otherwise wholly sensible personality. Woody spent almost eight years learning how to be a bomb hunter, longer than a vet or a doctor's training, and if he is to survive his six months in Afghan he will need both skill and luck.

Kev spells out the order of march, but the search team are already aware of what is expected of them. A soldier manning the entrance to Blue 17 pulls back a rudimentary gate and we patrol out in single file across the road and a bridge into the wheat field. The soldiers who remain in the compound look on silently with unsmiling faces.

I immediately feel hopelessly exposed but the rest of the soldiers appear calm, which offers some reassurance. The Taliban have been pushed back out of the area, but the reality is that an attack could come at any time. We will be in the same location for at least two hours, and that makes us vulnerable.

The wheat harvest is still many weeks away and the lush field affords a beguiling sense of calm. I am reminded of the fields and natural beauty that surround my home back in England. Compound 23, where the bomb is located, is 300 metres away. Up ahead I can see Sapper Richie Pienaar rhythmically swinging his Vallon in a 180-degree arc from left to right, leading the way.

The green, young wheat sways like a wave as a gentle spring breeze brings a few seconds of respite from the midday sun. I hear birds singing and the distant voices of children playing. It doesn't feel like a war zone.

Everyone in the patrol diligently follows exactly the same route. It is vital that we all stay in the safe lane, so I try to walk in the footsteps of the soldier in front of me, but after about 70 metres it becomes impossible.

My heart is now thumping in my chest and the adrenalin is coursing through my veins. I can feel the sweat running down my face and soaking my shirt beneath my body armour. I've never felt so vulnerable in all my life and I'm convinced that we are all about to be flattened by a huge explosion. I'm doing exactly what I promised my wife and family I wouldn't after Rupert was killed.

Richie alone is responsible not only for his safety but also that of every member of the patrol. It is an enormous weight to carry for such a junior soldier but he does not seem to be the least bit burdened by the task. If he misses a bomb the chances are that either he or another member of the team could be injured or killed. We move through the wheat field so fast that it feels like a sprint. Inside my head I'm shouting, 'Slow down! Slow down!' I can't see how they can possibly detect a buried bomb going at this pace – it seems almost suicidal.

The search team halts in the area which Kev had previously designated as the incident control point. My legs are shaking from a rush
of adrenalin, then I'm suddenly overcome with an enormous sense
of relief. I have been on patrol many times before – as a professional
soldier with the Parachute Regiment in Northern Ireland and as a
journalist in Iraq and Bosnia. I have been under fire and I have
learned how to cope with fear, but nothing compares to what I have
experienced in the past few minutes. For the first time since I arrived
in Helmand I am beginning to understand just how powerful a
psychological weapon the IED has now become, and how vital the
bomb-disposal teams are to the success of the whole mission in
Afghanistan. The IED is a weapon of terror. It is the ultimate weapon
in asymmetric warfare and its use on the scale now deployed by the
Taliban was completely unpredicted by British commanders and
NATO alike.

There is a few minutes' pause before the isolation search of the
compound. Those remaining in the ICP drop their packs and take
up fire positions, and those who smoke quickly light up. It dawns on
me that I'm not the only one who is sensing the danger of the task.

Once again Richie leads the way as the isolation search starts.
Woody follows him closely and begins eyeing his target. The soldiers
are looking for wires or pieces of string leading into the compound
as well as buried pressure-plate IEDs. The Taliban know that an IED
operator is at his most vulnerable when he is working on a device
and when possible they will always try to kill him. Classically, the
insurgents will bury a bomb near to another device which can be
detonated either by pulling a command wire or detonating the
device by means of a power source, such as a battery. Command
wires running up to hundreds of metres have been found in
Helmand and several soldiers have been blown up while conducting
the isolation. Some of the command wires found in Helmand have
been almost too thin to detect. To assist them in this most dangerous
of tasks, specialist searchers are equipped with a special detecting
device.

I look around, still feeling slightly anxious that the field could contain one or more IEDs. Kev seems to sense my nervousness. 'This is one of our easier jobs,' he tells me. 'Ten-liners tend to be easier because you know where the device is. We've been told that the Taliban once occupied this compound and used it as a firing point but when they got pushed back they left a device there, hoping to take out either us or the ANA. I think they were probably targeting the ANA because hopefully no British soldier would ever enter a compound once used by the Taliban through the front door. They normally leave them in doorways and this what they have done here, so it should be relatively straightforward. Saying that, most guys tend to get killed or injured on the routine jobs.'

Kev sits down, rests his rifle between his legs, and begins chewing on a piece of green wheat. He loosens his chin-strap, while another member of the search team establishes radio communication with the main base. 'Is this area secure?' I ask Kev, armed with the knowledge that just a few weeks ago a member of the battlegroup was blown up and suffered a double amputation while crossing a similar field.

'I'm very confident that there are no devices near us now,' Kev says calmly. 'The middle of a field is one of the least likely places they will put anything.' I'm tempted to tell him about Lance Sergeant Cumberland, but I'm reminded of Kev's fearsome reputation and decide to keep my thoughts to myself. Kev has been with the search team for only three months, having been sent out to Helmand to replace another RESA who had to return to the UK, but it is clear who is boss.

One of the soldiers has been chatting to one of his mates about compensation. The team were blown up a few weeks ago and the soldier is complaining about ringing in his ears. He asks Kev whether he will be entitled to any compensation when he returns home. 'Dunno, mate,' says Kev. 'The compo rules have changed. It depends how bad the injury is and whether you are going to recover. You'll have to wait until you get back to the UK, then go and see a doc.' Kev is clearly the 'daddy' of the team. The soldiers are his responsibility both in the field and during downtime on base. He is expected to have an answer to every problem, no matter how small.

'Have you had a tough tour?' I ask. 'It's had its moments,' Kev replies. 'These lads have had a tougher run than me. We got blown up in a Warrior ten days ago. We were going up to Patrol Base Pimon [a small British outpost on the edge of the desert]. It was just a routine job, nothing exciting. We were the fourth vehicle in a convoy and you would think you were pretty safe. We were moving along a track, one that we had used before, and bang! we hit an IED. The Taliban must have been watching for a while, reckoned it was becoming a well-used track, so they put an IED in the ground and we drove over it. It blew the track off the Warrior and dented the rear of the vehicle. The blast lifted the whole vehicle off the ground. We all got stiff necks but we got off quite lightly. If it had been something like a Viking I think that would have been it. The blast would have taken us all out. The device was only about 15–20 kg of HME but that's enough. If it can do that to a vehicle, imagine what it can do to a body.'

Boonie, the IED team's No. 2, who is sorting out the equipment he believes Woody will need later in the task, chips in. 'You would get the same effect from about 1.5 kg of military explosive. So 20 kg of their stuff will have the same effect. You don't need much to immobilize a vehicle. Twenty kilos of HME, which they can knock up pretty quickly, will give you an M-Kill on an armoured vehicle and then you have got another job on your hands to recover the vehicle and that will make you vulnerable to ambush. These guys know what they're about. I think some people forget that they have been doing this for a long time. They're not scared of us, they will take us on whenever they can. The Taliban will always find a way to counter our drills. They have low-metal and no-metal content bombs – they are always evolving. Sometimes they have the advantage, and sometimes we do.'

Boonie is fair-haired and his skin is yet to be burnished by the Helmand sun. He looks more like a fresh-faced sixth-former than a front-line soldier, an observation he is used to, so he takes no offence when I mention it. When I ask him how he ended up in Afghanistan, he replies, 'I always wanted to join the Army and I did quite well in my GCSEs and so when I went to the recruiting office I was told about being an Ammo Tech – it sounded great. You get quick promotion, and you get to do some really interesting stuff, so I went for it. I've been in four years and I'm already a corporal and I will become an IED operator providing I pass all the courses. This is my first major deployment. We've done two months but it feels like two weeks, we get bounced around so much, which is good but exhausting. We are working pretty much every day, going out on jobs. We've had some hairy moments, but I feel pretty safe much of the time. We come in from one job and go straight back out. That's OK at the moment but I should imagine we'll be pretty tired by the end of the tour. Our workload is a bit higher at the moment because our ECM operator, Corporal McCluggage, known as "Baggage", is sick at the moment.'

Our conversation is ended by the arrival of Woody, who has completed the isolation search. He looks happy and relaxed. He breezes over to where I'm sitting and, slightly out of breath, says, 'The search team and myself have conducted a search of the area,' he explains in between gulps of water from a plastic bottle. He then bends over and pours some over the back of his head. 'That's better,' he says, then stands upright and continues, 'I've also cleared a safe area for me to work in. From what I can see there are no wires running into the compound. I'm pretty confident we would have picked up any if there were. What we've also decided to do is move the ICP just over there.' He points at an area of the field some 10 metres from where we are standing. 'The guys will clear a safe lane to it and then clear the ICP. Moving the ICP will make it easier for me to work – there's no point in being uncomfortable when you're working. Also the guys are pretty well protected here because if anything does go wrong when I'm working the blast will be confined within the compound. Which is good news for them but not so good for me.

'I've no idea what type of bomb is in there at the minute – all I know is that there is a large charge. I'll now go and make my manual approach. My guess is that it's likely to be a pressure-plate IED. I could be wrong but I don't think so. After we move the ICP, that will be me going down the road.' By this Woody means going in to defuse the bomb. It is the moment of greatest danger but also of greatest challenge. Woody will be on his own, every decision will be his alone to make. It will be his wits against the bomb maker's and all he will have to rely on is his own skill and good luck. It is what the ATOs live for. Woody explains the impracticalities of wearing a bomb suit. 'To get into that compound I've got to climb over an 8 ft wall, so you can see that there is no way I could wear a bomb suit on this job. It's already getting hot just wearing body armour, so you can imagine what it would be like wearing that thing. It weighs about 50 kg in total. So you can imagine what it would be like carrying an extra 50 kg out here. I would be too hot, I wouldn't be able to climb over walls, and if I got shot at I wouldn't be able to get away quickly enough. It's just impractical, and anyway, if the bomb goes off and I'm kneeling over it, a bomb suit isn't going to help me.'

Woody prepares for the most dangerous and difficult phase of the mission. He alone will have to enter the compound, unprotected except for body armour and helmet – little defence against 20 kg of explosive. At this stage the only information he has is that there is a device in the doorway. He must assume that there could be one or more bombs buried inside the compound, rigged in a way to kill the ATO. His tools for this job include his ceramic knife, a paintbrush and a special electrically fired gun which is used to remotely cut wires. For extra personal protection he will also take his rifle, even though it will be an additional encumbrance when climbing the wall.

'I had a quick look over the wall and it's a real mess in there,' he says. 'It's pretty overgrown, so I'm going to have to hack through some brambles and then conduct my own search inside.' He then turns to the searchers, who are chatting among themselves, and says, 'Can I have Valerie, please?'

'Valerie? Who's Valerie?' I ask.

'Valerie Vallon – it's my lucky charm,' says Woody. 'I always take the lead searcher's Vallon when I do my own clearance. So I christened it Valerie Vallon. It's worked so far. I've only been blown up twice and I escaped without a scratch both times.'

Richie drops down besides me and blows out hard. Beads of sweat are leaving dark tracks on his dusty face. He pulls out a set of Army-issue wraparound sunglasses, places them on his face, and leans back. 'That was hard work, man,' he says as he wipes the sweat from his face. At 28 he's older than the other soldiers and more self-assured, but he has the demeanour of a man who has just about had enough of the war. Richie, who is from Zimbabwe, joined the Army in 2003, when he enlisted in the King's Own Scottish Borderers. 'I enjoyed being in the infantry but I thought the engineers might offer more of a challenge.' His story is interrupted by one of the other searchers sitting opposite, who shouts, 'Thought joining up would stand him a better chance of getting a British passport.' The team all howl with laughter, but Richie waves away the comments. 'You're all just jealous, just jealous.' More raucous laughter from the others follows.

'Right, that's me going down the road,' Woody announces to the ICP, and then turns to me and explains what he is about to do next. 'What I'm going to try and do is find the power source and then isolate the various components. Should be straightforward enough. Joe, you ready?' he shouts to his infantry escort. The laughter which filled the ICP only a few moments ago has now evaporated. All eyes are on Woody as he prepares to approach the bomb.

'Kev, you happy?' he asks.

The burly sergeant gives a reassuring nod. 'If you are,' he responds.

Woody switches on the Vallon, and says to the whole team, 'See you in a bit.' He is now a picture of concentration, like an Olympic diver at the edge of the 30 metres board, silently going through his finely honed routine. He is about to enter the death zone, and the drama of the situation is intensified by the silence that has descended upon the rest of the team. His jaw is fixed and he stares silently, almost lost in thought, running through his routine, before stepping off, with Joe following closely behind.

No one speaks for a few minutes, as if out of respect for what is being undertaken, then Richie casually continues with his story. 'I was back in Zim in August and I'm going back when I leave the Army at the end of November. I've started my own business – it's a sort of welding company. I just hope that the country is still functioning when I return. Things have improved since we got the US dollar – before that I thought it was over. But now there is at least food on the shelves and you can buy petrol, but the political system is fucked.'

Woody has now disappeared into the compound and Joe is kneeling down with an ECM box by his side while he watches the surrounding countryside. But Richie has spotted something. 'Hey,' he shouts over towards Joe after noticing that he has placed his Vallon on the ground to his side. 'Bad drills, buddy, bad drills. You've cleared the ground to your front but not your side. If you carry on doing that you're going to get caught out. One day there will be a device there and you'll be in for a fucking big surprise, man. You can't afford to fuck up in this place, eh?'

I ask Richie whether he has enjoyed serving in Afghanistan. 'Enjoy isn't the word I'd use to describe it. Nobody enjoys Afghan, man, not unless you've got a screw loose. What's to enjoy? The place is riddled with fucking IEDs and the Taliban are trying to fucking kill you every single day. You work your bollocks off every day not knowing whether you are going to make it back, so enjoy, no, but it's been an experience.

'But I'm with a good bunch of guys and we've had our moments. We've had some good times, mostly the banter back in camp when we've got some downtime, but otherwise it's pretty shit. It's just about getting through it – you know things can go wrong at almost any time so you just hope you're going to make it back.

'The worst bit was when Loz was killed – that was our lowest point, that hit us really hard, harder than I think any of us were expecting. He was our team commander, a fantastic bloke – exactly the sort of commander you'd want in Afghan. So when he died, and the way he died, was a real blow.'

Corporal Loren Marlton-Thomas, known as Loz, was the commander of Brimstone 45 until Sunday, 15 November 2009, when he was killed in action. Loz was 28 and married when he was killed in what was to become one of the most tragic and horrific incidents to befall the bomb hunters. Loz was one of the most popular search team commanders in the task force and was instantly recognizable by his large, round face and ready smile. He had been Army barmy all his life, according to his wife Nicola, and had once considered joining the Paras but believed his skill set was best suited to the engineers. He was killed while on a routine mission near Gereshk, just two weeks after Staff Sergeant Schmid was killed and during one of the worst periods for the CIED Task Force.

Richie's eyes are cold and almost emotionless as he describes the death of his close friend. It's clear to me that his emotional reserves have been exhausted by the death and injury of too many of his comrades, by the horror of waking up to the news that someone you were speaking to a day earlier has been blown to pieces. I have seen that look before, in the eyes of other men who have watched friends die. It is unmistakable. It is the cold, distant look of someone who has witnesed violent death.

Richie continues, 'We were on a ten-liner. It was a fairly normal job, just routine. The infantry wanted us to search an area so that they could get greater freedom of movement. That's routine work for us, nothing unusual. It was normal drills. We found a device and we pushed back to search an ICP. The ICP, which was a few yards from a canal, was searched and cleared. Everything was going fine, man – you know, nothing unusual. Then Ken, the ATO, stepped on a device, and bang. No one is really quite sure what happened. Was the bomb inside or outside the ICP – who knows?'

Initially members of Brimstone 45 thought they were under RPG attack. Those standing close to the seat of the blast were knocked off their feet, while others were left momentarily stunned and deafened by the noise from the explosion. At first there was silence. The sound of the explosion was just a distant rumble, and then the screaming started. It is still unclear whether a device was missed during the search of the ICP or if Ken Bellringer accidentally stepped outside of the cleared area.

WO2 Ken Bellringer was lying motionless on the embankment, paralysed through fear and injury. The first to spot him was Richie, who was horrified by what he saw. Ken had almost been cut in two – his legs from the hip downwards had disappeared and in their place were two charred stumps. His eyes were open but he was unresponsive and possibly dead. Ken's lower abdomen had been ripped open and his bowel was exposed. He had also suffered severe damage to his hands.

Richie knew that where there was one bomb there could be more, and it was vital that he clear a path to Ken so that the medics could try to save his life.

'There was this huge bang and then utter confusion,' he says. 'At first you are just stunned and then it dawns on you that someone has obviously stepped on a bomb. Several people were hurt but Ken was clearly the worst and then Loz was missing and at that stage all sorts of things are going through your head.

'It was a pretty fucking horrible day, pretty fucking horrible. Ken was in a coma for a month or so. I was there when it happened. It was the worst thing I had ever seen. It was a fairly routine task, something had been found, we did the isolation as normal, and then yeah, it was a simple task and it went wrong. That is the sort of shit that can happen out here – that's Afghan. Ken was lying down on the embankment, he wasn't moving. His legs had gone and you're thinking, oh shit! I can't remember whether he was conscious or not, but he was in a bad way and all the time you're thinking, this can't be real. One minute everything was cool – the next you're in hell.

'The medics ran in and treated Ken before the dust had settled. They put tourniquets around his legs, stopped as much of the bleeding as possible, and basically kept him alive. We then extracted the casualties back to the our previous ICP, which was 30 metres away, then the MERT [medical emergency response team] came in to take the casualties away. Then more reinforcements came in to look for Loz.'

It took almost twenty-four hours to find Loz's body. The injuries he suffered were even greater than those Ken, who survived, suffered and he was probably dead before he hit the water.

Richie continues, 'In our team Gaz was injured, our platoon commander was injured, the IEDD team No. 2 had a damaged eye and smashed teeth, and the ECM operator was battle-shocked. I had to tell my parents because it was on the news that a soldier from 33 Engineer Regiment had gone missing. I didn't want them to think it might be me.'

The searchers are a superstitious bunch, possibly because of the death of their commander. Every one of them, apart from Kev, carries a lucky charm. Richie has a coin lodged beneath the padding of his helmet, which was minted in the year of his birth. 'Loz found it and gave it to me. He told me to keep it close and it would keep me safe – and up until now it has.'

Sapper Gaz Homewood, another of the searchers, wears rosary beads around his neck, which I initially thought was a carefully crafted tattoo, Sapper Dan Taylor-Allen carries a lucky stone and Corporal Adam Butler has a St Christopher medal, a lucky threepence which is something of a family heirloom, and a crucifix. Joe also carries a crucifix, while Lance Corporal Michael Brunt has a St Christopher medal in his helmet. The soldiers are utterly convinced that the crosses, medals and charms have worked, because they have survived.

'They all have their ops kit as well,' Kev adds, laughing and convinced that they are talking nonsense. 'They always make sure they wear the same kit every time they go on an operation.'

I'm immediately reminded of *The Dirty Dozen*. I hadn't noticed it but Kev is absolutely correct. The search teams' uniforms are torn and threadbare, in some cases restitched by clumsy hands

'I always have two uniforms. One I will wear in camp and the other on ops. I've had these trousers the whole tour and they're now falling apart. Look,' says Richie, pointing at several strips of black masking tape holding one of his trouser legs together. 'Once you believe that something is giving you some good luck you don't want to change it. It's like me being lead searcher: so far so good, so why change it? If it works, don't fuck around with it. Not in Afghan, not until you need to.'

As the searchers chat among themselves, Woody is hacking his way through the brambles, clearing a path to the doorway where the IED has reportedly been buried. He is being forced to search by trying to spot IED ground sign. He is looking for anything out of the ordinary, like disturbed earth or patches of dead grass.

Back in the ICP the conversation enters the surreal and the subject turns to football. John Terry, the Chelsea and former England captain, and Ashley Cole, the Chelsea left back, are in the headlines for all the wrong reasons. Richie is appalled at the way Cole treated his wife Cheryl. 'Ashley Cole had the hottest chick in the country and he blew it. What a dick. Can you believe that? Cheryl Cole is a goddess.'

Gaz offers up an explanation. 'Yeah, but the reason why he was playing away was because her mother-in-law was living in the house at the time. Who wants to shag the missus when the mother-in-law is sleeping in the next bedroom?'

'They are all the same fucking overpaid knobs,' complains Richie. 'I get paid £64 a day to find IEDs and they get paid 100 grand a week to play football. Why is that fair? People think football is pressurized but if you want some real pressure come out here and be the lead searcher in the team.'

After twenty minutes of searching Woody discovers the IED in the doorway. It's a straightforward pressure-plate anti-personnel IED designed to kill or blow the legs off the victim – soldier, policeman, civilian, boy, girl.

Woody, working with the dexterity and intensity of a vascular surgeon, eventually picks out a wire connecting the bomb to the power supply. It's the breakthrough he has been hoping for. He loads the IED weapon and carefully positions it so that when it is fired by Boonie back in the ICP, the bomb should, in theory, be neutralized. There are no time limits. As bomb hunters say, short cuts are the quickest route to an early grave.

Woody returns to the ICP and explains to Kev and Boonie the layout of the device. The explosive is contained within a yellow-plastic 5-litre palm-oil container, the detonator has been improvised, and the pressure plate is relatively standard, although it contains very little metal.

Taking off his helmet, Woody wipes the sweat from his brow. He is red from the heat and his eyes are bloodshot. He explains, 'The device is definitely big enough to kill a soldier, that is what it was designed to do. It was a classic booby-trap, if you like, just placed in front of the door. The insurgents were hoping that someone would just walk into the compound, possibly as part of a route search, and would step on the device. It was probably aimed at either the ANP or ANA – I think they know by now that British soldiers don't walk through the doors of derelict compounds, especially those that were former Taliban firing points.'

'Controlled explosion in figures five,' announces Boonie. Five seconds later he remotely fires the IED weapon. A loud pop echoes around us. The wires are cut and the bomb should now be safe. But as there is always the risk of a secondary device Woody must take great care.

He leaves the device to 'soak' for a few minutes. The amount of time an ATO allows the device after he has remotely cut the wires is up to him. Some wait ten minutes, others might wait thirty minutes or even an hour. A lot depends on the operational situation.

Woody leans back and is almost lost among the green stalks of young wheat. He clasps his hands behind his head and closes his eyes, and I think he is about to take a quick nap, but then adds, 'The Taliban know that we carry out certain actions when we are working on a bomb. They know we return to the device after a certain amount of time, so you need to vary the time you return. It's all about not setting patterns, otherwise one day you are going to get caught out. They have already tried to booby-trap devices, to target the opera- tors. They might put another switch into the main charge so that if you try and lift the main charge out by hand then the device could explode. So we always try and remove the main charge by remotely removing it, which means pulling it out with a bit of rope and a hook so that if it does go bang you're OK.'

After several minutes Woody prepares to extract the bomb from the ground using a hook and line. It's an unsophisticated piece of kit but it works perfectly well. It allows the bomb to be pulled from the ground from a distance. ATOs have learned to their cost over the past thirty years that most of the actions they make while defusing bombs should be done from as far away as possible. By using the hook and line, Woody can pull the bomb out of the ground from more than 50 metres away if necessary. If there is a second bomb it will detonate now. But the ground is rock hard and it takes the combined strength of Woody and Boonie to pull it out. Everyone waits for an explosion which doesn't come.

Woody returns to the compound with Corporal Richard Lacey, the weapons intelligence specialist, who photographs all of the components so that they can be studied in detail later. The pressure plate and the detonator are retrieved and placed in plastic bags for further forensic examination, but the explosive will be blown up inside the compound.

Corporal Adam Butler, the acting team commander, who took over when Loz was killed, has soft, kind eyes and the demeanour of a man who encourages others through gentle persuasion rather than aggressive shouting. He has a rich country accent and despite his age

Staff Sergeant Karl 'Badger' Ley at the end of his six month tour in which he defused 139 bombs. He later won the George Medal.

Corporal Kelly O'Connor, No.2 operator with Brimstone 31, carrying a Dragon Runner.

Corporal Kevin Boon, No.2 operator in Brimstone 32, prepares to carry out a controlled explosion.

Armoured Ridgeback used by Lieutenant Colonel Roly Walker, commanding officer of the Grenadier Guards, which was blown up by an IED in February 2010. No one inside was injured.

A bomb hunter attached to the Grenadier Guards battle group confirming the location of an IED (left), and a soldier marks a cleared safe lane with yellow spray paint during operation Moshtarak.

Soldiers from A Company, 4 Rifles in Sangin march in single file along a route being cleared by a Vallon operator.

Company Sergeant Major Pat Hyde (standing) of A Company, 4 Rifles with his team. They were blown up at least twelve times in five months in Sangin.

Staff Sergeant Gareth Wood prepares his equipment before defusing an IED, with Lance Corporal Joe Rossiter acting as his bodyguard in the foreground (centre right), before returning all smiles after the IED is neutralized in a controlled explosion.

Top left Lead searcher Sapper Bradley Knight from Brimstone 42 sets off on isolation clearance.

Above Members of Brimstone 42 in Forward Operating Base Shawqat after successfully completing their first bomb hunting mission.

Left Sapper Richie Pienaar, lead searcher of Brimstone 45, relaxes after clearing a safe rout to an IED.

Below Staff Sergeant Gareth Wood and Royal Engineer Search Advisor Kev O'Dwyer discuss the best route to the location of an IED.

An improvised detonator used by the Taliban in Helmand.

Pressure plates, vital components of IEDs, discovered by British troops in a raid on a bomb factory during Operation Moshtarak.

Taliban IED composed of explosive in yellow container, pressure plate and battery pack. This would be powerful enough to kill a soldier or disable a vehicle.

Lieutenant Craig Shephard, the commander of 5 Platoon, No.2 Company, 1st Battalion Grenadier Guards, who was awarded the Military Cross.

The soldiers from 5 Platoon, No.2 Company, 1st Battalion Grenadier Guards, who fought at the Battle of Crossing Point One.

Members of Brimstone 42 take cover behind a Warrior armoured vehicle during a controlled explosion.

Staff Sergeant Gareth Wood with his Military Cross, November 2010.

Captain Dan Read, killed in action in Musa Qaleh on 11 January 2010.

Staff Sergeant Olaf Schmid, who was posthumously awarded the George Cross.

Staff Sergeant Kim Hughes and Christina Schmid, the widow of Staff Sergeant Olaf Schmid, with their George Cross citations, March 2010.

– he, like the others, is only in his twenties – is now on his second tour in Helmand. I ask him what life is like for a high-risk search team. 'You get used to the dangers but you never get complacent,' he tells me. 'We know what the Taliban are trying to do and we just have to stay one step ahead. Team work is our route to making it out of Helmand alive. If someone makes a mistake, then he or all of us could be killed or injured. We can't afford to have a bad day or switch off, so the pressure can be phenomenal, but I think we've all grown used to that. We all share the same risk, but Richie, as the lead searcher, does more searching, so I suppose you could argue that he is more at risk. He was the lead searcher when Loz was alive and so I decided to keep him as the lead when I took over. It's not good to change things around too much.

'But sometimes I might switch it around if we are doing lots of searches in one day – just to give Richie a rest. The other day when we did a route search there were quite a lot of isolations. We ended up doing about eight isolations over about seven or eight hours. Richie was in and out of the ditches all day long and so we changed things around a bit just to give him a break. You've got to rest them, otherwise they can go stale.'

The lead searcher is something of a talisman for the team, because their lives depend on him. Soldiers are very superstitious and it is very important that his mates believe Richie is a naturally lucky person. His role is to lead the way – he has to be 100 per cent focused 100 per cent of the time, and he admits, 'It can be pretty tiring some-times. The risks? You take a risk every time you cross the road, eh? I don't really think about it. I suppose I just get on with the job and hopefully everyone makes it back. I don't really worry too much about it. You've got to be good at the job, you've got to learn quickly because the Taliban aren't going to give you a second chance, and I think you need that little bit of extra luck sometimes. You can be the best searcher in the world but one piece of bad luck and you could be killed. It's got nothing to do with bad drills, just bad luck. In Afghan you always want to be lucky – being lucky is better than being good. Plenty of guys good at their job have been killed out here but the lucky ones survive.

'I've had two close shaves in vehicles where we have been blown up, and Inkerman was pretty intense because there are so many threats. It's very unpredictable and the Taliban will take you on all the time. The last time I was up there there was more pressure because they had been targeting isolations. So you've got to be really on the ball. In some areas the risk is less but in Inkerman and Sangin you can get channelled into alleyways, so the threat is greater.'

'Sangin is an absolute hell-hole,' Adam adds in agreement. 'It's basically one big fucking minefield. The Taliban will take you on wherever and whenever they can. When you get told you're going to Sangin – it's like, "Shit!" All anyone wants is just to get out of there alive. No one gives a fuck about hearts and minds, you just want to get out in one piece.'

Adam is married with a young son whom he misses terribly. As we chat in the ICP he talks longingly of his family back home, especially little Alfie. When he shows me a picture of his son I notice small tears beginning to form. 'I can't wait to see my little lad, he's a lovely boy,' he says, almost lost in thought. 'I think about him all the time. He means the world to me. Sometimes I miss him so much it's almost unbearable. That's the thing about kids – you really miss them, but thinking about them just makes you sad. He's only three and I've already deployed on two six-month operations since he was born. I've already missed a third of his life – and nothing will bring that back. For me that's the hardest bit. Part of you thinks, I don't want to do this any more, I want to watch him grow up and be with him. I want to play football with him and read books at night. That's not much to ask, is it? I just want to be a normal dad. The thing which really scares me, more than any IED, is how my family would cope if anything happened to me.'

Adam first served in Afghanistan in 2007 on Operation Herrick 6. He says that the war was different, what he calls a 'stand-up fight'.

Now, he says, and his views are echoed by many soldiers, 'It's a dirty, nasty little war.' He continues, 'IEDs are everywhere and that has increased our workload massively. On Herrick 7 we only had two search teams, now we have a lot more, but we are still out every day. Personally, I haven't seen any real improvements in this place since I was here last. I know Nad-e'Ali is safe now, but look at the manpower that was needed to secure this place. What did they say? Something like the biggest heliborne assault for fifty years, over 4,000 British troops. There are now checkpoints everywhere and you've got guys staging on 24/7, the blokes are really hanging out – there is no way you can do that in every AO. And if they are going make this place safe then you have to do that everywhere – that's a massive undertaking.'

When I ask Adam whether he thinks Afghanistan is worth the sacrifice, he replies, 'That's a very difficult question to answer.' Waving his arms around, he asks, 'Is this worth Loz's life? I don't think so. I don't think it's worth the life of a single British soldier. The politicians talk about sacrifice and duty but they are not the ones out here doing the fighting. Sacrifice is a lot easier to talk about when you're not the one making it. But we are professional soldiers and we have got a job to do, so we get on and do it. We do it for each other – that's it. The bottom line is, if we all do our jobs to the best of our abilities, then we've got a good chance of getting out alive. That's the same for everyone.'

Kev interjects and explains the true feelings of soldiers in Afghanistan. 'To be honest, I think many of the lads try not to think about the whys and wherefores too much – we just crack on and get through it day by day. Every day you stay alive you're a day closer to getting home.'

The death of Loz returns to the conversation and the ICP falls silent. Adam was on a four-day Mastiff commander's course when his boss was killed and it is clear that his absence on the day has led to some feelings of guilt. 'Part of me wishes I was there because, you never know, it may have been different, maybe Ken wouldn't have stepped on the bomb and Loz wouldn't have been killed, but I know you can't go through life thinking of all the what ifs. I knew Loz really well, he was such a great bloke, and we all miss him a lot. It was a really difficult time. The whole team took part in his repatriation ceremony back to the UK. We all carried his coffin onto the plane, which helped us come to terms with what happened and it allowed us all to say goodbye – but it was pretty heartbreaking. You can imagine how it must feel – we all came out together and then just before we go on R&R our commander is killed. It was shattering. Guys are getting killed all the time but you never think it's going to be one of your mates, and when it does happen it's the worst feeling in the world. We still talk about him quite a lot and then there will be things which remind us about him. I think that's quite important. We'll have a laugh and say, "Remember when Loz did this and that?"'

Adam is staring into the distance and he begins to sound sad and regretful. 'We had quite a shit R&R, to be honest,' he says, with his head now resting on his knees. 'You think it's going to be this great release, but at the back of your mind you know that you are coming back out to this place. It made life at home pretty difficult. I kept arguing with my missus over little things. I think I was still pretty stressed. You expect everything to be great when you go back but you soon realize that life hasn't stood still. Your family has a life too and it's pretty hard for them when you're away too. We think we have it hard, but it's a bloody nightmare for the wives and families. It's six months of gut-wrenching worry and you turn up in the middle of it and say, "Hi, I'm home," and they're glad you're home but you're also messing up the routine, upsetting the kids, and they know you're going to bugger off again in a couple of weeks.

'I think it was because of what happened to Loz and knowing that you are coming back out here, so you can't relax. R&R is vital, you need to get home, you need a break. I would rather we did a longer tour but less frequently, like nine months but every three years – I think if that was on the table the blokes would go for it. We'll be back here in two years. None of us want to come out here again.

Everybody in our team knows someone who has been killed or injured. One of our mates, Dave "The Leg" Watson, was killed on New Year's Eve. He was knocking down the wall of a compound as part of an operation. It was nothing really dangerous, just a straight-forward operation, and he stepped on an IED. The blast blew off three limbs – he was a triple amputee and he died on the operating table. He was a brilliant bloke, the fittest man I knew.

'And there was Captain Dan Read. He was a great bloke for an officer. He came up through the ranks and he had a good under-standing of the lads, although the officers in our trade are all pretty good. Anyway, his team were taking part in a route clearance in Gereshk district centre – again a routine task, nothing you would call dangerous. An IED was found and they set up an ICP and searched it, just like we've done today, but somehow an IED was missed – there was a pressure-plate device in the ICP and the WIS corporal, James Oakland, stepped on it and was killed instantly. Dan Read was injured in the blast – he took some frag in the chest and arm – and so were a couple of other guys. The worst thing was that Jim had actually been sent out as a battle casualty replacement and had been in Afghan for about three months when he was killed.'

Captain Read, 31, passed his High Threat course in August 2009 and immediately began his pre-deployment training for Operation Herrick 10, before arriving in Helmand the following month. He was injured just nine days before one of his friends, Staff Sergeant Olaf Schmid, was killed in Sangin. Captain Read told his family and wife Lorraine that he felt guilty about leaving his IED team, known as Team Illume, while he recovered, and so with the blessing of his wife and mother he returned to Helmand in December 2009 in a bid to 'get back on the horse'. On 11 January, after having dealt with more than thirty bombs, he was on a routine task in Musa Qala and was attempting to defuse a bomb when it detonates and he was killed instantly.

Woody returns to the compound for the next phase of the opera-tion – blowing up the home-made explosive. ATOs never recover explosive, because it could be unstable and it has limited forensic value, so it is always destroyed *in situ*. As Woody makes his way back to the compound with a packet of plastic-explosive detonation cord and a detonator, Adam tells me about the feared no-metal bombs which the Taliban have created.

Brimstone 42 was one of the first units to discover the no-metal IED, or wooden bomb. Lacking any metal content, these devices are extremely difficult to detect, which is why all soldiers must be able to recognize ground sign. The team were dispatched to Kajaki to conduct a search of an area after a suspected Taliban bomb team was observed acting suspiciously.

Adam goes on, 'If the IEDs are all-metal you have got every chance of finding them, but these lads are making IEDs with low or no metal. When we first arrived we were told about the low metal content with carbon rods and we were all shitting ourselves, then we got sent up to Kajaki and found the wooden one. One of the lads, Sapper Dan Taylor-Allen, found one while he was sitting in the ICP. The device was attached to a 20 kg main charge in a 20-litre palm-oil container. If it had detonated it would have killed everyone in about a 15-metre radius.'

Dan, one of the biggest but also one of the quieter soldiers in the team, explains that the team were conducting a search using special-ist equipment, which is supposed to be able to find devices with no metal content. The soldiers had finished searching the ICP and were relaxing when Dan noticed something about 2 in. from the heel of his boot.

'I was sort of kicking the stone away with my foot when I saw a shape,' he explains. 'I brushed the stones away and I saw a yellow container and then the pressure plate – the wooden box was right by my heel. We were literally sitting on the bomb. It was a 20 kg main charge – that would have taken out a Mastiff. If it had gone off there wouldn't have been anything left of me or anyone near me. But I wasn't really that fazed. I just thought, good job I didn't step on it.'

'Afterwards you sit around and say, what if? But it didn't go bang, so what's the point in worrying about it? That was a couple of months ago and we haven't seen any more of those since, but we know some have been found in Musa Qala – they're just another bomb.'

I learned about the 'no metal' bombs back in Camp Bastion but their existence has been kept secret from the British public, although the reason for such secrecy was lost on Adam. 'We know the Taliban have got them and they know we know. So what's the big deal?'

Undetectable land mines are nothing new, even if they do terrify the infantry. The German Army developed a non-metal anti-personnel mine in the Second World War and during the Cold War most NATO and Warsaw Pact countries produced anti-personnel mines with few or no metal components. All the Taliban have done is make an improvised version – the wooden IED.

The device is a wooden box consisting of a small cavity and a plug or plunger which can be compressed by the weight, of, say, a human being or a vehicle. Inside the box is a small piece of explosive and a piece of det cord which is linked to a main charge. When pressure is applied the explosive inside the box detonates and almost simultaneously the main charge detonates.

Kev, who has been monitoring the mission, rejoins the conversation. 'As far as we are concerned, it's just another device and if you stick to the rules and listen during your training you can detect them. The easy way to stop getting blown up is to stay off the tracks. We keep telling soldiers, "Stay off the tracks, that's where the Taliban plant bombs." We do the training with soldiers and we try and drum it into them. Some listen, some don't.'

I ask Kev whether there is any intelligence to suggest that the Taliban are planning to increase the sophistication of their IEDs. 'I don't think they need to,' he says dismissively. 'They can achieve what they want to achieve with what they are using now. They don't need to increase their sophistication. From their point of view they are killing soldiers and they are restricting our freedom of movement with a very simple device. It's too easy for them at the moment. Too easy to make and bury IEDs. By keeping it simple they are effective. I don't think the British public really get it. They probably think that the Taliban have made these incredibly sophisticated bombs which we can't detect. The fact is we find 80 per cent of them, or so we think. But there are thousands of bombs out there somewhere and we won't get them all, and that is what the Taliban are counting on.'

Woody returns to the ICP and hands the wires which will complete the explosive circuit to Boonie, who connects them to the firing pack and issues the warning: 'Controlled explosion in figures five.'

Every one one of us in the ICP is ordered to crouch down and prepare for a large bang. That's an understatement. The blast is huge and I can feel the thump of the shock wave in the pit of my stomach. There is no bright-orange flash, just a mass of earth rising 30 ft into the air. It's impossible to believe that there would be anything left of a victim unfortunate enough to detonate the bomb.

As Woody returns to the compound for a final time to ensure that all of the home-made explosive has been detonated, a warning comes over one of the radios alerting us to suspicious movement in the wood line around 800 metres to our north and close to an area where there are thought to be some small pockets of Taliban. Woody returns happy that his job is done. 'That's another one under the belt,' he says to himself.

'Job done,' announces Kev to everyone before turning to me and saying, 'We have been working together for two months and we've done maybe fifty jobs, possibly more. Some of the jobs just go on and on. We've done route clearance which can last all day, sometimes several days. Fortunately this one was routine.'

'Yeah, it was routine,' agrees Woody. 'But it's the routine jobs that some people have been killed on. You can get very comfortable in what you are doing. You do the same thing every day and at some stage you will switch off and make a mistake, so it's the routine jobs which will catch you out.'

The whole IEDD team is now back in the ICP and Kev announces that we will be moving out in two minutes. While Boonie is packing away the ATO's equipment and the searchers are hauling on their packs, the distant rattle of machine-gun fire pierces the still afternoon air. 'A fifty,' says Adam. He means a .50-calibre heavy machine gun, and so it should be outgoing rather than incoming fire. But Richie says, 'Or a Dushka.' The DShk is a 12.7-mm Russian-made heavy machine gun which has been used by the Taliban.

'Right, let's get a move on,' shouts Kev. 'Same order of march. Richie, you lead. Let's go.' Once again we are in single file, marching at speed across the wheat field, but this time taking a different route back to Blue 17. As we patrol back the firing continues. Whoever is shooting it is at least 2 km from us and therefore not regarded as a threat.

The team moves back into the patrol base and Woody tells Lance Sergeant Hunt that the mission has been successful. The searchers are now visibly more relaxed, talking and laughing among themselves, smoking cigarettes and gulping down fresh, ice-cold water. Clearing one IED has taken upwards of five hours and involved more than thirty soldiers. No one knows how many IEDs litter the tracks, fields and hamlets which make up Helmand, but the best estimates put the number in the thousands.

It has been a long, hot day for the men of Brimstone 45. In the next forty-eight hours, providing there is a helicopter available, they will fly out of Nad-e'Ali and return to Camp Bastion. It will then be four days on HRF and then back home, via twenty-four hours' 'decompression' in Cyprus, to their families, wives and girlfriends. They have almost made it.

Chapter 6: **The Lonely Walk**

'I was almost killed the other day.'
Staff Sergeant Gareth Wood, ATO, 11 EOD Regiment, Royal Logistic Corps, serving with JFEOD Group

'If you're lucky, and I mean really lucky, you will leave Helmand with your team intact – no one killed or injured, no amputees. But you know you are going to get blown up, you know you are going to get shot at. You will have close shaves and you just have to hope that luck is on your side. But there are only so many rolls of the dice you can have before you get a double six. We all know that, but we train ourselves not to dwell on what might happen. I suppose you could say that we are living in denial but I don't think there is any other way of getting through Afghan other than to have that sort of mentality.'

Woody and I are chatting over a cup of Army tea in one of the two steel-reinforced bunkers that serve as the canteen for the 150 soldiers operating from FOB Shawqat, the main headquarters of the Grenadier Guards battlegroup, to which Woody and his team are currently attached. It's around 8 p.m. and the soldiers have finished their evening meal, a chicken curry followed by semi-frozen Black Forest Gateau, all washed down with an orange-coloured, sickly sweet squash. Curry is an Army staple – back in Camp Bastion the food halls where the soldiers eat offer it as a menu choice every day – but in Shawqat curry is a rarity and always a crowd-puller. It's comfort food, it reminds the soldiers of home.

The bunker is lit by a series of low-hanging fluorescent lights emitting a dull-greenish hue. On one wall is an electric fly-catcher which periodically spits out a series of cracks every time a fly is zapped. The previous evening soldiers were betting on how many flies would be killed in one, five and ten minutes.

A 50-in. flat-screen TV fills a wall at one end of the building where three young soldiers sit engrossed in *The Hurt Locker*. It's one of the many oddities of life in Helmand that many soldiers appear to relax by watching war films or playing violent computer games.

Woody looks over his shoulder and stares at the TV for a few seconds. Then he turns to me and a wide, toothy grin creeps across his face. 'Hollywood,' he says, shaking his head. 'You just knew they weren't going to get it right. You wouldn't last five minutes if you behaved like that out here.'

I've now been with Woody and his team for over a week. I've seen him pull bombs from the ground after hours of toil. I've seen him tense, frustrated, angry and relieved, and I've listened to him talk long-ingly of his wife and 3-year-old twin daughters. But with so much to live for and so much to lose, I still can't quite understand why Woody is a bomb hunter. Helmand province, the largest in Afghanistan, is without doubt currently the most dangerous place on the planet. Woody knows the risks. He is horribly aware that a simple mistake, a momentary lapse in concentration, can spell disaster. He is no stranger to death. One of his best friends, Staff Sergeant Olaf Schmid, was killed in Helmand while Woody was completing his High Threat course.

Woody's face is friendly and burnished to a rusty light brown by the hundreds of hours he has spent exposed to the desert sun. His eyes are quick and alert and his face carries a happy smile. The dirt and sweat have been washed away but the fatigue of war has taken its toll. His cheeks are hollow, he admits to often being too exhausted to eat after a particularly difficult job, and, like most of the ATOs oper-ating in Helmand, he has acquired dark rings beneath his eyes.

To date Woody's team have been blown up twice and he can't remember exactly how many times they have come under fire since they arrived in January 2010. He thinks, though he can't be certain, that he and his team have disposed of something like thirty bombs. But Woody tries not to count. I have never met a soldier who is not superstitious, and Woody is no different. Staff Sergeant Olaf Schmid and Captain Dan Read both counted the number of bombs they defused, and both are dead, Woody tells me. He is now convinced that counting bombs brings bad luck.

Woody's first brush with death occurred when he was part of the High Readiness Force in early March 2010. His team were flown by helicopter into FOB Inkerman to clear two recently discovered IEDs. The base was named after the Inkerman Company of the Grenadier Guards, under whose watch it was established in June 2007. It sits right on the edge of the fertile green zone and was built to interdict Taliban movement towards Sangin district centre. At the time the base held the dubious distinction of being one of the most attacked in Helmand. I have been embedded in Inkerman twice before, in 2007 with 1st Battalion Royal Anglian Regiment and in 2008 with 2nd Battalion Parachute Regiment, and on both occasions the base came under Taliban attack.

The IED threat in the Sangin area is so high that ATOs are only sent on attachment to the resident battlegroup after they have completed at least two months in Helmand. The same rules, however, do not apply to the HRF who fly in, do the job, and fly out.

For bomb hunter callsigns Brimstone 32 and 45, the high-risk search team, the mission, on paper at least, appeared to be relatively routine. Two bombs had been located in the area, a pressure-plate device on Route 611, the main transit link between FOB Inkerman and Sangin district centre, some 8 km to the south, and one closer to the base.

'We were on HRF and were choppered into Inkerman the night before,' recalls Woody, between sips of hot, sweet tea. 'We were briefed on the task – it was basically a clearance op. We worked out our plan and we were all happy – well, as happy as you can be in Sangin.'

The bomb hunters left at first light in a convoy of Mastiffs supported by soldiers under the command of Company Sergeant Major Pat Hyde of A Company, 4 Rifles, a man who had developed the reputation of being a bomb magnet after having been blown up at least twelve times in five months.

Woody continues, 'We got up in the morning at first light and headed south down Route 611 towards Sangin, where the first job was. The plan was to deal with that bomb, then return to the one closer to Inkerman and deal with that. But no job in Sangin is ever what you think it is going to be. We had been told that the first bomb was effectively a pressure-plate device but when we got there we discovered that there was a pressure plate and also a command wire linked to the bomb. Since the device was first discovered the Taliban had come in and changed it. It seems they had been monitoring the area and had obviously seen that it had been discovered. Once that had happened they knew that it would have to be cleared. It was on the 611, so it couldn't be ignored. And the only people who clear bombs are ATOs. The route is overlooked by a number of patrol bases, so the enemy shouldn't have been able to get anywhere near it, but somehow they did. The Taliban are pretty cheeky in Sangin.

'The main charge was an anti-tank mine and I think they had basically modified the device so that it could be detonated by command pull or by pressure. I think the idea behind the command wire was the hope that they might get a kill when a soldier made an approach during the confirmation.'

Despite the complication of the double trigger, Woody and his team were able to deal with the device relatively quickly. The soldiers knew the threat was high and that the risk of attack was very real, so no one wanted to hang around a minute longer than necessary. The isolation searches had to be quick but thorough. By late morning the troops were heading back towards Inkerman to complete the second and final task.

Woody explains, 'We identified the area where the second device was buried – the soldiers from the Rifles had pinpointed it. The Mastiffs secured the area and we began clearing it. After the ICP was secured, the search team went out and began the isolation, a wide search of the area around the location of the bomb to ensure it was free from command wires.'

Above the ICP was a small outcrop on which sat an old, abandoned compound. Locals had recently been digging for rock in the area, possibly for use on their own homes. While the troops were preparing for the next stage of the mission they noticed a young boy, aged around 10, with a dirty face and matted hair, watching them closely. The soldiers waved and the boy, smiling, waved back.

A few of the troops shouted, *'As-Salaam Alaikum'*, the traditional Pashto greeting, which translates as 'God be with you' but also serves as a simple 'hello'. The boy's face lit up and he gleefully shouted back, 'Hello, soldier.' Everyone laughed and relaxed. The boy's presence was, on the face of it, reassuring. But in Sangin nothing is quite what it might at first seem, and many soldiers believe the Taliban operate there with the sympathy and support of the local population.

'I wasn't really taking much notice,' says Woody. 'We'd just come back in off the isolation and people were sorting their kit out, dropping their bags, and I was concentrating on what I was going to do next, which was the first approach – going down the road. I was in my zone and the security of the area was the responsibility of the infantry.'

Woody and Kev, the RESA, were discussing the best line of approach, while some of the search team began to relax and light up cigarettes. Richie, the lead searcher, was folding the stock of his Vallon when the ridge line above them erupted and the ICP was hit by a volley of rocks and shrapnel. Punched by the blast, Richie fell to the ground holding his groin as a large plume of dust and smoke enveloped the soldiers. 'Contact IED. Wait, out,' was frantically dispatched over the radio as the sound of thunder echoed around the valley. 'It was an almighty explosion, a fucking great bang,' recalls Woody, now more animated than he had been earlier. 'We were all showered with rocks and shit. It was really close, you could feel the shock wave. The detonation was about 30 metres away, and that's pretty close. Your ears are ringing, your nose is running, there's dust in your eyes, and you're wondering who's been hit. I can smile about it now, but at the time you're thinking, what the bloody hell was that?'

Richie was rolling around on the ground, his knees bent up to his chest, shouting, 'Shit, shit, shit,' still unsure how badly he'd been injured. Sapper Dan Taylor-Allen ran over, grabbed Richie and asked him if he was hit. 'In the nuts, man,' said Richie. 'I've been hit in the fucking nuts.'

Dan was joined by other members of the team, who told Richie to stop moving and quickly examined him. A wound in the groin from a piece of shrapnel can rupture the femoral artery and cause death within minutes. But whatever had hit Richie had not broken the skin: it had just given him one hell of a painful whack in the testicles. As they searched through his trousers they discovered the tip of a .50-cal bullet.

'Initially we didn't have a clue what had happened. We were all pretty shaken up. We called in the contact but we didn't want to move up to the high ground because the likelihood was that we would be hit by the Taliban. Although we were pretty shaken up we still had a bomb to pull out of the ground. So there was nothing else to do but to push on with the job.'

Woody continues, 'From the intelligence we gained afterwards we think that the Taliban had dicked us as we came into the area and while we were doing the isolation clearance word got back to the local Taliban. Two guys were seen in the area on a motorbike and we think they set an improvised claymore mine – which was basically a lump of explosive with lots of pieces of metal in there – like the .50-cal bullet tip which hit Richie. They set the device up – it would have been a compound pull or a command wire – gave the wire to the boy, told him to pull the wire when they disappeared down the road, and fucked off. They may have given him a few dollars or something, I suppose, as a bit of an incentive – that or threatened to kill his family. So the lad, who a few minutes earlier had been smiling and waving at us, pulls the wire and bang – we get blown up. If it had been 10 metres closer we would have taken some casualties. That's the sort of shit that can happen in Afghan.'

Intelligence obtained later suggested that the Taliban had proba-bly been monitoring the progress of the bomb hunters from the moment they left FOB Inkerman several hours earlier by using the well-established 'dicking screen'. It's almost certain that the bomb used against the patrol had been constructed some days or possibly weeks earlier but had been reconfigured to attack an opportunity target. Woody explains, 'Command wires are pretty basic but very effective. The bomber just waits for a target and then touches the end of a wire against a battery and bang. The bomber can be over the other side of a wall from a bomb, or 100 metres away. The command pull is also pretty effective too. The command pull is generally a bit of string which will go to a command pull switch, generally a drinks bottle of some sort with a bare wire loop inside so there are two wires looped over each other on the insulated part and when you pull them they move to the uninsulated part, the circuit is completed, and the device functions. That device was either a command wire or compound pull.

'There was no time to think about what might have been, so instead of shitting ourselves we all had a good laugh. We couldn't believe that it was a child that did it. We were only waving at him a minute earlier – little bastard tried to take me out. So we went and searched down and found the device, which was a command-pull IED, and we dealt with that. It was a couple of anti-tank mines, so about 10–15 kg of explosive. We sorted that out and then went back to Inkerman – and that's a fairly normal day out in Sangin.'

I suggest to Woody that having just been blown up is probably not the best preparation for defusing a bomb. 'Wouldn't it have been safer to call in another team, given that you were all probably shaken up?' I ask.

A knowing smile creeps across Woody's face. 'In an ideal word, yes,' he says. 'Another team would have come in and finished the job. But we don't have that luxury. This isn't an ideal world – this is war and we don't have the men. So yeah, we have to do things you wouldn't otherwise expect to do. We were the ones on the ground. We knew where the device was, so you ask yourself, "Can I still do this?", and I don't think any of us thought we weren't up to it. It just wasn't an issue. If we hadn't disposed of it someone else would have had to do it.'

Woody grew up in a dull, uninspiring Staffordshire mill town, where he says 'there was absolutely nothing to do'. He moved schools when his parents parted and ended up in the Army because he 'couldn't be arsed' to work at school. But despite his lack of interest in all things academic, he still managed to gain nine GCSEs. His school's careers office offered little that stimulated his imagination and so one day after school he ventured into the local Army recruiting office for a look. It was a path that has been taken by hundreds of thousands of other young men and women over the years: the search for a vocation with a bit of spice. Woody was interested in learning a trade and with his clutch of decent GCSEs the Army welcomed him with open arms and a big, fat smile.

'When I went to the careers office they give you a test and based on that test they give you a list of jobs you can do. So I went home with a big list of all the units or corps you could join. I originally chose to join the Royal Electrical and Mechanical Engineers. I thought, best get a trade, and then later I learned about what the RLC get up to, and I thought, I'll have some of that, and I then switched to become an ammunition technician. And I've never looked back. It's a pretty intensive job, you get quick promotion, but there are lots of courses and exams and after about seven years you can start looking at becoming an ATO. At first you start off as a No. 2 operator, where you learn all about the kit and look after the ATO, drive the robots, and then you move on to becoming an operator.

'Our job is very different to the sort of bomb disposal done by the Royal Engineers. They tend to focus on regular munitions, hand grenades, aircraft bombs, mines, that type of thing, but there is a bit of crossover now and we've got some bomb-disposal officers going onto the High Threat course. Our job is IED disposal. You can look in a textbook and see how an aircraft bomb works. You can't look in a textbook and see how an IED works. For a start it's buried in the ground so you don't even know what you are dealing with. You have to use all your training, all the intelligence, all your experience to work out what bomb you think it is. The bomb at Blue 17 was always going to be a pressure-plate device – it was in a doorway, it's a derelict building and was a former insurgent firing point. British troops are equipped with electronic counter-measures equipment, so my guess would be that they are not going to put a remote-controlled device in a place like that. The insurgents know we have ECM, so they don't target us with remote-controlled devices, they keep them for the Afghan Army or Police. No command wires were found in the isolation, so, by that stage, you know that the device is really going to be a pressure-plate or pressure-release and I knew all that before I even got to the bomb. But there's always the chance that you could be wrong and you always have to be conscious of that.'

Woody's very first mission took place in late January 2010, curiously inside the British base in Musa Qala, which had recently been expanded to accommodate more troops. The new area was searched for IEDs and some were found, but unfortunately others were missed and Woody was sent in to clear them.

Musa Qala had been a war zone for decades. In the 1980s the Soviets and the Mujahideen fought for control of the area for much of the war. Even today, Russian trench systems are still occasionally used by the Taliban to attack the US forces now based in the area. By January 2010 areas not under the direct control of the British had become laced with IEDs. Their use on such a massive scale helped the Taliban to hold ground and limit the movement of ISAF troops. As well as having a psychological impact, the IED also had a significant military effect; it is what the Army calls a 'force multiplier' – in other words, it allowed the Taliban to punch above their weight.

The historic strategic importance of Musa Qala is undeniable. As a population centre, it is regarded as a valued prize by both ISAF forces and the Taliban. And before the current conflict, Soviet generals fought many battles in the area against the Mujahideen. Vast areas of the region are effectively no-go areas because of the threat from Soviet-era 'legacy' mines. British troops from 16 Air Assault Brigade first arrived in Musa Qala in May 2006 and remained there until October, fighting the Taliban almost daily. The Musa Qala base was separated from its helicopter landing site, which often made both resupply and casualty evacuation impossible when the base was under attack. The HLS was frequently declared 'red' and the soldiers of the Royal Irish Regiment, who in late 2006 had almost become a forgotten fighting force, lived with the knowledge that commanders would not risk losing a helicopter and its crew to save the life of a wounded soldier.

The British had entered Helmand in 2006 horribly under-equipped, under-strength, and with virtually no intelligence and no coherent plan as to how they were going to pacify the region. Lieutenant Colonel Stuart Tootal, who commanded the 3 Para battlegroup, admitted in 2006, 'It wasn't that our intelligence was wrong – we just didn't have any intelligence.'

By the summer of 2006 the 3,300-strong British force in Helmand was fixed in the areas of Sangin, Gereshk, Musa Qala, Lashkar Gah, Nowzad, Garmsir and Camp Bastion. With no ability to manoeuvre and no reserve, their only choice was to stand and fight. Of all the areas where British troops were based, Musa Qala was the most difficult to hold, because of the difficulties of resupply, and so it was sacrificed. In October 2006 a controversial deal was struck between the local leaders, the British and the Taliban whereby it was agreed that under a truce both the Taliban and the British troops would withdraw from the area. And, in one of the most extraordinary scenes of the Afghanistan War, the entire 150-strong British force pulled out of the area in a convoy of Afghan trucks known as 'jinglies'. The truce lasted barely into the New Year and by February 2007 Musa Qala was back in the hands of the Taliban until they were forced to leave again by a major NATO operation to retake the area in December of that year.

Talking about his task at Musa Qala, Woody says, 'Your first job is always going to be a bit weird. I wasn't exactly scared but you feel a bit nervous, and obviously you don't want to get killed on day one. The last thing you want is people saying, "What a tosser – he got killed on his first job." I was totally confident in my skills, and my preparation before coming out was excellent, so I was pretty confident. I knew that I would be able to deal with whatever I found.'

The shortage of bomb hunters in Helmand meant that there was little time for Woody and his team to acclimatize before undertaking their first mission. Within hours of Brimstone 32 completing their RSOI (Reception, Staging and Onward Movement Integration) training, they were declared ready for operations and became the High Readiness Force, under orders to be ready to move at a moment's notice. 'I made sure we spent plenty of time on the barma lanes [the area where soldiers practise searching for bombs, or 'barma-ing'] in Camp Bastion. It was just knocking the dust off, really. I wanted to make sure that I was happy with my drills – digging in the Afghan desert is different to digging in Warwickshire.' Woody is referring here to the Defence Explosive Ordnance Disposal, Munitions and Search School at Kineton.

On 30 January 2010, just twenty-four hours after finishing the theatre training package, Brimstone 32 got their first mission. Woody was having a brew with his team members when the Operations Warrant Officer appeared with the details of the ten-liner, handed it to Woody, and said, 'Your helicopter leaves in forty-five minutes.' The report revealed that a pressure-plate IED had been discovered and that, unusually, the bomb was actually within the perimeter of the camp.

'Straight away you switch into automatic,' says Woody. 'The butterflies are there in the pit of your stomach because you don't want to make a hash of it, but as well as a few nerves there is also a feeling of "Great. Job to do – let's get on and do it."'

'You always wonder what your first job will be like but it's never going to be what you expect, and this was exactly that. I had been to Helmand before on Herrick 8 and 9, so I knew what to expect. We went into Musa Qala DC [district centre] and the device was in a patrol base to the south of the main base in the area. We arrived the night before, met the OC, got a brief on the job, and then we were told that there were another eight IEDs that they wanted us to clear. Happy days. It's never just the one bomb – once they've got you there, there's always more work to do. That's basically the same wherever you go. The ten-liner says one bomb and when you get to the location you find that every device which has been found in the past month now has to be cleared. Sometimes you can do it, sometimes you can't.'

Once on the ground Brimstone 32 were told that the area had been cleared before the expansion of the camp but at least one bomb had been missed and there was every possibility that there might be others. The IED Woody's team had been sent to remove had been found purely by chance in the middle of the vehicle park. Somehow, and no one was quite sure how, it had been missed by man and vehicle alike for several weeks.

'It was between 20 and 25 kg – that is a fairly big IED. That is going to give you an M-Kill on a Mastiff or an armoured vehicle but it could also take out a lot of blokes out in the open. You could easily have a situation where a group of guys are standing around prior to a patrol and one of them detonates the device and then you would have a mass-casualty incident.

'Soldiers had been driving within millimetres of it – that's no exaggeration. I don't know how it was missed. There are some pretty

lucky guys wandering around up in Musa Qala. The bomb had probably been there for a couple of months. It was in an area where you
would expect IEDs to be. It was in an area of high ground, which is
why we built there. It was a good tactical position and the Taliban
probably knew we would move into that area. Classically, they put an
IED there and, amazingly, it was missed on one of the searches.'

When Woody arrived at the base he discovered that the bomb
wasn't a pressure-plate IED but an improvised Russian land mine,
known as an MUV. He explains, 'An MUV fuse is a pressure switch
that can be victim-operated – that is, a soldier stands on it or it can
be detonated by a trip wire which when tugged will pull out the pin,
just like pulling the pin out of a grenade. What the Taliban do is that
they take out the safety pin and put a matchstick in so that it can be
used like a pressure plate. When someone stands on it the matchstick
breaks, the switch goes into a detonator and straight into a main
charge underneath. It's instantaneous, the speed of the detonation is
8,000 metres per second, so you stand on it and boom, you're dead.
From the Taliban's point of view the MUV fuse is great because it
doesn't need a power source, so they can be left all over the place and
the insurgents can bury and forget them. No batteries to die away, so
they will always remain a threat.

'Sometimes the device will have a bit of a booster between the
detonator and the main charge, which can be det cord wrapped
around a metal cooking pot, which gives it a massive signature
[Vallon alarm], so they should be easy to find. Once you've found
them, then it's just a case of separating the components and destroying them. That's what I did in this case. I was working in a controlled
environment – there was no ICP to secure, no need for isolations, so
I just separated the components and it all went according to plan.
Then we found another one on the HLS and you think, how lucky
are these guys? First the car park and then the HLS.'

The US bomb-disposal teams operate as part of Task Force Paladin and are known as Paladin Teams. When Woody arrived at Musa
Qala he discovered that Paladin Teams were also taking part in the

clearance operation. The Paladin Teams are three-man units and, according to Woody, their main role is clearance rather than exploitation. 'The Paladin Teams will search up to the IED – put a charge on it, back off, and bang! But British operators will always try and recover some of the IEDs – that is one of our main roles. We have philosophies and principles as to how we operate which must always govern every mission, and they are: life, property, normality, and forensics. That's the order of priority, and we can swap property and normality and sometimes forensics all around, but life is always paramount. Ultimately that's our job: to preserve life.'

One of the greatest challenges ATOs face is the threat of complacency – not through any lack of professionalism but simply because the vast majority of the devices they deal with are pressure-plate IEDs. All ATOs have strategies and techniques to help them guard against the risk of complacency, and Woody was no exception. His technique was to focus on the often minute differences between devices.

'Every bomb is different – even though they have the same characteristics. You never know where all the components are going to be, some may be stretched out – for example, the power supply could be several metres away. Other bombs will have all the components close together, almost on top of each other, and may actually be hidden in a different way. The device may be poorly built, which could make it very unstable, or it may have been in the ground a long time and may have deteriorated and all it needs for it to function is for someone to start dislodging something. So the matter of quality control actually plays into the hands of the Taliban.

'Then you get some devices which may have a pressure-release switch with a pressure plate, so it can go off if you put pressure on or take pressure off. What the Taliban try and do to catch us out is put a number of pressure-plate devices down a route, so you get quite comfortable, and then they will throw a cheeky one. So you might arrive at the site and there in front of you is a pressure-plate IED. So no dramas – normal stuff. You have the pressure plate, power source and main charge, and then in parallel to the circuit there might be a pressure-release switch with a bit of rock or metal weighing it down. And this is all buried under the ground, so you move or someone moves the bit of rock to get a better working position, and bang, you're dead.'

Woody laughs, then goes on, 'There was this one time where I had to deal with a pressure-release device which had been in the ground for a while. It had been found by soldiers who had conveniently put loads of rocks around the device, which was their way of marking it, and you think, brilliant, now which stone has got the bomb under it? It was one of those classic situations where someone is trying to be helpful but actually making your job very difficult. I'm always aware that not every device I come across is going to be a pressure-plate, so you need to keep your wits about you. I'm not so nervous when you come across a new type of bomb. The way I look at it is, that's another one ticked off the list. There are a lot of different devices out there, so you want to find at least one of each fairly early on. That gives you the confidence to know that you are going to be able to deal with anything you might come up against – or at least that's what you tell yourself.'

But in bomb disposal there is never a 100 per cent guarantee of success or survival. Luck always has a part to play. Staff Sergeant Olaf Schmid, who now has almost legendary status in the EOD world, was a close friend of Woody's. Both were men at the very top of the profession.

'Oz was a one-off,' says Woody. 'I'd known him since he was an ammunition technician when he first joined the trade. He was a great laugh and a bit of an animal with a drink inside of him. He would come up and lick your face. He was a genuine soldier, he loved it, every minute.'

Like many soldiers who knew Oz Schmid, Woody was devastated when he learned of his death. The news was broken to him while he was driving from his home in Stoke to Didcot. 'I was in the car and I got this call. It was something like, "Got some bad news for you,

Woody. Oz is dead." I was utterly stunned. I just couldn't believe it. I got the news just before I hit this big roundabout and I kept going round and round it, thinking, this can't be happening. I still can't really believe that's he's gone. I've been so busy since he was killed that I've hardly had time to take in what's happened and then every now and then his death hits home and you realize he's gone for ever.

'Oz was a good ATO, he was an assault IED operator, the same as me, so that's an extra string to your bow, and there are not many that have got it. He had passed his High Threat and he had done quite a few IEDs and he loved Sangin, and no one wants to go to Sangin. It's horrible and he loved it, which tells you a lot about the sort of bloke he was.

'Oz's death was the start of a really bad period for us all. First there was Gaz O'Donnell in 2008, then Dan Read, and that was bad enough. Then Oz was killed and two weeks later I was on a course and I got a text saying that Corporal Loren Marlton-Thomas had been killed and WO2 Ken Bellringer had been badly injured and his legs were broken. Then, a few hours later, I got another text, which said that Ken had lost both legs below the knee, then another which said they had gone right at the top. And back in the UK you're thinking, what the fuck is going on out there?'

On New Year's Eve Sapper Dave Watson, a high-risk searcher, was killed during a patrol close to Route 611 in the area of PB Blenheim, just south of FOB Inkerman. The blast blew off both his legs and an arm and he later died of his wounds. On 11 January Captain Dan Read was killed and on 8 February WO2 Dave Markland was blown up and killed in one of the shaping operations prior to Operation Moshtarak. A week after Dave Markland was killed, Sapper Guy Mellors was blown up during a clearance patrol, again on Route 611, near PB Ezaray, a few hundred metres from the point where Dave Watson had been killed.

I'd met Dave Watson a few months earlier in November 2009, while I was on an earlier embed with the Grenadier Guards battle-group. I accompanied him on a routine change-over of troops south of Nad-e'Ali district centre. The journey to the base was only about 6 km but it took the Mastiff convoy almost six hours. Every few hundred metres the vehicles would stop and the soldiers would begin another search. Many of the troops going into the base were very inexperienced and, frankly, scared. I could see that Dave's calm confidence was a great boon to the young soldiers who were also helping in the search for bombs. He was a friendly and warm soldier who impressed me enormously. The spate of deaths shattered morale in the EOD world. It wasn't just the bomb hunters who were struggling with the losses, but also their families, wives, mothers, fathers, husbands, sons and daughters. More bomb hunters had now been killed in just a few weeks than in the past thirty years.

Woody tells me, 'All those guys killed and injured in such a short space of time – there had been nothing like that since the 1970s in Ulster. I knew all the ATOs, some I knew very well and they were good operators, just as good as me, and you can't help but think if it can happen to them then it can happen to me. The thing is, in Afghan you don't have to do anything wrong to get yourself killed – you can't say, "His death was caused by a mistake." You can be doing everything correctly and be killed – it's just the way it is in Afghan.'

Every time an ATO or any soldier is killed by an IED an investigation is conducted to try to establish the sequence of events that led to the death. But there are often significant problems in trying to piece together that sequence of events and work out what the bomb was composed of.

'There are many explanations as to what happened to Oz,' Woody tells me. 'It could have been another command wire that was missed, it could have had a booby-trap. You never really know because that bit of the bomb has functioned as intended and when that goes off all the components get destroyed – there's nothing left.

'We know that when Oz arrived there were three main charges in the area. He dealt with one, he was dealing with another one when he got killed, and there was another one remaining which his No. 2 dealt with to make the area safe so that his body could be extracted.

Other than that there are just a few explanations as to what happened. An investigation is conducted and you try and establish first of all whether all the proper procedures were followed. Did they do all the things they were supposed to do, such as a proper isolation? But it's very rare that you can nail it down to one specific event. I know Oz had been quite ill before he died. He had D and V for at least a week, ten days before he was killed. D and V is pretty grim and that would have taken its toll. All of the guys killed died around the four-month point. That might have just been a coincidence but it may be that they had become exhausted by the workload. We used to do four-month tours at one time. Four months in Iraq and four months in Afghanistan. I think the Army saw it as a way of getting eight months on operations out of us. Now that Iraq is over we are doing six-month tours in Afghan and that is a long time, very long – like I said before, there are only so many times you can roll the dice before you get a double six. Oz had dealt with a fair few bombs, sixty-four in four months, and he did twenty-three in one day and was killed. But Badger [Staff Sergeant Karl Ley] did 139 in six months and went home. So how do you explain that? It's just luck, I suppose – good luck if you make it, bad luck if you don't.'

I didn't come across a single ATO who complained about his workload, even though they are some of the most hard-pressed troops in Helmand. But it was painfully clear that vastly more bomb hunters were needed in Afghanistan. The shortage has been caused, in part, by a recruiting cap a few years ago – a purge which was imposed upon the Royal Logistic Corps by the bean counters in the Ministry of Defence.

The search for additional resources within the EOD world has been dubbed by some as the 'Oz Schmid effect'. Following Oz's death the press became mesmerized by the stoicism and fortitude of his wife, Christina, and suddenly bomb hunters were big news. For the first time it became clear to the public that ATOs were being pushed well beyond the limit of what could ever reasonably be expected of them. Ripples of panic ran through the government and the

Ministry of Defence, who were worried that they would be seen as doing too little to counter a threat which was killing and injuring soldiers every day, and so the order went out that more ATOs needed to be trained. What the politicians failed to grasp, however, was that the job of an AT or an ATO is a trade. ATs are trained to store, handle and work with all types of explosive and ammunition – and only part of that trade is IED disposal. It can take up to seven years for a soldier of non-commissioned rank to become fully qualified in IED disposal. In an attempt to boost numbers, the Defence EOD Operators' course was created.

Explosive ordnance disposal is conducted by the Royal Engineers, the Royal Navy and the RAF, as well as the Royal Logistic Corps. The EOD groups within these units also carry out IED disposal, but only those who have completed the High Threat IED course are qualified to serve in Afghanistan, and the vast majority of these are members of the RLC.

Soldiers can train to become an Ammunition Technician (AT) from the age of 18. Officers at the rank of second lieutenant can also train to become an Ammunition Technical Officer (ATO). After five to six years' service ATOs and their equivalents in the other parts of the armed services, and lieutenants or junior captains who have around seventeen months' service, will be considered for the sixteen-week Defence EOD Operators' course at the Felix Centre, which is housed in the Defence Explosive Ordnance Disposal, Munitions and Search School at Kineton in Warwickshire. The course is also now open to any senior non-commissioned officer or junior officer from any other part of the armed forces who is shown to have the aptitude for bomb disposal.

Those who pass the course, around 50 per cent, will then be qualified for conventional munitions disposal, which can range from RPG warheads to Second World War grenades. They will also be qualified to deal with IEDs, but only in the UK and areas such as Cyprus, Gibraltar and the Falkland Islands. After a year's further training and experience of commanding an EOD team, some of the officers and

NCOs who demonstrate the right aptitude will be offered the opportunity to join the seven-week Advanced EOD Operators' course at Kineton, where they will learn how to dispose of IEDs primarily found in Helmand. Around 17 per cent of trainees pass the advanced course first time, while the second-time pass rate is around 40 per cent.

At the moment only those who have passed the advanced course can deploy to Helmand and undertake IED disposal, but that could change. There is a school of thought in the EOD world that believes that servicemen who have passed the sixteen-week Defence EOD Operators' course could also be deployed to Helmand but would be restricted to dealing with specific devices such as disposing of RPG warheads or IED which can be neutralized remotely using robots. It then follows that the more advanced operators would be available for the more dangerous IED-disposal missions.

Within the EOD world such a departure is proving controversial. Many ATOs believe that the gold standard for IED disposal should be the Advanced EOD Operators' course and that any change to that practice is exposing soldiers and the newly trained Defence EOD operators to very real risk. The other school of thought argues that there is a role in Helmand for those who have passed only the Defence EOD course. The US Paladin teams and the rest of the NATO IED disposal units are trained to the standard reached by Defence EOD operators, yet deploy to Helmand as IED operators. So, if that standard is good enough for the US and the rest of NATO, then why should it not be good enough for Britain? By setting the bar at a lower level than the British, US Marines are almost able to embed an IED operator with every platoon of thirty men. The British Army can only achieve embedding of a single ATO at battlegroup level – 1,500 men.

The question for the country's defence chiefs is how much risk they are prepared to take. There is no doubt that, from the MoD's position, the strategic harm which comes from the death of an ATO is far more damaging than the death of an infantry soldier. Over 300

British soldiers have been killed in Helmand and very few people in the country could name them all. Five ATOs have been killed and their names have a much higher profile. Interestingly, such a distinction does not exist within the US Marines, where the death of an IED operator is treated with no greater or lesser importance than that of a Marine.

Financial incentives are also being offered to ATOs who have completed one tour in Afghanistan but agree to a further four years' service, which could include another tour in Helmand. Those who sign up will be paid an extra £50,000 over four years in addition to the extra £15 a day ATOs receive as part of their skills pay.

But increasing numbers of ATOs is not the sole answer to the problem of dealing with IEDs. Bomb-hunting teams always deploy as an eleven-man unit composed of the IED disposal team and the search team. One cannot deploy without the other. Producing additional ATOs is only half the battle. Additional high-threat searchers will also need to be trained, an issue which hasn't yet been resolved.

'There is only one ATO in the Nad-e'Ali battlegroup – me,' Woody says with more than a hint of exasperation. 'This place is absolutely saturated with IEDs and yet there is only one ATO – one IED disposal team, one search team. That means you come in off one job and you immediately go out on another. There are always more jobs than there are ATOs. Every battlegroup has a stack of devices for us to deal with. You are constantly in demand – you are doing planning for the ops, going to O-groups [Orders groups] and I have still got four reports to write. I will go out tomorrow and I'll have to write up some more reports. It's not just doing the bomb, it's all the other stuff that goes with it, the administration, the planning.

'Six months is a long time but as long as you are managed correctly it's about achievable. But it's tough – there are no easy tours in Helmand – and I think some ATOs might struggle, especially if your team has suffered casualties. You need to trust the people above you, and you need to believe that the headquarters will not put you in somewhere if you are too exhausted. Trouble is, we're always knackered – it's part of the job. We always say an ATO never has trouble sleeping but there can come a point when you are so knackered that you can become a danger to yourself and that's when you need people above you to step in and say, "We're pulling you out for a rest." But then that will put greater pressure on other ATOs. We will always be rotated around the various operational areas so that you don't get stale – and also because they all have different operational tempos.

'Sangin is very busy, it's horrible. You wouldn't last six months in Sangin – you would either be a nervous wreck or be dead. I will go to Sangin at some stage. If I'm honest, I'd rather not, but you have to take it as it comes. The devices being laid in Sangin are not really any different to anywhere else, there are just more of them and the insurgents based there will target ATOs. The Taliban also have a very effective dicking screen. You will be watched every time you are on a job. For example, you always pull a device out of the ground using a hook and line and not by hand. If you pulled a bomb out of the ground by hand in Nad-e'Ali you might get away with it, but not in Sangin. Try that in Sangin and you will die. You might get away with it once but the Taliban will be watching and it will be, "OK. So he pulls it out by hand. OK, we'll use that." And next time you did it – and I mean the next time – it would be bang, you're dead. They will target routine, they will target obvious routes, they will target our casevac procedures. They know there are only so many places where you can put an HLS if you take a casualty, so they will target that too.

'Sangin is different. The ground is different – on one side you have a sniper threat and on the other you have lots of hamlets and alleyways, so it's really easy to channel soldiers into killing zones. And I think the Taliban are different too. They come in from Pakistan. They will have a play, try new ideas, new tactics. They all want to prove themselves, the foot soldiers and commanders, so you get taken on nearly all the time. Once they've proved their worth in Sangin, they get sent elsewhere in Helmand – that's the current theory anyway.

'There are also a lot of checkpoints for troops to man, so you don't have the depth in numbers you might have in other areas and that can also be exploited by the Taliban, giving them greater freedom of movement. So a lot of the time, for the soldiers and the ATOs, Sangin is a real struggle. But it's not the only area which is dangerous for ATOs. We've had guys killed and injured in every area – it wasn't only Oz who died in Sangin. Gaz O'Donnell died in Musa Qala, Dan Shepherd was killed in Nad-e'Ali, Ken Bellringer lost his legs in Gereshk, and Dan Read was blown up in Musa Qala. So yes, Sangin is dangerous, but so is everywhere in Helmand. You've always got to try and stay one step ahead – it's cat and mouse. The Taliban aren't stupid. They will take you on if they think they can get away with it. I've been out on jobs where the support from ground troops has been brilliant. When we cleared 6 km of Route Dorset, which is on the eastern edge of Nad-e'Ali, we had four Vikings, six Scimitars and a Danish tank. The isolation was split into two: we had twenty blokes on each side of the road. We had fast air up as well. If I was the Taliban I would be thinking, do I want to take these guys on? Answer: no. But then I've been on similar jobs and all we've had is a Mastiff and half a dozen soldiers because that is all that can be spared. And you know that the Taliban will think, let's have a go. They will use multiple IEDs in ambushes, they will target casevac routes, and if your drills are bad you will be targeted too.

'The Taliban know how we react when we have a contact – they have seen it. A guy gets blown up and loses both legs – there's a lot of panic and shouting, the adrenalin is pumping, he's close to death, and at the forefront of everyone's mind is getting him out of the killing zone and back to the HLS. The Taliban know this, so they target the route to the HLS. Now, if in the midst of all this panic, blood, gore and mayhem you charge off to the HLS you will become a casualty too. It's happened here many times. Guys have died rescuing their mates because they forgot the basic drills. Rather than slowing everything down and making sure they carefully clear the route to the HLS, the fog of panic descends and then bang, you've now got one double amputee, another couple of severely injured guys, and possibly some KIAs – and that's a big mess. We've to constantly make sure that we play by our rules and not the Taliban's, we fight on our terms, not the Taliban's. But that's one of those things which is far easier to say than do.'

Woody falls silent and stares into the empty paper cup he has cupped between his hands. Just as I'm about to ask if everything is OK, he lifts his head and says, 'I've got a bit of a confession to make.' There is a slight curl at the ends of his top lip and I intuitively realize that he is about to explain that something almost went wrong on an operation a few days ago. I remember Woody having a serious conversation with the WIS and Kev, the RESA, after he returned from the compound for the last time. Shortly after their conversation finished, I asked Woody if everything was OK. 'I'll tell you later,' was all he said.

'I was almost killed the other day,' he says without the slightest hint of either bravado or concern, 'and I've been going over in my mind whether I could or should have done anything differently and the bottom line is, I couldn't – I was just lucky.'

Woody is referring to the operation a few days earlier when he had to climb over the wall of a compound which had at one time been a Taliban firing point and had since been booby-trapped with a pressure-plate IED. The compound had become very overgrown with brambles and weeds, which meant that Woody was forced to hack his way through to the doorway where the bomb had been buried.

As he approached the doorway he could see a wire protruding from the compound's earth floor. He immediately knew it was linked to the power pack. 'When you are faced with that sort of situation, you make a mental assessment of where you think the various components are located. You can do a bit of searching with the Vallon. That will give you a general idea of where the device is located but you can't narrow the location down in the way that you can with the hand-held metal detector. So I set about working and I placed the IED weapon on the ground near the battery, I was happy with that, and I started uncovering the rest of the device. What I hadn't realized at the time was that the pressure plate was directly beneath the weapon. The problem was – and this is always the problem you face as an ATO – the device was very poorly laid out. You try not to have any preconceived ideas of how a bomb might be set up but you have to go in with some sort of basic plan and the acceptance that the bomb is designed to kill people. Whoever buried it didn't want it to be found – or at least that is the premise you work on. I had picked up quite a strong metal signature in the doorway, so that's where I assumed the pressure plate would be. But it wasn't. It was right beneath where I was working. I didn't realize that until I returned to the compound after I had extracted everything. When I returned to the compound with the WIS he asked where and how the device was laid out so he could write his report. I said, "The explosive was there, the pressure plate there, and the power pack there." And that's when the penny dropped and I realized that I had placed the weapon on top of the pressure plate. The pressure plate was low metal content. It was effectively made of cardboard – there was almost no metal signature and it had two thin wires running along the inside. It was the thinnest wire I'd ever seen on a pressure plate. The device was very cleverly made but was really poorly placed, which suggests that the person who made the bomb was not the person who laid it out – same tactics as the IRA. The bomb maker is the more valuable asset, so why risk him?

'Looking back, I could have caused the device to function and if it had blown up I would have been killed – no doubt about that.'

Woody laughs as he makes this last point but I also sense concern. He knows, as I know, that he did everything by the book, he followed all the rules, all the procedures, and used all the experience he'd built in Helmand to find and defuse the bomb. But he still came close, too close, to being killed.

Again smiling, he adds, 'It didn't play on my mind at the time, but I have thought about it a bit since coming back. It's just one of those things really, and I suppose I got a bit lucky. Maybe that's another life I've lost.'

While life for bomb hunters in Helmand is clearly dangerous and demanding, Woody, like most ATOs, believes that it is the wives, families and girlfriends back home in the UK who really suffer. For many of the wives the pressure and worry are sometimes too much to bear.

'There is a saying in the Explosive Ordnance Disposal world that EOD actually stands for "every one's divorced".' Woody laughs as he says this, but he's also being serious. After the special forces, whose members spend months away from home or on courses sharpening their killing skills, bomb-disposal operators have the highest divorce rate in the Army.

'We all know guys whose marriage has gone tits up because they put the job first. I don't want that to happen to me. I want to have a family life. The missus wants me to leave. I could join the police force – it's better money and I wouldn't have to come back to Afghan. I would go home every night, and that's very tempting. Guys are getting killed and injured every day by the bombs I'm defusing. It's not me who is feeling the pressure, it's the wife. She's the one whose heart stops when there's a knock on the door or the phone rings. None of us thinks about the dangers but we all know they're there, niggling away at the back of your mind, and I suppose now that I've got children you start to question what you're doing. I've got twins and I want to see them grow up – I don't want to miss too much of their childhood.'

It is the separation from their families which most soldiers seem to struggle with, especially at the beginning of a six-month tour. No married soldier, no matter how experienced, gets used to saying goodbye. Even the toughest, most battle-experienced sergeant major goes watery-eyed when talk turns to families back home, and Woody is no different.

He continues, 'There are a few of them who are mad for it [bomb disposal in Afghanistan] but most ATOs just want to get the tour done. I've never met an ATO yet who has finished his tour and wants to come back – it's the stresses and dangers that eventually get to you, they get to everyone, especially when guys are getting killed and injured. If you survive the tour out here as an ATO you know you've been lucky – good at the job, yes, but lucky too. On Op Herrick 10 there wasn't one team that hadn't been blown up. I've been blown up, Dan Perkins [another ATO] has been blown up, Captain Rob Swan was pinned down by snipers, Badger was under fire, Harry French's team had two guys taken out by a grenade lobbed over a wall. The thing is, none of us were doing anything wrong. That's just the way it goes out here.'

The soaring rates of amputees returning from Helmand because of the surge in the Taliban's use of IEDs has inevitably led to conversations among the bomb-hunting fraternity about whether life is worth living after surviving a double or triple amputation.

Woody gives me his view on the subject. 'None of us really ever discusses how we would feel until you hear that someone has been hurt and has lost both legs and sometimes both legs and an arm. And then someone will say, "I wouldn't want to live like that." The thing all the soldiers are scared about is losing their balls – you hear people say, "As long as I don't lose my balls, I could cope, but if I lose my legs and my balls I'd rather be dead." And I've thought about that too. I've asked myself the question: would I want to live with no legs and no balls? We all know that you're going to have a lifetime of struggle. But I always say, well, at least I would be able to cuddle my children – they can't take that away and that's worth living for because that's the best feeling in the world. Anyway it's pretty rare for ATOs to lose our legs because we are normally right over the device, so if an IED detonates it's usually all over. Ken [WO2 Bellringer] was standing up when he stepped on a pressure plate, so he's fortunate because he survived even though he had terrible injuries, but he will be able to cuddle his children again.'

Woody falls silent again, lost in thought, perhaps about his twin daughters back home. *The Hurt Locker* has now finished and the soldiers are leaving, some to get some sleep, others for sentry duty on the front gate.

'Right,' Woody says, slapping his hands on the table. 'Time for bed, I think. We've got another job on tomorrow. A route clearance – probably several bombs on the road. Should be interesting. Can sometimes get a bit cheeky out there. You up for it?' he asks with a smile.

'Yep, I'm up for it,' I reply.

Woody finishes his tea and adds, 'We've got a new search team coming in tomorrow, so that should be interesting. Now I'm going to finish my reports and get my head down.'

Chapter 7: **Murder at Blue 25**

'It was like being hit with a sledgehammer. It just didn't seem real. One second everything was normal, the next there was chaos and death – it was that quick.'
Lance Sergeant Peter Baily, Signaller, Grenadier Guards

I awake to the news that a soldier who was badly injured in February by an IED in Musa Qala has died the previous evening, 15 March 2010, at Selly Oak Hospital in Birmingham. Captain Martin Driver of 1st Battalion Royal Anglian Regiment was blown up while on patrol and suffered a double amputation of his legs as well as serious injuries to other parts of his body. Shortly after he was injured he was evacuated back to the UK and survived for a further three weeks before succumbing to his injuries. It must have been a terrible ordeal for his family but it is a tragedy which has been played out hundreds of times over the past four years.

One more life lost, one more family shattered. At the back of my mind I'm thinking, what's the point? Captain Driver, like all of those who have died before him, will no doubt be called a hero and I'm sure he was – anyone who spends six months fighting the Taliban is a hero as far as I am concerned – but who will remember him or his family's suffering in five years' time? Captain Driver's loss is another reminder that death in Afghanistan is never far away. Since I arrived two weeks ago, five soldiers have been killed

and at least a dozen more have been injured, the majority by
IEDs.

By 7.30 a.m. I'm back in FOB Shawqat's vehicle park, waiting to
leave on the next IED mission. Warrior drivers are gunning their
engines in preparation for this latest mission and the air is thick with
the pungent smell of diesel. Woody is standing at the centre of a
small group of soldiers and I can see from the look on his face that
there is a problem. The incoming search team – callsign Brimstone
42, nickname Team Stallion – has just arrived as expected, but the
helicopter which has flown them in has also extracted the old search
team. The plan had been for the two search teams to work together
for at least a week so that the outgoing team could pass on all of their
knowledge of the local area to the incoming team. That process will
now not take place and, to make matters worse, half of Brimstone
42's kit was put on board the wrong helicopter and is sitting in
Sangin.

And so Brimstone 42 are about to go out on their very first
mission with almost no understanding of the ground or the local
Taliban tactics.

'It's not what I would say is ideal,' says Woody out of earshot of
his new team. 'It's their first job and they are going to go into it
cold. They are a good bunch of lads and some of them have been
on operations before, but Afghan is different. You don't get a
second chance here. Fuck up out here and you're going home in a
body bag.'

Brimstone 45 have been called back to Camp Bastion earlier than
expected because they are needed to man the High Readiness Force,
which is regarded as a greater priority than having them remain in
Nad-e'Ali and show their replacement team the lie of the land. If
there were more bomb-hunting teams available, commanders would
not be forced to make difficult compromises like this.

For many within the bomb-disposal world, however, shortages of
bomb hunters is nothing short of scandalous, given that it has been
obvious since 2008 that the production and deployment of IEDs

against NATO forces, especially in the south of Afghanistan, has been part of the Taliban's main effort.

In 2008 WO2 Gaz O'Donnell, then a George Medal holder (later awarded a posthumous Bar) and a veteran of both Iraq and Afghanistan, confided in me that he was amazed that there were just two IEDD teams in Helmand – back then the main war effort was in Iraq, where roadside bombs were killing British troops every week. Gaz and other members of the EOD group were staggered that senior commanders in the Ministry of Defence in London did not view Helmand as a high-threat IED environment even though the numbers of IED incidents had increased by more than threefold in two years. In 2004 there were just 304 IED incidents – an incident means a find or a detonation – in the whole of Afghanistan. In 2009 the number of IED incidents had risen to over 10,000, the vast majority of which occurred in Helmand. Gaz told me at the time, 'It suits the MOD to be able to say that Helmand isn't a high-threat area because then they can justify the numbers. Iraq is a high-threat environment, so there are a lot more IEDD teams in Basra. If they admitted that Helmand was a high-risk area too, then they would have to increase the number of ATOs here as well. The problem is that there aren't enough ATOs for both operations and we have got the short straw.'

Six weeks after Gaz vented his frustrations to me in August 2008, he was dead and became the first ATO to be killed in Helmand. The number of CIED teams and search teams has increased fivefold but there are still too few and the consequence of this is that practices such as the team handovers, which are designed to save lives and prevent injury, are abandoned.

A message comes via the operations room informing Woody that our mission has been delayed by at least an hour. A few soldiers grunt disapprovingly but most are indifferent to the news. Brimstone 45 have a whole six months ahead of them, so why complain about an hour's delay? Like the soldiers around me, I take off my body armour, drop it against the wheel of a Mastiff and use it as a makeshift seat. Rushing only to wait is part of Army life, especially in a war zone. I'm staring absent-mindedly out across the vehicle when I notice Lance Sergeant Peter Baily, one of the survivors of an incident which became known as 'Murder at Blue 25', heading towards the operations room.

The killings took place on Tuesday, 3 November 2009, a day which began as it always did for the soldiers located at the small British Army patrol base known as Blue 25. The soldiers rose from their beds in the hour before dawn, made tea, loaded their weapons, and waited for the Taliban to attack. It had been the same routine every day for the past two weeks – and the Afghan police whom the troops had been sent to 'mentor' joined them.

Led by Regimental Sergeant Major Darren 'Daz' Chant, a living legend within the Brigade of Guards, the sixteen-strong unit had been detached to Blue 25 in a last-chance bid to shore up relations between the local population and the Afghan Police. The police were so utterly hopeless that there was every chance that the local population would turn to the Taliban to uphold law and order unless urgent and drastic action was taken. The plan had worked well. The presence of the British soldiers had helped to partially restore the locals' confidence in the police, who also seemed to appreciate the effort being made by the Grenadiers. But by the middle of the afternoon five British soldiers would lie dead and another six would be injured at the hands of a policeman whom they thought of as a trusted friend. Even in a war as dirty as that being fought in Helmand, the murders were a despicable act and had the potential to undermine the delicate relationship between the British Army and the Afghan Police. As the details of the mass killings broke in the UK, many newspapers questioned the whole nature of the mission in Afghanistan, with several asking why British troops were risking their lives for a nation where individuals employed by the government could act with such treachery.

When the Grenadier Guards battlegroup arrived in Nad-e'Ali in September 2009, Lieutenant Colonel Roly Walker, the battlegroup commander, knew that if he was to fulfil his orders to secure Nad-e'Ali and separate and secure the population from the insurgents he would have to work hand in glove with the Afghan security forces, namely the police and the military.

'The three legs of the stool were the International Security and Assistance Force [ISAF], the Afghan Army and the Afghan Police,' he explained over a coffee one morning in March 2009 while I was embedded with his battlegroup in Nad-e'Ali. 'We knew that we would have to work with them all if we were to be successful in Nad-e'Ali and if we wanted to make real progress. What I didn't know when we arrived was that one of the legs of the stool, the police, was rotten, rotten to the core.'

Up until late 2009 the Afghan National Police had not received anything like the same levels of strategic investment afforded to the Afghan National Army and were widely regarded by those British military commanders unfortunate enough to work with them as at best a bad joke and at worst a liability which threatened to undermine the Army's efforts to win hearts and minds. In Helmand, as in much of Afghanistan, the police were an utter shambles. Many of the officers were addicted to opium and would routinely sell their weapons and ammunition – even to the Taliban – in order to fund their habit. In one case a police unit sold all its supplies of bullets and rockets to insurgents. A few days later the same group of insurgents attacked the police and several officers were killed.

The police were ill-disciplined, untrained, poorly led, and would openly 'tax' or steal from the local population, often because they had not been paid by their commanders. Corruption within various units was rife, and young teenage policemen risked being sexually assaulted or raped by senior commanders. While ISAF had concentrated its efforts on building up the Afghan Army, the police had been left to wither on the vine, and for that a price was being paid.

While relations between the British Army and the Afghan soldiers were based on mutual respect, most British soldiers regarded the country's police as being worse than useless. But there was some sympathy for the police's predicament. Whereas the Afghan soldiers were often recruited from areas outside of Helmand and lived in barracks or secure camps, the police lived a dangerous life among the people they were supposedly protecting and were often easy targets for the insurgents.

Shortly after the first elements of the Grenadier Guards battle-group arrived in September 2009, reports began to emerge of some of the dangerous everyday antics involving the Afghan police, which often left the locals in a state of abject terror. Village elders began to complain about the goings-on in one police checkpoint where almost every day the force would be high on drugs and often fire wildly down a road used by civilians.

British soldiers working close to or alongside Afghan police offic-ers had to always be prepared to factor in the unexpected when plan-ning operations, as Lieutenant Mike Dobbin, of Queen's Company, Ist Battalion Grenadier Guards, explained. An incident which took place on 7 October 2009 typified the problems the British soldiers faced when dealing with the Afghan police. 'During a routine patrol in Basharan area, my platoon, which at that time was partnered with the Afghan police, found an IED on a major route in the area,' he explained while giving a summary of his experiences of working with the Afghan police. 'We were unable to destroy the device because there was no bomb-disposal team with us, so we marked the area with green spray paint to bring it to the attention of locals and to stop anyone driving or walking over it. All of this was much to the frustration of the police, who simply wanted to tear it out of the ground and blow it up.

'It was clear to us that the insurgents, knowing we had discovered the device, were likely to come back, take it out and replace it in another area with the aim of killing British or Afghan troops. We therefore planned with the police to return that night and ambush them while they did this. At around 9 p.m. I led a twelve-man team up to a cemetery in the area, which was around 500 metres away from the IED's location. Overwatching the cemetery was a police checkpoint with good arcs of observation across the open ground.

The Afghan police knew that we were in the area and that an ambush was being planned. As the patrol pushed on through the cemetery, approximately 300 metres from a checkpoint, the police opened fire, pinning us down with a heavy weight of rocket and machine-gun fire. Eventually, through a series of mobile telephone calls and radio messages, the police became aware that we were actually friendly forces and they stopped their firing, but it was clear that our position had been given away. There was a clear lack of understanding between ISAF and our Afghan partners. We later found that the police unit in the checkpoint were lazy, untrained and highly addicted to opium.'

Another example of the police's ill-discipline came to light one lunchtime at the police training college in Lashkar Gah, Helmand's provincial capital. The college was divided into two, a junior term and a senior term, the latter of which were afforded special privileges, such as being first in the queue for meals. During one lunchtime, scuffles broke out between the two sets of students after the junior term managed to get into the lunch queue first. A British soldier who was overseeing the process intervened and tried to restore order, only to have both sets of students turn on him. Those among the crowd who had weapons cocked them and threatened to shoot the young corporal. Order was restored only when the soldier grabbed a rifle from one of the trainees and with a single swift blow managed to knock him out.

One evening early in the tour, the commander of Queen's Company received a message disclosing that a police checkpoint in one of the local communities was perilously close to falling to the insurgents. Two police outposts, one on each side of it, had apparently fallen earlier that day and five Afghan police officers had already been killed at this checkpoint, and during the recovery of the injured soldiers the police's casualty evacuation vehicle had been destroyed by an IED.

Lieutenant Dobbin explained, 'My platoon crashed out in three vehicles at about 1800 hours with orders to hold the checkpoint until dawn. We met some police at a nearby checkpoint and they led us to a point where we took over in the more armoured vehicles due to the IED threat. We rolled into the village at about 2200, driving in on black light – that is, using night-vision rather than white headlights. It's great for covert insertions but can make driving very tricky. We came to a crossroads at the centre of the village and had to turn quite a sharp corner. The first two vehicles got round with no problem, but the third must have pushed a little over to the left because as it turned the road gave way and the Mastiff slipped into an irrigation ditch. The vehicle weighs 20 tons and many roads in Helmand are not capable of bearing such a weight. Members of the Royal Electrical and Mechanical Engineers spent several hours using their incredibly powerful recovery vehicle to pull this out.'

The situation in the village was very complex. There were several police commanders, working independently rather than together, and a sizeable Taliban force which had been emboldened by a series of dramatic successes against the Afghan police.

Lieutenant Dobbin continued, 'That night we tried to understand the situation … there were three police stations on the one crossroads. The Taliban had attacked them with machine guns and rockets from seven separate firing points surrounding the crossroads. The three stations, one in the tower, one in a mosque and one in a school, each had their own problem. The tower had poor policemen, lots of weapons and limited ammo; the school had good policemen, few weapons and limited ammunition; the mosque had poor policemen, good ammo supplies, few weapons. Annoyingly, the three commanders would not speak to each other or distribute the resources.

'I split my men, five to each station, and we sat out the night with no attacks. The following day it became clear that many of these police were high on drugs and fairly ill-disciplined. Then something remarkable happened. A police commander whom I had heard of but never met walked into the village at the head of an Army patrol with a civilian, who was clearly under arrest. The police officer,

Lieutenant Daoud, caught an insurgent red-handed connecting a battery to an IED and was about to blow up the patrol, which was composed of soldiers from the Duke of Lancaster's Regiment.

'I chatted to him about what had happened and he then told me this amazing story of how, just days earlier, he had been blown up by an IED while travelling in his police ranger [a four-wheel-drive Toyota], resulting in the death of the other two officers in the vehicle. He survived with only minor injuries. A week before that he had been walking to the police station on his own when he was ambushed by eight Taliban gunmen. He took cover in a small shop on this crossroads and had the locals filling his magazines with ammunition while he kept the Taliban away. He was hugely respected by the locals because he was forceful in his zero-tolerance approach. The ISAF mentor who worked with him said he was outstanding but because of his tribe he was not the commander of the checkpoint. He was extremely blasé about being attacked and ambushed and almost killed and, as with other competent police commanders, realized that he was a wanted man by the Taliban.'

Lieutenant Dobbin, a fresh-faced 24-year-old and one of the most inexperienced but highly regarded junior officers in the battalion, also forged a close relationship with another capable Afghan police-man, Commander Israel.

'He was an extraordinary individual, very brave and very capable and highly regarded by both his men and the population, but bizarrely he seemed quite happy in the knowledge that he would not be alive for much longer. Both Israel and Daoud had the air of a European ski instructor, weathered, relaxed and totally unfazed by fairly extreme situations. Both men were relatively quiet individuals. I think Daoud was local. I know Israel was a local to the area in which he served.

'During one patrol with the Afghan Army we were being watched by the insurgents and could hear them chatting on their radios (our interpreter was listening in and translating for us). Over the radio they began to talk about the fact that they could see Israel with us and what they would do to him if they caught him – he was clearly well known to them for them to pick him out from an eighty-man patrol. When we told him what they were saying he just smiled and carried on. That was the type of character he was and I had a great deal of respect for him.'

It would be wrong to condemn the entire police force as an incompetent and corrupt organization – that was almost the whole picture but not quite. There were a few commanders of quality who often demonstrated outstanding bravery which within the British Army would have been worthy of official recognition. But it was clear that officers like Daoud and Israel were the exception rather than the rule. Within weeks of arriving in Nad-e'Ali, Colonel Walker knew that he would have to invest a great deal of time and effort in improving the local police if he was to make headway in the battle for hearts and minds.

Nad-e'Ali is a large, highly populated area of central Helmand. It covers an area of 250 sq km and has a population of around 200,000. Colonel Walker's battlegroup numbered 1,500 men, which gave him just six men for each square kilometre of ground.

It was clear almost immediately to the Grenadier Guards that Nad-e'Ali was not a hotbed of insurrection; instead the Taliban exploited local grievances between the farmers and some of the more powerful figures in the community. The Taliban offered an alternative, and possibly more secure, existence which, in some cases, managed to capture the public's imagination. The local population had relatively simple demands – they wanted to be able to farm safely by day and night and have freedom of movement within the district – and they would ultimately support whichever side could deliver.

By the time the Grenadiers arrived in September 2009, the insurgents had managed to create a series of screens and guards which kept ISAF troops away from the people the Taliban were trying to control. Colonel Walker explained to me how he set about the task of separating the local people from the Taliban and making life more secure for them. 'We had to prove to the people that the Afghan government was more effective at providing for their needs than the Taliban were. We had to make them active participants in the success of their community. Everything we did would be done by, with and through the Afghans. Each of my six company groups were tasked to protect the community of the main population centres, which we had asked the governor to identify, and then we set about creating freedom of movement between them to stimulate the return to normality.

'The second part of the plan was to work with the Afghan security forces and merge ourselves into one single entity with the single purpose of defeating the insurgents. The last object of the plan was to defeat the insurgents when we met them. One of our greatest concerns was civilian casualties. We observed and were told that the insurgents would deliberately seek us out in a fight to goad an over-reaction in order to kill civilians, so I had to ask the men to react with courageous restraint when attacked by insurgents, so as to reduce the risk of civilian casualties, and often they would have to walk away from a fight. But I did ask them to observe the enemy's vulnerabilities and their predisposition to set patterns in our area, a crime I would not tolerate among my own soldiers but which the Taliban were happy to tolerate, and thus we would try and seek to discredit the Taliban fighters in the eyes of the community they would claim to be protecting. By discrediting the Taliban you create the conditions for reconciliation and reintegration. So the rules were pretty simple: don't kill civvies and ruthlessly pursue the insurgents on our terms.'

If the strategy was to succeed, the Grenadiers would have to work with and develop the capability of the police and, most importantly, get the public to trust them. One of the areas where they began this process in earnest was in the hamlet of Shin Kalay, which is sited on one of the main transit routes into the district centre, about 2 km west of the main British base. The local police commander was corrupt and brutal and had almost single-handedly managed to turn the entire population towards the Taliban. He was replaced by the senior police commander in the district, but the police unit had failed to build a working relationship with the local population, who had started to drift towards supporting, or at least accepting the presence of, the Taliban.

Colonel Walker set about taking the Taliban's influence away from the district centre, clearing a route to the Nahr-e-Burgha canal, and building a protected community around Shin Kalay. These changes would allow the Grenadiers to build a central belt of prosperity that would then serve as a example to the rest of the district of the advantages of going along with their government.

In addition Colonel Walker decided to embed elements of his tactical headquarters within the police unit in Shin Kalay, who would act as mentors for the officers and help them win the trust and respect of the locals. The battlegroup's tactical headquarters was composed of a mixed bunch of soldiers with a variety of different skills whose role on operations was to 'fight' the battle by establishing a communications network, assist with casualty evacuation, ammunition resupply and prisoner handling, as well as providing a bodyguard for the commanding officer.

WO1 Darren Chant, as leader of the small force at Blue 25 on the outskirts of Shin Kalay, was a man who set high standards and demanded that the battalion's officers and men adhere to them. On a previous tour of Afghanistan in 2007 he carried a wounded soldier in full kit for 2 km across uneven ground, all the while chatting about drinking, fighting, and his beloved Inkerman Company. Two members of the Royal Military Police, Corporals Steven Boote and Nicholas Webster-Smith, were also part of the team. Also present was Sergeant Matthew Telford, the regimental police sergeant, who was effectively the second-in-command of the patrol base and was known as 'the daddy'. 'If you had a problem you went to see him and it would get sorted, and it worked the other way too. If he had a problem he would come and see you. He was a giant of a man,' recalled Lance Sergeant Peter Baily, 31, a veteran of twelve years' service, another member of the team. The Grenadiers, like all Guards regiments, do not have the rank of corporal. The equivalent rank in the Guards is Lance Sergeant.

Also serving with the tactical headquarters were Lance Corporals Liam Culverhouse, William 'Woody' Woodgates, and one of the battalion's Fijian soldiers, Lance Corporal Peniasi 'Nammers' Namarua. Junior members of the unit included Guardsman James Major, who had been with the battalion for just under a year and at just 18 was one of the youngest members of the unit, Guardsman Steve Loader and Guardsman Pete 'Treacle' Lyons.

When the Grenadier Guards arrived at the police compound, a former pharmacy, they were greeted by an ill-disciplined and shoddy bunch, some of whom wore police uniforms while others wore their own clothes. The compound was dirty and bullet-riddled. The police kept irregular hours, carried dirty weapons, were dishevelled, and clearly lacked respect for themselves and one another. Almost immediately Sergeant Major Chant began to stamp his authority on the situation. He explained to the commander that he was there to help and improve the police's relationship with the locals, but it was clear to everyone, including the police, that life was about to change.

Forty-year-old Daz Chant was a physically imposing man with a huge character. Those who knew him said he was a 'force of nature' who was 'cast from the original model of the Guards sergeant major'. He was ultra-fit and Para-trained, having once served with the Path-finders, a specialist reconnaissance unit of 16 Air Assault Brigade. Within the battalion he was feared and loved in equal measure. He worked hard and played hard and expected everybody else to do the same. Back in Britain his wife, Nausheen, whom he had met at the Royal Military Academy at Sandhurst when she was a civilian admin-istrator there and he was an instructor, was pregnant with their first child.

The arrival of Chant and his team was a life-changing event for the Afghan police. The 'please yourself' ethos which typified the core of the police's command structure was over. The twelve-man police unit would report for duty every day, in uniform, looking smart – no arguments. Within a week the unit had been transformed. The compound 'stood to' every morning before first light, the police saluted Sergeant Major Chant whenever they saw him, but, most remarkably of all, their relationship with the local community began to change.

'The sergeant major was in his element,' recalled Colonel Walker. 'He had the police eating out of his hand. He had turned this rag-tag bunch into a unit which was relatively well disciplined. They were turning up for work on time, in uniform, wearing the proper head dress, with clean weapons. He had managed to instil a bit of pride. He also managed to make an impact with the locals, who would come up to him and tell him their problems, calling him Mr Daz.

'After about two weeks I told Sergeant Major Chant that I was going to need him back at the headquarters, I had other things for him to be doing, but he kept saying, "Just a few more days."'

On that fateful November day at Blue 25, as the soldiers stood to at dawn they spotted some suspicious movement of civilians in a couple of empty compounds which had previously been used as Taliban firing points. They had patrolled down to the site a few days earlier and ringed the murder holes in the walls with white spray paint so that in the event of an attack they would be able to easily identify the firing positions.

The Taliban had launched a couple of attacks against the base in recent weeks and Daz Chant wanted to be ready for anything. As the dawn sun began to climb into the cloudless Helmand sky, the haunting sounds of the call to prayer echoed around the kalay. Rather than wait for the Taliban to attack, Daz decided to seize the initiative and quickly issued orders for a patrol down to the abandoned compounds. The patrol was fully 'kitted up' and prepared for anything the Taliban might throw at them. But an extensive search of the compounds found nothing. Whoever had been there had gone. With the excitement over, the soldiers withdrew back to the base and began their usual morning routine. The British soldiers washed and shaved and had their breakfast of Army rations and hot, sweet tea, followed by a first cigarette of the day for those who smoked.

After breakfast Lance Sergeant Baily and Sergeant Telford recced a set of emergency helicopter landing sites close to the base which could be used if a casualty evacuation proved necessary. The location of these sites would be changed every few days just in case they were identified by the Taliban and booby-trapped with IEDs.

At around 9 a.m. Daz Chant and his men went out again to picket, or guard, the main route to allow a British Immediate Replenishment Group, a supply convoy of armoured vehicles, to safely pass through Shin Kalay. But on this occasion the police refused to go on patrol with the soldiers. Such acts of petulance were nothing new. Afghan soldiers and police officers alike would often refuse to go out on patrol with the British soldiers, usually claiming they were too tired. Route clearances are long and boring but always potentially dangerous. A route must be cleared of IEDs before a convoy can pass through, and it was little surprise that the police had no interest in joining the soldiers. The Grenadiers used to call the practice of guarding the route 'street lining' in reference to their ceremonial duties back in London, where they would stand at attention on either side of the road waiting for a Royal cortège to pass.

While the soldiers were picketing the route, Sergeant Telford and Lance Sergeant Baily were preparing a lesson on how to use trip flares. The device uses the light of the flare to illuminate an area of tactically important ground, such as a track or a stream crossing. The flare ignites when a wire 'guarding' an area of ground is 'tripped'.

Daz was keen for the soldiers to receive some sort of military training every day to ensure boredom wouldn't set in and to keep the soldiers sharp. The lessons was planned to take place at around 3 p.m., when the soldiers had finished lunch and completed some general duties. Just before the patrol returned, Lance Sergeant Baily, the tactical headquarters signaller, who was responsible for all communications, had noticed that one of his radio antennae was broken. The only way of establishing communication with the main base was to move the radio set onto the roof and hope for a better signal.

The relationship between the soldiers and the police had been pretty good. But there was one individual, named Gulbuddin, whose behaviour and attitude had started to irritate some of the soldiers, especially Lance Corporal Culverhouse. Gulbuddin was likeable enough but had the annoying habit of grabbing some of the soldiers' backsides, which on two occasions had almost led to a fight. His behaviour forced Sergeant Major Chant to have words with the police commander. On one occasion the Afghan grabbed Culverhouse from behind and tried to force him to the ground. The lance corporal reacted angrily and a scuffle broke out which only came to an end when Sergeant Telford stepped in.

After lunch Lance Sergeant Baily, who by now had established a radio link with the battalion headquarters, was joined on the roof by Lyons and the two RMP corporals, Steven Boote and Nicholas Webster-Smith, and the four of them shared a welfare box of goodies such as cheese and onion crisps, biscuits and boiled sweets sent to the troops by members of the Women's Institute. It was a sunny, late autumn day and for a few moments the soldiers forgot about the war, the constant fear of death and the Taliban as they relaxed together. The talk was of home leave, wives, girlfriends and the English football premiership.

Baily stayed up on the roof, leaning against a wall reading a well-thumbed paperback while keeping an ear open on the radio. Down in the small courtyard below the soldiers began to assemble for the lesson, sitting on a small wall which had become the communal gathering place. In one of the buildings where the troops slept, Lance Corporal Culverhouse and some of the other soldiers were having a competition to see who could catch the most mice. Then, without warning, the killing began.

A volley of machine-gun fire split the still afternoon air. Another longer burst followed, then another and another. The deafening sound seemed to fill the compound and could even be heard at FOB Shawqat, nearly 2 km to the east.

Daz Chant was the first to die. It is thought that he was less than 2 ft away from Gulbuddin, who moments earlier had been on guard duty, when the Afghan fired the first volley. The burst struck Chant in his unprotected flank. Assuming they were secure within the confines of the compound and among comrades, none of the soldiers was wearing body armour. Sergeant Telford, 37, died next, killed almost instantaneously by the same burst of fire from Gulbuddin. Steve Boote, 22, was shot through the head in a second burst of fire and also died. Young Jimmy Major, 18, had also been hit several times and was close to death, as was 24-year-old Nicholas Webster-Smith.

Gulbuddin fired burst after burst into the bodies of the dead and the wounded before moving into the troops' sleeping quarters. The soldiers instinctively ran for their weapons when he burst through the door and fired another burst from his AK-47 into the corridor. Russian-made 7.62-mm short rounds ricocheted off walls, causing even more chaos and confusion.

Lance Corporal Culverhouse was hit six times in the first burst, with bullets striking him in the head, both arms and both legs. Lance Corporal Woodgates, Guardsmen Lyons, Bone and Loader and Lance Corporal Namarua were also hit by the same lethal volley. They didn't stand a chance.

'I remember getting hit in the face with something and I remember shouting and swearing,' recalled Lance Corporal Culverhouse, who lost an eye in the attack. 'I remember saying, "Fucking hell, what was that?" and I covered my face and turned around to see the back of an Afghan, one of the police officers, shooting the lads. It just all went so fast, and then when he saw me he just basically unloaded a magazine, firing at me. He only managed to hit me six times. Thank God.'

Culverhouse was lying face down in a bloody, crumpled heap on the ground when Gulbuddin walked over to him. The wounded soldier, by now in agony, squeezed his eyes shut tight, held his breath, and prayed.

'The guy came and checked that I was dead. I heard his footsteps and I could hear dust being kicked away from his feet. And then it stopped, and then it went back, so I don't know what he was doing at the time. I know he must have been checking I was dead because he stood over me. When I was playing dead, I was thinking, he's going to shoot me again, he's going to shoot me again. But he didn't.'

Up on the roof, Lance Sergeant Baily's initial thought was that either the compound was being attacked by someone very close or one of the soldiers had opened fired at an insurgent.

'I was a bit confused because when you come under fire you usually get a crack where the bullet passes close by, but I didn't get any of that. I sent an initial contact report to HQ: "Contact. Wait, out." That's when the screaming started. I heard screaming downstairs and I thought, someone's giving orders down there, but then it became apparent that it was a painful scream, a really agonizing, grating scream, the sort of thing you hear when someone's in a lot of pain. It will live with me for ever.

'The best thing that I could do was to stay on the roof until someone tells me what has happened. As the radio operator my job is to stick by the radio come what may. I'm the link to the outside world and, apart from anything else, I had left my body armour, helmet and rifle in the ops room downstairs. Then there was another burst, this time from inside the accommodation. That's when I thought, fucking hell, someone's inside and they are shooting. At first I thought the Taliban had managed to get inside the base and were attacking the soldiers. It was really confusing and you can imagine the sense of panic.

'I dived into the sangar behind me and the guy on duty was armed with a general-purpose machine gun, I saw his rifle behind him, so I grabbed hold of it and waited for the Taliban to attack us. Then one of them came up the stairs and said, "One of the ANPs has just gone mad and is shooting everybody. We need medics. People have been hit." I got straight onto the radios and began feeding the information back to the headquarters.'

The whole shooting incident lasted around thirty seconds. A thin veil of blue gun smoke hung over the central courtyard. Nine of the sixteen British soldiers were dead or injured.

By this stage Gulbuddin had already fled the compound and disappeared into the surrounding countryside, leaving in his wake a scene of bloody chaos. Neither the British troops nor their police counterparts had time to react. Many of those injured had not even realized that they had been shot by a member of the police. Shortly after Gulbuddin fled, the Taliban began shooting at Blue 25, an act which has led to the suggestion that Gulbuddin was a Taliban agent and the attack was part of a well-coordinated plan. There is no real evidence to support such a claim and the Taliban could have simply been responding to the sound of shooting inside the base.

Meanwhile, in the area where the soldiers slept, one of the beds had caught fire. A round had ignited something in one of the rooms and ammunition was starting to explode. There was a real possibility of a major fire breaking out. Fuel jerry cans were close by but further damage was prevented by one of the interpreters, who grabbed the cans and moved them to another room.

Up in the sangar, Pete Baily sent a request for medics. He also sent one of the soldiers down to the scene of the crime to find out the full extent of the casualties. 'I needed to know who had been hit and where. I needed that sort of information so that I could get the ball rolling. At this stage I still didn't know that we had fatalities.'

When the soldiers returned to Baily, they broke the news that Sergeant Major Chant was dead. 'I was in a different world at that time,' Baily recalled. 'It was like being hit with a sledgehammer. It just didn't seem real. One second everything was normal, the next there was chaos and death – it was that quick. I was reeling. Nothing made sense. The thought going through your mind was, this isn't real, it can't be happening. I thought, now I'm in charge, and I was terrified. My initial instinct was to man that radio and get any information I could back to the headquarters – that was my job. At one point it was like a training session where you are suddenly hit with all of these different scenarios to see how you would react. It just felt like that, it was unreal.'

Daz Chant and Sergeant Telford had been killed instantly. Guardsman Major hung on for a little while longer. He had been hit in the torso but a bullet had passed through his head. His friend, Guardsman Alexander Bone, had tried to keep him alive but his wounds were simply too grave. Corporal Boote had also been shot through the head and had died instantly. Despite sustaining severe injuries, Corporal Webster-Smith made it onto the helicopter, but died later.

Lance Corporal 'Woody' Woodgates was the most seriously injured. One bullet had hit him in the leg and two more had hit him in the lower back and exited his body through the stomach. 'He was carried upstairs and placed in the sangar,' Lance Sergeant Baily explained. 'The whole situation was still really confused and the rooftop was the safest place to be. The gate was open, the police had gone, we had mass casualties and there was always the chance of a follow-up attack. The only thing going through my head was: get the guys to cover their arcs [of fire], look after the wounded, and pretty much wait for the cavalry to arrive. Woody was in a really bad way and at one stage I didn't think he was going to make it. He was in a lot of pain and all the medical kits were downstairs. He was screaming for water and morphine and was drifting in and out of consciousness. I put Woody in the sangar on his own because he was the most seriously wounded and I had one guy looking after him. I kept talking to him, encouraging him to hold on, telling him he was going to be OK. At one point he stopped talking. I had thought he was gone, dead. I was shouting out his name and then I went to have a look in the sangar. There was blood everywhere but he was still alive.

'At that stage I wasn't really sure how many dead and injured there were. Liam was downstairs, he was too badly wounded to be moved, and one of the terps [interpreters] stayed with him. I was really scared at the time and I just grabbed hold of that radio like it was a

lifeboat and started passing over all the information. I sent the
message to the headquarters that Sergeant Major Chant was dead.
He had his own callsign, which was "Mongoose 99 Charlie". I sent
the message "Mongoose 99 Charlie is down", which meant that the
sergeant major was dead, then I sent "Mongoose 96 is down", which
was Sergeant Telford. I was just in automatic mode. I knew that the
HQ would want to know as much as possible; they needed to know
who was killed and injured and it was down to me to pass on as
much info as possible.

   'The radio operator at the other end was fantastic, he was very
calm and simply said, "Yep, Roger." He didn't panic at all. Every time
I sent over details of the dead and injured I just got a "Roger" – and
that's what I needed. God knows what they thought was happening
in the ops room, it must have been mayhem. I can't remember a lot
of what I said or what I did. The adrenalin was pumping and things
happened so quickly, but I do remember passing over the callsigns of
the dead.'

   Back at Shawqat the news was greeted with disbelief, but immediately, like a well-oiled machine, the operations officer and his team
began organizing the casualty evacuation. An emergency air medical
evacuation request was sent to Camp Bastion informing the hospital
that there was a mass-casualty situation with at least four dead and
four T1 – the highest level – casualties with multiple bullet wounds.

   The order was simultaneously given for the soldiers from the
Operational Mentoring and Liaison Team, the OMLT, pronounced
'omlet', who formed the Quick Reaction Force (QRF), to charge
down to Blue 25 to assist with the casualty evacuation and to help in
the event of a full-scale Taliban attack.

   Lieutenant Colonel Walker was out visiting another checkpoint
when he was told that there had been a contact at Blue 25. The colonel's convoy was only 5 km away from the incident but the threat
from IEDs buried along most of the transit routes effectively meant
that it would take at least an hour to reach the stricken troops. In
November 2009, as it is today, only routes which are overwatched by

ISAF troops, the police or the Afghan Army are effectively risk-free. All others must have every inch checked by troops equipped with mine detectors. Any IEDs discovered are then 'marked and avoided' or cleared *in situ*. There was no ATO in the commanding officer's convoy – being such a rare asset, the ATO and his IED disposal team were already deployed on another operation.

Speaking in the immediate aftermath of the attack, Colonel Walker, who was clearly still shaken by the deaths of his soldiers, told me, 'We heard over the radio that there was a contact at Blue 25. It took two or three seconds to sink in and I thought, damn, that's my team. We were told that it was under attack and I felt, well, if it's under attack, I know the position, it's fortified, the boys will be in it, the sergeant major will be all over it – I'm happy. Patrol bases and checkpoints were being attacked pretty much every day so when the contact report came over it wasn't really anything to worry about – it wasn't an unusual event.

'I was almost inclined to say, "OK, fine, no matter, give me an update when it's over." Then we were told that it was serious and that there were casualties. We immediately headed off [towards Blue 25] and then it came over the radio that there were ISAF dead, which is just chilling when you hear that as a commanding officer.

'It trickled in that there were three dead and that it was a mass-casualty situation, which sounded horrific. Then we were told that there were four dead and the remainder were seriously injured and the evacuation was taking place. At that point your heart just sank. We were only 5 km away, but on these roads, with the threat of improvised explosive devices, that is around forty-five minutes to an hour away.

'So we made our way down and going through your mind is the worst – you're asking yourself, who's dead? I knew there were four dead and I knew that they had been shot from inside the base. But that was all I knew.'

The scene within the courtyard resembled a slaughterhouse – four dead soldiers lying down together, with gaping wounds caused by the effect of a high-velocity round at close range. The soldiers who witnessed the carnage were almost paralysed with shock.

Lance Sergeant Baily recalled, 'It was surreal. Something in me took a step back and let the training kick in. When the lads told me that the sergeant major and Sergeant Telford were dead something in me just said, "You're in charge now, mate," so I got on with it. So I detailed guys out in their firing positions and waited for the operational mentor and liaison team to arrive. When they got there I made sure they knew where the emergency helicopter landing site was – the helicopter was inbound at that point. I was also on the radio for the whole time. When the chopper came, we covered the arcs to make sure that the insurgents weren't about to attack the casualty evacuation. When the helicopter did arrive there was some sporadic gunfire from a tree line a few hundred metres from the base, but it was short-lived and had no effect.'

The OMLT medic arrived and immediately set about categorizing the wounded into those who would survive and those who were close to death. He also had to confirm that those who had been assumed to be dead were actually dead. Even for a trained medic the scene was shocking.

Lance Sergeant Baily described the courtyard of the compound where the killings took place as a 'scene out of a murder movie'. 'It was absolutely horrific – those memories will never leave me. There was blood everywhere and kit all over the place. The dead were just lying where they fell.'

The need now was to get the seriously injured back to Camp Bastion as quickly as possible. The living were the priority, not the dead; they would have to wait. The most seriously injured, Lance Corporal Woodgates, Lance Corporal Culverhouse and Corporal Webster-Smith, who was by this stage very close to death, were the first to be extracted by helicopter. The rest of the injured were taken back to FOB Shawqat in an armoured Pinzgauer vehicle, at which point it was discovered that one of the bullets had nicked an artery in Lance Corporal Namarua's leg and he had started bleeding profusely, but the blood flow was quickly stemmed by the medics who had arrived with the OMLT troops.

Lance Sergeant Baily and those not injured then began the process of clearing the rest of the rooms in the compound to make sure that there were no other gunmen hiding. 'After we cleared the rooms, I had to go through a list of all the guys we had at the base and categorize them as either dead, injured or alive. I was pretty much on autopilot at that stage. The guys who had survived uninjured were sitting around smoking. They were very quiet, I don't think anyone was speaking. One of the guys looked at me and I said, "Are you all right?" and he broke down, so I went over to him and gave him a hug. It was the only thing I could think of at the time. I then looked at the terp and he started crying too, and I gave him a hug as well. I thought to myself at that stage, I can't cry now, I've got to keep it together for these guys.'

Meanwhile Colonel Walker headed straight for his headquarters, where on arrival he was met by the senior major, Andrew James, who had known and served with Daz Chant for the past eighteen years.

Colonel Walker continued, 'I was met by the Senior Major when I arrived back at Shawqat. The look on his face told me everything and he said that the sergeant major was dead. It was a desperate blow, but by that stage I somehow had kind of expected that to be the case; no one had mentioned his name before that. And then he explained that Sergeant Telford had been killed, a very gentle man, and that one of the [Royal Military Police] corporals had been killed and that Guardsman Major had been killed.

'Jimmy Major had just joined us and was going to be 19 in a couple of days' time, and this was his first tour. Then later, some time after, I learned that the second RMP corporal had died, and your heart sinks. It was a treacherous act, it was monstrous. Gulbuddin was a man the sergeant major had helped train and they were killed then, when they were unarmed and off their guard. So you take a pause, you take a breath, and realize you have got to take control of the situation and deal with the living.'

Colonel Walker went down to the regimental aid post and visited the casualties, during which time the survivors began to arrive back at the main base. The injured and some of the survivors were in a state of shock; others became very emotional as the enormity of what had just happened began to sink in.

The colonel, who was originally commissioned into the Irish Guards, had come to rely heavily upon Sergeant Major Chant, whom he described as 'my conscience, my right-hand man'. He went on, 'From the first day that I took over command of the battalion through to the day the sergeant major died I would consult him on every significant decision concerning soldiers or the regiment.

'The tragedy is that as I was going through the formalities of writing up notes on the incident my instinct was to turn to the sergeant major and say, "Right, what do we do about this?" But obviously he's not there and that's when you realize you are on your own at that point.

'I missed him very, very quickly and I still do, but for the battle-group he was a really big personality and this will come out in the telling as people remember him. He has left us a great legacy; every word he said will be remembered. Yes, he was a living legend, but my God now he is preserved.'

Back in the safety of the camp the survivors had to relive the horrific events by writing formal statements which would form the basis of an inquiry by the Royal Military Police Special Investigation Branch.

It was at this stage that Lance Sergeant Baily came close to breaking down for the first time since the attack. 'I was writing down what had happened and I looked up and one of my mates from the signal platoon walked in. He had this moustache he had been growing and because I had been away for two weeks I hadn't seen it. I looked up at him and I was just on the cusp of crying when I noticed the moustache and I just burst out laughing and said, "What the hell is that?" It was literally a "laugh or cry moment".

'There have been a couple of times when I came very close to crying but I just got a grip of myself and said, "No, not yet." I made a pact with myself that I wouldn't let it affect me until I get home. I told my wife what had happened on the phone before the news broke, and said, "This has happened but don't worry, I'm OK."

'That night when I went to bed, I closed my eyes and I was back on the roof again and I was thinking what a complete idiot I was for not having my body armour and helmet. I did get to sleep and there have been a few nights when I couldn't sleep. I've spoken to a few people about events but really only when I felt that I needed to. Sergeant Telford was a good friend and I knew how hard losing a good friend was going to be. I had known him since I joined the Army and I have lost other friends before – two were killed on our last tour here in 2007. Having been through that experience before, I knew that I had just got to crack on and do my job.'

Slowly the news began to circulate that Corporal Webster-Smith had also died and that Lance Corporal Woodgates was in a very critical condition. Many of the soldiers who knew the dead were reduced to tears, while others were angry and felt a sense of deep betrayal that a police officer could cold-bloodedly murder men who had been helping him bring law and order to his country. There were fears that some soldiers might exact some form of retribution on members of the police. But the Grenadiers reacted with the utmost professionalism. There was no reaction, no calls for retribution, just a deep sense of personal loss.

The wounded were soon confronted by mixed emotions: elation at their survival but also guilt arising from the belief that they may have been able to do more.

Guardsman Loader, who a month earlier had lost one of his best friends when Guardsman James Major was killed, was mystified as to how he survived the attack with just a single bullet wound to the hand. 'I don't know how we managed to get out of that situation and still manage to be here, all right, talking and walking. I have never,

ever seen so much blood in my entire life, all over the floor, all over me, all over my legs, all over my hands. It's lumps of blood. I've never seen lumps of blood before like I did then.

'It's hard to explain, I just really do not know how we survived. Someone must have been watching over us. Because I thought that was it. So many times, at so many points, I thought that was it. I've never been so scared in my life. Every single move that I made, the thought before it was, what if I do this and I run into him? I mean, so many thoughts of, what if I do this and because of this it's the reason that I die today? So there was so much going through my head, my whole body was in overload. I didn't know what to think, didn't know what to do.'

Lance Corporal Namarua, who had been hit twice and was incapacitated, also pretended he was dead as the policeman ran around shooting. 'That's when my mind started going about my little one and my wife, and have I done enough, you know, with the insurance,' said Nammers in the days after the attack. 'I was the last one to get shot, it's like my fault for not getting the bloke. I feel guilty for not doing anything. You know, I should have killed him. I should have killed him that day.'

Guardsman Lyons, who had also been shot in the hand, said it was just luck that he survived and others didn't. 'You know it's just the luck of the draw, whether it's you or not. And this time I got lucky. That's what it comes down to, just luck.'

Despite the tragic events of 3 November there was no time for the soldiers to mourn and little time to dwell on the events of that day: life was simply too busy. The soldiers needed to remain focused, because lives depended on it. When I arrived at the base twenty-four hours after the attack there were no outward signs of the tragedy except that the Union Jack was flying at half-mast and the names of the dead had already been added to a plaque in a courtyard close to the operations room. I assumed, wrongly, that the soldiers' morale would be at rock bottom but there was nothing to indicate the trauma of forty-eight hours earlier. It was only when I spoke to individual soldiers that the pain of recent events bubbled to the surface and eyes became watery with grief.

The incident led to a cull of poor policemen, and there were a lot of them. Three senior commanders, all known to be corrupt, were dismissed and a massive round of drug testing was undertaken. All those who tested positive were sacked. After the cull, just thirty-five serving police officers remained in the whole of the Nad-e'Ali district. By the following March a new police training college had been established in the area and over 500 new officers were trained. Despite some advances, however, corruption and drug abuse are still endemic in parts of Helmand, the police force is still largely illiterate, and public trust in the organization remains low.

Suddenly the vehicle against which I am leaning thunders into life and someone shouts, 'Be ready to move in five minutes.' I stand to put on my body armour, tighten the chin-strap of my helmet, and wait to be assigned a vehicle for the move.

The hour-long delay seems to have heightened the tension among the search team. The casual confidence of Brimstone 45, who a few days earlier breezed through their final mission, is absent. Apprehension is etched on the faces of all the soldiers. The younger members of the team look slightly lost and have an awkward demeanour. There is no banter, no horseplay. The troops' pristine uniforms and pallid complexions only seem to exaggerate their vulnerability to what awaits them beyond the wire. All eight know they are about to enter a war zone, where the threat is deadly and hidden and there is every chance that not all of them will make it back home in six months' time.

Chapter 8: **New Arrivals**

'Afghanistan is just like Iraq – hot, dusty, and full of people who
want to kill you.'
Staff Sergeant Simon Fuller, Royal Engineer Search Advisor

I'm strapped to the seat of a Warrior armoured personnel carrier
opposite Staff Sergeant Simon Fuller, Brimstone 42's RESA, who has
just joined up with Woody's team. Simon, a tall, heavily built veteran
of two tours in Iraq, is bullish. 'It's good to get out on the ground so
soon,' he says. 'This is what we wanted.' But his slight stammer makes
me wonder whether the opposite is true.

The inside of the vehicle is ridiculously cramped and swelteringly
hot. Most of the loose equipment, such as ammunition boxes, water
and radio batteries, has been tied to the vehicle's floor or sides in an
attempt to reduce injuries in the event of an IED strike. The force of
the blast can be so great that heavy items like batteries can fly around
the cramped interior at lethal speeds. It is for the same reason that
we are all strapped in as well.

Simon is from 36 Engineer Regiment, based in Maidstone in Kent.
The regiment has been involved in Helmand since the inception of
the Afghanistan campaign and the Royal Engineers have paid a heavy
price. Members of the corps have been blinded, paralysed, and
suffered brain damage and multiple amputation. The Royal Engineers are at the forefront of every battle, every campaign, clearing

routes through which others can pass. On D-Day in Normandy in 1944, some of the first troops to hit the beaches were members of the corps who were charged with breaching the numerous German minefields while under murderous machine-gun fire. Today in Helmand it is often the men of the Royal Engineer Search Teams who clear routes so that British troops can advance and engage with the enemy.

The bomb hunters depart the base in a convoy of three Warriors. Woody and Simon are sitting side by side in the lead vehicle and I am squeezed between Corporal Arianne Merry from the Weapons Intelligence Section, and the interpreter, Mohammed. Everyone is wearing body armour and helmets. It's a tight fit even though the vehicle is meant to carry at least seven passengers in addition to a gunner commander and driver. The Warrior was designed for warfare in the 1980s when the enemy was the Soviet Union and the battleground might have been north Germany. It might not have been designed for war in Afghanistan, but it's a good compromise. To date no one travelling inside a Warrior has been killed by an IED, although tragically several drivers, who are probably the most vulnerable to the effects of a bomb blast, have been killed and seriously injured. As well as offering good protection, the Warrior is armed with a 30-mm Rarden cannon, which fires a variety of munitions, including high explosive, and a 7.62-mm coaxial chain gun.

Within minutes of leaving the base everyone is dripping with sweat. The Warrior's twenty-year-old air-conditioning is broken and is blowing out hot rather than cold air and the temperature quickly soars to well over 50°. Inside the vehicle it feels like a fan oven is on full blast.

I ask Simon for his first impressions of the country. 'Afghanistan is just like Iraq – hot, dusty, and full of people who want to kill you,' he shouts above the roar of the engine. There is general laughter, and the tension which accompanied our departure from the base eases slightly. Arianne complains about the heat and fans herself with a magazine. She first served in the Royal Navy for four years, then left and was a member of the Territorial Army for five year before becoming a regular soldier. Arianne's job as the weapons intelligence specialist is to photograph the IED *in situ* and recover and analyse as much of the bomb as possible.

Thirty minutes later we arrive at our destination – a long, straight stretch of road about 8 km north of FOB Shawqat. The outside temperature is close to 30° but it feels beautifully cool in comparison with being shut inside the Warrior. Sweat is pouring down Simon's face and as he wipes it away with the cuff of his sleeve he looks at me with a slightly embarrassed smile and says, 'Still haven't acclimatized.'

The enemy are believed to be around 1,000 metres due north of where the IED is located, just beyond an area known as 'Yellow 9'. The bomb hunters will be in the Taliban's range for as long as Woody and the searchers are working. The road has been secured by around thirty soldiers from the Right Flank company of the Scots Guards, who are lying and sitting on either side of the road, ready to repel an attack.

It's going to be a long, sweltering day for the guardsmen as there is absolutely no shade and no chance of keeping cool. Providing security during an IED clearance is one of the jobs most loathed by soldiers, and now I can understand why.

Behind the first vehicle in the convoy, Corporal Andy Hurran, the search team commander, is shaking out his team for their first mission. Equipment is being checked and rechecked before the isolation search begins. The bomb is just 100 metres directly to the north. The vehicles have stopped next to one of the many hamlets which are dotted about the Green Zone. In almost any other country such tranquillity might be described as heavenly.

The soldiers are objects of fascination for children and old men, who stop and stare. Women and teenage girls are never seen, and the younger men are working in the fields or fighting alongside the Taliban. On the left side of the road, down by a clear, free-flowing stream, children are playing and laughing, waving at soldiers, and begging for sweets and pens.

Arianne describes the scene as 'good atmospherics'. 'Children are playing, there are farmers in the fields, there's a bit of traffic – it's everyday routine,' she says. 'The local people will be the first to notice that the Taliban are moving into the area, and then the locals will disappear. It will happen very quickly. One minute they're doing their daily business and the next minutes they have gone, and that's when the Taliban will hit us.'

The search team have gathered around Andy, who stands well over 6 ft tall and has a cool, calm demeanour. It is clear that the team will rely heavily on his leadership over the next few hours. The tension among the team is palpable.

The area behind the Warrior is chosen as the ICP but no one seems quite sure what to do until Woody says that the ICP should be cleared of devices. It is as though nervousness has dulled the senses and the months spent in training have been forgotten, albeit temporarily. Simon and Andy swing into action, cajoling and urging their men to 'switch on'.

The soldiers move slowly and hesitantly until Simon begins to bark a series of orders. 'Bradley, you clear down to the river, and then come back into the vehicle from the front. Adam [Lance Corporal Adam McLean, another member of the REST], you do the same from the other side. 'The search is slow but uneventful and once the ICP is clear Andy calls the team in for a final briefing.

'Right, lads, listen in,' says Andy. 'The device, as we know, is about 150 metres up the road. What we know is that there was a callsign barma-ing a route from Yellow 21 to Yellow 25, when they were approached by a local who said there were at least three IEDs on the road. They did a clearance and got a loud tone just up the road from here. The first thing we are going to do is an isolation. Bradley' – Andy looks directly at Sapper Bradley Knight – 'you happy with everything? Vallon working correctly, kit sorted, happy to go?' Bradley nods but his apprehension is clear for everyone to see. No one comments, probably because they all share the same fears. 'Right, good. We're moving off in two minutes. You all know the order of march. It's our first job, so everyone take it easy, take your time, stay switched on.'

The team are just about to move off when Bradley, who at the age of 20 is already married with two children, announces that his mine detector is not working. 'For fuck's sake,' says Lance Corporal Israel Shankar, one of the many Fijians in the British Army. He has intense, piercing eyes and the build of a rugby forward. 'Have you got it turned on?' 'Course I have,' Bradley responds angrily. 'OK, I'm good to go now,' he says, but his movements are stuttering and he seems uncertain. Shankar, who is second in the order of march, wades in again. 'Bradley, fucking wise up, man! You're the fucking lead searcher, now get a fucking grip and switch on.'

Just before he departs on the isolation Woody turns to me and says, 'This is going to take a long time. But that's not a problem. It's the same for everybody on their first job. Everything will be done slowly and methodically. There's no rush, we've got a good bit of fire support here, so I really want the guys to get their confidence.'

Just as Woody finishes speaking, the alarm on Bradley's Vallon sounds. He swings the detector repeatedly over a patch of ground about 10 ft down the embankment, just at the water's edge, very close to where Woody and I are standing. 'I've got a double tone,' shouts Bradley, his voice breaking with fear. A double tone usually indicates a pressure-plate IED. Everyone stops and no one speaks. I'm holding my breath. If it is a device and it were to function now, most of us would be killed or injured. Bradley sweeps the Vallon over the same patch of ground again and everyone can hear its high-pitched whine. He is unsure what to do next. 'Either check it out or mark and avoid,' shouts Woody, who is clearly the only one not panicked by the prospect of being blown sky high. 'Have a look around you,' he adds calmly. 'It's unlikely to be a device down there, so close to the house opposite, so I would mark and avoid.' Bradley moves off into the distance, stumbling every few paces on the steep embankment. He is followed by six team mates.

'Watch your spacing – don't bunch,' shouts Andy, sliding down the embankment. Spacing is vital. Soldiers don't want to be so close to the man in front or behind that if he detonates a bomb the explosion will kill or injure others. But if the troops are too far apart, especially in close country, the patrol will lose its cohesion and run the risk that soldiers will become detached in the event of an attack.

The killing zone of an IED is dependent on the amount of explosive, the nature of the ground, the depth at which it is buried, and the fragmentation. The men of Brimstone 42 are subconsciously making these evaluations while at the same time searching for hidden IEDs.

With Woody on the patrol, Boonie, the team's No. 2, begins to prepare the equipment needed to neutralize the bomb. After three months of working together, sleeping inches away from each other, and defusing around thirty bombs, Boonie knows exactly what equipment Woody will need to tackle this latest device. He opens what is known as Woody's 'man bag' and begins to select various instruments. He checks the hook and line which will be used to pull the bomb from the ground from a safe distance and checks all the remote equipment being used to neutralize the device.

An hour later Woody and the team return, the isolation search completed. There are no other devices in the area and no command wires. In theory the bomb 150 metres up the road is now hermetically sealed within a security bubble.

The isolation has allowed Woody to get 'eyes on' the patch of ground where the device, which he believes to be a pressure-plate IED, has been concealed. But from what he has seen on the ground he now thinks the bomb could be one of a number connected in a chain designed to take out an entire British patrol. 'I think there could be at least three bombs along there,' he tellls Simon, pointing back over his right shoulder with his thumb. 'What I want to do is remove the first entirely, then defuse the second and the third.'

Simon nods his agreement. 'Seems like the right plan. Anything you want me to do?' 'No,' replies Woody. 'Not much you can do really.' He then turns to his No. 2 and says, 'Three bombs, Boonie. I'll sort the first, blow it, and then see what happens. Should take about half an hour. Where's the lead searcher? I want his Vallon.'

Bradley appears with his mine detector, looking slightly bemused. 'Right,' Woody says, taking it from Bradley. 'I christen this Vallon Valerie and from now on this is the one I'll use every time I go down the road.'

The searchers look puzzled. 'What are you talking about, Woody?' asks Simon.

'Valerie Vallon was my lucky charm with the last search team,' says Woody. 'I always used the lead searcher's Vallon and I've never had a problem. But they've taken Valerie with them, so I'm christening this one Valerie too.'

Woody sips some water from a plastic bottle, removes a few key pieces of equipment from his man bag, and tucks his ceramic knife into the front of his body armour. He is calm but focused and I can't help wondering whether he says a silent prayer and has one final thought of his wife and twin girls before taking the lonely walk to the bomb.

All eyes are fixed on Woody as he walks down the safe lane, man bag in one hand, Vallon in the other. The men of Brimstone 42 are pensive and silent. This is the first time any of the newly arrived team have seen an ATO defuse a bomb in Afghanistan. Within a few minutes Woody is a distant, lonely figure shimmering in the heat haze. His vulnerability is clear and frightening – he is the definition of the sitting target. Apart from the infantry escort, Lance Corporal Joe Rossiter, who is also doubling as the ECM operator, Woody is on his own, armed only with a 9-mm pistol – effective range about 30 metres. He clears a safe, working area around the bomb before crouching down into what, from a distance, looks like the foetal position. He is trying to make himself as small a target as possible while still being able to work.

The earth is baked rock-hard by the sun and it takes at least thirty minutes of digging, chipping and scraping before Woody finds a wire. He picks at it with his ceramic knife for a few minutes and then flicks the dust away with his paintbrush. It is painfully slow work and Woody's body temperature must be going through the roof. It's difficult to imagine how he can maintain his concentration, but a mistake now could be fatal. I'm watching him through the weapon sight on one of the soldiers' rifles. Every few minutes he stops and wipes the sweat away from his eyes, then continues working. After twenty minutes he stops and rests the front of his helmet on the ground for a few moments' respite before resuming the excavation.

A few minutes later Woody manages to locate what he believes is a wire connecting the power supply to the detonator. He carefully positions the IED weapon he will use to 'attack' the bomb and walks back to the safety of the first Warrior with a wire trailing behind him. Boonie moves forward, connects the wire to the firing pack, and shouts, 'Controlled explosion in one minute.' There is a distant crack and then nothing – the sound everyone wanted to hear. A few minutes later Woody is back in his familiar crouching position, digging away, trying to isolate the pressure plate. It is a long and laborious process, made all the more difficult by the knowledge that somewhere in a distant field or tree line the Taliban are waiting and watching. In theory, time should not be a factor in any IED-disposal operation, but it is in Helmand. The longer an ATO spends on the ground in the open the more time the Taliban will have to plan and mount an attack. Balancing speed and safety is a constant challenge for bomb hunters.

As the sweat begin to trickle into his eyes, Woody eventually locates the device and carefully but firmly pushes the hook underneath the pressure plate. This is one of the most dangerous phases of the operation. In all probability the bomb is a straightforward pressure-plate device, but Woody is aware that it could be booby-trapped with a secondary pressure-release switch. A single sudden move could be enough to cause a detonation. With the hook safely in place, Woody stands, tucks his tools into the front of his body armour, and begins walking back down the cleared lane, unreeling a coil of rope behind him. Boonie is waiting at the front of the Warrior, ready to help in the extraction of the device. The pair have carried out the same procedure more than thirty times and now they move into position, Woody in front, Boonie behind, grabbing the thin rope between them without the need for a single word. After three powerful tugs the pressure plate is pulled clear. The two men silently stare into the distance, waiting for an explosion which never comes.

Woody returns once again down the safe lane to retrieve the pressure plate and to position a fist-sized lump of military-grade plastic explosive next to the yellow palm-oil container containing the main charge.

'It was a 20 kg device, or thereabouts,' he says. His eyes are red with sweat and dust. 'It was designed to take out a vehicle – it would easily take the track off a Warrior and if you were in a Mastiff you would know about it. If someone had stepped on it, they would have been killed. We are basically big bags of water, so you can imagine what would happen if you stepped on 20 kg of explosive.' He holds up the pressure plate by a wire in the same way that a fisherman might show off a prize catch. The pressure plate is about a foot long and an inch thick, with two white plastic wires at one end. 'That's what will do the damage – it's a ball-bearing pressure plate – works in the same way as a conventional pressure plate but the circuit is made by a ball bearing and a wire – simple but deadly.'

Although Woody managed to find the bomb and the pressure plate, he hasn't been able to locate the power pack and he appears slightly deflated. Every ATO likes to recover as much of a bomb as possible – it's all part of their individual battle against the Taliban bomb makers. There is always the chance that a piece of forensic intelligence may be obtained from a power source or a pressure plate, so no bomb hunter feels entirely satisfied unless he manages to locate the whole device.

'I can't for the life of me find the power pack,' says Woody, frustration written all over his face. 'It may not actually be there, of course, but the ground is so hard it's difficult to tell. But I absolutely hate it when I can't find something. I feel as though the Taliban have got something over on me. I see it as all part of winning individual battles and if we all win our individual battles, then we will be OK and make it back. The bottom line is that the device may not have had a power pack attached. The bomb may have been placed there some time ago and the insurgents could have been planning to attach the power supply some time in the future. Who knows?'

Boonie prepares to blow the main charge. Twenty kilos of home-made explosive is a big bomb, and although we are all about 100 metres from the device everyone gets into cover either inside the vehicles or standing in their lee. 'Standby, firing,' shouts Boonie, and seconds later there is an earth-shaking boom. Lumps of earth rain down upon us and the front of the convoy is engulfed in a plume of choking brown dust.

Woody goes forward with Arianne to check that all of the HME has gone. There's nothing left apart from a huge hole on the side of the road. The WIS photographs the site of the devices and the surrounding countryside. She wants to build up a picture of why the Taliban bomb team chose this particular spot. She and other intelligence staff in the CIED Task Force will then try to answer a number of questions. Are there Taliban sympathizers in the area? Can the bomb location be easily monitored? Is the route being used too frequently by NATO forces? All the intelligence gleaned will be fed into a database which one day, when enough information has been gathered, may lead to the identity of the bomber. With the bomb cleared, there is a tangible decrease in tension among the members of Brimstone 42. In their eyes they are no longer rookies. After six months' intensive training they have just completed their first mission and everyone is relieved that it went smoothly.

'That's the first one under the belt,' says Simon. 'The lads won't be as nervous as this now – they've broken the fear aspect. This is some-thing we can build on. We were probably a lot slower than what Woody is used to, but we will improve and the lads will get quicker. From here on out we've got to maintain this level of professionalism, remain switched on for the next six months, remember all of what we learned in our training, and make sure that we all return home in six months' time.'

The job of the bomb hunters for this particular mission is now complete, but before the Brimstone team can return to the safety of FOB Shawqat they are sent on another mission. The ANP have found several IEDs close to Patrol Base Pimon and, rather than marking and leaving them *in situ* for an IED team to clear, they have risked injury or death by pulling them out of the ground and bringing them into the base. Woody has been tasked with disposing of them.

PB Pimon is the home of the Right Flank company of 1st Battalion Scots Guards. The base sits high on the left shoulder of the Grenadier Guards' area of operations, on a line which demarcates the desert from the Green Zone. It's also an area which has been heavily laced with IEDs and is regarded as one of the most dangerous areas of the Nad-e'Ali district. There are only certain routes in and out and the Taliban have planted IEDs on all of them at one time or another.

With everyone now back in the Warriors, we move off towards Pimon. It's less than 5 km away but we are being forced to take a more circuitous route because of the threat on some of the roads and tracks which have not been secured by either the ANA or the ANP.

As soon as the large armoured door on the back of our Warrior closes, the temperature again begins to soar. Within minutes everyone is sweating buckets. The vehicle commander offers a cursory apology. 'Sorry about the air-con,' he says in his thick Glaswegian tones. 'We've tried asking for spare parts but there aren't any. There's such a shortage of working vehicles and they aren't going to take this one off the road just because the air-con's fucked.'

'How do you cope when you're on a long trip?' asks Simon.

'You just have to,' replies the commander. 'If it gets really bad we pour water over ourselves, but that's about it. We can't exactly stop, get out and have a breather. We had a lad who passed out with heat stroke the other day, and we nearly had to call the MERT out. Luckily we were returning to the FOB, so we went straight to the medical centre and he was carried out and put on a drip. So this will have to be fixed by the summer otherwise someone is going to end up dead.'

After we've been bouncing around in the back of the Warrior for a few minutes, the conversation dies away to nothing. It is simply too hot to talk. Eyes begin to close and tired faces are intermittently illuminated by shafts of sunlight piercing the dark, dusty interior. Beneath my body armour and helmet I can feel my body temperature soaring. Then, just when I think I can't possibly take any more, we arrive at Pimon and the sense of relief is extraordinary. The electrically powered armoured door can't open quickly enough and a blast of cool, fresh desert air quickly fills the Warrior.

'That heat was fucking unreal,' says Woody. 'Absolutely insane. An hour inside one of those and you would be next to useless.'

The five of us stumble out of the rear of the Warrior, pulling our sweat-soaked body armour from our limp bodies. We all look exhausted and dishevelled and frankly not fit to do anything. I wonder how soldiers would cope if ambushed by the Taliban and forced to dismount from the vehicles after travelling inside for an hour or two. My trousers are soaked through with sweat and Simon's face is a frightening puce colour. Woody looks as though he has stepped out from a shower, and even Mo, the terp, who comes from Kabul and is used to the harsh Helmand summers, is complaining about the heat.

'Let's go and find some cold water,' says Woody, 'and then sort out these bombs.' PB Pimon is a massive camp, at least equal in size to FOB Shawqat, and is home to around 150 members of the Scots Guards and a detachment of Gurkhas. From the fortified sangars it is possible to view both the fertile Green Zone and the stark, brown desert, between which the camp lies. Of all the bases I have visited during numerous trip to Afghanistan since 2002, Pimon is the bleakest. Most bases are Afghan compounds which have been extended and fortified by the engineers, but Pimon seems to have been built on a vast expanse of flat land in the middle of nowhere. It is not a welcoming place and I can tell already that I will be pleased to leave.

As we walk across the sun-bleached gravel I notice a lone soldier furiously working out on a punchbag. It is an almost surreal image. He is dripping with sweat and as we pass by he stops, smiles and says in a thick Scottish accent, 'Believe me, it helps,' then continues punching.

Woody tells Simon to get his men to clear an area outside the camp where the devices are to be blown up. He warns him that even though we are now within the confines of the camp everyone must treat the area beyond the wire as though they were inside enemy territory. 'A few weeks ago a guy was killed walking to the ranges just outside Camp Bastion. The insurgents had been watching us beyond the wire there and probably thought, that's an opportunity target. Maybe the troops had become a bit slack and weren't clearing the areas properly, and the Taliban probably assumed our guard would be down because the ranges are so close to Camp Bastion – a massive base with thousands of soldiers, and let's face it, who would think that the Taliban would have the balls to plant a device there? But after every range practice you get locals coming up to the ranges to collect the empty bullet cases and melt them down and sell the stuff.

'Someone managed to get a device in and bury it without being seen, and from their point of view they got a result. The next morning a group of new guys go up to the range as part of their training package and someone steps on the bomb. They should have cleared all the way there and cleared their range area. Maybe they did and missed it, and maybe they didn't. The guy who died had only been in Afghan a week – that's not a good way to go. So make sure they don't get too relaxed – the threat is everywhere. If it can happen in Bastion, it can happen here.'

Simon acknowledges Woody's concern and heads off to brief the search team.

The soldier to whom Woody is referring was Lance Corporal James Hill of 1st Battalion Coldstream Guards, who was killed on 8 October 2009, just a week after he arrived in Helmand.

After meeting the base commander, Major Iain Lindsay-German of the Scots Guards, I accompany Woody to the Unexploded Ordnance, or UXO, pit just outside the main defensive Hesco wall of the base. Our small unit of four is led to a small, designated area where two yellow palm-oil containers are sitting in the dust.

'Who brought them in?' Woody asks one of the guardsmen.

'The ANP, a couple of days ago. They said they found them on a track, pulled them out of the ground and brought them in. They pulled the detonators out with their hands. Can you believe it?' says the soldier, shaking his head.

Now Woody is bent over one of the palm-oil containers, looking but not touching. He has found the hole housing the detonator and he is peering inside. 'I don't know why the ANP feel the need to dig these out of the ground and bring them in. They won't listen and it's not as though they haven't taken casualties. They've had guys killed and injured, they know the risks, and they still keep doing it. We keep telling them, "Just mark them and tell us and we'll sort them out." Do they listen? Do they fuck.'

Woody explains that although the ANP are not yet issued with mine detectors they are very good at spotting ground sign or manage to persuade the local population to tell them where bombs have been hidden.

'That one's safe,' he says, pointing to the larger of the two containers before carrying out the same forensic examination of the second bomb. Two minutes later Woody declares that both bombs are safe. He explains that the ANP disconnected the pressure plates, the detonators and the power sources when they were discovered a few days ago, but his examination was to ensure there 'weren't any surprises for us'.

He continues, 'The other reason why we want the ANP to mark and avoid and then tell us is because by the time they've pulled them out of the ground they've handled the det, the pressure plate, the power source, so there is virtually no chance that we can get any forensics. Part of the problem is that the ANP are always trying to demonstrate that they are fearless and strong. We used to get the same problem with the Afghan Army but they are a much more professional outfit now and they've got the message. Strength and courage are really important in the Afghan culture and they think that we might question their courage if they find a bomb and leave it. Instead they pull it out of the ground, risking life and limb, and bring it in as if to say, "Look how brave I am."'

Unfortunately for the ANP, the Taliban have noticed their propensity for perceived bravery and have started to modify basic pressure-plate devices by attaching a pressure-release switch. This is nothing sophisticated and can be as basic as the type of switch which turns on the interior light of a car. The unsuspecting ANP officer who finds the bomb will cut the power supply from the pressure plate in the belief that the bomb has been rendered safe, only for it to explode when he releases the pressure by pulling the bomb out of the ground.

Woody lifts up the larger of the two containers and says, 'That one weighs about 20 kg. That would have been enough to take out a vehicle.' Pointing to the other, he adds, 'That's got about 10 kg of HME. That would definitely kill or injure. At the very least it's going to take your legs off and it would probably destroy a smaller vehicle. So we've got two bombs, one larger than the other, and we know that they were placed along the same stretch of track, so that makes you wonder what the Taliban were trying to achieve. I think they were probably trying to take out a vehicle and then get another casualty with the small device in a follow-up clearance.'

Warriors have been used elsewhere in Helmand since 2007, but they have been in this part of the province for only a matter of weeks. The Taliban are masters of observation. Whenever any new unit, piece of equipment or type of vehicle arrives in an area the local commander will almost always start a small-scale intelligence-gathering operation before attempting to carry out an attack. The Taliban will simply watch, wait, record, and then react.

Although there is some migration of Taliban tactics across Helmand, some units of insurgents can become quite insular and dislocated from the main Taliban central command. If the Taliban were a pan-Afghan cohesive force conducting mutually supporting operations across Helmand and the rest of the country, they would pose a much greater threat to NATO. But since 2006, when British troops first entered Helmand, their tactics, although often deadly, have never really moved beyond 'shoot and scoot'.

Sitting down by the two bombs, Woody begins to explain how the Taliban are becoming increasingly sophisticated in some of their attacks. 'One of the current concerns is that the Taliban will try and take out a Warrior – that would be a bit of a coup for them. The Warriors have only been in this part of Helmand for a few weeks and we know the Taliban are looking and watching. They have all the time in the world, so it is easy for them to put a device in with a certain amount of explosive, say 10 kg, and wait and see what effect that will have on a Warrior. The type of vehicle you have will reflect the size of the main charge the Taliban use. Taliban tactics aren't haphazard; they may have been a bit like that a couple of years ago, but not any more. They are still basically hit-and-run but with a lot of thought behind them. They will put a 10 kg device in the road and see what happens. The next day or week another one will go in with 15 kg and then another with 20 kg, until they get the desired effect, and they will build their tactics around what happens. They're in no rush, they have no timeframe, they are always going to be here. The clock is ticking for us, not them.'

Woody is ready to dispose of the two bombs but the search team have failed to materialize. I can sense his frustration but he keeps his thoughts private. Rather than wait for the searchers to turn up, Woody decides to reconnoitre an area 200 metres to the front of the base, in what is effectively no man's land. I watch him disappear into the distance, clearing the ground in front of his feet with the Vallon. One of the Scots Guardsmen with our team senses my concern for Woody and assures me that he is pretty safe. 'He will be covered by the sangar and the boys up there have got a .50-cal HMG and a 7.62-mm GPMG and a sniper.'

Ten minutes later Woody returns to the perimeter wall. 'Right, I've found a site – it's about 200 metres north from here. Boonie, I'll need a couple of sticks of PE and we'll blow the two bombs together. Any sign of the search team?'

'Haven't seen them,' replies Boonie.

In the world of IED disposal it is vital that rules and procedures are followed to the letter and that when an order is given it is acted on. Every member of the IEDD and search teams must have an absolute understanding of their role and that of every member of the team. Woody likes to run a relaxed ship but that method of leadership will only work if everyone toes the line. 'OK,' he says to no one in particular, 'there are going to have to be words.'

Twenty minutes later Woody returns and tells Boonie that the bombs are primed and ready to be blown. He has placed a couple of sticks of military-grade plastic explosive between the two containers and attached a detonator to a length of det cord which is connected to the PE. Woody hands Boonie a length of wire the end of which is connected to the detonator 200 metres in the distance. Our small party moves back inside the camp and takes cover behind an 8 ft Hesco wall.

'Get ready for a loud bang,' says Woody, now smiling again. Boonie shouts, 'Controlled explosion in figures two,' then repeats the warning. Two minutes later he presses a black button on his green firing box and, almost instantaneously, a massive explosion fills the air around us. I can feel the force of the blast in the pit of my stomach and within a few seconds pieces of the desert which have been sucked into a large mushroom cloud begin to shower down on us. The massive explosion was caused by just 30 kg of home-made explosive and it seems almost impossible that anything, apart from the largest and most heavily armoured tank, would escape either total destruction or severe damage. The effect on a human body would be devastating. 'If you stepped on something that big you would be vaporized,' says Woody. 'You would be literally blown to pieces, but the pieces would be very small. There wouldn't really be anything left to send home.'

It almost defies belief that the Taliban can make something so devastating with items that can be found on practically every farm in Helmand. Although ammonium-nitrate fertilizers were banned by President Hamid Karzai in February 2010, it is estimated that there are hundreds of thousands of tons of the material in circulation in Afghanistan. More is smuggled across the border from Pakistan and Iran every day and it is estimated that it will take years before supplies in circulation are exhausted. It strikes me that banning ammonium-nitrate-based fertilizers is nothing more than a cosmetic act. In Northern Ireland they were banned from the early 1980s and the Troubles still rumbled on for another decade, with fertilizers still forming part of the main ingredient of the IRA's home-made bombs.

With the bombs cleared it's time to return to Shawqat. Everyone is looking forward to a rest and a shower, but then a message comes over the radio during the journey back that another IED has been found on the same route which Woody cleared a few hours earlier. 'It's going to be a long day,' is his only response as he closes his eyes and falls into a deep but short-lived sleep.

Within half an hour our convoy has returned to the area where today's operation began several hours earlier. I'm reminded of the film *Groundhog Day*. Standing in the doorway is the silhouetted figure of a 6 ft 2 in. Scots Guards sergeant. He greets Woody with a firm handshake and ready smile. 'Back already,' he says. 'Missed it too much,' replies Woody, who manages to conjure up a smile even though he is exhausted.

The sergeant immediately emabrks on a faultless but speedy briefing on how the suspected device was discovered. 'We were doing a route clearance from Yellow 21, which is about 500 metres to our rear. It was a routine task and we were clearing using our normal drills. It was quite a lengthy task. We had a four-man barma team and two hedgerow men to cover the outside and two covering the inside of the road. The Vallon men interlocked their arcs to make sure the whole route was being covered. As we advanced up this road, Guardsman Warren Forrest got a high reading on his

Vallon. He went straight into his confirmation drills. He walked back, drew a line in the sand, and then started his confirmation from there. It was a very brave thing for a young guardsman to do. He then started digging to try and confirm that there was a device. But the ground was very hard. We couldn't get a confirmation. That's about it.'

The soldier, a guardsman – the most junior rank in the Brigade of Guards – appears from behind the Warrior seconds after the sergeant calls for him. He looks too young to be in the Army.

'Hello, mate, I'm Woody, the ATO. Your sergeant says that you think you found something up the road,' says Woody. 'Can you tell me exactly what happened and what you saw? But tell me your name first.'

'I'm Warren. We were pushing along the track,' the soldier replies in a strong Glaswegian accent. 'I had got about 100 metres from here and I got a tone on the Vallon. I checked the Vallon and then shouted, stop. Marked the site and told the sergeant what I had found. It was a very similar tone to one I got before, a few days ago, when I found another PP IED.'

Guardsman Forrest then takes Woody to the bomb's location, around 100 metres forward of our position. When Woody returns a few minutes later he is not convinced that the soldier has found an IED.

'If I was a betting man I would bet that it's just a piece of metal in the ground,' says Woody, rubbing his chin. 'The ground feels rock solid, so the easiest and safest thing to do is break up the ground with some PE and then go and have a look. I've got a couple of pounds of PE I could use, but that might be a bit much. The idea is to blow up the ground rather than make the device function. If there is something there and it goes off when I blow up the ground, I'll be able to tell from the explosion. There is a big difference between a piece of PE and a 10 kg device. I'm going to try and carry out a further confirmation myself, but if I can't then I will use some PE. There is no ground sign, so if there is anything there it was buried a long time ago. I'm going to try and locate it with the hand-held detector and place the PE by the side of it.'

With the poppy harvest just a few weeks away, the Taliban have been placing IEDs in poppy fields in the hope that they will deter the ANP from destroying the crop. It is a tactic which is only partially successful. Woody explains that the Taliban will also hide bombs in trees which are effectively improvised claymores designed to decapitate soldiers, or bury them in the walls either side of alleyways. 'They will put an IED anywhere to try and catch you out – not just in the ground – so you have to think three-dimensionally.'

Just before Woody 'goes down the road' for the second time, several soldiers standing on one of the Warriors begin shouting aggressively. A civilian motorcyclist with a pillion passenger is rapidly approaching. One of the soldiers immediately shouts, 'Boss, miniflare' to his platoon commander in the vehicle to our rear. The platoon commander fires a red flare and the interpreters begin shouting at the motorcyclist to stop. It is a moment of heightened tension. If the civilian fails to stop, warning shots will be fired, if time allows, otherwise the soldiers will resort to lethal force. Suicide bombers have used motorcycles to target and kill several British soldiers in the past few months and no one is prepared to take the risk. I look round and can immediately see about a dozen grim-faced soldiers, fingers on triggers, ready to let rip at the motorcyclist and his burkha-wearing passenger if they fail to stop. Fortunately the civilian has taken heed and slowly comes to a halt with a look of bemusement on his face. I wonder if he realizes how close he has just come to being shot dead.

As we wait for Woody to return, swallows are swooping above our heads and two soldiers discuss the merits of having a dog with young children. 'I might get one for the wee nipper when I get back. He'll love it. He'll think Christmas has come early,' says one. 'A lot of work, though,' says the other. 'Yeah, I know, but worth it just to see the look on the young lad's face when you walk in with a wee puppy in your arms and say, "Here's your doggy, son."'

Their reflections on life back in the UK are interrupted by Woody, who tells the crouching soldiers that an explosion is imminent. 'Take cover,' shouts Boonie. 'Controlled explosion is about to take place. Everyone happy?' he asks, before shouting, 'Standby, firing!' A loud bang follows, but it's PE and not Taliban explosive which has detonated.

Woody returns to the site of the detonation and carefully searches through the broken hard mud – there is no device. The Vallon's alarm was reacting to some discarded pieces of metal, as he suspected.

When he comes back he looks fatigued and has a wry grin on his face. 'There was nothing there, just a few bits of metal in the ground. I don't blame the soldiers, they are just following the procedures, and it's right that they do, but every time I have been called out on a double tone there has been nothing there. It's slightly frustrating but I can understand why I have been called in. The soldiers can't get into the ground to confirm the presence of a device because it is too hard and they can't mark and avoid because they are here to clear this route. It's just one of those things. But if you don't have over-watch on a route, then two days after you clear the devices the Taliban will put them back in the ground. We should only clear routes that are going to be overwatched, otherwise the soldiers should use alternative routes. I'm not being precious but we are a pretty rare asset out here and a little bit more thought should go into how we are used. We are not here to clear every single device – just the ones that are either a risk to us or preventing movement of our forces. The Taliban want to get you bogged down clearing everything and sometimes I think we are falling into that trap.'

As we walk back to the Warrior for our journey back to FOB Shawqat, the sense of achievement among the soldiers is obvious. Smiles, which have been absent for a large part of the day, suddenly emerge on relaxed faces. Brimstone 42 were confronted by the first of the many challenges that will dominate every day of their lives for the next six months and they have had the best of all possible starts.

'The lads did well. It was quite slow at the beginning, which is what you would expect and want really, because the last thing you would want is for the team to rush the job, but on the whole I'm pleased. I think we'll make a good team,' says Woody as we walk back to our Warrior. By the time we arrive back at FOB Shawqat, most of the soldiers are too tired to talk. Weapons are unloaded in the firing bay and the search and IEDD teams silently disperse in the hope of a good night's sleep in preparation for another mission tomorrow.

It's 8 a.m. the following morning. Woody had been hoping for a slack day to sort out some personal administration and catch up on some report-writing, but it's not to be. Over the past few weeks members of the ANP have been arriving at the gates of the compound belonging to the Nad-e'Ali district governor, Habiullah Khan, with a wide variety of unstable and highly dangerous unexploded munitions, such as RPGs, mortar bombs and artillery shells. These explosives which have failed to function are called 'blinds' by the British troops. Some of the munitions have been used recently against the British by the Taliban, while others are believed to be remnants of the Soviet invasion. Woody has been tasked to 'dispose' of them. It is a routine job both he and Boonie could do without.

Woody, Boonie, the Intelligence Officer of the Duke of Lancaster's Regiment, which will be relieving the Grenadier Guards in the next few weeks, and a member of the Weapons Intelligence Section rendezvous at the ANP headquarters with Wali Mohammed, the regional head of the National Directorate of Security, the Afghan equivalent of MI5. Wali Mohammed is a shrewd character with sharp eyes and a ready smile. It is said that he has connections with everyone who matters, including the Taliban, and little happens in Helmand without his knowledge. For this former Mujahideen commander, the AK-47 and the RPG used to be the weapons of choice, but these days his battles are fought using a pair of mobile phones. I have met him many times and he's is always polite and warm. But what you see with Wali is certainly not what you get. Governor Habiullah Khan might be the official head of the Nad-e'Ali district, but I have always been left with the feeling that Wali is the real power behind the throne.

Wali tells Woody that all of the bombs and main charges were found by the ANP in the area of Shin Kalay, a small hamlet with a strong Taliban presence a few kilometres from FOB Shawqat. We are led outside to a haul of artillery shells, rockets, mortar rounds and IED main charges. All of the munitions have been fired and are in a relatively unstable state. One of the ANP officers moves over to the pile, picks up an RPG warhead, studies it, then drops it casually on the ground, much to everyone's alarm. Back in the UK, unexploded ordnance would never be treated with such disdain. Out of the corner of my eye I can see the intelligence officer backing away with a look of sheer terror on his face. Woody immediately tells the interpreter to warn the ANP officer to treat the blinds with a little more respect.

I ask Boonie whether the blinds are safe. 'They should be, but you shouldn't be chucking them around like that,' he tells me. Woody smiles at me and adds, 'Unnerving, isn't it?' The hairs on the back of my neck begin to rise.

Speaking through the interpreter, Woody patiently tells Wali Mohammed about the danger of soldiers bringing in blinds and the need to treat them safely. 'These are very dangerous items and could explode if not treated correctly. Your men should be told that these need to be handled with care. They don't always have to bring them in. They could leave them where they are and we would go and destroy them. That is the safest way.' Wali smiles and explains that he understands but his men have grown up in a country littered with mines and rockets and they hold no fear for them.

The blinds will be taken back to the British base and kept there securely before being taken into the desert and destroyed with a load of other unexploded ordnance, while the palm-oil containers, the main charges of the IEDs recovered by the ANP, will be destroyed in an adjacent field.

We walk to a corner of a field where there is a 10-ft-deep irrigation ditch running the length of the field, about 600 metres from the camp perimeter. The two large palm-oil containers each hold around 10 kg of HME. Woody prepares the plastic explosive which will be used to detonate the HME and begins moulding it into a ball. Rather than using an electric detonator, he is using a strip of fuse wire.

'When we light this,' Woody tells the interpreter, pointing at the fuse wire, 'we have two minutes to get away.' The terp repeats the message and there is nervous laughter among the ANP. Seconds later Woody lights the fuse and we all start walking across the field at a brisk pace, occasionally looking back over our shoulder. Woody stops walking and begins to give a countdown – thirty seconds, twenty seconds, ten seconds – and, right on queue, detonation, the ground in the distance rising up like a scene from the First World War.

'That would ruin your day if it went off underneath you,' he says. Non-survivable on foot, it would blow a Jackal in two and would do serious damage to a Mastiff, so it's pretty nasty stuff.

Chapter 9: **The Battle of Crossing Point One**

'It was like *Zulu*. The Taliban just kept coming and coming.
It was suicidal. The more they sent, the more we killed.'
Dean Bailey, 5 Platoon Sergeant, No. 2 Company,
Grenadier Guards battlegroup

The IED had been the Taliban's weapon of choice since the middle of 2008, but among NATO troops in Afghanistan, especially the British in Helmand, casualties caused by blast only really began to soar in early 2009. The volume of bombs being laid by the Taliban was completely unpredicted, and initially this turned the conflict into a stalemate.

By the time I was embedded with the Grenadier Guards in March 2010 almost every soldier serving in the dozens of different FOBs and PBs which peppered the Helmand landscape had encountered an IED in one capacity or another. The IED was a weapon all soldiers rightly feared but, in the best traditions of the British Army, commanders believed that the best way to defeat the significant psychological effect the IED presented was offensive action.

This approach was typified by what became known as the Battle of Crossing Point One, which took place in November 2009, just hours after the brutal murders of five members of the Grenadier Guards battlegroup at Blue 25.

It was in that same month, during a previous embed with the Grenadier Guards, that I first learned about the events at Crossing

Point One. I had intended to visit the soldiers at the time but so ferocious was the battle that it was too dangerous to fly in by helicopter.
Reluctantly, I had to wait another four months, until March 2010, to
discover what befell a small, isolated group of British soldiers who,
with guile and cunning, out-thought the Taliban and used the insurgents' favoured weapons – the IED – against them. One afternoon I
sat down with members of No. 2 Company, who told me how they
fought and survived one of the most extraordinary battles of the
conflict to date. This is their story.

Morale was low, probably the lowest it had been. The men of the
Grenadier Guards battlegroup knew that they would take casualties
during their time in Afghanistan. Soldiers learn to live with the
knowledge that in the Army death is part of their way of life. But no
one had expected that British soldiers would be killed by those they
were trying to help.

The deaths at Blue 25 were a hammer blow for the battlegroup.
The gunman, Gulbuddin, had killed without mercy and the Taliban
were gloating, claiming that he was one of theirs, a spy who joined
the police with the sole aim of killing British troops.

But up in Luy Mandah, in the north of Nad-e'Ali, British soldiers
were about to strike back. Major Richard Green, the officer
commanding No. 2 Company, 1st Battalion Grenadier Guards, had
been planning an ambush which would exploit the Taliban's fond-
ness for attacking the casualty evacuation chain. It is important at
this juncture to make clear that the ambush, which would have
dramatic consequences, was not an act of retribution. The ambush
was supposed to have been launched some weeks earlier but it was
aborted for logistical reasons. Major Green was also determined that
when it was launched the risk to the local population would be zero.
Countering the insurgency, as he constantly told his men, would not
be achieved by killing or injuring local people.

Attacking the casevacs was a popular Taliban sport, especially
when the injured soldier was the victim of an IED. The Taliban knew
that British soldiers would at times act recklessly in order to save the

life of a severely wounded colleague. The Taliban had watched and
learned well. They had studied British tactics and had been able to
predict their actions. Now it was time to turn the insurgents' tactics
against them. So, on the evening of Tuesday, 3 November, just hours
after the murder at Blue 25, a plan which had been in the pipeline for
some time came into action.

In the short while that the Grenadier Guards had been in
Helmand they had learned to live with the fear of knowing that they
risked life and limb every time they left the safety of a base. The
maxim 'Knowledge dispels fear' is often cited by instructors in the
armed forces when training soldiers for dangerous tasks such as
parachuting and bomb disposal, but in Helmand fear often plays a
vital role. In many cases fear is an essential element in staying alive.
Fear prevents complacency and promotes respect for the enemy's
capabilities. Practically every soldier fighting on the front line has
either witnessed or knows of men who have been blown to pieces or
suffered horrendous, life-changing injuries through being blown
up.

Vast areas of Taliban-controlled Helmand had effectively become
minefields where soldiers literally feared to tread and in some bases
units were sustaining 20 per cent casualties. Towards the end of 2009
the volume of IEDs being laid by the Taliban had fixed the British
troops within specific boundaries from where the insurgents would
attack and ambush at will. By the end of the Grenadiers' tour, in
March 2010, the battlegroup alone would have experienced some
1,000 IED incidents. Movement beyond these boundaries was at best
highly dangerous and at worst suicidal. Small incursions into enemy
territory risked unnecessary casualties among the British forces and
threatened to damage or undermine the morale of the troops.

But under General McChrystal's strategy of protecting the civilian
population centres, it was imperative that ISAF did not remain inside
fortified compounds, safe and secure but isolated from the people
they were supposedly trying to protect. The butcher's bill for such a
strategy was high and the highest price being paid in the autumn of

2009 was that paid by the British. The casualty rate of the British force in late 2009 and early 2010 outstripped that of every other NATO country in Afghanistan, including the United States.

In September 2009, No. 2 Company were deployed to the northern tip of Nad-e'Ali, in an area known as Luy Mandah, where they relieved the soldiers of 1st Battalion Welsh Guards, who had fought in Operation Panchai Palang. The battalion suffered many casualties and the Welsh Guards were also the first regiment to lose their commanding officer, Lieutenant Colonel Rupert Thorneloe, in the Afghan War.

Number Two Company's headquarters was FOB Waheed, which was essentially a large fortified compound sitting on the junction between the Luy Mandah Wadi and the Nahr-e-Burgha and Shamalan canals. The area had once been the centre of a thriving community with a bazaar but it had long been deserted by the time the Grenadiers arrived. It was now Taliban territory, with a small, transient civilian population who worked on their farms during the days and returned at night to their families in more secure parts of the district.

The company were based in three locations in the Luy Mandah area. As well being the company headquarters, FOB Waheed was the base for 6 Platoon, along with interpreters, mainly from Kabul, a Fire Support Group (FSG), an additional Fire Support Team (FST) from 1st Regiment Royal Horse Artillery, a section of Grenadier Mortars, an Electronic Warfare Detachment and two sections of engineers.

The soldiers of 5 Platoon and elements of the FSG were located in a compound known as Crossing Point One, while 4 Platoon, with elements of the company headquarters, were housed at another nearby location, known as Crossing Point Luy Mandah.

When the Grenadiers arrived in Luy Mandah they entered a hostile environment. The company headquarters and its two satellite bases were surrounded on three sides by various insurgent groups, who were well armed and composed of experienced fighters, while to the north was the desert. The vast majority of locals had fled, and some of those who had remained were probably sympathetic to the Taliban. The area was also one of the few in Helmand where ISAF troops did not partner either the Afghan Army or the Afghan Police.

Nevertheless, life ticked along for No. 2 Company, and they enjoyed being detached from the battalion headquarters and out of sight of senior officers and the thunderous voice of Regimental Sergeant Major Darren Chant. The painful heat of the late summer was behind them and the soldiers quickly established a routine. Boredom had yet to raise its head as it was still early in the tour, and quiet periods were inevitably ended by a shoot-and-scoot attack by the Taliban. But everything changed in early October.

Although only 20, Guardsman James Janes was, in the eyes of many of the more inexperienced soldiers in 6 Platoon, an old hand. He had previously served in Helmand in 2007 and was widely trusted by everyone within the unit, especially his commander, Lieutenant Alex Rawlings, and platoon sergeant, Chris Dougerty.

Jamie fulfilled a long-held ambition when at the age of 16 he was selected for training at Harrogate Foundation College before moving on to complete his infantry recruit training at nearby Catterick. Although one of the youngest on the course he passed out with little difficulty and was posted to the Grenadier Guards. While the rest of the battalion deployed to Helmand in 2007, Jamie, still only 17, was forced to wait until his eighteenth birthday before he could join his mates in the province. Two years later Jamie volunteered to become one of the platoon searchers. Jamie's job was to be point man, searching ahead for IEDs with a Vallon mine detector, putting himself at risk not only from hidden bombs but also from insurgent snipers. Despite the dangers, Jamie relished the challenge.

On 5 October 2009, by which time the company had pretty much established their presence in Luy Mandah, Jamie's section was attached to an Irish Guards multiple of around sixteen men. A platoon of 'The Micks', as the Irish Guards are fondly known, was attached to the battlegroup as much-needed reinforcements. The mission that day was to conduct a patrol in the area of Checkpoint

Luy Mandah. The plan was to move along and clear a track, which had not been used for many months, up to a canal bridge, and obtain any intelligence from local farmers, if there was any, before returning back to their base. The route took the troops directly into what was effectively Taliban-controlled territory. On one side of the track, which was around 5 ft wide, was a canal and on the other was a small wall forming the boundary of a pomegranate orchard. In any other circumstances it would have been an idyllic setting, but that day the track became a route into hell.

The platoon moved along the track in three distinct groups, each led by a Vallon operator at the head of an eight-man section. The guardsmen forming the lead element of 4 Platoon quickly began to identify suspected IEDs on the track. It was immediately clear that the route had been heavily mined. Jamie's section, which was bringing up the rear, moved along the track carefully, giving the marked IEDs a wide berth. By the time the platoon had reached the canal bridge, at least six IEDs had been identified.

The patrol moved down into the canal, where the cold water was waist-deep, and continued with the patrol for around 50 metres before turning back. Jamie was one of the first out of the water. The bank was slippery with wet mud and each soldier needed help climbing out. As each soldier was hauled out Jamie pointed out the location of a marked IED. What happened next remains unclear but there was a massive explosion, caused either by Jamie stepping backwards on to another unmarked device or by vibrations through the ground from the presence of several soldiers in a confined area which triggered an IED. The blast was massive, resulting in the traumatic amputation of Jamie's arms and legs. Also injured in the explosion were Lance Corporal Gareth Harper and Guardsmen David Clark and Jordan Pearson.

Despite his horrific injuries, Jamie was still alive. But he was very close to death and, unbeknown to the soldiers at that time, he had just minutes left to live. The loss of blood from a quadruple amputation would have been rapid and massive. Jamie's chances of survival were poor, but his fellow soldiers fought hard to keep him alive. He received immediate medical attention and his huge blood loss was controlled by the application of four tourniquets to what was left of his shattered limbs. It was now urgent to get the wounded guardsman to a secure HLS in order that he could be evacuated back to the field hospital at Camp Bastion. But within minutes of 6 Platoon's withdrawal they came under a fierce Taliban rocket and machine-gun attack. Bullets raked the ground beneath the soldiers' feet and zipped through the air above them. Rocket-propelled grenades crashed and exploded among the troops, some detonating in the air about their heads, showering them with razor-sharp slivers of white-hot shrapnel.

It was a bitter fight made all the more desperate by the knowledge that Jamie's young life was ebbing away. The twenty or so soldiers who made up the patrol were almost completely surrounded and pinned down. Back at the company headquarters Major Richard Green ordered the FSG and their three Mastiff armoured personnel carriers, which were at the time conducting a routine administration run between Waheed and Crossing Point One, to make their way to the contact point and assist with the casualty evacuation. The urgency of the situation was not lost on the FSG. They had heard over the radio that the injured soldier was a quadruple amputee. As soon as the vehicles arrived at the contact point they began to attract Taliban fire.

Guardsman Robert Ashley, who fought in the attack, described it as 'the most fierce battle I've ever been in. We were almost completely surrounded.' After four years of fighting, insurgent commanders had acquired a detailed understanding of British tactics. The Taliban knew, for example, that after an IED strike British troops would normally call in a helicopter evacuation if the casualty was seriously wounded, as was normally the case with an IED. The Taliban also knew that the British would do everything in their power to save a wounded comrade no matter how severe his injuries. It was an act the insurgents could exploit.

Rather than randomly laying IEDs, the Taliban began to plan their ambushes to second and third levels. For example, IEDs would be planted not just along a track but also on all possible casualty extraction routes and on likely helicopter landing sites. Furthermore, the Taliban began to follow up IED strikes with ambushes – as in the attack on 5 October 2009. With Taliban fire raining down on the soldiers, the heliborne medical teams were unable to land close by and were forced instead to land inside the company headquarters. Back at the ambush site, the troops loaded the injured onto the Mastiffs, while the gunners in the vehicles' turrets laid down a heavy weight of fire. At one stage Guardsman Josh Shelton was suppressing four different Taliban firing points.

It took thirty minutes for the soldiers to fight their way back to the base, by which time Jamie's vital signs suggested that he was probably dead. The fact that he had survived for so long was testament to his inner strength and to the incredible work of the combat medics who accompany every patrol. 'Is he alive?' asked Major Green as he helped carry the wounded soldier from the Mastiff to the waiting helicopter. The look on the medic's face showed no answer was needed. Major Green was horrified by Jamie's injuries but kept telling him to 'hold on'. The reality, however, was that Jamie was already dead. His brain had stopped functioning and the flickers of life which the medics had identified were his vital organs closing down.

Within seconds Jamie was on board the helicopter and in the hands of a surgeon and a team of paramedics. As the dust storm kicked up by the departing helicopter began to settle, the exhausted soldiers began to arrive on foot back at FOB Waheed. They were shattered, many were covered in blood which was not their own, and others were carried to the medical centre for the treatment of their wounds.

No one spoke because there was nothing to say. Jamie hung on for a few minutes longer before his shattered body could fight no longer. An hour later No. 2 Company were told the news they had expected: Jamie was dead, and everyone in the company was devastated. There were many tears and many questions, and company morale took a beating. But the platoon was back out on patrol the next day and the day after that. Now wasn't the time to mourn; that would be done later, in the Guards Chapel in London, after the soldiers had returned home. And so life continued for No. 2 Company at a steady pace; steady for Helmand, that is. Every day or so they would be attacked by the Taliban, sometimes twice a day, and then on 3 November news began to filter into their base that five members of the battlegroup had been gunned down by an Afghan policeman.

Within a few hours of the deaths at Blue 25, Major Green decided to press ahead with the IED ambush. The orders for the launch were sent to Lieutenant Craig Shephard, who was charged with ironing out the finer points of the operation before its launch. Later that night, sipping instant coffee in the secure confines of Crossing Point One, Lieutenant Shephard, Sergeant Dean Bailey and Company Sergeant Major Pete Downes put the finishing touches to the plan. The murders at Blue 25 and the death of Guardsman Janes had dented morale. Both events had shocked No. 2 Company, but especially the nature of Guardsman Janes's death. And there was sheer outrage at the murders of the five members of the battlegroup and at the gloating propaganda of the Taliban, who later claimed that the rogue policeman was a Taliban agent.

Lieutenant Shephard was not cast from the same mould as the average Guards officer. With his close-cropped hair and muscular arms, he took pride in his physical appearance and harboured an ambition to join the Guards Parachute Platoon, which forms part of 16 Air Assault Brigade.

'It was a case of thinking out of the box,' he explained to me during a period of relative quiet between operations. 'We knew the Taliban would not be able to resist attacking a casevac, so it was a case of, how do we exploit this?' In the weeks in which 5 Platoon had been based in Luy Mandah, the soldiers had managed to gather a great deal of intelligence about the Taliban's routine, number of fighters, favoured firing positions and location of IEDs on Route

Jupiter, one of the main transit roads through the area. Every time there was an explosion, intercepted Taliban radio chatter revealed that the insurgents assumed an IED had been detonated. All intelligence suggested that the best way to ambush the Taliban was to set up a fake IED strike. There was also a need to blow a hole in a wall which ran alongside Route Jupiter as it was providing the Taliban with cover during firefights. So a decision was taken to kill two birds with one stone: blow a hole in the wall and attempt to lure the Taliban into the ambush.

Lieutenant Shephard prepared the plan, then briefed Major Green and the rest of the platoon. One of the key concerns was the prospect of locals being caught up in the ambush, so Major Green insisted that no phase of the operation was to be launched without his express approval.

At 6.30 p.m. on 4 November troops began the first stage of the operation when the FSG set off on a night patrol. The soldiers had ditched their desert-pattern uniforms, opting instead for the green camouflage, which was considered more appropriate for the time of year. Everyone had been briefed on the plan and both night and day-time rehearsals had been undertaken. Section commanders had also planned a series of contingencies to cover, for example, what action soldiers should take if someone triggered an IED during the operation or how to respond if part of the patrol was ambushed by the Taliban. Every eventuality had to be accounted for so that every man would know how to react should the mission be compromised.

Using excellent field discipline and barely making a noise, the troops managed to get into the area of a building known as Compound 26 without being seen. Other elements of the FSG – the machine-gunners, snipers and Javelin anti-tank missile operators – moved into position. Once the fire base was established, Sergeant Bailey set off with his team and moved into a position of overwatch on Route Jupiter, while Lieutenant Shephard's team moved beyond them into another location. While passing through the garden of one of the compounds, Guardsman Rose, a member of Shephard's team, spotted a potential IED. It was a moment of tension but everyone was aware of the need to keep the momentum of the operation going, so the IED was 'identified and avoided'.

'We continued and began to head south,' said Shephard. 'We reached an overwatch position on a bank south-east of Compound 50. I left Sergeant Roderick Tracey with the bulk of the multiple on overwatch to the south and south-east. Guardsman Peter Shields, Corporal Harry Noorhouse, Corporal Ronnie Parker, who led the engineers' section, and his assistant and myself moved south into the open field adjacent to Jupiter. Shields Valloned up to Jupiter and with the four of us using optics we observed the surrounding area from a very exposed position. It took Shields seemingly for ever to Vallon a route across Jupiter. We knew it was riddled with IEDs, so we had to be extremely careful. In reality it took Shields about ten minutes to clear 20 metres, but it felt like an eternity.'

Once the route was cleared, Corporal Parker moved across the road and began to prepare the explosive for the fake IED strike. Meanwhile Sergeant Bailey's and Lance Sergeant Tracey's teams monitored the surrounding area for Taliban activity. But there was a problem. Corporal Parker had only 25 metres of detonation cord, which effectively put him well inside the explosion's danger area. To survive he would have to face away from the blast, eyes closed and mouth open. Corporal Parker was unconcerned about the risks, but Lieutenant Shephard was worried.

'I checked with Corporal Parker and he assured me he would be OK. I then checked with Rich [the company commander] and he was happy,' Shephard said. 'Twenty seconds later ... bang, a massive explosion, which felt powerful enough to wake up the entire province. Corporal Parker upped and ran to me. Lance Sergeant Tracey and my group linked up with Sergeant Bailey. We threw red cylooms [luminescent markers] onto an obvious location to simulate the casualty evacuation. It was then a case of a quick head check to make sure that we had everyone together, and then it was best speed to

Sergeant Bailey and back to our base. Sergeant Bailey was directly behind us and we were back in the base within fifteen minutes. Everything had gone like clockwork. By this stage the FSG were receiving Icom chatter. The plan was working. The Taliban were planning to move up what they described as a "long-barrelled weapon" – the game was on, the Taliban had taken the bait, and it was a case of watching and waiting for the time to strike.'

The turbaned Taliban figures, AK-47s and Dragnov sniper rifles at the ready, emerged into the failing light of dusk on the hunt for injured British troops. Back in Compound 26, the snipers steadied themselves and waited for their targets to appear. Each sniper had a spotter using night-vision equipment – the night-time battlefield offered no hiding place for the enemy. Four hundred metres to the front two snipers spotted two armed men moving towards known fire positions. The snipers brought the cross-hairs of their telescopic sights to bear on the now stationary targets. Both snipers went for head shots, and the two insurgents fell dead. Their rifles were fitted with sound suppressors, which dulled the sound of the shots and so caused fear and panic in those who saw comrades fall.

The time was now 8.30 p.m. and Lieutenant Shephard moved onto the roof of Crossing Point One, where Sergeant Dave Claxton and Sergeant Thomas Loader were watching and waiting, armed with highly accurate Javelins. More insurgents moved into known firing positions but the Grenadiers were waiting. Shephard went on, 'When the Taliban showed themselves, Sergeant Claxton and Sergeant Loader began to do what they do best. There was a whoosh, followed by a cheer – all the soldiers knew that a rocket was on the way. Two Javelins were fired, killing four enemy. Sergeant Claxton fired another missile through a murder hole, killing at least one more. Back in Compound 26, a sniper killed another insurgent. It was now the turn of the guns [heavy and medium machine guns] to join in.'

Red tracer fire from 7.62-mm and .50-cal machine guns streaked across the night sky, with flares and the occasional explosion silhouetting insurgents against compound walls. There was no hiding place for the Taliban. Those who hid inside compounds risked being blown to pieces by Javelin missiles, while those who chose to stand and fight or run were cut down by machine-gun and sniper fire.

'By the end of the evening we had accounted for ten enemy dead, W even managed to shoot through the hole in the wall caused by our fake IED blast. Everyone made it back to XP1 [Crossing Point One] safely. It was a fantastic result. Ten enemy killed and two IED finds. We were all suitably chuffed. It was the best possible response to the dreadful events of just a few hours earlier. You could see by the look on the soldiers' faces that this was the best possible response to what had happened at Blue 25. It was a case of "roll on tomorrow".'

When the men of 5 Platoon eventually made it to their beds, they slept well, exhausted by the fears and excitement of battle. But, unknown to the men of No. 2 Company and especially 5 Platoon, it was not the end but just the beginning of one of the most intense periods of fighting of the entire six-month tour.

At that stage, in early November 2009, a large force of Taliban, al-Qaeda, Chechen and English-speaking south Asian fighters had come together in the Luy Mandah area with the aim of disrupting the second round of Afghanistan's presidential elections, but when these were cancelled the insurgents turned their attention to the British.

Initially No. 2 Company had occupied two checkpoints in the area, Crossing Point One and Checkpoint Luy Mandah, both of which had been attacked several times earlier in the tour. Major Green decided to close down Checkpoint Luy Mandah because it served little purpose, and the troops from 6 Platoon would be more useful bolstering the force at FOB Waheed. But that was not how the insurgents viewed the development. As far as they were concerned the decision to abandon Checkpoint Luy Mandah was the result of Taliban attacks. So now Crossing Point One became their target instead.

On the morning of 5 November, after what the soldiers called 'the night of nights', Lieutenant Shephard and Sergeant Bailey set off at 8 a.m. on a short clearance patrol into the southern area surrounding the base. The Grenadiers were still buoyant from the previous evening's success and were keen to get back on the ground. The patrol moved out in two groups of nine, one led by Shephard, the other by Bailey. As the soldiers left the safety of the base, the Taliban Icom chatter started. Somewhere in the surrounding countryside the insurgents were watching and reporting the movements of the British troops. The patrol's route led south across a deep irrigation ditch and into the fields beyond. It was a warm, sunny morning, there was little wind, and the birds were singing as the soldiers pushed south. Without warning, the firing started and cracks of RPGs and machine-gun fire tore the air. The fire was heavy and accurate. The tables had been turned and it was the Grenadiers who now had unwittingly walked into an ambush.

Shephard's team dashed for cover and took up fire positions in a tree line as Taliban bullets sliced through the air around them. The platoon was now split, with Bailey's team hiding in cover some 150 metres to the west. Before the attack the soldiers had seen what they had assumed to be three farmers working in one of the fields, who had abandoned their trailer when they saw the British moving into the area.

'I remember thinking, we were observed moving out, so is this the start of some sort of planned retribution for last night?' recalled Shephard. 'Sergeant Bailey was fixed in a ruined compound, taking fire, so I moved my team back 150 metres towards him with the idea of creating all-round defence. So we had Sergeant Bailey's men facing east and south-east and my guys facing west and south-west.'

Back at Crossing Point One, Sergeant Loader was already on the roof preparing the Javelins, searching out the insurgents' firing points. Within a few minutes high-explosive missiles were smashing into compounds just a few metres in front of the soldiers who were trapped out in the open. But rather than withdraw, the Taliban seemed to intensify their fire. 'We were fixed in our positions and taking masses of fire,' said Bailey. 'We couldn't move, we could barely lift our heads to return fire. If we had tried to break away we would have been cut to pieces.'

Once the first contact report had been sent, Major Green immediately crashed out the FST in the three Mastiffs, to help in the extraction of Lieutenant Shephard and his platoon. On their arrival, the Mastiffs began pounding the Taliban firing points and parts of Route Jupiter occupied by the enemy. 'With the help of Lance Corporal Gaz Pendlebury, my Mortar Fire Controller, I planned to lay down smoke and use the Mastiffs to cover our extraction, with Sergeant Bailey's team moving first,' he said. 'But then the Taliban opened up from the south. It was plain that we were being surrounded. Part of you thinks, they have got some balls trying this on, especially given the kicking they got last night. They were up for it. They wanted revenge and they had the momentum.'

The Taliban had managed to get within 40 metres of Sergeant Bailey and began attacking both Grenadier teams with RPGs. The rockets at first fell short but then the Taliban found their aim. The real fear now was that a casualty at this stage would bring the extraction to a halt and lead to further casualties. Sergeant Bailey explained, 'Where you get one casualty you can easily get two, then three, and then you can't move and that's when there is a real fear that you could get overrun.' Smoke rounds were also dropping perilously close to the British troops and were becoming a liability. Bailey's section successfully made it to a compound close to the base and were almost safe. But Shephard's team were still out in the open and taking fire and had they remained in that position casualties would have been taken.

Shephard scanned the area to his front and spotted an irrigation ditch 50 metres away. He gave the order for the soldiers to peel off one at a time and make for the ditch while others provided covering fire. It was a move straight out of the training manual and it worked to perfection – almost. As Shephard and the last two members of his team, Guardsmen Reiss McDonald and Shaun Darville, were bringing up the rear, the Taliban spotted them.

'The weight of fire coming at us forced us to hit the deck,' Shephard recalled. 'The rounds were between us and above us, just inches above our heads. We had airburst RPG going off. I have to say that it was terrifying. The ground was alive with bullet splashes. We were trapped and I was amazed that none of us were dead.'

The momentum of the battle had swung in the insurgents' favour and there was a very real risk that the three soldiers trapped in the open could be killed or injured. It was now up to Sergeant Bailey to turn the tide of the battle. He recalled, 'We hit back, firing at everything that moved or what we thought might be a firing point. There weren't any civilians in the area, so we didn't have to worry about collateral damage. It was a crazy situation – like something out of the movies. The weight of fire from both sides was incredible.'

The enemy fire began to subside and Lieutenant Shephard fired a 66-mm light anti-tank rocket at a group of Taliban fighters attempting to outflank his team. The rocket exploded among the insurgents, and no further movement was seen. Just when the 5 Platoon soldiers thought they had the measure of the enemy, the Taliban hit back and relaunched the assault. Shephard continued, 'I told the other two soldiers to put down a huge rate of fire and then prepare to move – it was now or never. McDonald moved first, then me, then Darville. It was a textbook move from the Brecon School of Infantry but it worked. We all got out alive and moved quickly back into Crossing Point One.'

But the battle was far from over. Although the soldiers had managed to get back into the base, the Taliban continued to press home the attack. 'You couldn't make it up,' Sergeant Bailey said. 'There were four sangars in the corners of our compound, all being hit at the same time. It was 360-degree warfare. It seemed that we were taking hits from everywhere. It was just like *Zulu* – that is what was going through my head at the time.'

During the heat of the battle, and out of sight of the soldiers within the base, a group of enemy fighters began an audacious bid to break into the compound by using the cover of an irrigation ditch to move up to one of the compound's rear walls. Fortunately one of the soldiers in a sangar spotted them and alerted Sergeant Bailey.

With little thought for his personal safety, and knowing that drastic action was required, Bailey, with two of his corporals, filled their ammunition pouches with grenades, fixed bayonets and charged 50 metres across a field to reach the wall behind which the enemy were preparing their attack. The three soldiers, separated from the enemy by the thickness of a high mud wall, listened and waited. On the other side of the wall a Taliban commander briefed his men.

'I looked at the guys and pulled a grenade out of my pouch,' Bailey went on. 'The other two did the same. No one spoke. We all knew what had to be done. I pulled the pin and held onto the handle and waited for the others to get ready and then said, now, or something like that. We lobbed white-phosphorus grenades into the ditch from behind the wall. There was a crack and a fizz and a bit of screaming, then silence. It worked. We killed or injured them all. The threat from that line of assault was over. There wasn't any sense of jubilation in knowing that we had killed them – it was just something we had to do. If they had breached the wall we would have taken casualties. So it was them or us.'

Bailey returned to the inner perimeter, moved to the roof and began searching out more targets. After half an hour Apache attack helicopters arrived and began engaging the Taliban positions with their 30-mm cannons and Hellfire missiles. 'We closed the TIC [troops in contact],' Shephard explained. 'I was emotionally and physically drained and just relieved that we had managed to get the platoon in safely. It took the whole company and good fortune to get us back. Amazingly successful the previous night and an amazingly lucky escape the following morning. Nevertheless, it was still successful in certain aspects. We got another twelve to fourteen KIA and captured two Taliban suspects. One had a battery pack and wiring while the other was found trying to delete all the numbers from his phone – my guess is that they were almost certainly Taliban. Despite the intensity of the fighting there were no civilian casualties. We fought ferociously, but everything was controlled and cleared through Major Green.'

That afternoon Lieutenant Shephard patrolled back to FOB Waheed to discuss the morning's events and talk about the accuracy of the Fire Support Teams, which had been a concern with the smoke rounds landing so close to the troops during the initial contact. It was a positive and friendly discussion, with egos put to one side so that everyone could learn from mistakes. Major Green had fostered an open and constructive debate where the theme was always 'how to improve our fighting ability and save lives'. After the discussion Lieutenant Shephard moved to the operations room, only to hear his platoon sergeant, Sergeant Bailey, announce over the radio that Crossing Point One was 'in contact'. 'I thought, great! – they're in contact and I'm up here. Major Green told Sergeant Rob Pointon, of Support Company, to deploy the Mastiffs to Crossing Point One and I jumped on board. Within a few minutes I was back and went straight to the roof.' Major Green added, 'I wanted Craig back at the checkpoint. I believed that it was vital for Lieutenant Shephard to return to XP1 so that he could respond to my orders, keep me informed of the situation, and ensure that the return of fire was proportionate and controlled.'

The scene which greeted Lieutenant Shephard took his breath away. 'When I got up on the roof, my first reaction was, "Oh my God!" There was this roar of battle which you could feel thumping in your chest. Sergeant Loader, Pearson, Shields and others were all engaging targets. Down below the Mastiffs opened up with .50-cals. But it wasn't all one-way. We were taking rounds and ricochets on the top roof. Guardsmen Robert Chiswell and Reiss McDonald looked stunned. Rounds were passing between them.'

Within minutes of the contact initiating, mortar rounds soon began landing on the Taliban fire positions and it wasn't long before the FSTs were guiding attack helicopters and the heavily armed US A-10 Thunderbolts onto Taliban positions.

Despite the weight of the twenty-first-century weaponry being used against the Taliban, they did not flinch but rather reinforced their attack. The roof of the base was now drawing fire from 360 degrees, with the Taliban using every weapon at their disposal.

'It was terrifying,' said Shephard. 'But at the same time you're thinking, gleaming! This is what I joined the Army for.'

The grenade machine gun – a devastating weapon that can lay to waste an enemy position in seconds – was now brought into action and began belting out 40-mm grenades at a rate of 340 per minute. With unerring accuracy the gunner began launching the bomblets right into the heart of the Taliban strongpoint, where an enemy gun team was literally torn to shreds. The insurgents counter-punched with a seemingly endless supply of RPGs, while their machine guns peppered the British sangars with witheringly accurate fire. The thump of Taliban bullets slamming into walls reverberated around the compound. The two sides were slugging it out like two heavy-weight punchers, neither giving ground. As the battle continued unabated, the news that every guardsman wanted to hear had arrived. A NATO combat jet equipped with a 500 lb high-exposive satellite-guided bomb was en route. Cheers reverberated around the base.

'It was a relief when we were told that a 500-pounder was coming in. There was a boom and a cheer and jubilant whoops of joy,' said Shephard. 'But it was fairly short-lived. Once the dust had cleared, the shooting started again and it was more ferocious than ever. We were getting spanked and so were the Mastiffs. And you're there thinking, what the fuck do we have to do to stop these bastards?'

The soldiers on the roof readied themselves as the Taliban seemed to be moving forward in another seemingly suicidal attempt to over-run the base. Grenades were primed and bayonets fixed for the expected close-quarters battle. But the Taliban assault was met with a hail of murderous fire. Some of the enemy hit by the .50-cal rounds were cut in two, decapitated, or lost limbs. The ageing 66-mm anti-tank rocket which first saw service with the US military in Vietnam was also brought into action, scoring kills. Up in the sangars the barrels of the GPMG smoked with the heat of non-stop firing. Under normal battle conditions the barrels should be changed every 300–400 rounds to allow them to cool – but these were not 'normal battle conditions'.

The deafening roar of battle made communication almost impossible. It mattered not. Every man knew his duty and no one was found wanting. As long as Crossing Point One was under attack the soldiers returned fire.

As the sun began to slip below the horizon, the fighting continued into the cool of the evening. While Lieutenant Shephard controlled the battle from the roof, Sergeant Bailey ran from sangar to sangar with cases of ammunition, food and water, constantly urging on his soldiers. Piles of empty bullet cases formed mole-like hills around their feet – in a few short hours thousands of rounds had been expended. But the soldiers stood firm. They were in the fight of their lives and they knew it.

Then more good news arrived over the radio. Two A-10s were now heading into the fray. Slow and cumbersome, they turned their fire on Route Jupiter, the haunting groan of their seven-barrelled 30-mm cannon echoing around the countryside. Burst after burst of high-incendiary cannon fire turned the route into a terrifying inferno, a sight which was greeted with unbridled joy by the embattled Grenadiers. When the A-10s' ammunition was spent, two Apache attack helicopters joined the hunt and began picking off the Taliban with ease.

Finally, as darkness fell, the insurgents faded away. The air was thick with smoke and dust. Flares were fired high into the sky, illuminating an empty battlefield. The enemy dead and injured had been removed from no man's land. For a few moments there was an eerie silence. The soldiers, with the sound of gunfire still ringing in their ears, were too exhausted to speak. Another attack was expected

and they began recharging their magazines. Caked in dust and dried
sweat, they watched and waited. After fifteen minutes with no
incoming fire, the soldiers, apart from those in the sangars, were
stood down, some simply slumping to the ground. Some ate, a few
chatted, but the majority slept. Among the soldiers there was no
rejoicing, just relief that they had survived another day. Besides,
everyone knew the Taliban would be back. The Grenadiers had been
lucky: they had managed to kill another dozen or more Taliban
fighters without taking a single casualty.

That night Lieutenant Shephard wrote in his personal journal:
'Since arriving at XP1 no day been dull. Be it good arrests, small-
scale skirmishes to full-on 360-degree engagements. The guys passing through or permanently down there have been truly impressive.
The guardsmen and non-commissioned officers' work rates have
been beyond measure. I have never been so happy, satisfied or
impressed by the men and attachments No2 [Company] has at
present. Nothing can compare in my 24 years to the last two months.
Just knowing these guys has been a treat and a privilege, let alone
commanding them. They are all exceptional. The last 48 hours have
been remarkable and they have achieved a lot. The men remain
humble and almost indifferent about it. Be under no illusion this is
not because what happens at XP1 is insignificant, it's because it has
become normal for them. From the outside there is nothing normal
about it. Commanders have come up with ideas and schemes that
work. Forty-two enemy have been killed, if not more, and guardsmen have not been hurt in the process. Good timely decisions, a
company supporting every man in it, level-headed commanders
and luck have all played a massive part in the success of the last 48
hours. The biggest factor in our success in my mind is our guardsmen and senior non-commissioned officer standards – they are
exceptional, they are brave and they are all determined to succeed
here in Afghanistan. Parents, friends and my family should not
worry – I could not be in better hands surrounded by these
individuals.'

Lieutenant Shephard, who joined the Army in 2007, was offered commissions in a number of different infantry regiments but he opted for the Grenadiers because of the chance of serving in Afghanistan. 'Every platoon commander wants to come to Afghanistan and have "their fight". You want to test yourself in battle, to see if you can lead and do the job. But you have to be careful what you wish for. We were lucky. We were involved in some pretty major battles and we got away without any serious casualties.'

By the time 5 Platoon and their attachments withdrew from Crossing Point One, every single member of the unit had killed at least one member of the Taliban, some, especially the snipers and those manning the .50-cal, GPMG and automatic grenade launchers had killed many more. Such was the damage the Grenadiers inflicted on the Taliban during this period that the brigade headquarters was even asked whether the British should attempt some sort of communication with the Taliban to prevent further bloodshed.

On 10 November 2009 Major Green wrote in his daily report to the commanding officer: '15 to 20 insurgents attacked today and probably more would have attacked at last light if the Support helicopter escort of two Attack Helicopters had not been in the overhead. The question is: Do we keep destroying them in large numbers or do we try and persuade them we are not leaving? There are significant numbers of foreign fighters here so perhaps the "destroy" is the best option. The accuracy of the fire is an issue, as are the heavy weapons; hence the reason I often crash out the heavy Mastiffs, to split their fire, fix them with .50 cal and mortars and then destroy with snipers, Javelin and air. This is not how I would wish to prosecute the insurgents but because of the closeness to Crossing Point One (grenade range), the numbers and the accuracy of fire, I cannot just rely on the snipers and the occasional Javelin to defeat them.'

The fighting continued at the same intensity every day for the next two weeks. The Taliban would attack shortly after breakfast, stop apparently for lunch and then continue in the early afternoon until dusk. 'You could set your watch by them,' recalled Lieutenant

Shephard. 'There was a touch of *Groundhog Day* about it. We were wondering when they were going to stop – it was exhausting, I could see that the soldiers were knackered, and I was drained. There were times when I even wondered how long I would last. It was just unrelenting war fighting.'

In just eights weeks the platoon fired off forty-seven Javelin missiles, more than the rest of the Army in Helmand. In fact the Brigade headquarters in Lashkar Gah was forced to do a trawl of all British bases in Helmand asking for spare Javelins to be shipped to FOB Waheed. There were also some remarkable feats of military skill. The gunners on the Mastiffs became adept at engaging multiple targets while under fire and the snipers produced some remarkable long-distance kills, one of them managing to achieve a kill at night at a range of 980 metres, a record shot for the Grenadiers.

It was an exhausting and challenging period for every soldier in No. 2 Company, especially Major Green, who was fearful that severe battle fatigue might begin to take root among the soldiers at Crossing Point One. Many of them were already displaying some of the minor symptoms such as the 'thousand-yard stare' and hyper-alertness. However, given that the battlegroup was being stretched across the entire operational area, there was little Major Green could do apart from pulling some of his men out of the front line for a few hours' rest. 'I started to rotate the guys after a week. They were shattered,' he told me after the battle. 'But it was everything you wanted from leadership. The guys were tested to the limit – no one let me down.'

Two months after arriving in Luy Mandah, No. 2 Company handed over responsibility to an Estonian company before moving to PB Pimon. There were mixed feelings among many of the officers and men as they left the headquarters for the last time. Although everyone knew that the operational tempo within the Pimon area would be much lower and the environment relatively safer, many soldiers felt a sense of disappointment too. The battle of Waheed had been the making of No. 2 Company and had tested all the soldiers from the company commander to the most junior guardsman. Bonds between men of all ranks had been formed during their epic eight-week battle which would never be broken. Some of the soldiers were now closer than brothers; they owed their lives to one another. The battle had been an extraordinary journey that many would never experience again in the whole of their Army careers.

Chapter 10: **Going Home**

'Taliban bomb makers can put an explosive device together in a matter of minutes. Quality control is not an issue – they have adopted the mass-market strategy.'

I'm sitting in the dust adjacent to the HLS on the southern perimeter of FOB Shawqat, waiting for a flight back to Camp Bastion. The sun is shining brightly and the sky is a wonderful expanse of blue. The buzzard, the Army's name for the soldier responsible for coordinating flights for personnel, has just told me that there is a 50 per cent chance my flight might be delayed. I accept the news with a smile and a shrug. I'm feeling relaxed for the first time since I arrived in Helmand three weeks ago.

I'd said goodbye to Woody and the members of Brimstone 42 earlier this morning, before they departed for a week-long route-clearance operation in the south of Nad-e'Ali. Although routine, it will be a task fraught with risk and danger, but part of me wishes I were going with them.

Another long, hot, bloody summer beckons and the men of 1st Battalion Grenadier Guards are happy to be leaving, and not just because they've come to the end of a sixth-month tour. A growing weight of intelligence seems to suggest that the Taliban will attempt some sort of offensive over the next few months to try to recapture the ground lost during Operation Moshtarak. As part of the insurgents' information campaign they will need to demonstrate to the local population that they remain a force to be reckoned with.

The bomb-hunting teams of the CIED Task Force will be thrown into the thick of it. Ahead lie endless weeks of unimaginable danger. The stresses will be enormous and the soldiers will have to learn to live with the knowledge that they are now specific Taliban targets. It is an undisputable truth of this war that killing any soldier involved in bomb disposal guarantees more headlines than killing an infantry private, a fact not lost on the increasingly media-savvy Taliban. My admiration for the bomb hunters' courage and humility knows no bounds.

Equally worrying is the expectation that the Taliban will refine the manufacture of IEDs and begin developing a new generation of bombs similar to those used by Shia militants with devastating effect against British and US soldiers in Iraq. The devices, which were developed with the help of Iran, were highly sophisticated and in some cases used infrared triggers to detonate the bombs. The insurgents developed the technology to make explosively formed projectiles capable of penetrating armour. Although the Taliban currently lack the technological capability to make bombs of a similar sophistication, they have already launched a pretty effective campaign, so why change? Their bomb makers are already experimenting and are attempting to build more lethal anti-armour devices. An anti-vehicle device, known as a swarm, which fires hundreds of ball bearings at a concentrated area, has been developed by the Taliban, and although so far it has proved ineffective other such weapons are likely to follow.

Taliban bomb makers can put an explosive device together in a matter of minutes. Quality control is not an issue – they have adopted the mass-market strategy. If only 10 per cent of Taliban bombs injured or killed British soldiers that would be regarded as a success. The Taliban know that they will never beat the British or NATO in a straightforward fight – but neither do they need to. Their strategy is designed to undermine public support for the war in the

West, and it is working. Both Canada and the Netherlands plan to withdraw troops from southern Afghanistan very soon because of domestic political pressures. While there is huge support for troops in Britain, there is little appetite for continuing the war in Afghanistan. The British public have simply not bought the message that a stable, secure Afghanistan will make Britain a safer place to live, especially when a significant number of UK terrorist plots emanate from Pakistan.

NATO has now been in Afghanistan for almost ten years and the security situation seems to be worsening almost daily. Kabul is no longer safe, road routes into and out of the country are routinely subject to attack, and NATO's casualty rates have never been higher.

But it is not all doom and gloom. Since 2008, when the use of IEDs by the Taliban began to escalate, millions have been spent on countering the bombers. The SAS and the Special Boat Service (SBS), as well as other elements of the special forces, such as the Defence Human Intelligence Unit, which runs agents in Afghanistan, and the Special Reconnaissance Unit have been targeting the bombers, and with some success. In what has effectively become a covert campaign within an overt war, increasing numbers of bomb makers have been killed or arrested in SF strike operations. CIED training and the use of ISTAR assets have helped to save the lives of hundreds, if not thousands, of soldiers. Specialized armoured route-clearing teams have eased the burden on bomb hunters. British mentoring teams are training the Afghan security forces in counter-IED techniques and members of British special forces are helping to develop an Afghan equivalent of the SAS, which in time will begin to mount its own operations against Taliban bomb makers. In October 2010 General David Petraeus, the US commander of the NATO force in Afghanistan, said that American and British special forces had killed or captured 300 Taliban leaders in the past three months. Such losses cannot be sustained in the command structure of any organization, and it is significant that in the same month it was reported that a delegation of senior Taliban leaders had met for peace talks in Kabul.

But the Taliban will continue to make bombs while they have access to nitrate-based fertilizers, the main component of the explosive. The Afghan government banning of nitrate-based fertilizers in January 2010 came too late to have any real impact. Current estimates suggest that there is still enough nitrogen-based fertilizer in circulation in Afghanistan to manufacture 100,000 bombs. And then there is the problem of the many tons brought in every week through the numerous border crossings which encircle the country, some of which are manned for just a few hours a day. The reality is that, despite recent successes, British troops will continue to be killed and maimed by IEDs for as long as they are based in Afghanistan. Rather than removing the Taliban's ability to kill and maim using IEDs, the best for which NATO can hope is to limit the insurgents' ability to increase the volume and sophistication of bombs being developed.

Between March and October 2010 the number of IED incidents remained broadly the same as in the previous seven months and there was some intelligence to suggest that the Taliban were returning to more traditional means of attacking British troops. In some quarters within the British Army, although it would never be couched in such terms in public, such a development amounts to a success. In presentational terms, government-speak for propaganda, it 'plays' better if a soldier is killed by a Taliban bullet rather than a bomb.

My helicopter, an ancient Royal Navy Sea King, eventually arrives and I'm whisked away in a plume of white-grey dust for the twenty-minute flight back to Camp Bastion. Like most of the soldiers who make it to the end of their tour in Helmand, my focus now is to get home as quickly as possible. I've only been away from home for three weeks but it seems much longer. From what I have witnessed it seems to me that the war is never far away for the troops who live beyond the wire. Sleep is often disturbed by gunfire or the comings and goings of helicopters, and there is always the next patrol for which to prepare. There are no weekends, no days off, just a never-ending round of patrols and operations.

As we fly over the flat desert landscape back to the safe confines of Bastion, I wonder once again how soldiers cope with a six-month tour, especially the bomb hunters. A front-line tour is tough for every soldier, especially the very young, the 18-year-olds whose first experience of leaving the UK was to go and fight and, in some cases, die in Helmand. For those, and there are many of them, who have young children, being separated for so long must be almost physically painful. The infantry have it tough but in many cases the bomb hunters have it tougher, being bounced around Helmand from location to location without ever really being able to establish a routine. The monotony of routine is a vital ingredient for surviving Helmand. Soldiers like to establish a working pattern. Get up, go on patrol, sleep, eat, go on patrol, sleep, eat. Days soon begin to merge into one another and time begins to pass unusually quickly. But the bomb hunters are denied such 'luxuries'. The most they can hope for is to spend six weeks in a single location before they are sent to another part of the province where they are put to work for hours on end. It is little wonder that the bonds between these men are so close and the fallen are so deeply mourned.

Over the past few days a further five soldiers have been killed in action in Helmand. One, Lance Corporal of Horse Jonathan Woodgate of the Household Cavalry regiment, was killed when a grenade was lobbed over a wall during a patrol in Helmand. It later emerged that a young boy had been using a mirror to signal to the Taliban when British troops arrived in the area. It was not the first time insurgents had recruited young children to attack British soldiers. The other four soldiers were all killed by IEDs – confirmation, if any were needed, that this particular threat is as strong as ever.

During my embed with the bomb hunters and the Grenadier Guards, I have seldom heard soldiers complain about their lot or about the burden they carry. During wars for national survival like the First and Second World War, the burden was shared by the nation. Sadly that is no longer the case. General Sir Richard Dannatt,

Chief of the General Staff between 2006 and 2009, attempted to restore the balance, but much work needs to be done. We now live in a society where a Premier League footballer can earn over £100,000 a week and still complain that he is not being paid enough, while soldiers, sometimes earning less than a traffic warden, are daily risking their lives in the service of the nation. For me, irrespective of one's views on the war, such an imbalance is a grotesque distortion of the values of any civilized nation. Successive governments have continuously praised our armed forces as the best in the world but in terms and conditions of employment they have been constantly failed. Even today the care and treatment of injured veterans still relies on charities like Help for Heroes, the British Limbless Ex-Service Men's Association, the Royal British Legion, and the various service benevolent funds, as well as a host of other charities. But why? If our armed forces are held in such high regard, why is the treatment of those injured in the line of duty partly dependent on handouts from the public?

The helicopter lands on a grey tarmac circle close to the flight line of Camp Bastion. I jump to the ground and am buffeted by the downdraught from the chopper's blades. But I feel safe for the first time in almost three weeks. It is as though a weight has been lifted from my shoulders and I can feel myself smiling. I look at my watch. It's midday, and if I'm lucky and my flights aren't cancelled or delayed, I could be back home picking up my children from school at 3.45 p.m. tomorrow.

I have time for a shower, shave and change of clothes before reporting for the flight to Kandahar, along with over 100 soldiers, the majority of whom have just completed a six-month tour. Most will have lost a friend or seen colleagues injured on the battlefield. They all look drawn and tired and some are clearly exhausted. As we wait in a tent too small to cope with the numbers, a senior non-commissioned officer from the movements staff, the person responsible for making sure large packets of troops get from A to B, begins to brief the soldiers. He ends by saying, 'Form an orderly queue with officers

and NCOs at the front and the rest of the rabble behind.' The word
'rabble' hangs uncomfortably in the air. An unnerving silence
descends as all eyes turn towards the now clearly concerned NCO.
He is a sorry sight. His camouflage shirt is stretched across a
distended stomach and he is sweating profusely. He must be at least
two stone overweight and is probably too fat to complete a standard
infantry test. I wonder how long he would survive beyond the wire
of Camp Bastion, a place where, in all likelihood, he will never
venture.

Out of the corner of my eye I notice a corporal menacingly walk
over to the NCO, upon whom it has just registered that he has
insulted 100 or so soldiers who have spent the past six months
fighting the Taliban. The NCO backs away from the approaching
corporal. I fully expect punches to be thrown and I wonder whether
anyone will intervene. It is a moment of extreme tension. The
corporal leans forward and whispers something to the NCO, who
lifts up his hands in a conciliatory gesture. It is a pathetic spectacle.
The corporal, point made, returns to his friends muttering under his
breath, 'Fucking REMF.' The NCO backs away without anyone
giving him a second glance and the hum of conversation returns to
the tent.

The flight back to Kandahar is unremarkable except for the fact
that it is on time and by 3 a.m. I am on board an RAF TriStar, about
to fly back to the UK. The flight is delayed while injured soldiers on
stretchers are loaded on board and placed in an area which, when the
aircraft was part of a civilian airline, would have been the preserve of
first-class passengers. One of the injured is unconscious and looks
painfully white. He is fitted with an oxygen mask and appears to have
wounds to his legs. I wonder what the future holds for him. Soldiers
are now surviving injuries which just two years ago would have killed
them. Even some soldiers with ultimately terminal injuries can be
kept alive long enough to be flown home to the UK to allow their
family an opportunity to say goodbye. While I watch the injured
being taken on board, I begin to think about Rupert Hamer. I had

hoped that my embed would have helped me come to terms with his death but I now know that the only cure is time.

Somewhere over the Gulf, an announcement on the intercom informs us that as part of the RAF's 'beers for the boys' programme we are all entitled to a can of lager or bitter. A few of the more boisterous soldiers cheer. It's 6 a.m. The beer tastes good and I sleep soundly.

The TriStar enters UK airspace and down below I can see the green English countryside – and the contrast with Helmand is striking. It's almost like flying into another world, and suddenly I'm hit with a wave of euphoria. The aircraft lands at Birmingham Airport to offload the injured. The detour adds another hour to our journey but no one complains. The soldiers stare, some with watery eyes, as their colleagues are taken to the new Queen Elizabeth Hospital at Selly Oak, to begin another journey.

Finally, the Tristar lands at RAF Brize Norton and everyone is eager to depart and join loved ones. As we walk across the tarmac to the arrival lounge we are lashed by rain and wind, but it feels good.

There is no ceremony, no fanfare, as soldiers hug wives and children. The women look happier than the men, many of whom have left behind friends who will never return. 'Why them and not me?' some are no doubt wondering.

On the long taxi ride to my home in Kent I reflect on the war in Afghanistan and how it has developed. The mistakes, the setbacks and the successes, of which there are painfully few. After years of fighting in Helmand, we are told that NATO has a strategy capable of delivering progress. It is instructive that few, if any, generals or politicians will use 'victory' or even 'success' to define NATO's desired end state. Today the key phrase is progress. Progress, I suppose, allows a greater degree of flexibility than success or victory and, given that Afghanistan was the epitome of the failed state up until 2001, progress is easier to achieve.

David Cameron has decided that British forces will not play a part in combat operations after 2015. By then, in theory, the Afghan security forces should be able to cope on their own. Britain and other NATO countries will still have a mentoring role; they will still help to train and shape the Afghan Army. But what happens if the Taliban become more capable and the Afghan Army are unable to deliver success? Are British troops simply going to cut and run or refuse to leave their bases as the Taliban kill and butcher their way to Kabul? Where is the 'Plan B'? The reality is that NATO and the West are now drinking in the last chance saloon. This is the last role of the dice – there is no 'Plan B'.

As I walk through the front door of my house my two sons, Luca and Rafe, and Daisy, the family dog, attack me. I kneel on one knee and my wife joins the happy scrum. Tears well in my eyes as I think of all those who have died and what their families will miss.

Epilogue

Ten days after I left FOB Shawqat, Woody's CIED team, Brimstone 32, were dispatched on a short-notice mission to help extricate a Mastiff patrol which had become marooned in Taliban territory after striking an IED. The bomb hunters were flown by helicopter to a patrol base in the north of the Nad-e'Ali district before linking up with cordon troops who had moved into the area to help protect the stranded patrol.

The soldiers from 1st Battalion Royal Welsh battlegroup had become trapped in what was effectively an improvised minefield. The two Mastiffs were stuck on a narrow track bordered by a canal on one side and a high mud wall on the other, with at least one IED at the front and another at the rear. The challenge for Woody was to free the troops within the four remaining hours of daylight. Earlier the Royal Welsh troops had moved down the track as part of a routine security patrol. Some of the soldiers had dismounted from the vehicles to clear the road ahead with their Vallons. As they moved towards a track junction, an IED was discovered. With no room to manoeuvre, the patrol commander decided to withdraw, at which stage the troops came under Taliban fire. As one vehicle moved forward to engage the enemy it struck another, undiscovered IED. The blast blew a wheel off the vehicle but the crew and troops inside were unharmed. After the firing subsided, the long process began of reversing the vehicles, including the damaged Mastiff, back up the previously cleared route. A few minutes later another IED was found which had been missed on the route in. The troops were trapped.

'It took us forty-five minutes to clear a safe lane down to where the Mastiffs were stuck,' recalled Woody. 'Almost straight away you could see that it was a pretty good ambush site. I could see where the first IED was almost as soon as I arrived. It was a low-metal pressure-plate device with a remote power pack, which is why it was missed in the first search.' The bomb was pulled from the ground using a hook and line and the main charge of around 20 kg was blown.

The bomb hunters came under fire almost from the moment they arrived in the area. The accuracy varied: some of it was poor, but other rounds came close, hitting the wall along the side of the track just above the soldiers' heads. But returning fire was a problem for the British and Afghan soldiers on the cordon, who risked a blue-on-blue incident unless targets could be clearly identified.

The bomb hunters cleared a safe path down to the second of the two vehicles and discovered a further two IEDs. Woody isolated the power supply to each bomb and began attempting to extract the first device using the hook and line, but it was stuck fast.

Woody wrapped the line around his hand and told the other team members, Boonie, his No. 2, and Baggage, the ECM operator, to stop pulling, but the message wasn't properly heard or understood. And, determined to shift the bomb, the other searcher gave the line one last, violent tug. The bones in the first two fingers of Woody's right hand snapped like dry twigs and his palm was sliced open. He collapsed to his knees in agony.

Sergeant Simon Fuller, the RESA, assumed that Woody would have to be evacuated back to base and another ATO flown in. But Woody refused and insisted that a medic dress the wound, splint his fingers, and put his arm in a sling. Within fifteen minutes Woody, who was sweating with pain, was back at work. 'No one else was going to come in – there wasn't the time. So you just get on with it. I'm right-handed, so that presented a bit of a problem. I'd never defused bombs with my left hand before.'

Using just his left hand and while in considerable pain, Woody neutralized a further three devices in twenty minutes. With the track now clear the Mastiffs began to reverse slowly back along it. It was a process fraught with danger, especially for the driver of the damaged Mastiff, which was manoeuvring on just three wheels. A misjudgement could have easily caused the vehicle to tumble down the embankment into the canal. Manoeuvring 800 metres along the track took almost two hours, and by the time the patrol reached the edge of the cordon it was almost dark. The delay was caused by a fifth bomb, which had been missed on the initial move down the track. As with the previous four devices, Woody removed the power source and blew the main charge.

Exhausted but safe, the bomb hunters were flown back to FOB Shawqat later that evening. Woody's exploit that day were not forgotten. No one would have blamed him had he chosen to withdraw from the operation for medical attention. But he chose not to. He didn't want to leave his team behind and he wanted to finish the mission. It was a staggering feat of ordnance disposal by Woody, who for most of the operation was both under fire and in great pain.

After Woody returned from two weeks of much-needed R&R at the beginning of June, he felt as if he had landed in another country. The harvest, which had kept many 'part-time' Taliban fighters in the fields, was over and the number of attacks increased massively. On 27 June Corporal Jamie Kirkpatrick, known as KP, who was serving with 101 Engineer Regiment (EOD), was shot dead in the area of Nahr-e-Seraj. His death came at the beginning of a bloody six-week period for the CIED Task Force which saw the unit suffer three KIAs and about a dozen serious casualties.

On 8 July Woody's team returned to the patrol base line close to PB Malvern, east of Gereshk, in an area which in recent months had become increasingly kinetic. Woody knew the area well. Back in April his team had been blown up by a command-wire IED and his ECM operator had suffered minor shrapnel wounds. But 8 July would be different. The mission that day was to find and clear at least three command wires in a wood line some 200 metres from PB Malvern. Brimstone 32 woke at 4 a.m. and were ready for action at the outer cordon of troops, who had secured the area within the hour.

As the sun began to rise Woody and his team of bomb hunters began searching. During the isolation search of the area the team discovered three command-wire devices, none of which were the ones they had been originally sent to clear. By 8.30 a.m. a good part of the area had been covered and cleared and the team began the hunt for the final command wire. Woody told two of his searchers to move to a tree line about 5 metres from where he was standing. The soldiers moved off one behind the other, about 5 metres apart, in single file with the lead searcher at the front. The tranquillity of the early-summer morning was destroyed by a massive explosion. The lead searcher had stepped on a low-metal victim-operated IED. The force of the blast knocked Woody to the ground. Initially he and the team assumed they had been attacked by an RPG.

'There was this massive explosion. It was quite disorientating and I couldn't see a great deal because of the dust. The search team leader said that it had come from an area where his two searchers were working. I told everyone to stand still, grabbed a Vallon and began to clear a path up to the site of the explosion. My ears were ringing from the blast and I realized at this stage that someone had probably stood on a pressure plate.'

Woody inched his way forward, listening for the quietest of Vallon alarm tones. He knew that the bomb would have been missed only if it had had a very low metal content.

'I got to the site of the explosion and I saw the lead searcher sat there with no legs. I shouted back that he was alive and called for medics. I then began to search around the area of the crater to make sure it was safe and all the time in my head I was saying, oh my God, oh my God, because I knew I was going to have to get in there and sort him out. We were talking to one another. I was saying, "Don't worry, mate, you're gonna be OK, I'll be with you in a minute" – stuff like that.'

Once the immediate area was cleared, Woody jumped into the hole and began applying tourniquets to the shattered limbs.

'He was fully conscious, although in shock. There was no scream-ing, in fact he was being a bit humorous. He had been talking about buying a new car when he returned to the UK and he was saying stuff like, "Now that I've lost my legs I'll have to buy an automatic."'

The medics, who had accompanied the bomb hunters for the clearance operation, arrived within a few minutes and the casualty was evacuated back to Camp Bastion by helicopter. Woody contin-ued, 'It was pretty shocking, horrendous to be honest, not something I would like to experience again.' After the casevac, the search was abandoned and Woody's team were withdrawn back to Camp Bastion. Such was the damage to Woody's hearing that he was not allowed to deploy on operations for the rest of the tour, which ended at the beginning of August.

On 17 July 2010, just over a week after Woody's team was blown up, Staff Sergeant Brett Linley, a fellow ATO and close friend of Woody's, was killed while attempting to neutralize a device in the Nahr-e-Seraj area. He was 29 years old. The death hit Woody hard. In the space of a little over six months two of his closest friends had been killed and many more injured. Nine days later Sapper Mark Smith, 26, who was serving with 36 Engineer Regiment (EOD), who was also a member of the CIED Task Force, was blown up and killed in Sangin.

The deaths brought to a bloody close Woody's tour, during which time he was blown up for times and defused more than fifty bombs. He survived, he believes, because he was lucky. Like most of the ATOs I have interviewed for this book, Woody believes the tour length of six months is too long.

'At some time your luck has to run out, so the more bombs you do, the more risk you take. Four months would be fair. It wouldn't have saved Brett's life but some of the others might have made it back. We made it back because I had a brilliant team and we were lucky. But the war goes on.'

After returning to the UK I interviewed Staff Sergeant Kim Hughes, who won the George Cross in August 2009 for an outstanding act of gallantry. I wanted to know whether he thought the tour length of six months was too long for a high-threat operator. The interview took place in the presence of a senior officer, but Hughes was undaunted.

When he serving was in Afghanistan, Hughes found himself face to face with Bob Ainsworth, the then Defence Secretary, who was visiting the country. 'What would make a difference to your life in Afghanistan?' Ainsworth asked, no doubt hoping for an answer to which he could positively respond. 'More troops,' replied Hughes, who went on to tell reporters who witnessed the exchange, 'What was he going to do, send me home? It has been a ridiculously busy, ridiculously hard tour. We have lost two guys. Clearly more troops are needed on the ground, but then the same could be said for equipment.'

Staff Sergeant Hughes answered my question about the current length of the tour by recalling an incident which took place on his very first operation. 'On our very first job someone was shot – it was a one-in-a-million chance,' he said as we sat in a classroom at the Defence Explosive Ordnance Disposal, Munitions and Search School at Kineton. 'We were doing compound clearances on an operation. One of the guys went into a compound which was supposed to be clear, and was chased out by a dog. This thing was massive – it was the size of a bear, and one of my searchers, Sapper Harry Potter, spun round and shot the dog. If he hadn't the dog would have mauled the searchers. Unfortunately the round passed through the dog, hit the floor, ricocheted off the wall, bounced off another wall at forty-five degrees, and hit one of my searchers in the face. The bullet passed through his eye and went into his brain. He survived but he was in a bad way for a while. It was our first operation, and that wasn't good at all. It was no one's fault but it was the worst possible way to start a six-month tour. That's what can happen in Afghan.

'The bomb teams are out on the ground every day neutralizing stupid amounts of devices. But I always felt under control. I had a fantastic search team – I thought they were the best in theatre. I trusted them with my life. At the end of the tour we were all completely knackered. Six months is a long time for what we do in Afghanistan. We were all exhausted. I'd say it was too long; four months would be about right. Everyone who goes out to Afghan has a job to do, but going out neutralizing bombs day in day out is too long. It's not just bombs; it's being a soldier as well. Gone are the days when the RLC guys could say, "I'll leave that to the infantry." Now, in Afghan, whatever job you do, you are always a soldier first. During operations the bomb-hunting teams can expect to be in full-on contact with the enemy. They will be at the point when they are on their last magazine of ammunition, and then, when the firefight has been won, they still have to go forward to find and clear bombs and then come back to the base and do it again, every day for six months. I'd say it was too long, absolutely, much too long. Six months is a long time for doing what we do – it should be four months. The consequences of that, well, who knows? Would those guys still be alive today? I don't know. Four days later I had to take my team into Wishtan, an area in Sangin where lots of searchers had been killed and injured. I was pretty worried about the job. Two guys had been killed, Sergeant Paul McAleese and Private Jonathon Young. The soldier stepped on a pressure plate and was killed and the sergeant went in to get him and he was killed. For me that was one of the most scary jobs we did because then Wishtan was a very, very dangerous place.

'When I did the job for which I was awarded the GC I was at the five-month point and I'd defused eighty devices – that's a lot. I was pretty tired by then. Guys are going out every day clearing a ridiculous number of bombs.'

Every member of the bomb-hunting teams mentioned in this book will return to Helmand in the next two to three years for another six-month tour of duty.

Appendix

Lieutenant Colonel Roly Walker, the commanding officer of the Grenadier Guards, was awarded the Distinguished Service Order. His citation reads:

'Lieutenant Colonel Walker transformed a district of some 200,000 people from one of the most hostile in Afghanistan into one of relative peace and tranquillity. His sophisticated approach placed his Battlegroup at the cutting edge of population-centric counter insurgency, making it a byword for success and a role model for others to emulate. The Battlegroup, besieged by a mix of local and foreign Taliban, was attacked relentlessly for a month, sometimes by human wave assaults approaching the perimeter, ending with grenades thrown and bayonets fixed. The Afghan Army was under strength and the Afghan Police was at best ineffective, and at worst actively hostile. Undaunted, Walker set about analysing the complex social dynamics of Nad-e'Ali. He demanded restraint of his men, insisting that it showed greater courage not to use lethal force and indulge in pointless duels of fire. Walker understood that freedom of movement would allow economic improvement and forced the opening of routes and the building of bridges. The Kharotei tribe stopped fighting and their community was given protection and employment. Walker showed indomitable leadership in the early dark days, leading his Guardsmen to a striking success.'

Lieutenant Craig Shephard, the commander of 5 Platoon, No. 2 Company, 1st Battalion Grenadier Guards, was awarded the Military Cross. The following forms part of his citation:

'Lieutenant Shephard commanded his platoon from the patrol base for over a month at Crossing Point One, during which time he and his men sustained intense and constant insurgent attacks. The situation required exceptional levels of leadership, control and ingenuity. Shephard was personally credited with conceiving and executing a complex deception and ambush mission on 4 November 2009 against a determined and relentless insurgent force. When up to sixty insurgents attacked and tried to overrun a patrol Shephard was leading, he calmly brought in mortars "danger close" to his position and then began moving his sections back under cover of fire to the patrol base before following himself. His prompt actions and leadership undoubtedly saved his patrol many casualties. Shephard was calm and measured at all times, displaying immense bravery and leadership in the most kinetic and dangerous situations. Shephard's actions significantly contributed to over eighty insurgents being killed. Of crucial importance is the fact no civilians were killed or injured from his controlled and measured reaction. Shephard's judgement and clear thinking was of the highest order on his first operational tour, within a year of joining the battalion. Shephard displayed leadership, inspirational command, personal bravery under fire, and unflinching attention to duty.'

Staff Sergeant Gareth Wood, Royal Logistic Corps, was awarded the Military Cross for an action which took place in Helmand on 30 March, 2010. His citation reads:

'When a fully manned Mastiff Armoured Vehicle was struck by an IED, the stricken crew assessed their situation and it became apparent to them that, not only had they been struck by an IED, they were surrounded by them. Marooned in a minefield in hostile terrain, they were soon trapped under sustained and accurate enemy small arms fire. Staff Sergeant Wood and his supporting patrol flew by helicopter to the nearest patrol base, with only four hours of daylight remaining, to fearlessly set about rescuing their comrades. As heavy and accurate automatic fire rained down, Wood insisted that others took cover while he swiftly defused the first device. Still under fire, he moved on to the second device and wrenched it from the ground with his bare hands. In so doing he sustained a laceration to his hand and broke two fingers. He refused to be evacuated and insisted upon completing his task with nothing more than the crudest of first aid. With one arm in a sling and his fingers in a splint, Wood rendered safe a total of five IEDs, enabling the stricken Mastiff crew to extricate themselves under the cover of darkness through the path that he had single-handedly engineered.'

Staff Sergeant Karl 'Badger' Ley of the Royal Logistic Corps won the George Medal for his tour in Afghanistan. His citation reads:

'Staff Sergeant Ley has dealt with more Improvised Explosive Devices (IEDs) than any other operator in history. To date, Ley has made safe and recovered 139 IEDs across Helmand Province. In supporting the infantry's intensity of operations, Ley has willingly accepted an incredibly high level of personal risk, often having to deploy on foot with only what he could carry in his rucksack. On a 72 hour operation in November 2009, Ley defused 28 Victim Operated Improvised Explosive Devices (VOIEDs) and tackled 14 bombs. Ley painstakingly defused seven of the devices so that they could be recovered intact for technical intelligence purposes. This single day typifies the sheer determination, guile and awesome bravery of this man. During his six-month deployment Ley has been exposed to more than twice the number of IEDs than any one other High Threat IEDD

Operator, and with a limited number of available IED operators, Ley has worked tirelessly in the most hazardous of conditions, enduring both mental and physical fatigue, displaying unwavering dedication and conspicuous gallantry over a sustained period.'

Badger has since been promoted to Acting Warrant Officer (2nd Class).

The citation of Company Sergeant Major Patrick Hyde, who served in A Company, 4 Rifles from October 2009 to March 2010 and received a Mention in Dispatches, includes the following:

'Warrant Officer Class 2 Hyde has been involved in thirteen Improvised Explosive Device (IED) incidents and seven casualty extractions. Of these incidents six have blown up the vehicle he was in, three have been near misses and four have been strikes onto vehicles in the resupply convoy he was commanding. In addition to this his vehicle has sustained a direct hit with a 107 mm rocket which peppered him with shrapnel. Hyde has personally overseen the medical evacuation of ten members of the company group. In an area later found to be littered with IEDs and with no thought for his own safety, Hyde retrieved the casualty of an IED strike which had also critically injured the section commander. Hyde took command of the section, applied first aid and then evacuated the two casualties to a helicopter landing site in under 35 minutes. Hyde has repeatedly been at hand to treat, reassure and extract casualties. During the tour, Hyde has also been involved in the treatment and extraction of four mortally injured local children and numerous critically wounded locals. Hyde's selfless commitment and bravery in the face of continued enemy attack have been an inspiration, displaying exemplary gallantry, determination and his utter selflessness.'

Acknowledgements

This book would not have been possible without the cooperation, courage, generosity and patience of a large number of people, both civilian and from within the military establishment.

Sitting at the top of the list of those to whom I owe a great debt of gratitude is my agent, Humphrey Hunter. Quite simply, if it were not for Humphrey I would not have written *Bomb Hunters*, a book of which I am deeply proud. Humphrey became a friend and confidant, who, thankfully, also possesses the unique ability to treat me as though I were his only author. He was and remains always on hand for a friendly word of advice or an ear in which to moan, sometimes almost daily.

I would also offer my heartfelt thanks to Iain MacGregor, the editorial director for *Bomb Hunters*, for his inspiration, creativity, his ability to gently cajole, and also for keeping the faith during the brief occasions when I was in doubt. My deepest thanks also extend to the team at HarperCollins for their professionalism, enthusiasm and dedication in seeing the project through to its end. Richard Dawes, the copy-editor, also deserves to be singled out for special mention for his forensic examination of the manuscript.

Research for *Bomb Hunters* was primarily undertaken during several visits to southern Afghanistan, specifically the Sangin and Nad-e'Ali areas in Helmand, between August 2008 and March 2010. My great friend Rupert Hamer, who was tragically killed in Helmand in January 2010 while reporting for the *Sunday Mirror*, once said to me, 'To report the war you have to see the war.' His vision of war reporting became the abiding philosophy underpinning this book.

Helmand remains an area too dangerous for journalists to work in without the support, assistance and protection of NATO forces. *Bomb Hunters* would not be the book it is today if I had not been able to visit Helmand and interview and accompany soldiers performing their duties on the front line.

From the Army I would like to single out for specific mention: WO2 Gary O'Donnell GM and Bar, 11 EOD Regiment, Royal Logistic Corps, killed in action September 2008; Staff Sergeant Kim Hughes GC, 11 EOD Regiment, Royal Logistic Corps; WO2 Karl 'Badger' Ley GM, 11 EOD Regiment, Royal Logistic Corps; Staff Sergeant Gareth 'Woody' Wood MC, 11 EOD Regiment, Royal Logistic Corps; Lieutenant Craig Shephard MC, Grenadier Guards; Lieutenant Colonel Roly Walker DSO, Grenadier Guards; Major Richard Green, Grenadier Guards; Captain John Donaldson, Irish Guards (serving with Grenadier Guards); Colonel Gareth Collett, Royal Logistic Corps, head of Army Bomb Disposal. Also, all ranks of 1st Battalion Grenadier Guards, who fed, watered and kept me safe, and Colonel Huw Parry-Jones of the Ministry of Defence's Public Relations (Army). Thanks also to Toni O'Donnell and Lorraine Read, widows of WO2 Gary O'Donnell and Captain Dan Read respectively.

My deepest thanks are also extended to all ranks of the Joint Force Explosive Ordnance Disposal Group on Operation Herrick 11, the majority of whom spoke with unflinching honesty about life on the front line, and who were willing to allow me to accompany them on operations and generally get in the way.

From the Ministry of Defence I would like to thank James Shelly, the Head of News of the Directorate Media and Communications, who, with unerring foresight, identified problems before their arrival and helped negotiate the book's passage around and through the perilous waters of operational security. My thanks also to Sonja Hall of the Directorate Media and Communications and her small team of civil servants, who had the unenviable task of ensuring that all operational security, factual and personal security issues were identified and resolved.

I am grateful to Professor Sheila M. Bird of the MRC Biostatistics Unit in Cambridge for providing figures on combat deaths in Afghanistan.

I would also like to thank the brilliant photo-journalist Heathcliff O'Malley for the kind use of his photographs.

Lastly I would like to thank my wife Clodagh and my sons Luca and Rafe for never complaining when I wasn't the attentive husband or the playful daddy during the period in which this book was researched and written.

Glossary

AH – attack helicopter

AK-47 – Kalashnikov 7.62-mm assault rifle

AT – Ammunition Technician

ATO – Ammunition Technical Officer ·

BCR – battle casualty replacement

CBA – combat body armour

Chinook – RAF twin-propeller helicopter

CIED – counter-IED

det – detonator

Dragnov – Russian sniper rifle

ECM – electronic counter-measures

EOD – Explosive Ordnance Disposal

FOB – forward operating base

FSG – Fire Support Group

FST – Fire Support Team

GPMG – general-purpose machine gun

HLS – helicopter landing site

HME – home-made explosive

HMG – heavy machine gun

HRF – High Readiness Force

IED – improvised explosive device

ICP – incident control point

IEDD – improvised explosive device disposal

ISTAR – Intelligence, Surveillance, Target Acquisition and Reconnaissance

JF – Joint Force

KIA – killed in action

MERT – medical emergency response team

Mastiff – wheeled armoured personnel carrier

Merlin – RAF helicopter

M-Kill – mobility kill (when an IED disables a vehicle)

O-group – Orders group (where orders for an operation are issued)

PB – patrol base

PE – plastic explosive

PPR – personal role radio

R&R – Rest and Recuperation

REMF – rear-echelon motherfucker

Ridgeback – four-wheeled variant of Mastiff

RLC – Royal Logisitc Corps

RSOI – Reception, Staging and Onward Movement Integration

SA80 – standard-issue British Army rifle

SF – special forces

SH – support helicopter

UGL – underslung grenade launcher

terp – interpreter

VP – vulnerable point

Warrior – British Army tracked armoured carrier

WIS – Weapons Intelligence Section

WO1 – Warrant Officer Class 1

Index